ALL SUMMER LONG

ALSO BY HOPE LARSON

Madeleine L'Engle's
A Wrinkle in Time: The Graphic Novel

Compass South *(Four Points Book 1)*
Illustrations by Rebecca Mock

Knife's Edge *(Four Points Book 2)*
Illustrations by Rebecca Mock

ALL
SUMMER
LONG

HOPE LARSON

Farrar Straus Giroux
New York

For the weirdos and the part-time punks

Farrar Straus Giroux Books for Young Readers
An imprint of Macmillan Publishing Group, LLC
175 Fifth Avenue, New York, NY 10010

Printed in China by Toppan Leefung Printing Ltd.,
Dongguan City, Guangdong Province
Designed by Hope Larson and Andrew Arnold
First edition, 2018
Colored by MJ Robinson

Paperback: 10 9 8 7 6 5 4 3 2 1
Hardcover: 10 9 8 7 6 5 4 3 2 1

mackids.com

Library of Congress Control Number: 2017956974
Paperback ISBN: 978-0-374-31071-4
Hardcover ISBN: 978-0-374-30485-0

Our books may be purchased in bulk for promotional, educational,
or business use. Please contact your local bookseller or the Macmillan
Corporate and Premium Sales Department at (800) 221-7945 ext. 5442
or by e-mail at MacmillanSpecialMarkets@macmillan.com.

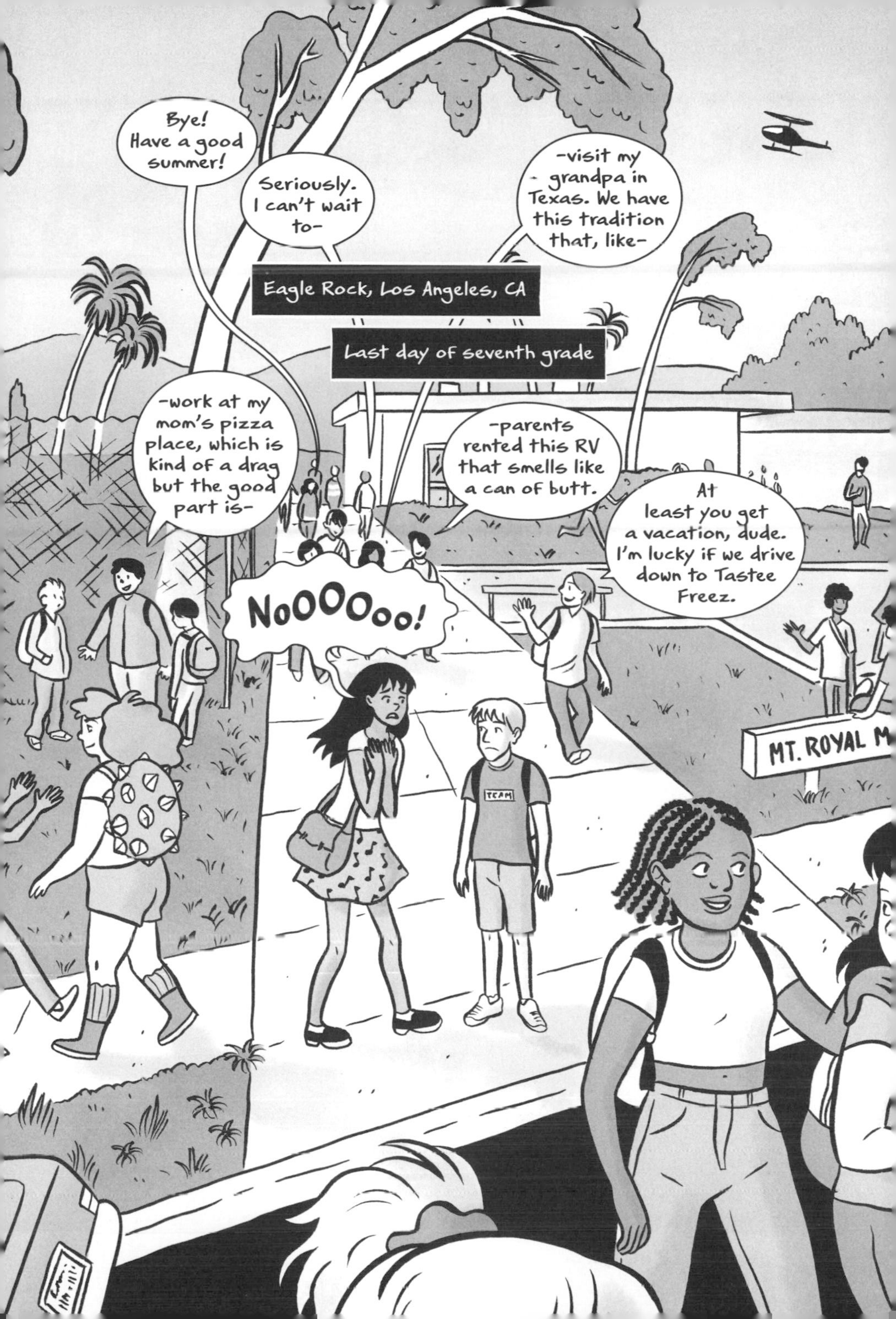
Bye! Have a good summer!
Seriously. I can't wait to-
-visit my grandpa in Texas. We have this tradition that, like-
Eagle Rock, Los Angeles, CA
Last day of seventh grade
-work at my mom's pizza place, which is kind of a drag but the good part is-
-parents rented this RV that smells like a can of butt.
At least you get a vacation, dude. I'm lucky if we drive down to Tastee Freez.
NoOOOoo!
TEAM
MT. ROYAL M

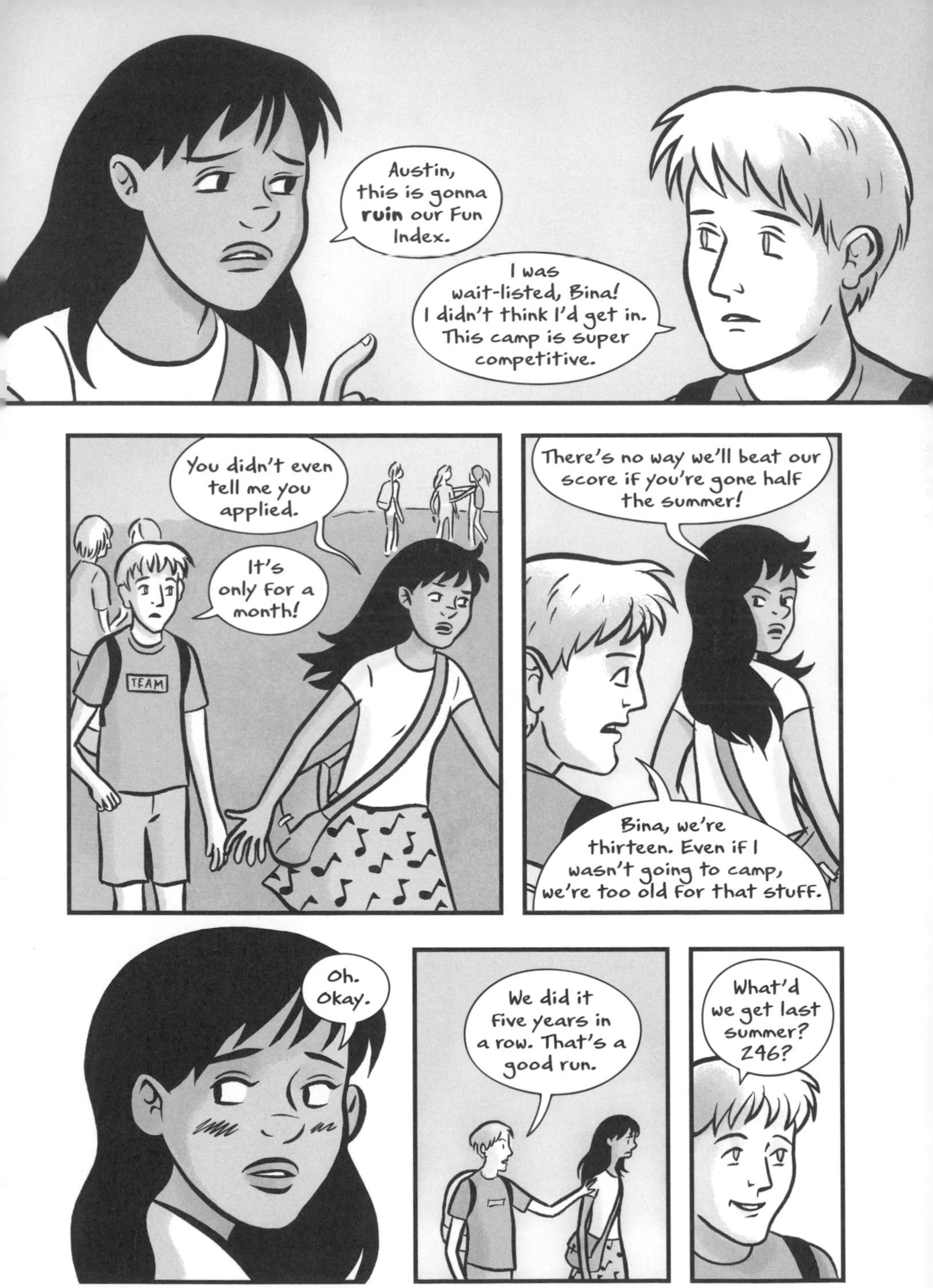
Austin, this is gonna **ruin** our Fun Index.
I was wait-listed, Bina! I didn't think I'd get in. This camp is super competitive.
You didn't even tell me you applied.
It's only for a month!
TEAM
There's no way we'll beat our score if you're gone half the summer!
Bina, we're thirteen. Even if I wasn't going to camp, we're too old for that stuff.
Oh. Okay.
We did it five years in a row. That's a good run.
What'd we get last summer? 246?

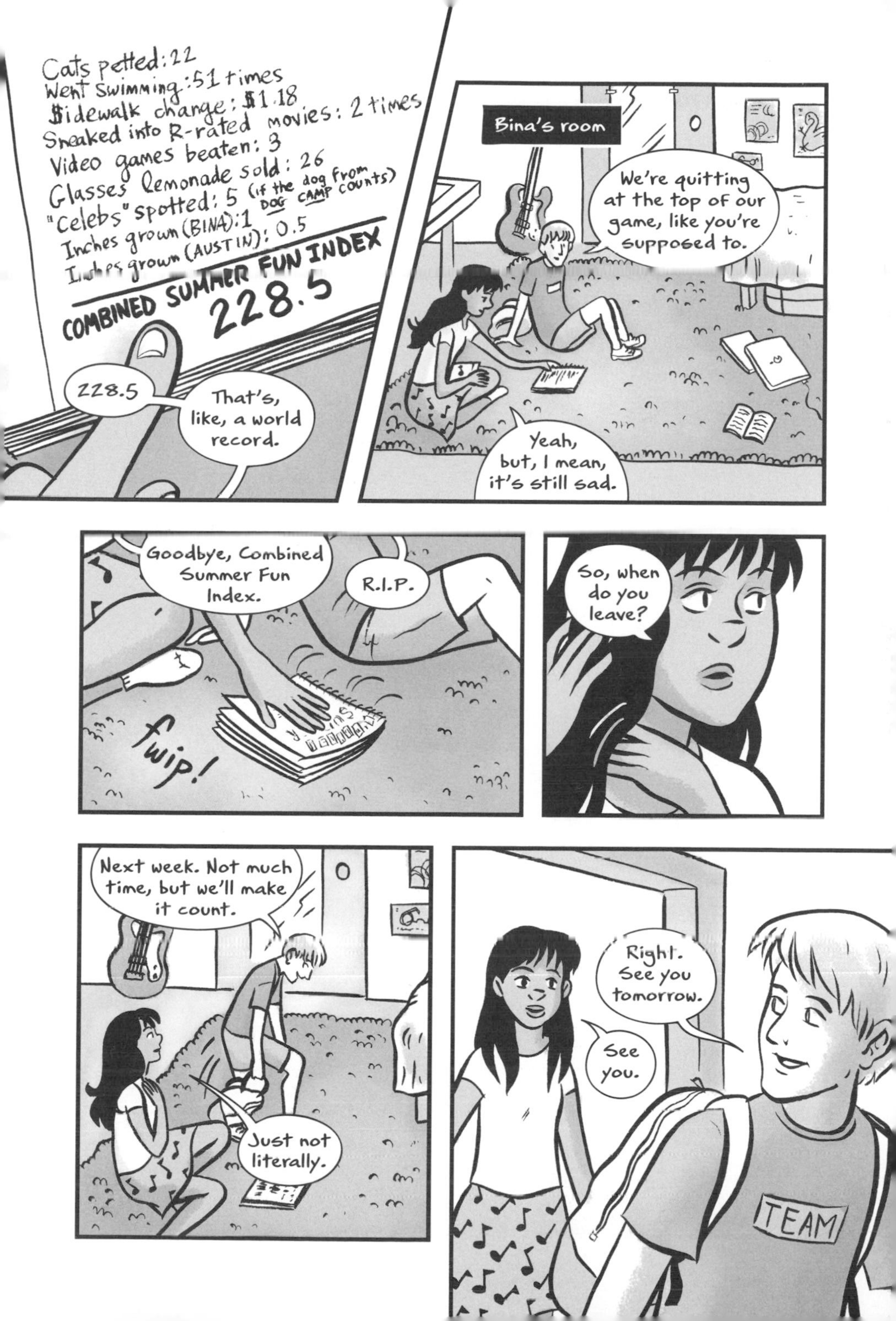

Cats petted: 22
Went swimming: 51 times
$idewalk change: $1.18
Sneaked into R-rated movies: 2 times
Video games beaten: 3
Glasses lemonade sold: 26
"Celebs" spotted: 5 (if the dog from DOG CAMP counts)
Inches grown (BINA): 1
Inches grown (AUSTIN): 0.5
COMBINED SUMMER FUN INDEX
228.5
228.5
That's, like, a world record.
Bina's room
We're quitting at the top of our game, like you're supposed to.
Yeah, but, I mean, it's still sad.
Goodbye, Combined Summer Fun Index.
R.I.P.
fwip!
So, when do you leave?
Next week. Not much time, but we'll make it count.
Just not literally.
Right. See you tomorrow.
See you.
TEAM

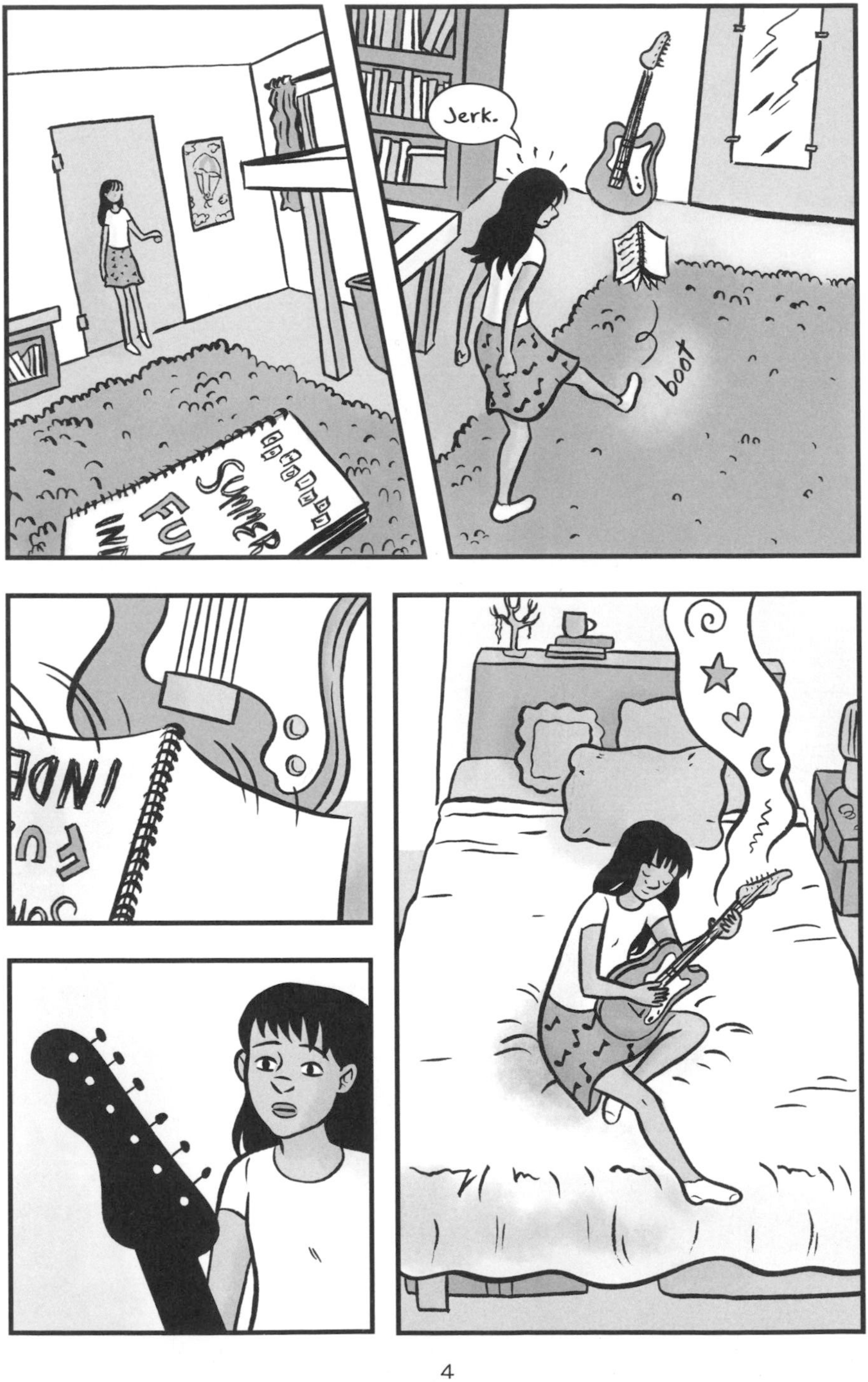
SUMMER
FUN
IND
Jerk.
boot
INDE
FU

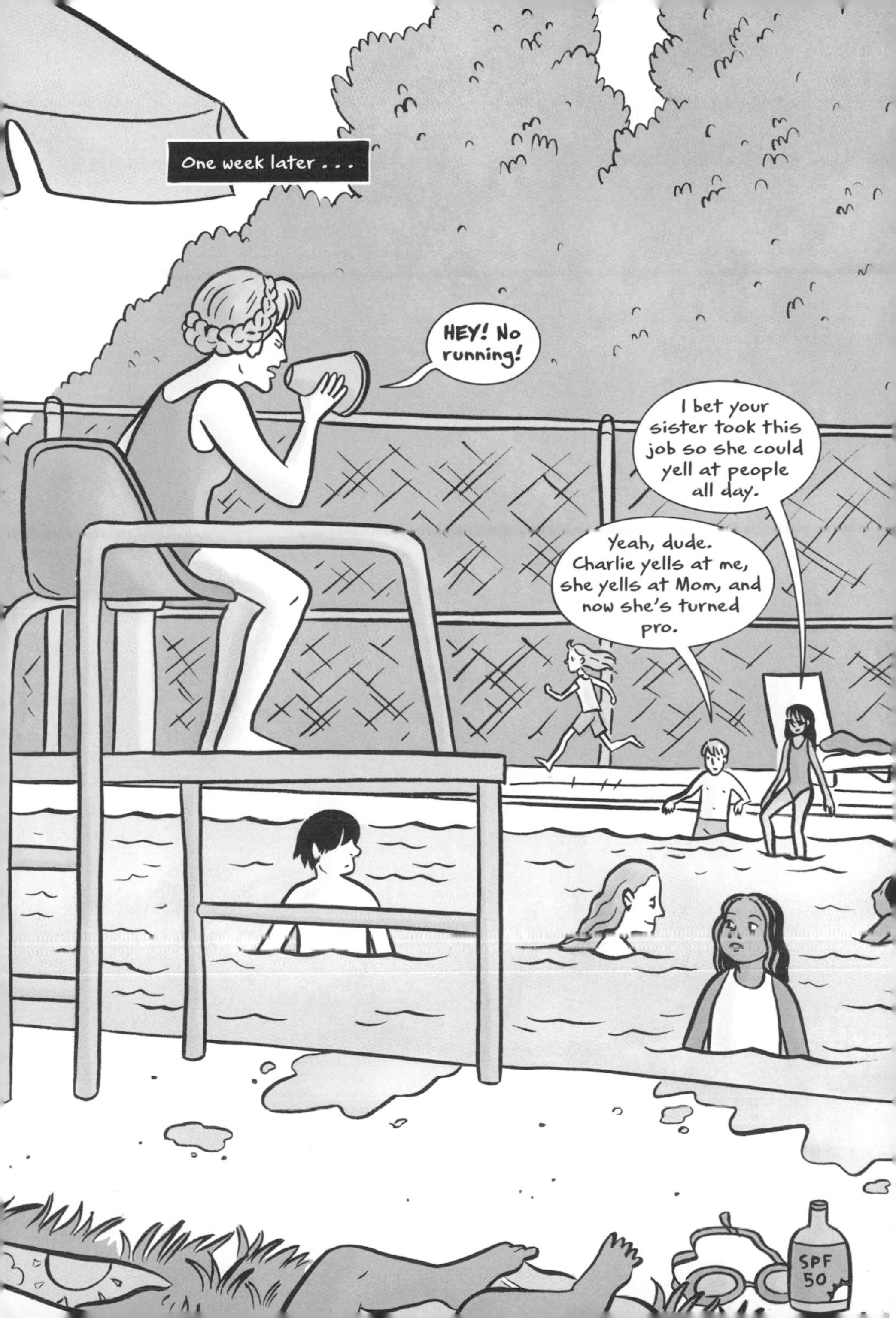

One week later . . .
HEY! No running!
I bet your sister took this job so she could yell at people all day.
Yeah, dude. Charlie yells at me, she yells at Mom, and now she's turned pro.
SPF 50

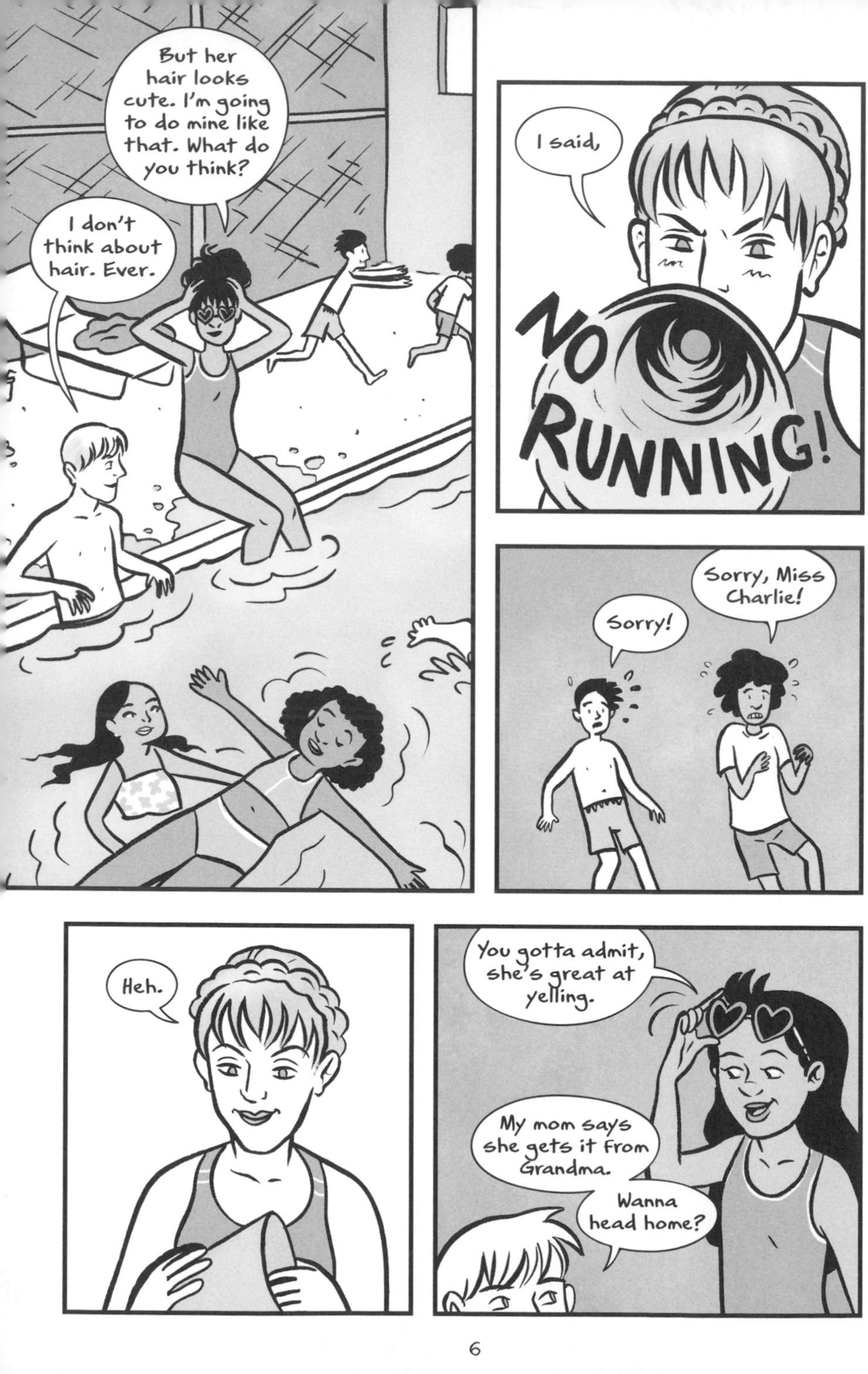
But her hair looks cute. I'm going to do mine like that. What do you think?
I don't think about hair. Ever.
I said,
NO RUNNING!
Sorry!
Sorry, Miss Charlie!
Heh.
You gotta admit, she's great at yelling.
My mom says she gets it from Grandma.
Wanna head home?

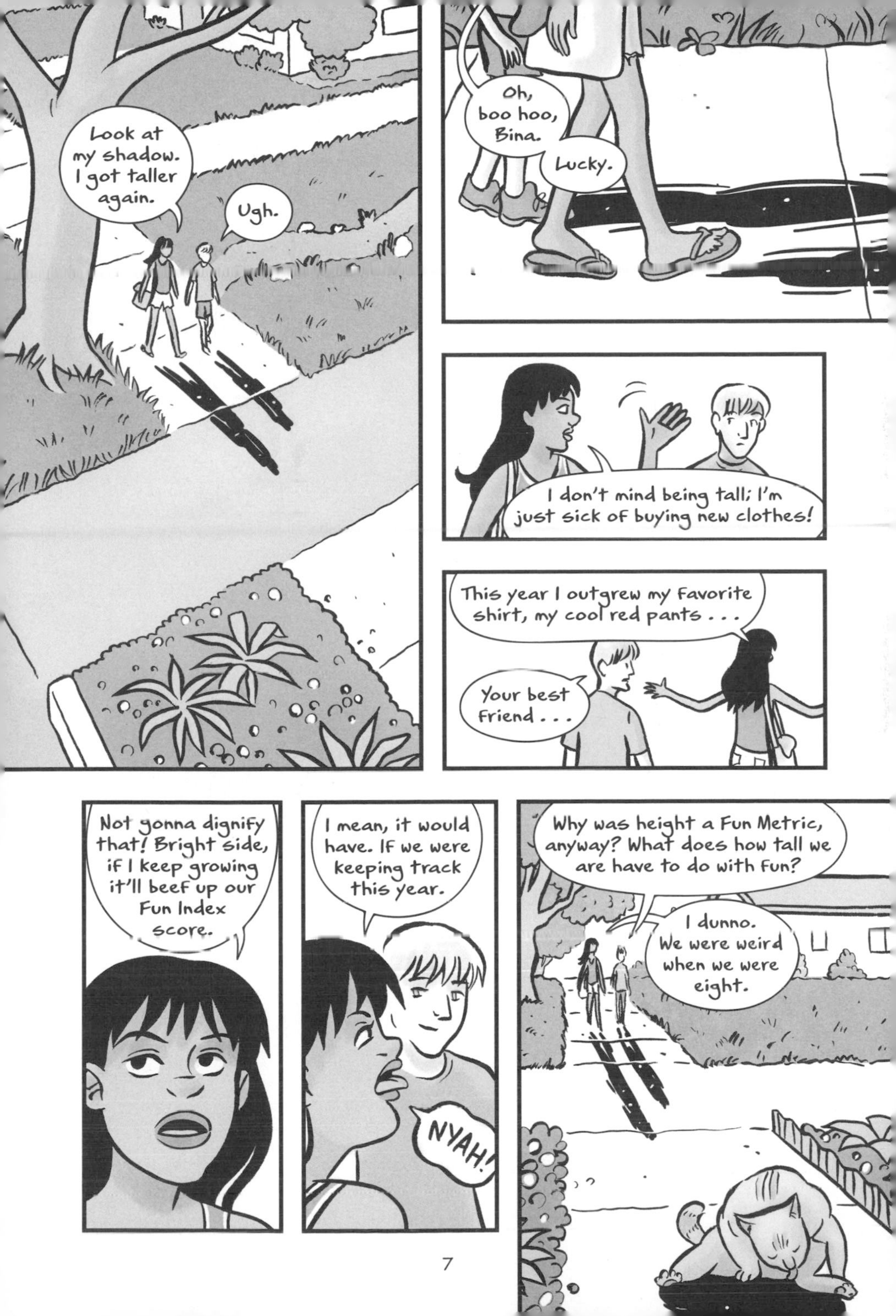
Look at my shadow. I got taller again.
Ugh.
Oh, boo hoo, Bina.
Lucky.
I don't mind being tall; I'm just sick of buying new clothes!
This year I outgrew my favorite shirt, my cool red pants . . .
Your best friend . . .
Not gonna dignify that! Bright side, if I keep growing it'll beef up our Fun Index score.
I mean, it would have. If we were keeping track this year.
NYAH!
Why was height a Fun Metric, anyway? What does how tall we are have to do with fun?
I dunno. We were weird when we were eight.

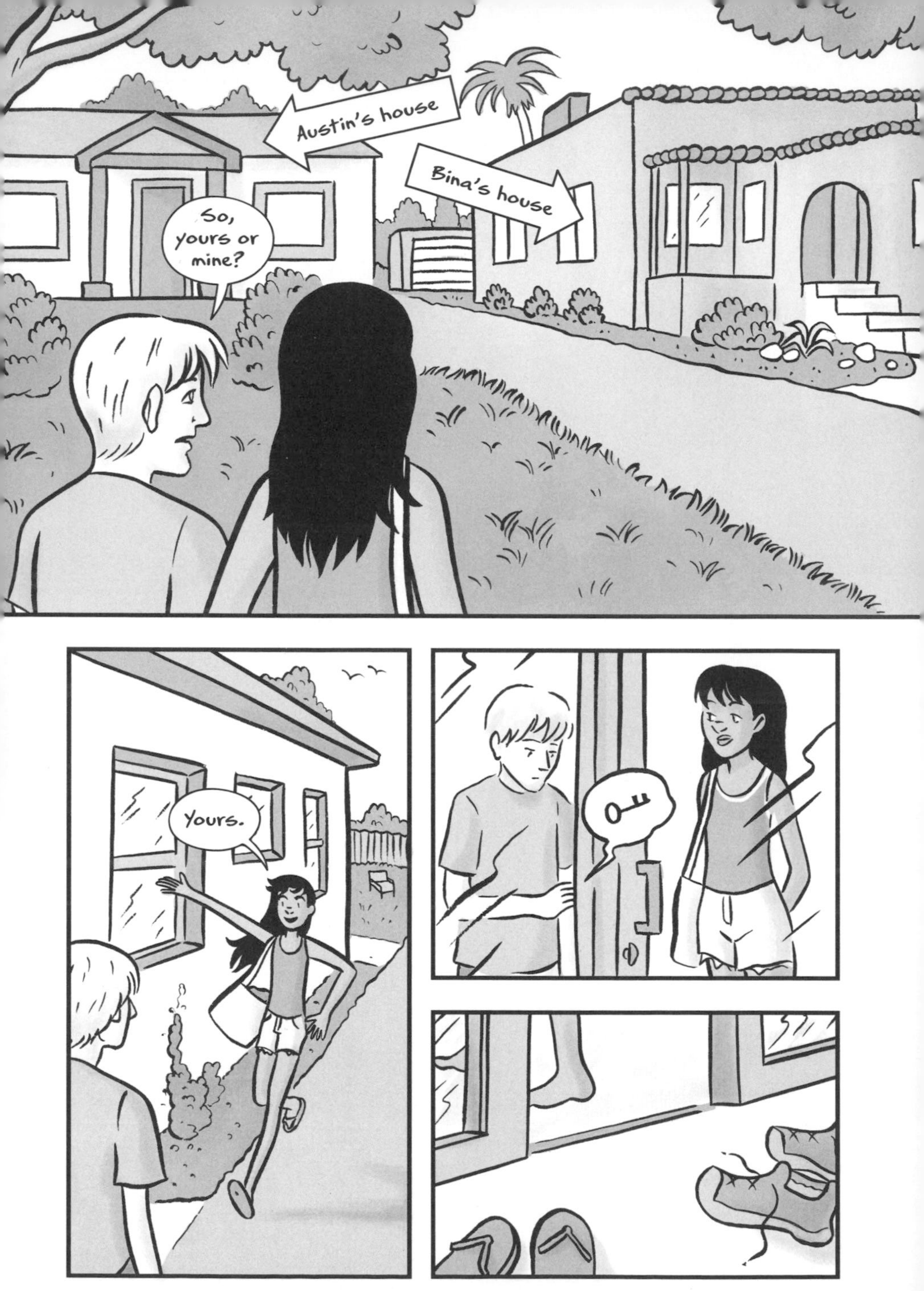
Austin's house
Bina's house
So, yours or mine?
Yours.

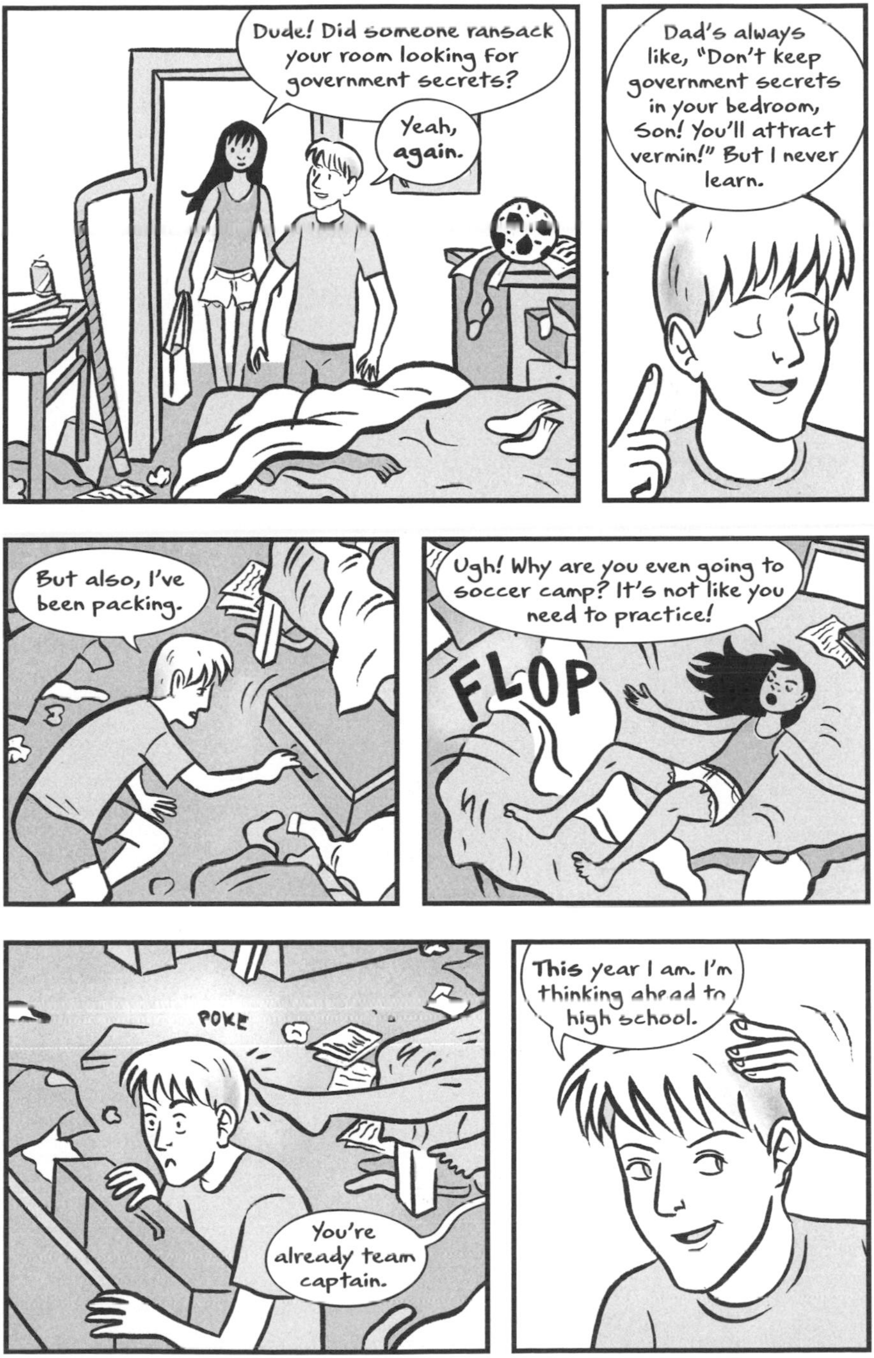
Dude! Did someone ransack your room looking for government secrets?
Yeah, again.
Dad's always like, "Don't keep government secrets in your bedroom, Son! You'll attract vermin!" But I never learn.
But also, I've been packing.
Ugh! Why are you even going to soccer camp? It's not like you need to practice!
FLOP
POKE
You're already team captain.
This year I am. I'm thinking ahead to high school.

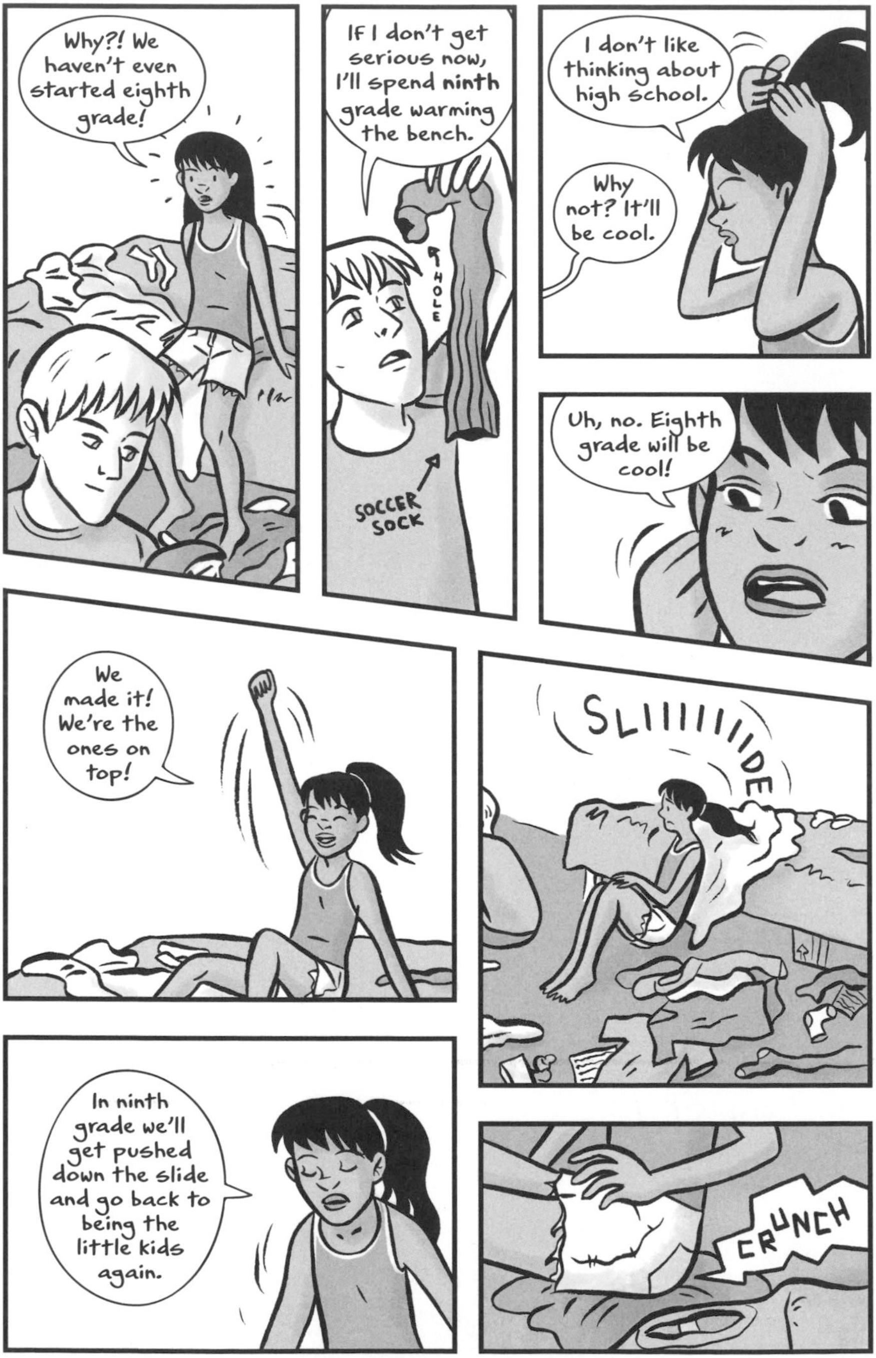
Why?! We haven't even started eighth grade!
If I don't get serious now, I'll spend ninth grade warming the bench.
HOLE
SOCCER SOCK
I don't like thinking about high school.
Why not? It'll be cool.
Uh, no. Eighth grade will be cool!
We made it! We're the ones on top!
SLIIIIIIIIDE
In ninth grade we'll get pushed down the slide and go back to being the little kids again.
CRUNCH

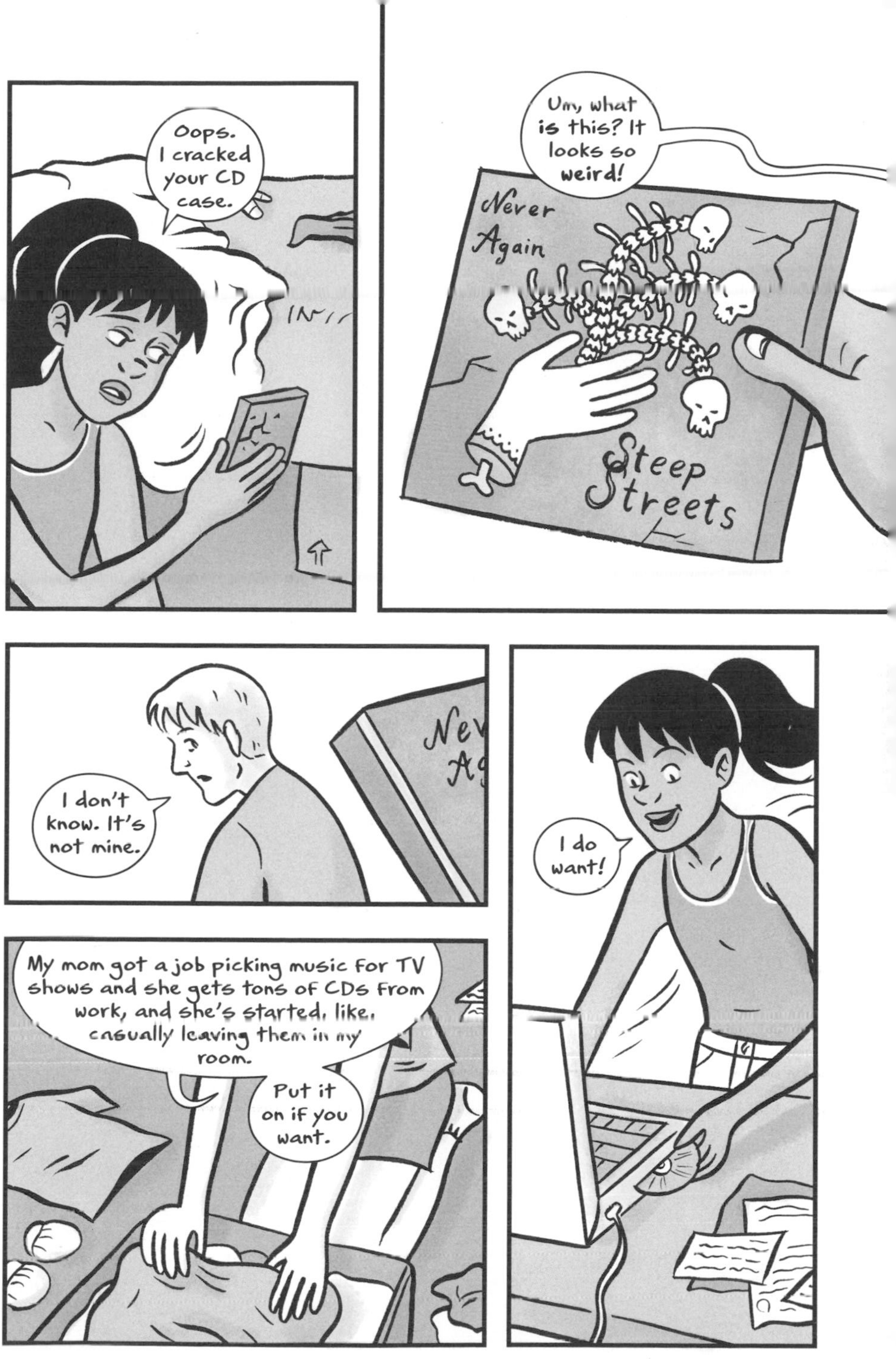
Oops. I cracked your CD case.
Um, what is this? It looks so weird!
Never Again
Steep Streets
I don't know. It's not mine.
Nev
Ag
My mom got a job picking music for TV shows and she gets tons of CDs from work, and she's started, like, casually leaving them in my room.
Put it on if you want.
I do want!

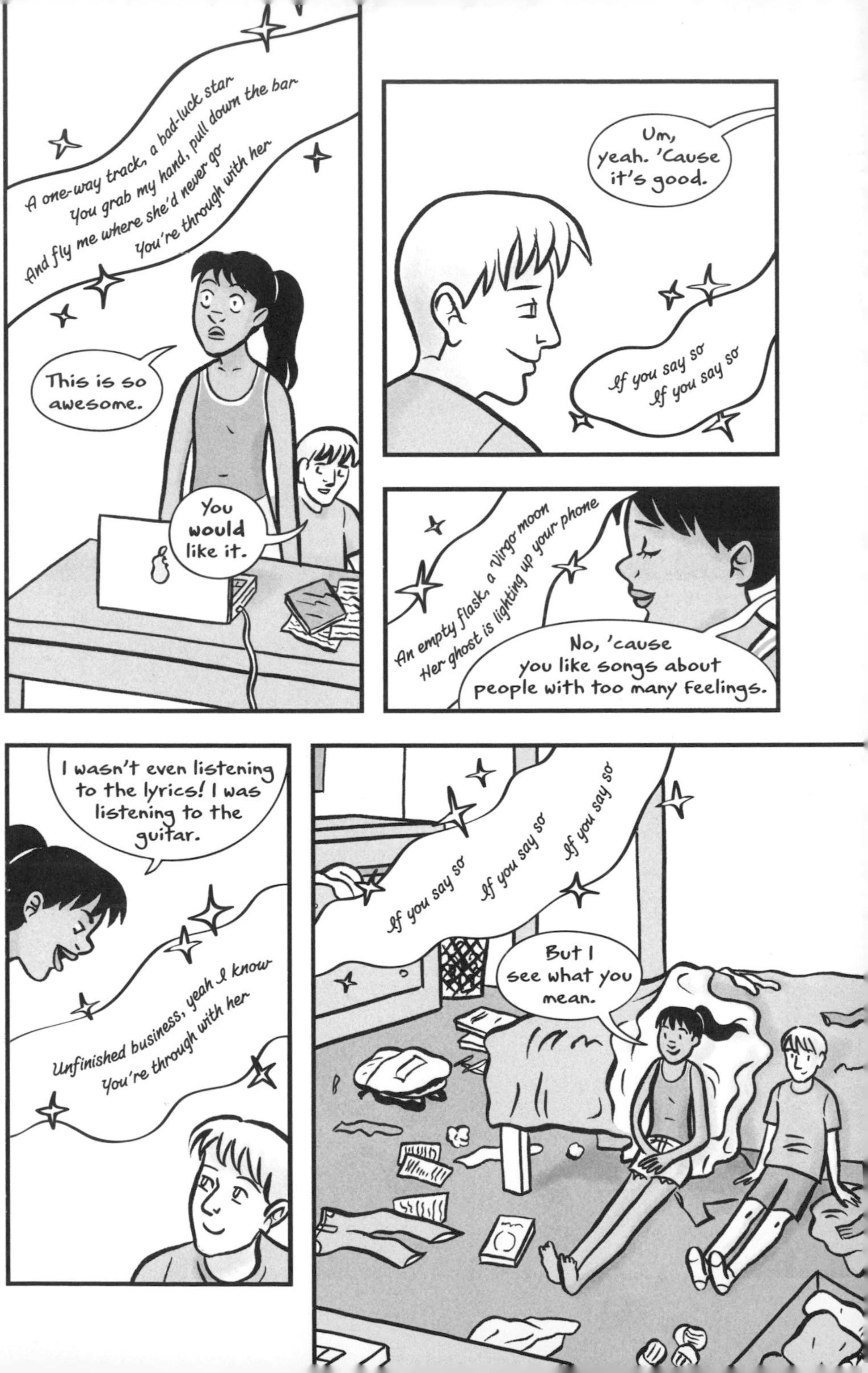
A one-way track, a bad-luck star
You grab my hand, pull down the bar
And fly me where she'd never go
You're through with her
This is so awesome.
You would like it.
Um, yeah. 'Cause it's good.
If you say so
If you say so
An empty flask, a Virgo moon
Her ghost is lighting up your phone
No, 'cause you like songs about people with too many feelings.
I wasn't even listening to the lyrics! I was listening to the guitar.
Unfinished business, yeah I know
You're through with her
If you say so
If you say so
If you say so
But I see what you mean.

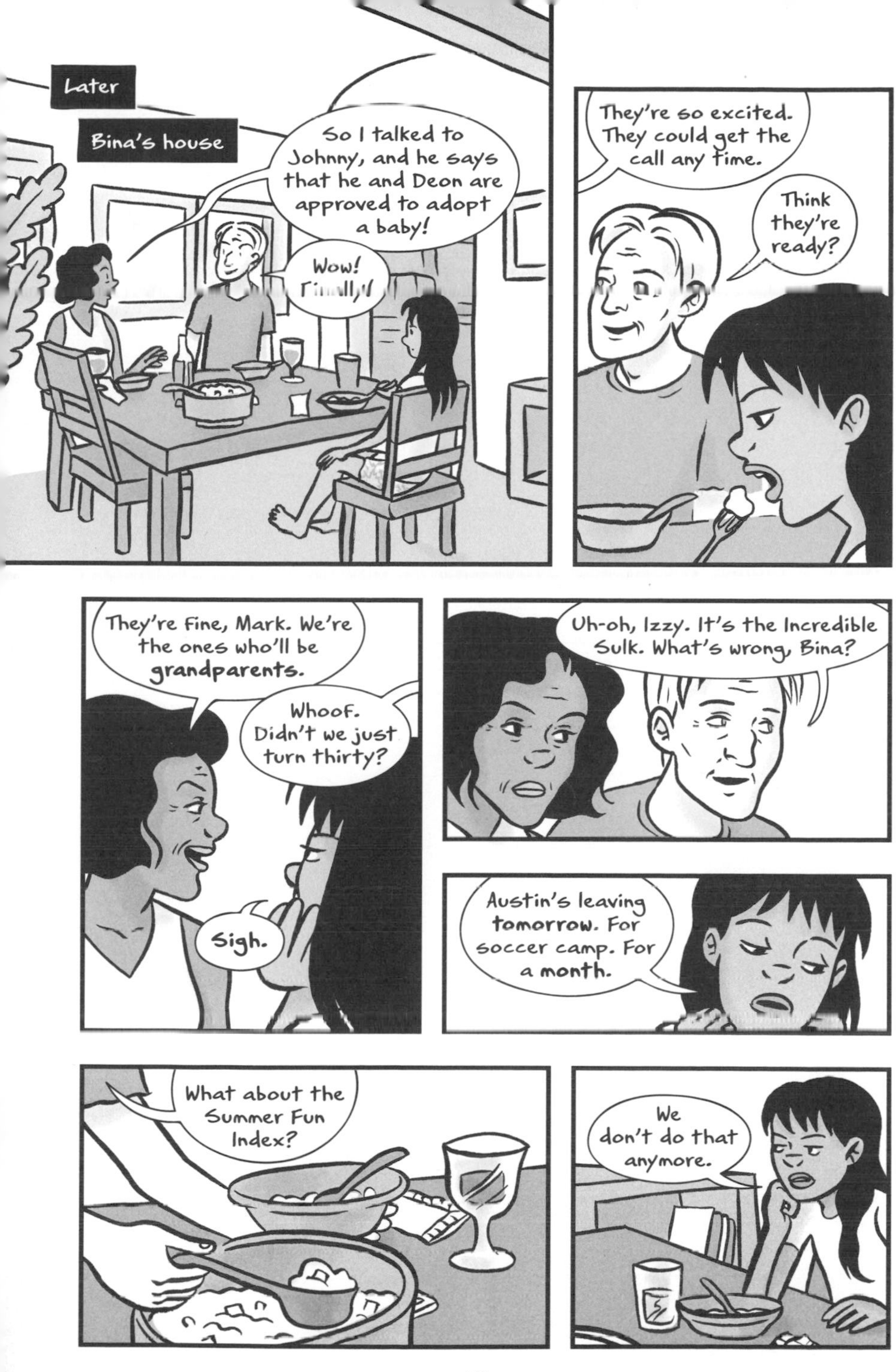

Later
Bina's house
So I talked to Johnny, and he says that he and Deon are approved to adopt a baby!
Wow! Finally!
They're so excited. They could get the call any time.
Think they're ready?
They're fine, Mark. We're the ones who'll be **grandparents.**
Whoof. Didn't we just turn thirty?
Sigh.
Uh-oh, Izzy. It's the Incredible Sulk. What's wrong, Bina?
Austin's leaving **tomorrow.** For soccer camp. For a **month.**
What about the Summer Fun Index?
We don't do that anymore.

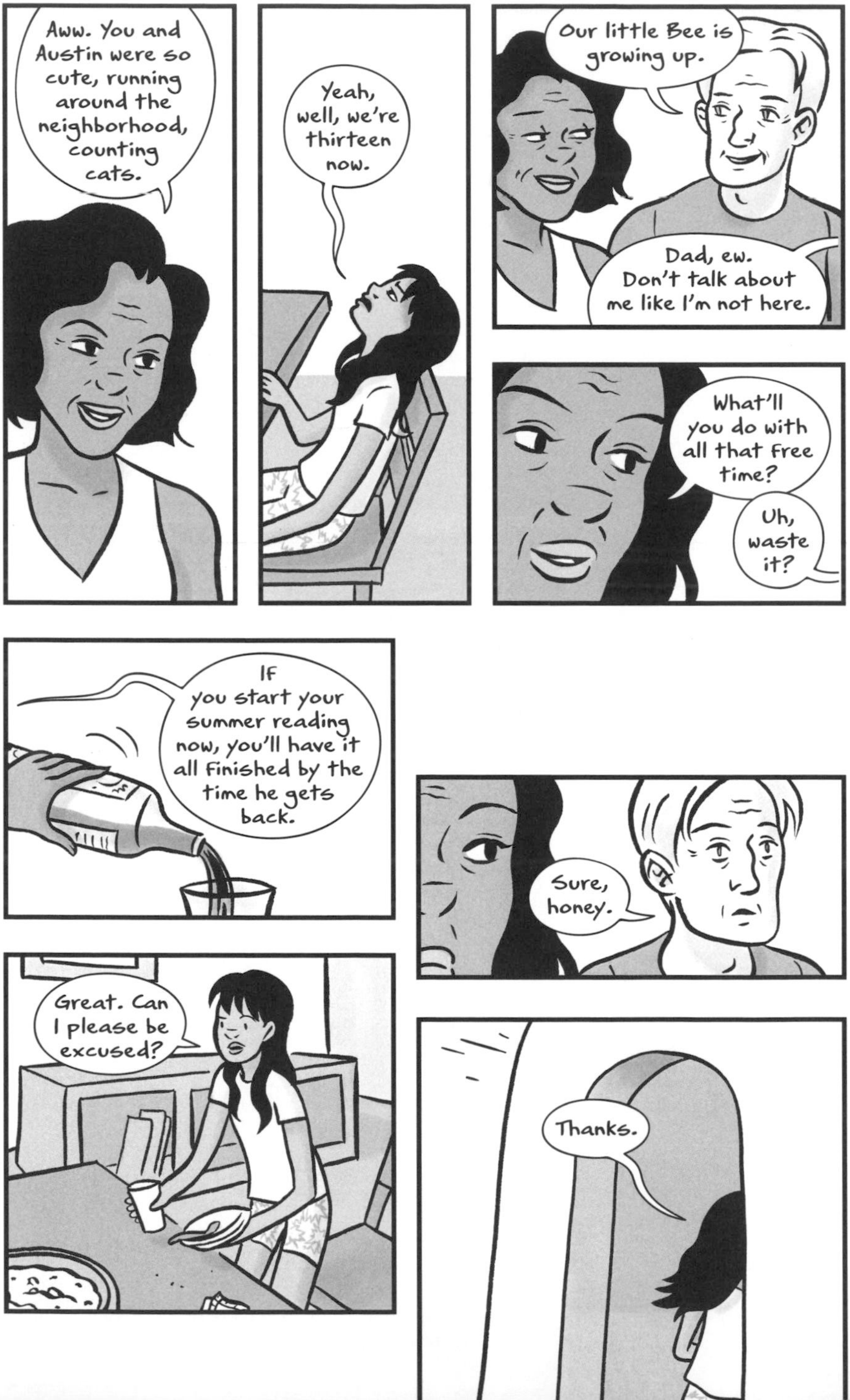
Aww. You and Austin were so cute, running around the neighborhood, counting cats.
Yeah, well, we're thirteen now.
Our little Bee is growing up.
Dad, ew. Don't talk about me like I'm not here.
What'll you do with all that free time?
Uh, waste it?
If you start your summer reading now, you'll have it all finished by the time he gets back.
Sure, honey.
Great. Can I please be excused?
Thanks.

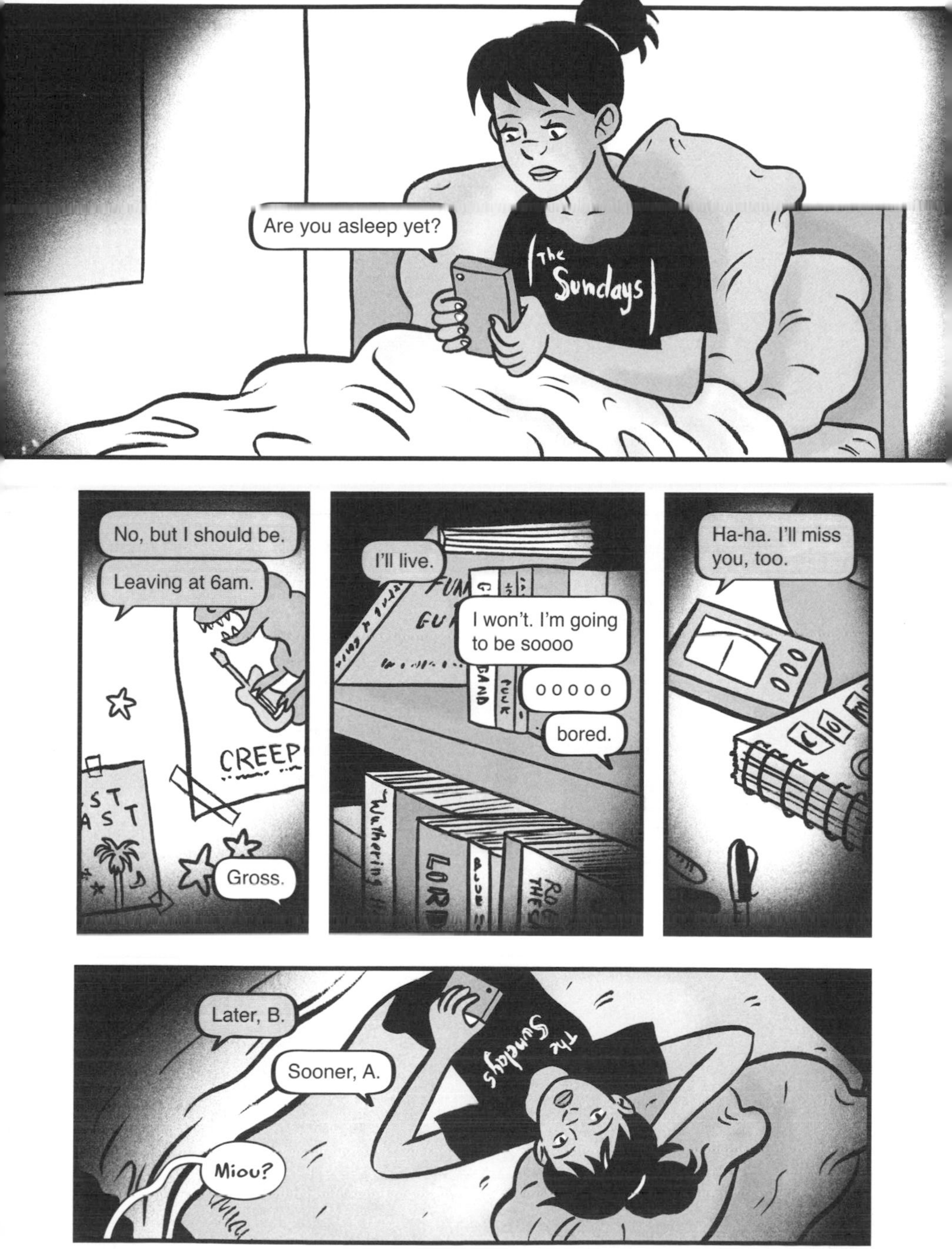
Are you asleep yet?
The Sundays
No, but I should be.
Leaving at 6am.
CREEP
Gross.
I'll live.
I won't. I'm going to be soooo
ooooo
bored.
Wuthering
Ha-ha. I'll miss you, too.
Later, B.
Sooner, A.
The Sundays
Miou?

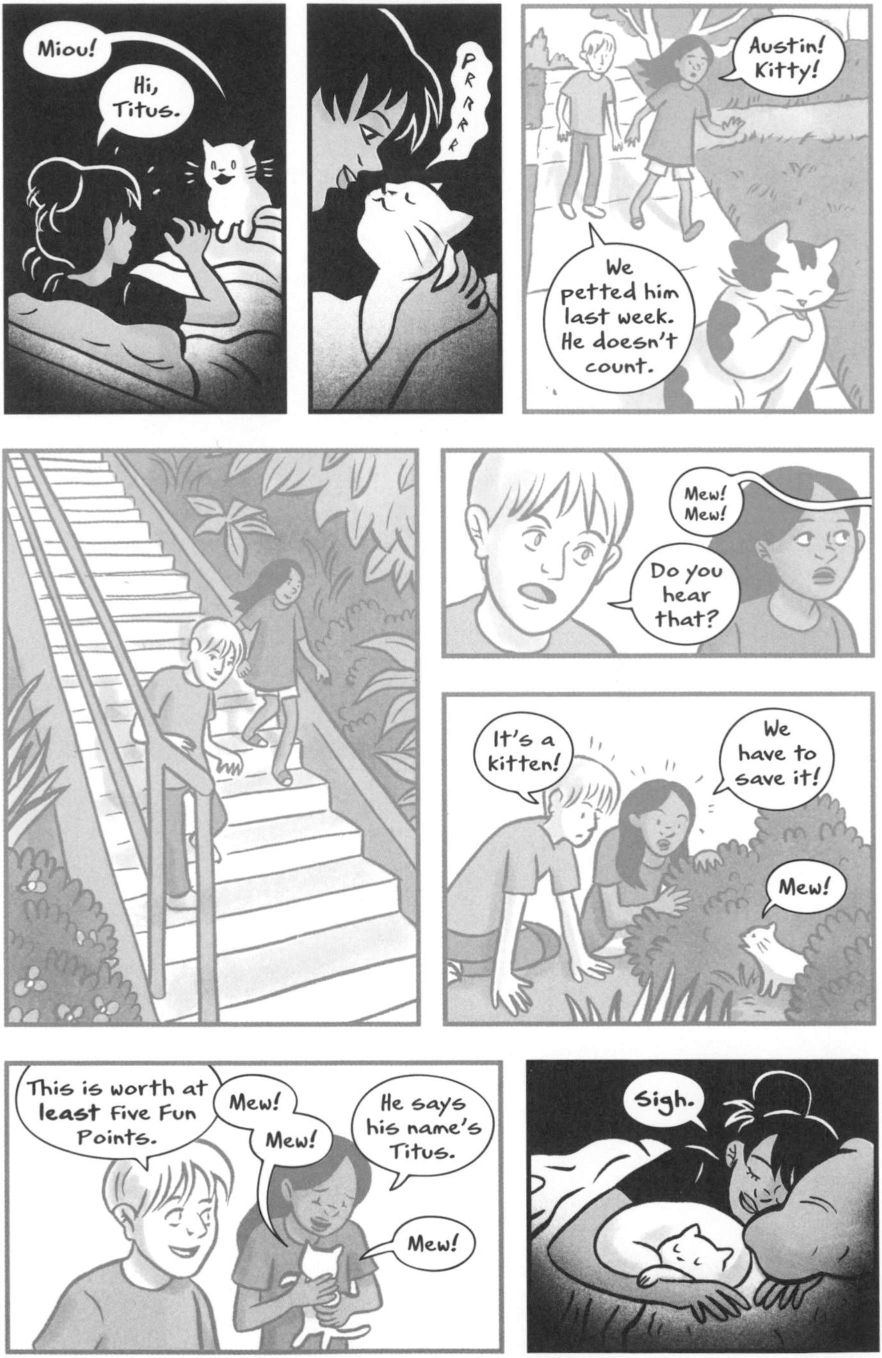
Miou!
Hi, Titus.
PRRRR
Austin! Kitty!
We petted him last week. He doesn't count.
Mew! Mew!
Do you hear that?
It's a kitten!
We have to save it!
Mew!
This is worth at least Five Fun Points.
Mew!
Mew!
He says his name's Titus.
Mew!
Sigh.

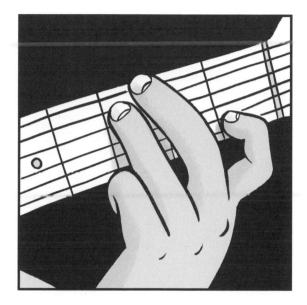

Week One

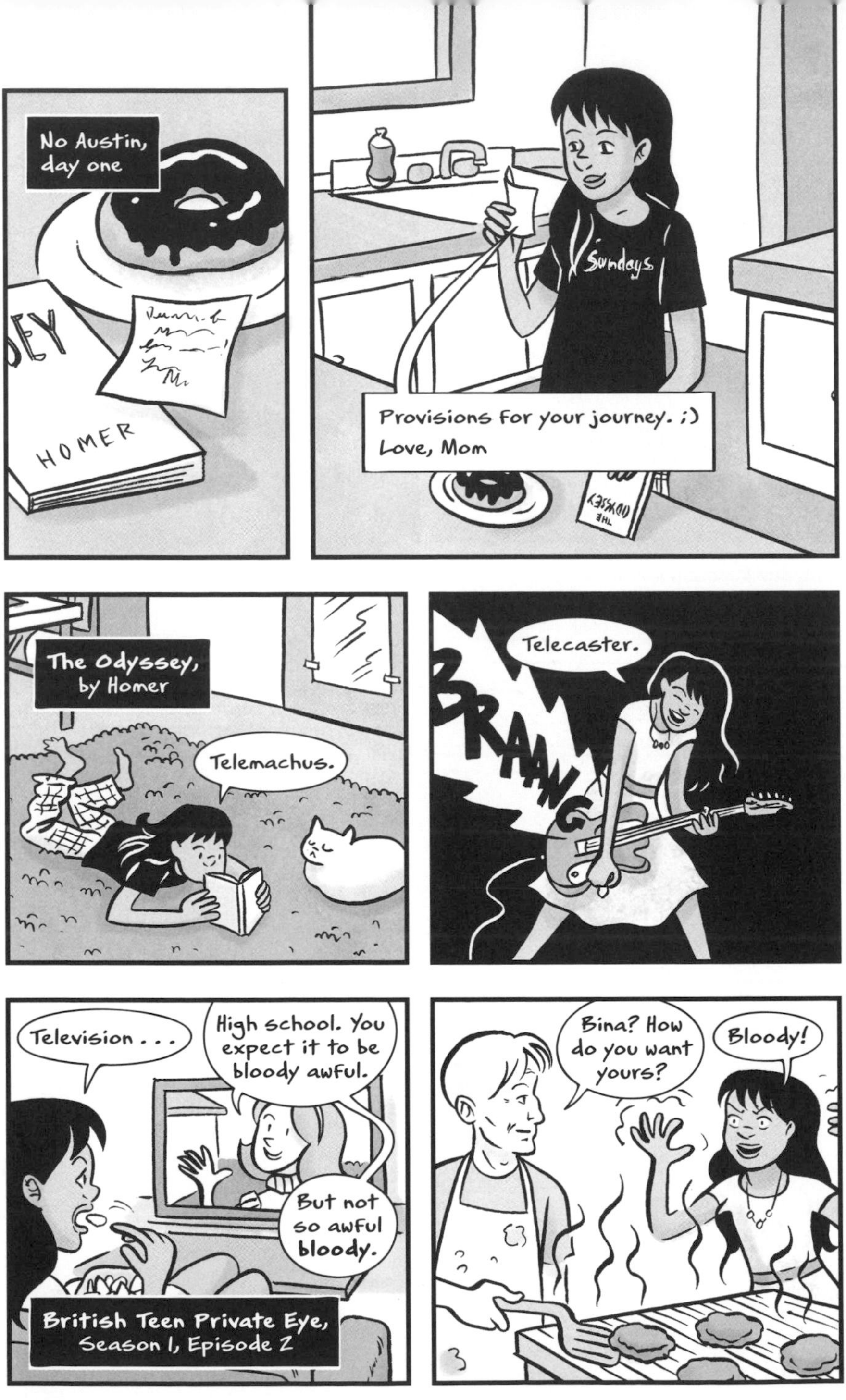
No Austin, day one
HOMER
Provisions for your journey. ;) Love, Mom
Sundays
The Odyssey, by Homer
Telemachus.
Telecaster.
BRAAANG
Television . . .
High school. You expect it to be bloody awful.
But not so awful bloody.
British Teen Private Eye, Season 1, Episode 2
Bina? How do you want yours?
Bloody!

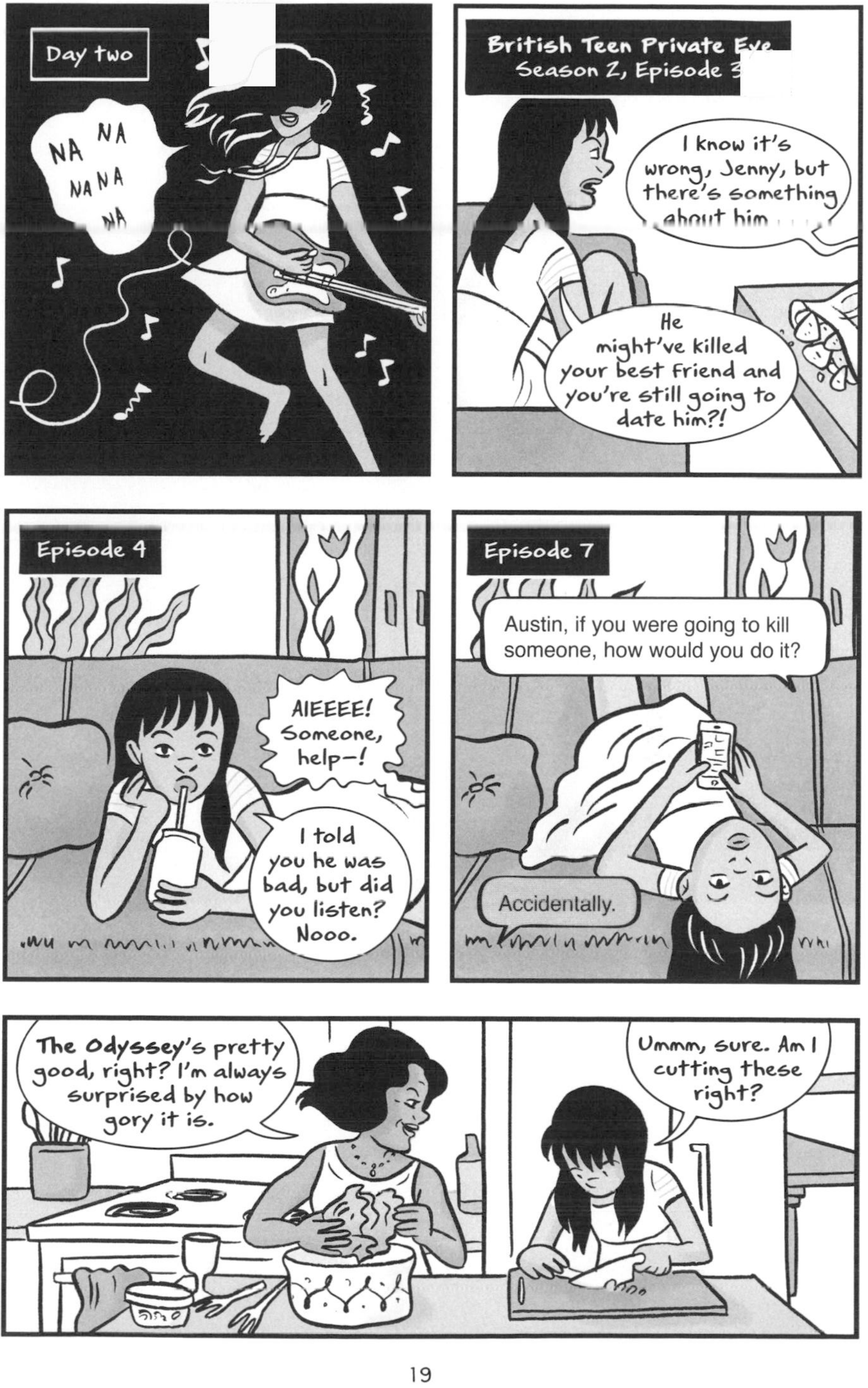
Day two
NA NA NA NA NA
British Teen Private Eye
Season 2, Episode 3
I know it's wrong, Jenny, but there's something about him
He might've killed your best friend and you're still going to date him?!
Episode 4
AIEEEE! Someone, help–!
I told you he was bad, but did you listen? Nooo.
Episode 7
Austin, if you were going to kill someone, how would you do it?
Accidentally.
The Odyssey's pretty good, right? I'm always surprised by how gory it is.
Ummm, sure. Am I cutting these right?

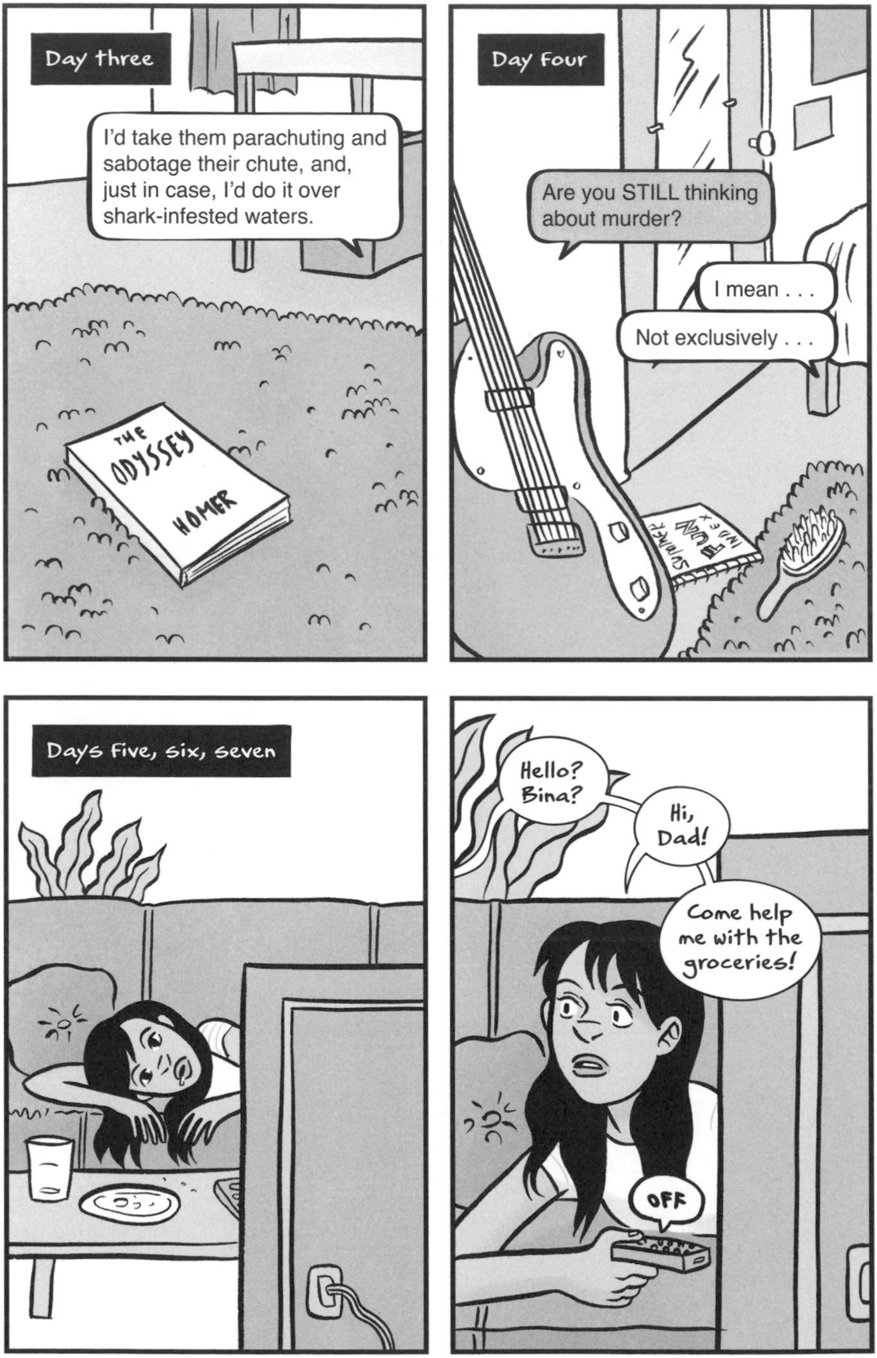
Day three
I'd take them parachuting and sabotage their chute, and, just in case, I'd do it over shark-infested waters.
THE ODYSSEY
HOMER
Day Four
Are you STILL thinking about murder?
I mean . . .
Not exclusively . . .
Days five, six, seven
Hello? Bina?
Hi, Dad!
Come help me with the groceries!
OFF

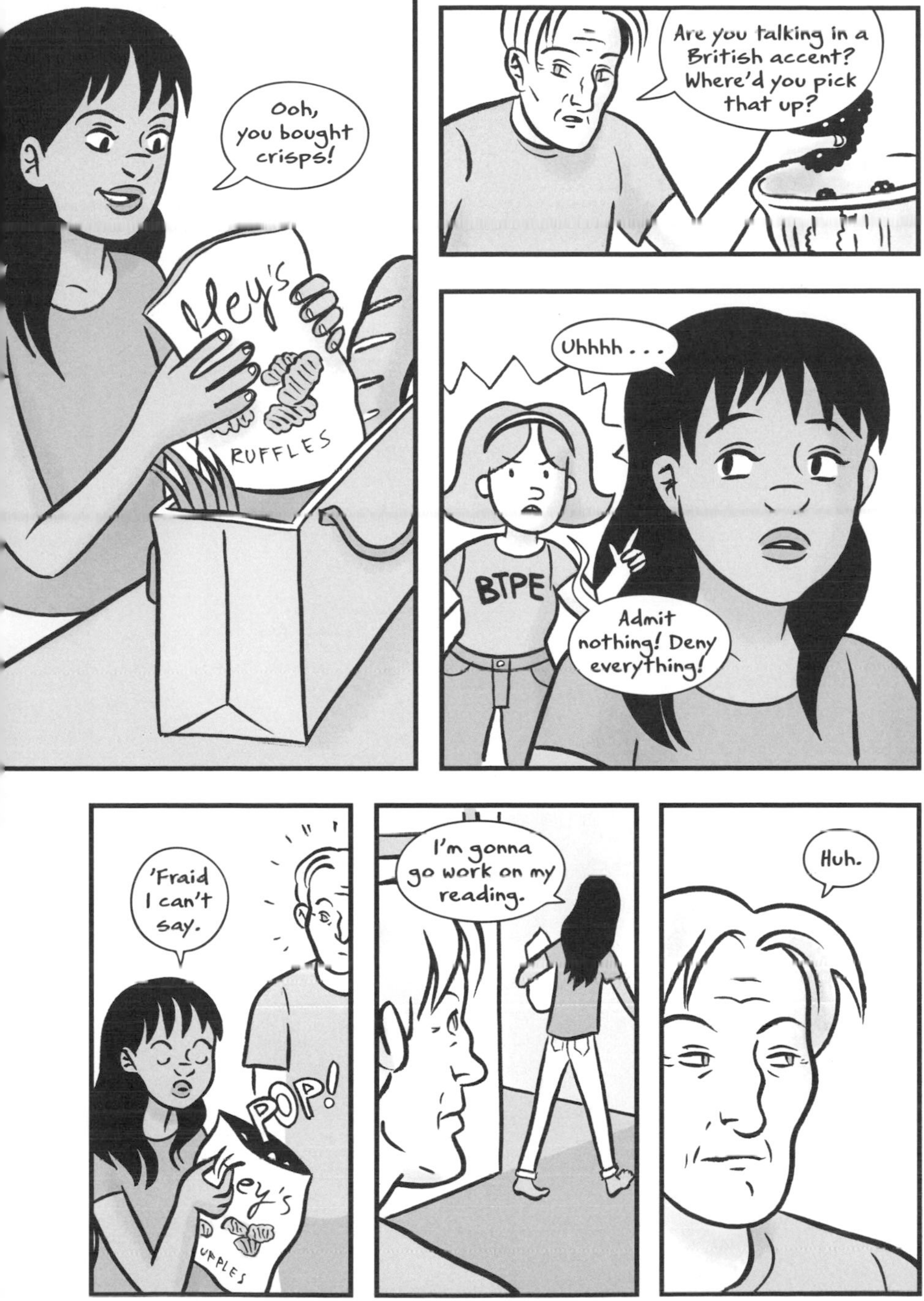

Ooh, you bought crisps!
Hey's
RUFFLES
Are you talking in a British accent? Where'd you pick that up?
Uhhhh . . .
BTPE
Admit nothing! Deny everything!
'Fraid I can't say.
POP!
Hey's
I'm gonna go work on my reading.
Huh.

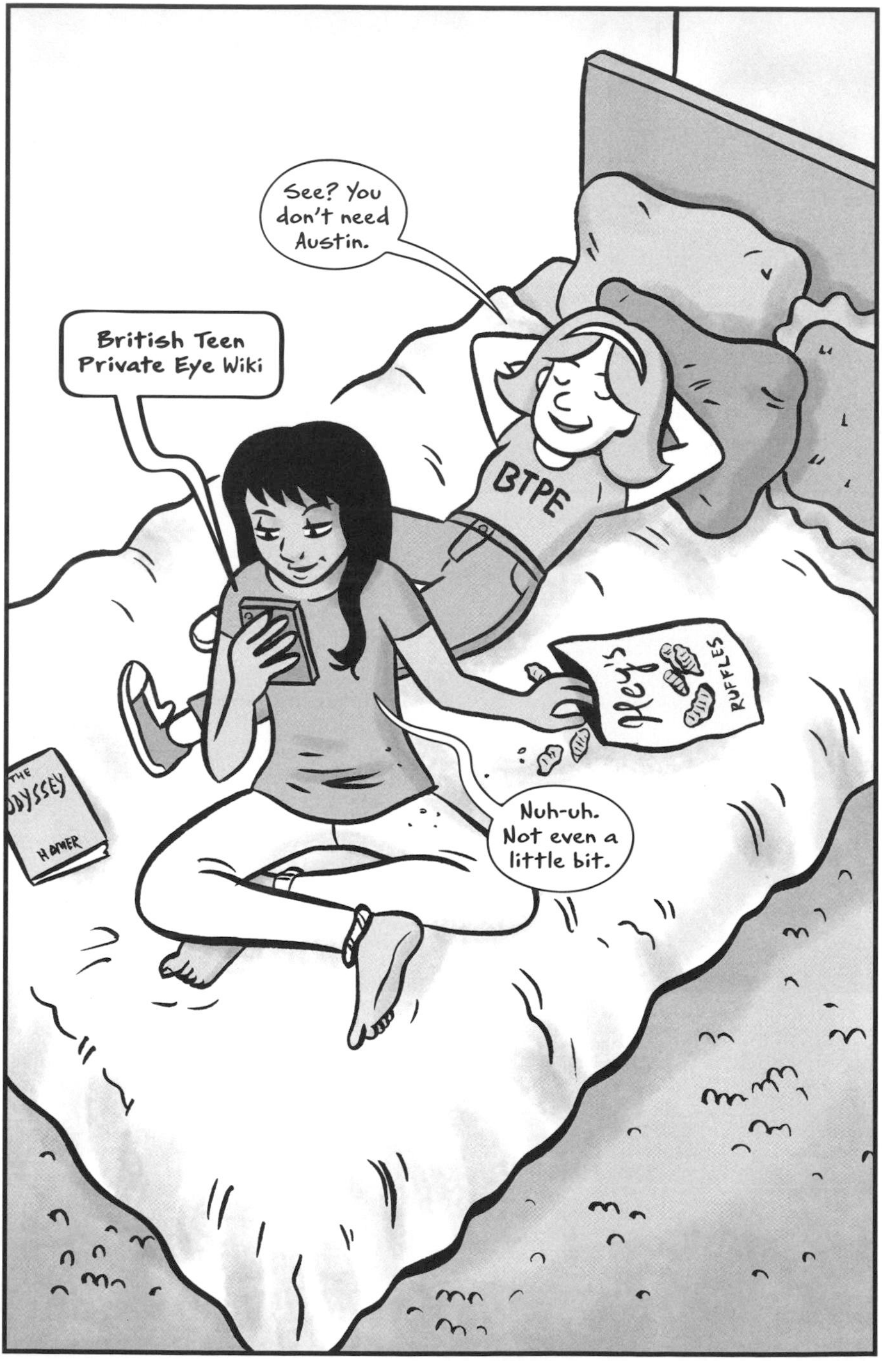
See? You don't need Austin.
British Teen Private Eye Wiki
BTPE
THE ODYSSEY HOMER
Ley's RUFFLES
Nuh-uh. Not even a little bit.

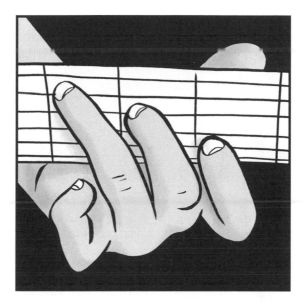

Week Two

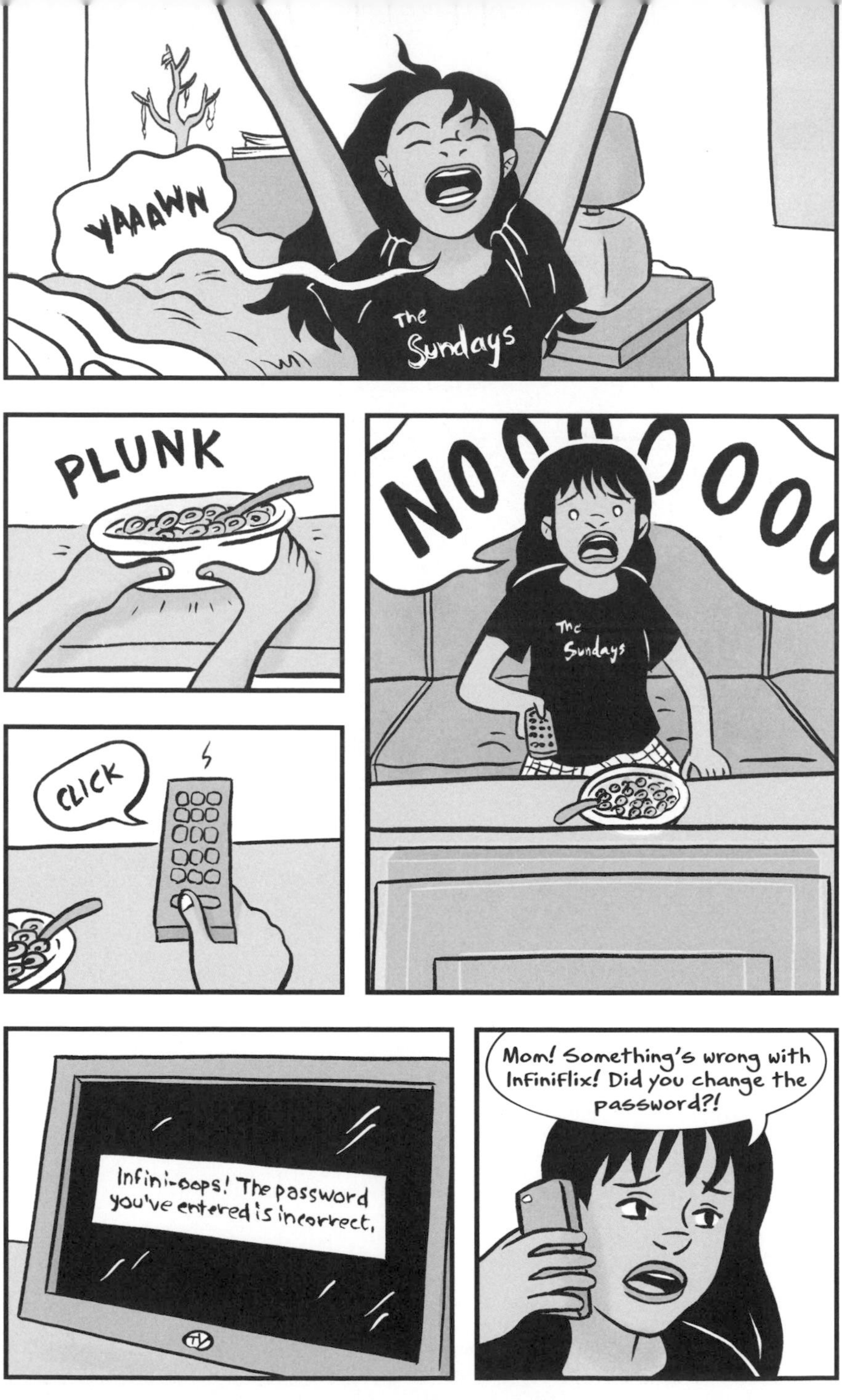
YAAAWN
The Sundays
PLUNK
NOOOOOOO
The Sundays
CLICK
Infini-oops! The password you've entered is incorrect.
TV
Mom! Something's wrong with Infiniflix! Did you change the password?!

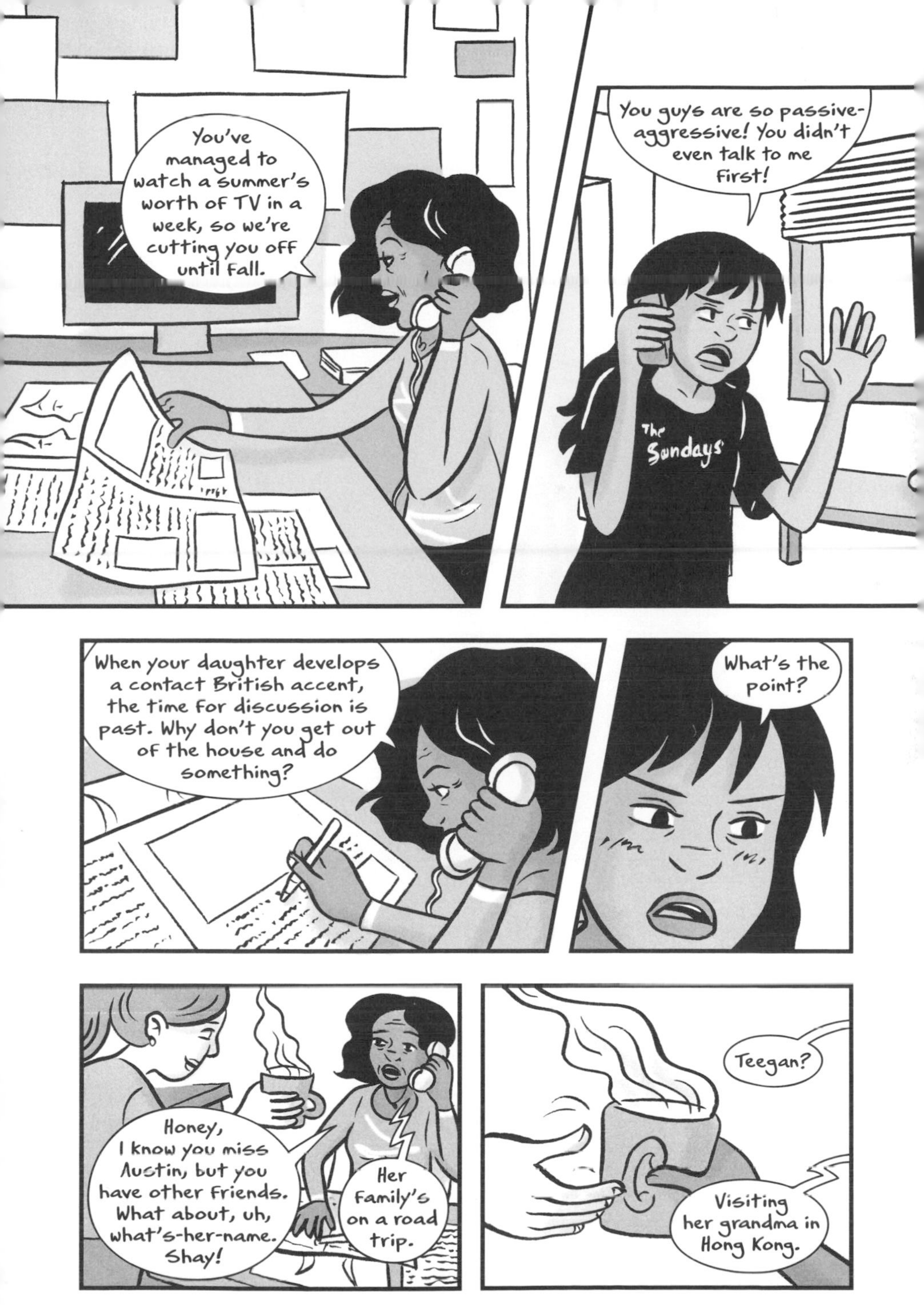

You've managed to watch a summer's worth of TV in a week, so we're cutting you off until fall.
You guys are so passive-aggressive! You didn't even talk to me first!
The Sundays
When your daughter develops a contact British accent, the time for discussion is past. Why don't you get out of the house and do something?
What's the point?
Honey, I know you miss Austin, but you have other friends. What about, uh, what's-her-name. Shay!
Her Family's on a road trip.
Teegan?
Visiting her grandma in Hong Kong.

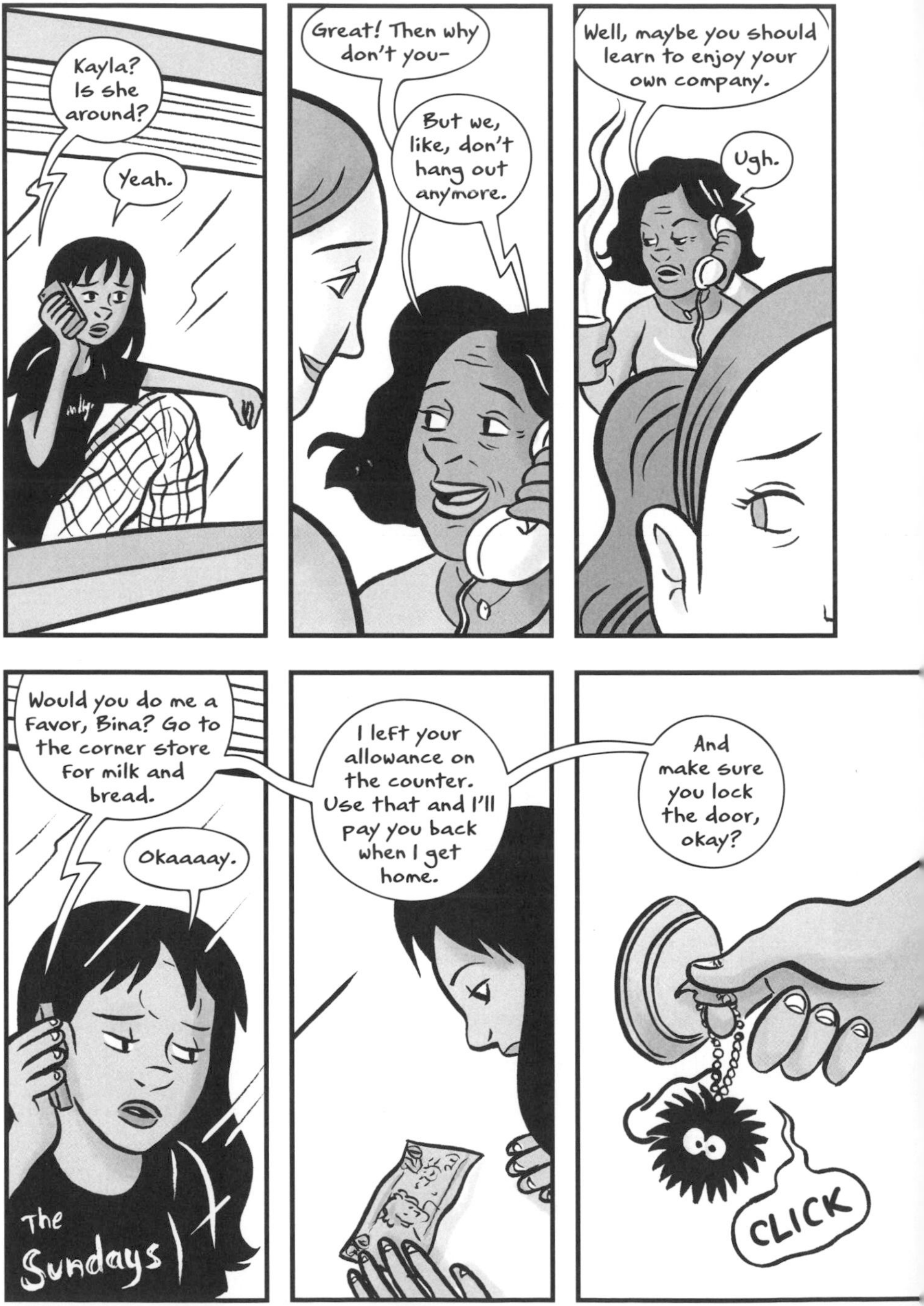
Kayla? Is she around?
Yeah.
Great! Then why don't you-
But we, like, don't hang out anymore.
Well, maybe you should learn to enjoy your own company.
Ugh.
Would you do me a favor, Bina? Go to the corner store for milk and bread.
Okaaaay.
The Sundays
I left your allowance on the counter. Use that and I'll pay you back when I get home.
And make sure you lock the door, okay?
CLICK

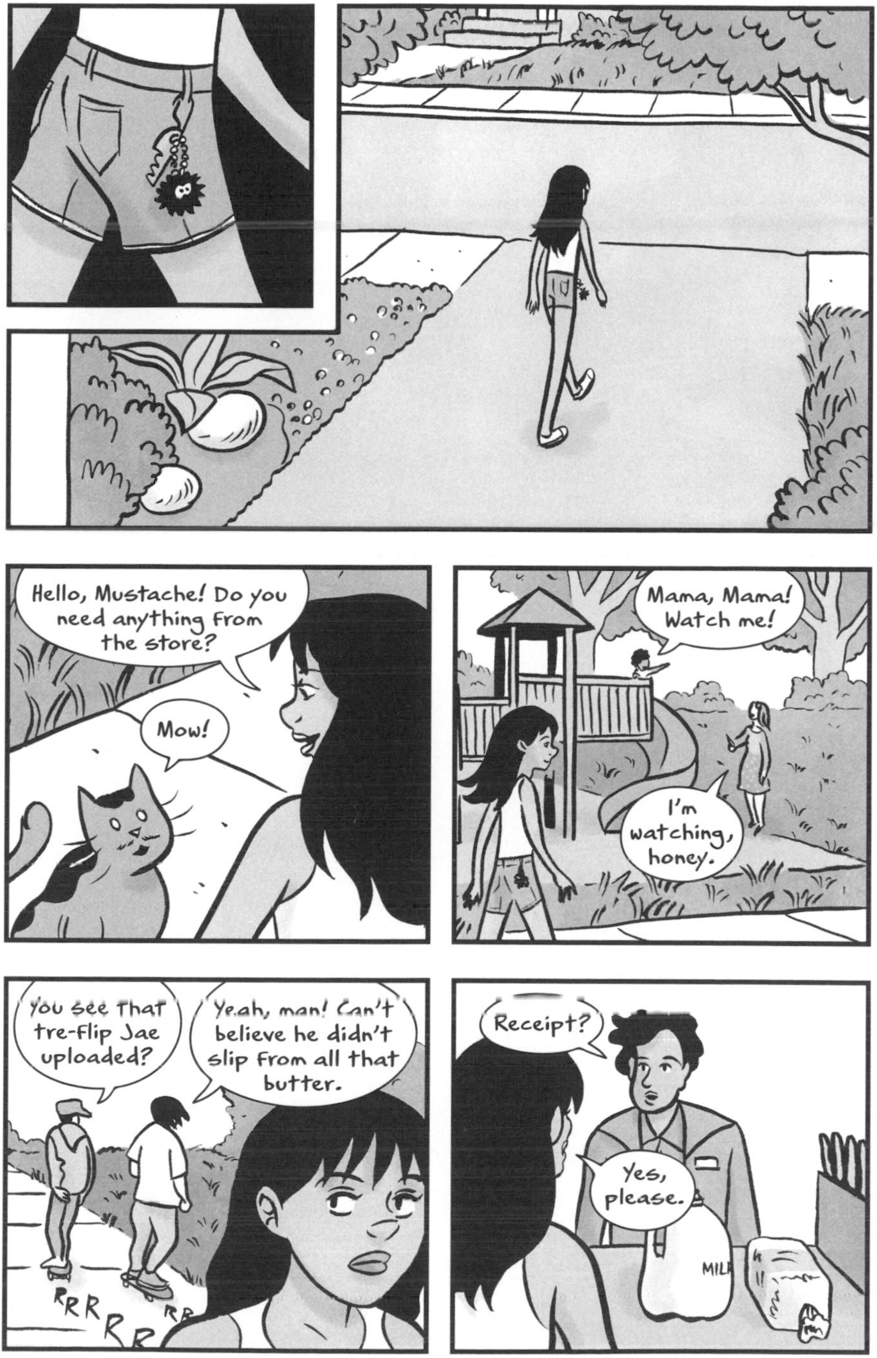
Hello, Mustache! Do you need anything from the store?
Mow!
Mama, Mama! Watch me!
I'm watching, honey.
You see that tre-flip Jae uploaded?
Yeah, man! Can't believe he didn't slip from all that butter.
RRRRR
RR
Receipt?
Yes, please.
MILK

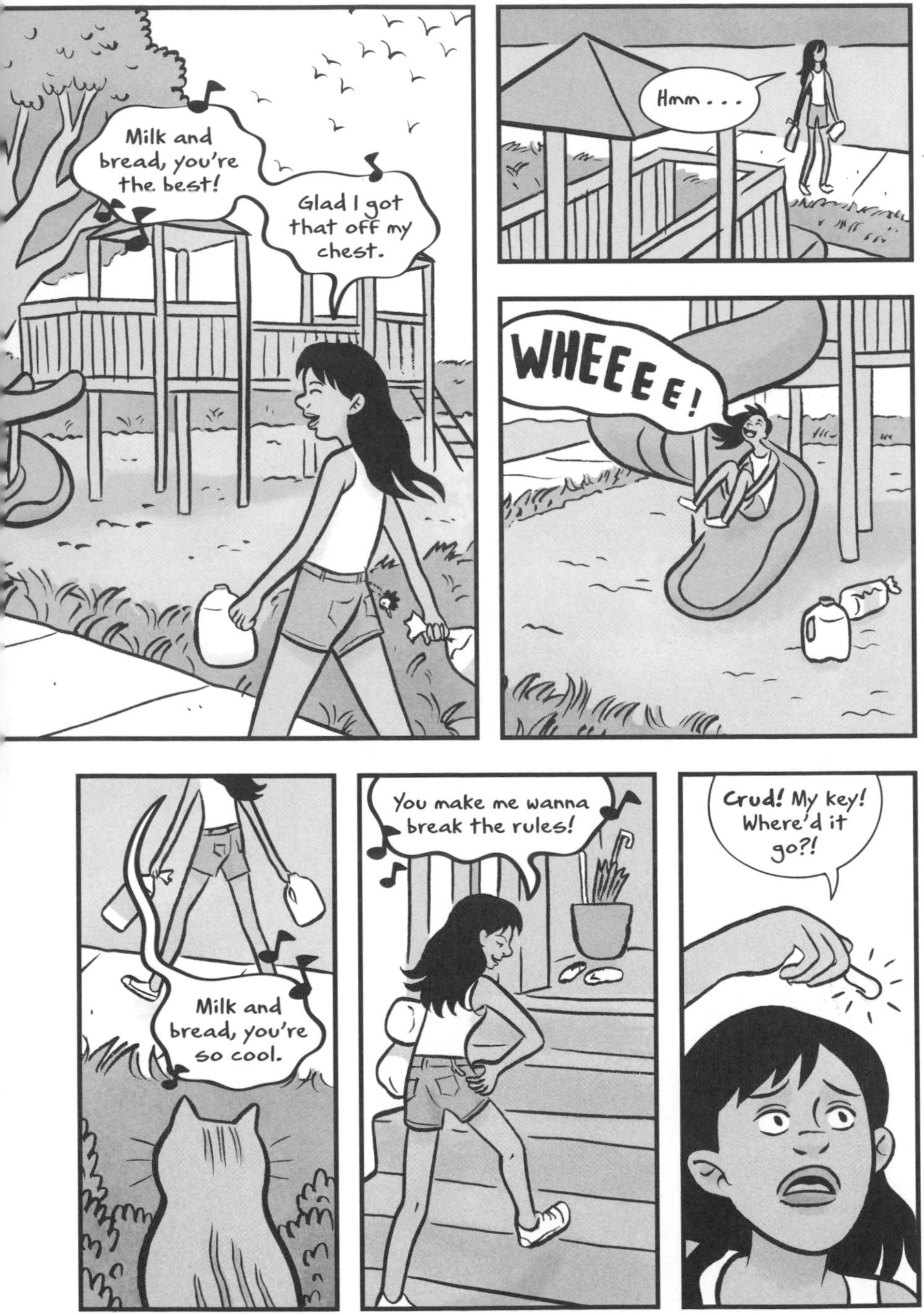
Milk and bread, you're the best!
Glad I got that off my chest.
Hmm . . .
WHEEEEE!
Milk and bread, you're so cool.
You make me wanna break the rules!
Crud! My key! Where'd it go?!

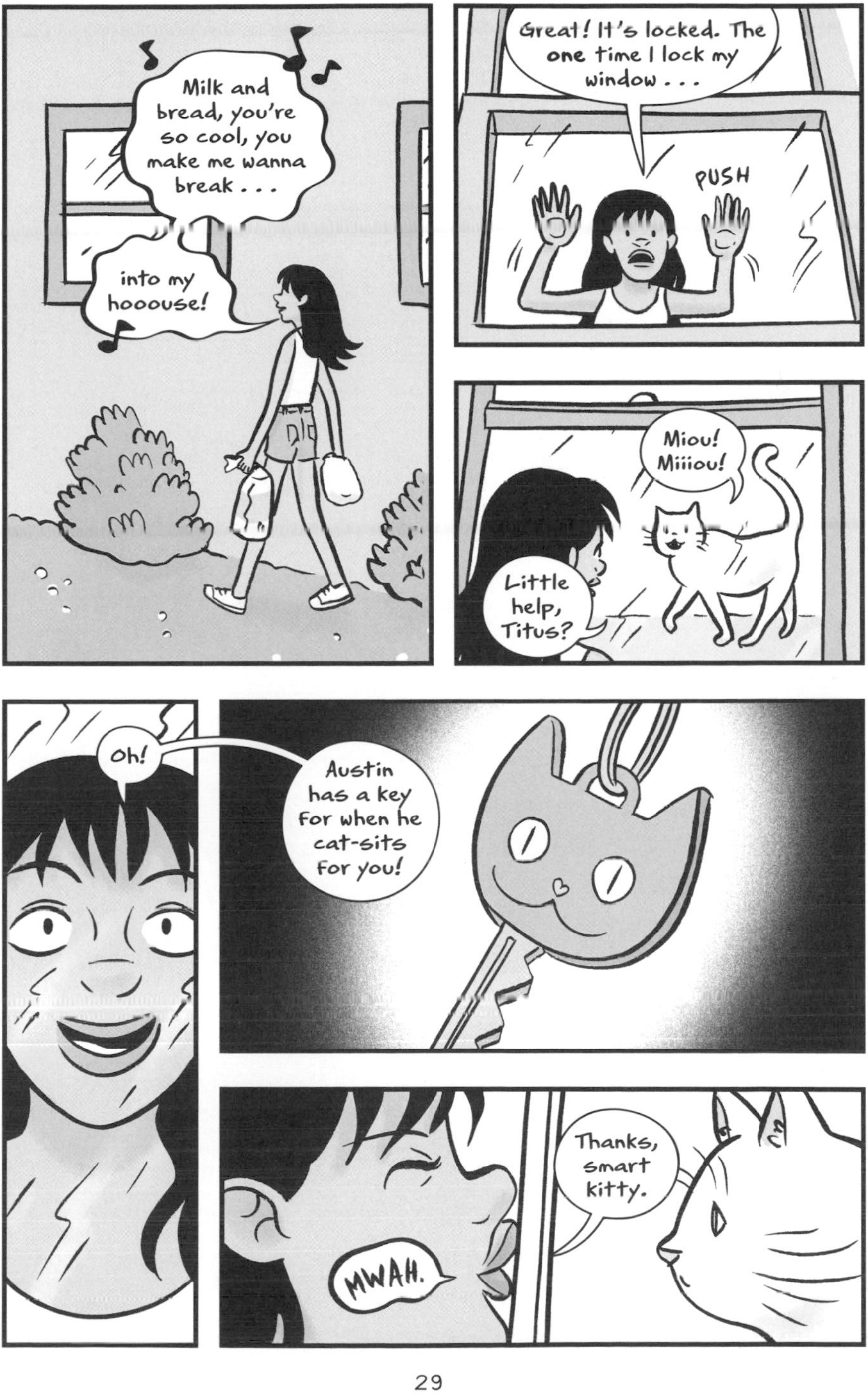
Milk and bread, you're so cool, you make me wanna break . . .
into my hooouse!
Great! It's locked. The one time I lock my window . . .
PUSH
Miou! Miiiou!
Little help, Titus?
Oh!
Austin has a key for when he cat-sits for you!
Thanks, smart kitty.
MWAH.

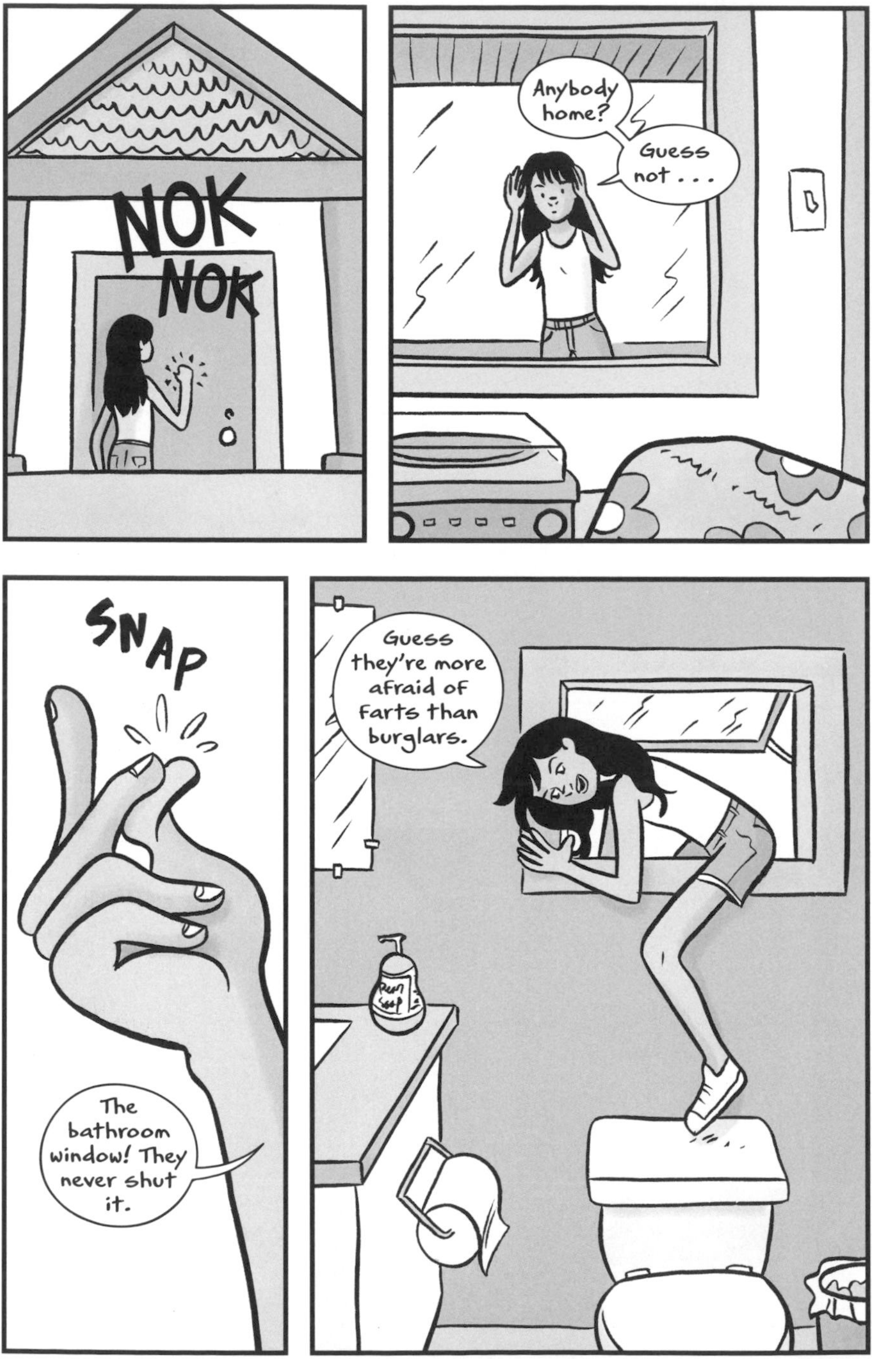
NOK
NOK
Anybody home?
Guess not . . .
SNAP
The bathroom window! They never shut it.
Guess they're more afraid of farts than burglars.

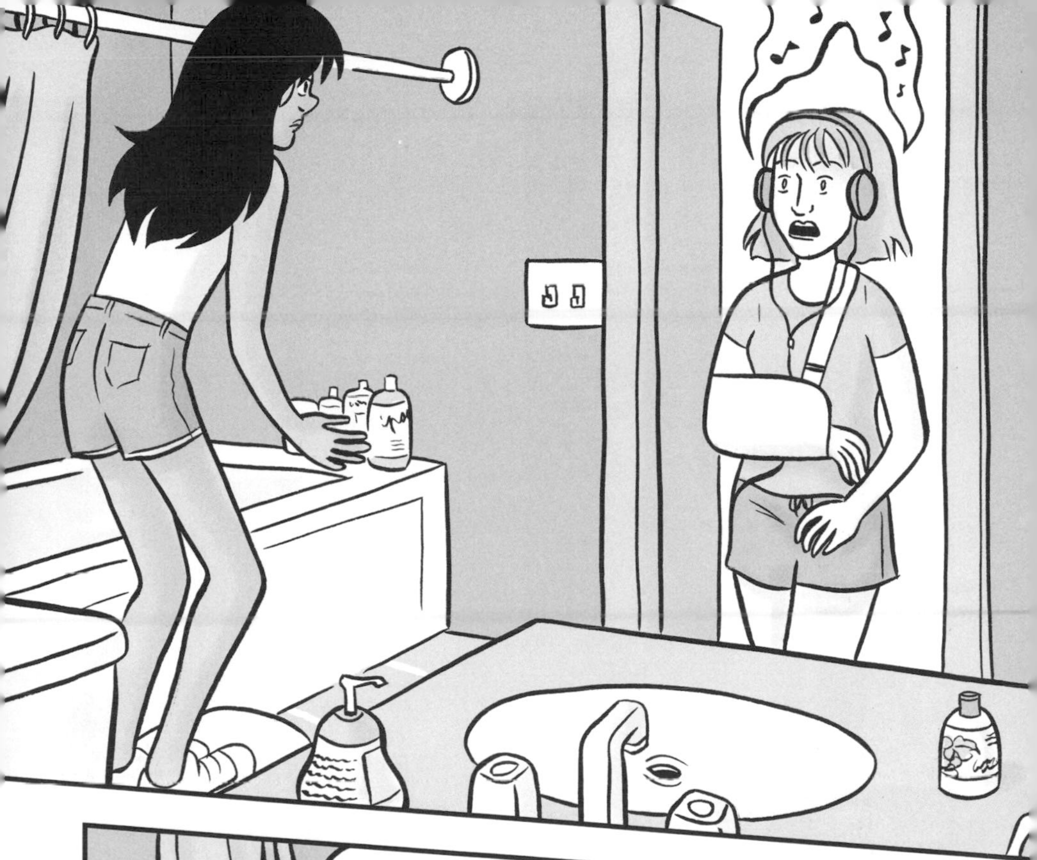
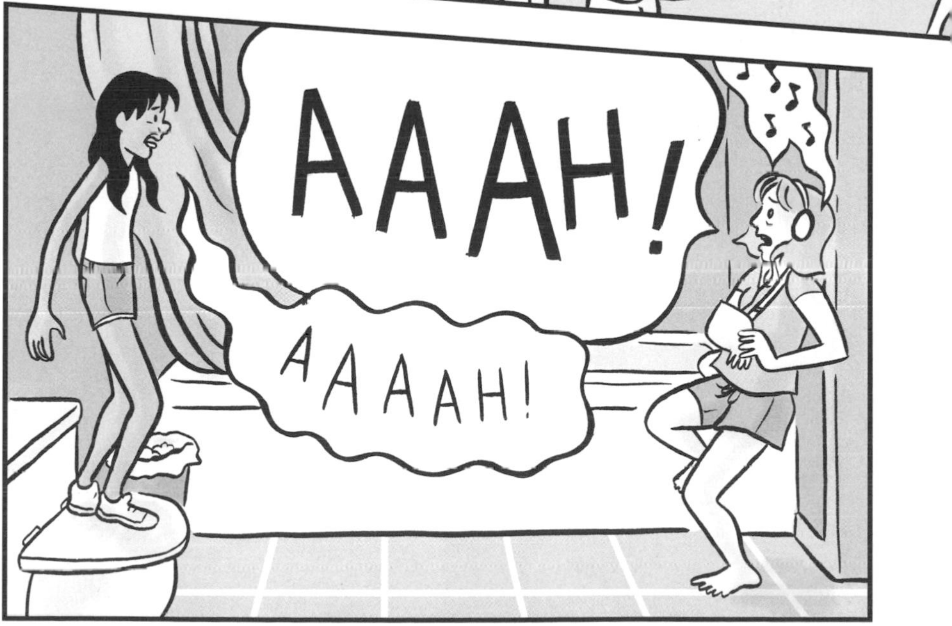
AAAH!
AAAAH!

I'm sorry! I-I didn't think anyone was home!
So you thought, "Hey! I'll just **break in**!"?
I'm locked out of my house, Charlie!
So go **break in** there!
I can't! It's like Fort Knox! But Austin has a key in his room. For cat-sitting.
SQUINT
Get down off the toilet. You're a stone-cold psycho and I kinda admire that.
Come get your dumb key.

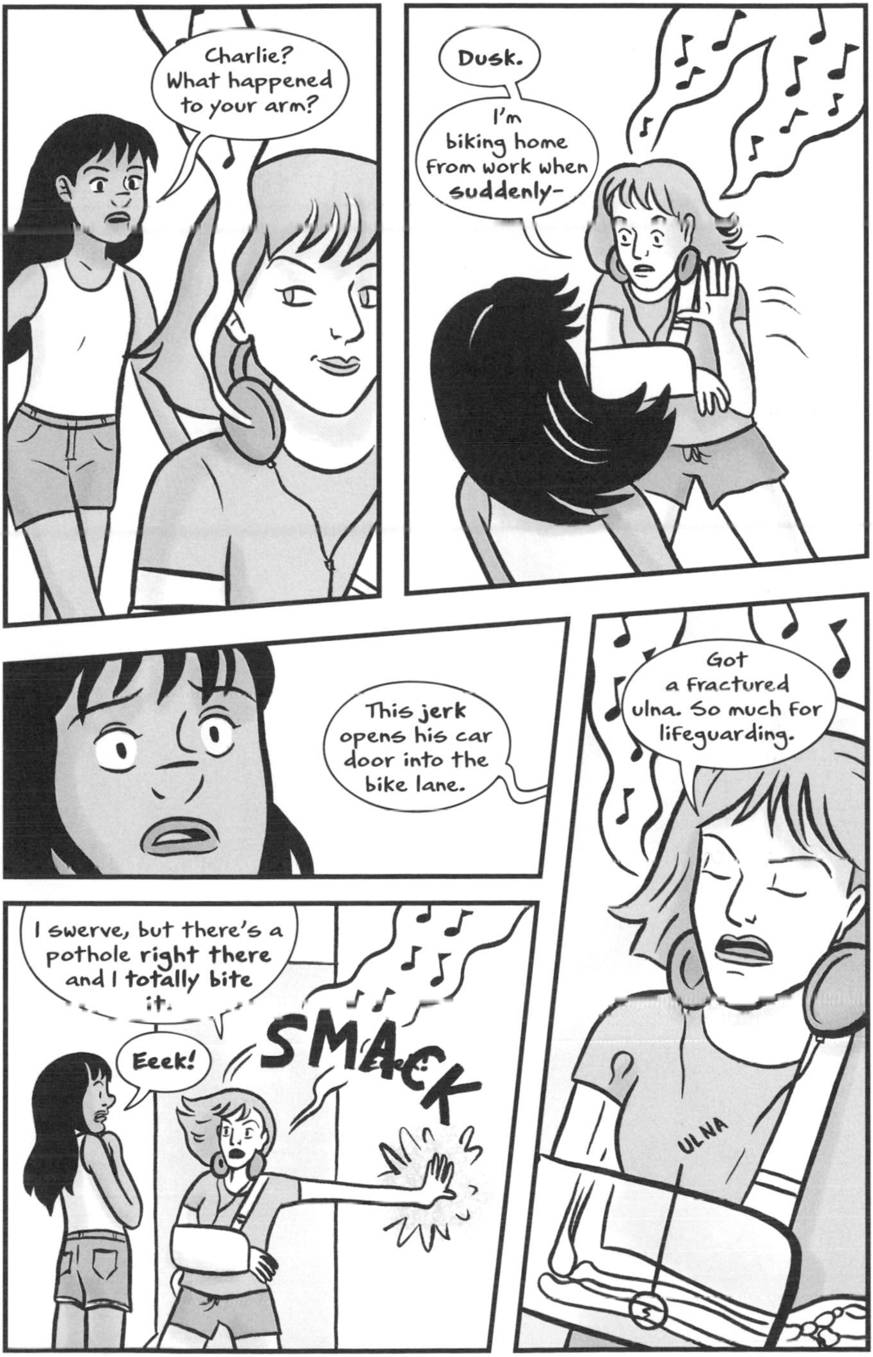
Charlie? What happened to your arm?
Dusk.
I'm biking home from work when suddenly-
This jerk opens his car door into the bike lane.
Got a fractured ulna. So much for lifeguarding.
ULNA
I swerve, but there's a pothole right there and I totally bite it.
Eeek!
SMACK

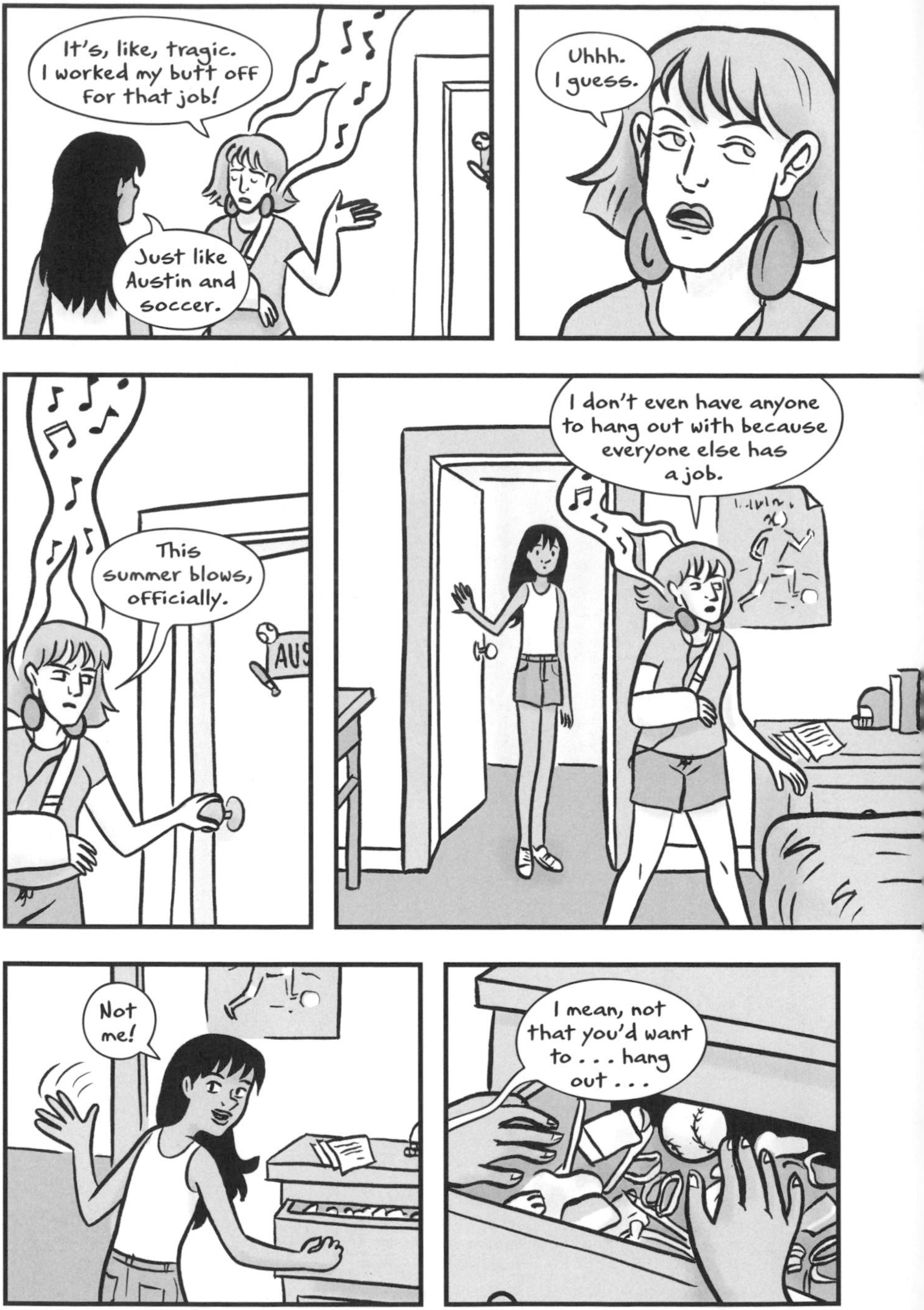
It's, like, tragic. I worked my butt off for that job!
Just like Austin and soccer.
Uhhh. I guess.
This summer blows, officially.
AUS
I don't even have anyone to hang out with because everyone else has a job.
Not me!
I mean, not that you'd want to . . . hang out . . .

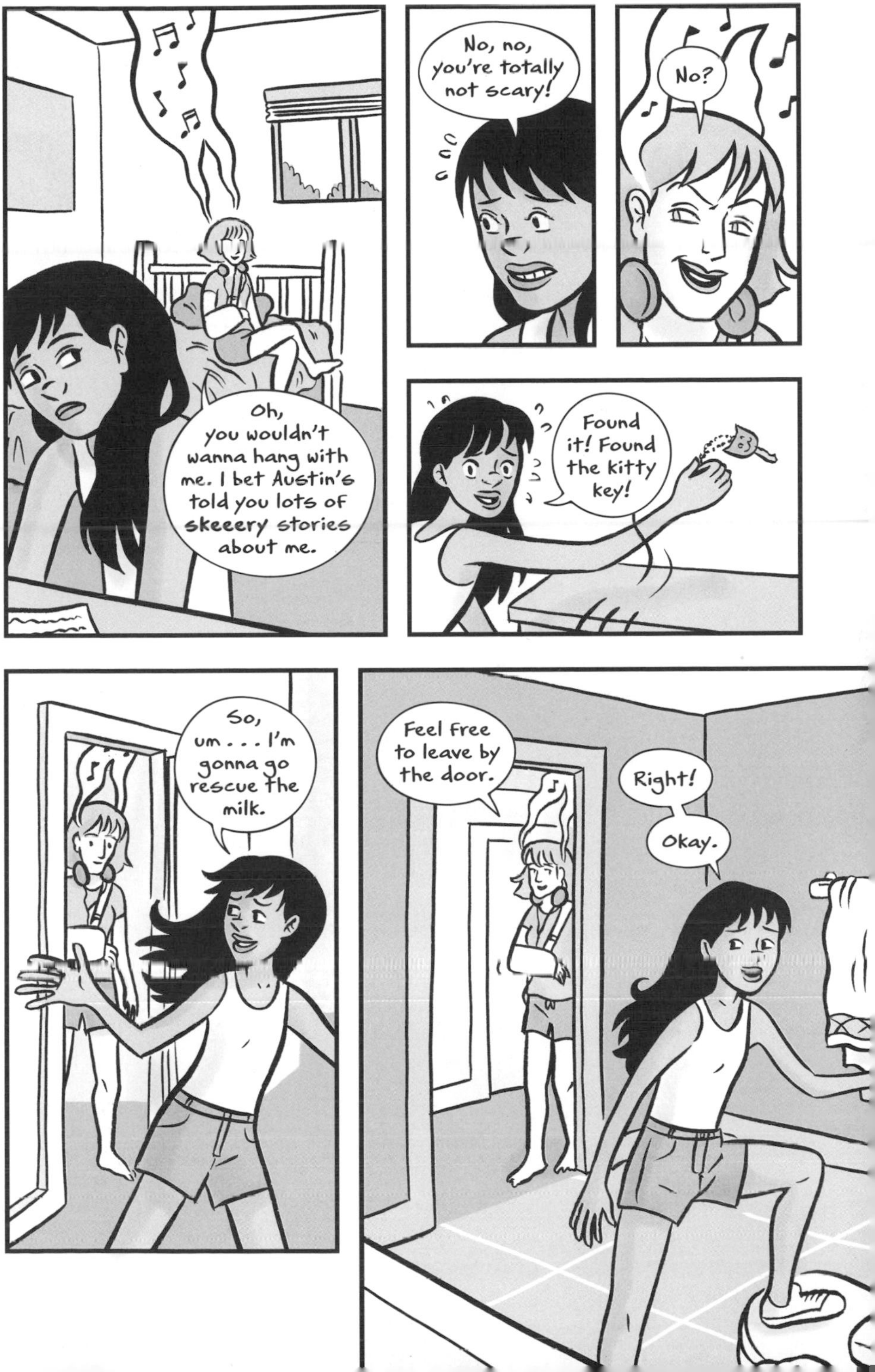
Oh, you wouldn't wanna hang with me. I bet Austin's told you lots of skeeery stories about me.
No, no, you're totally not scary!
No?
Found it! Found the kitty key!
So, um . . . I'm gonna go rescue the milk.
Feel free to leave by the door.
Right!
Okay.

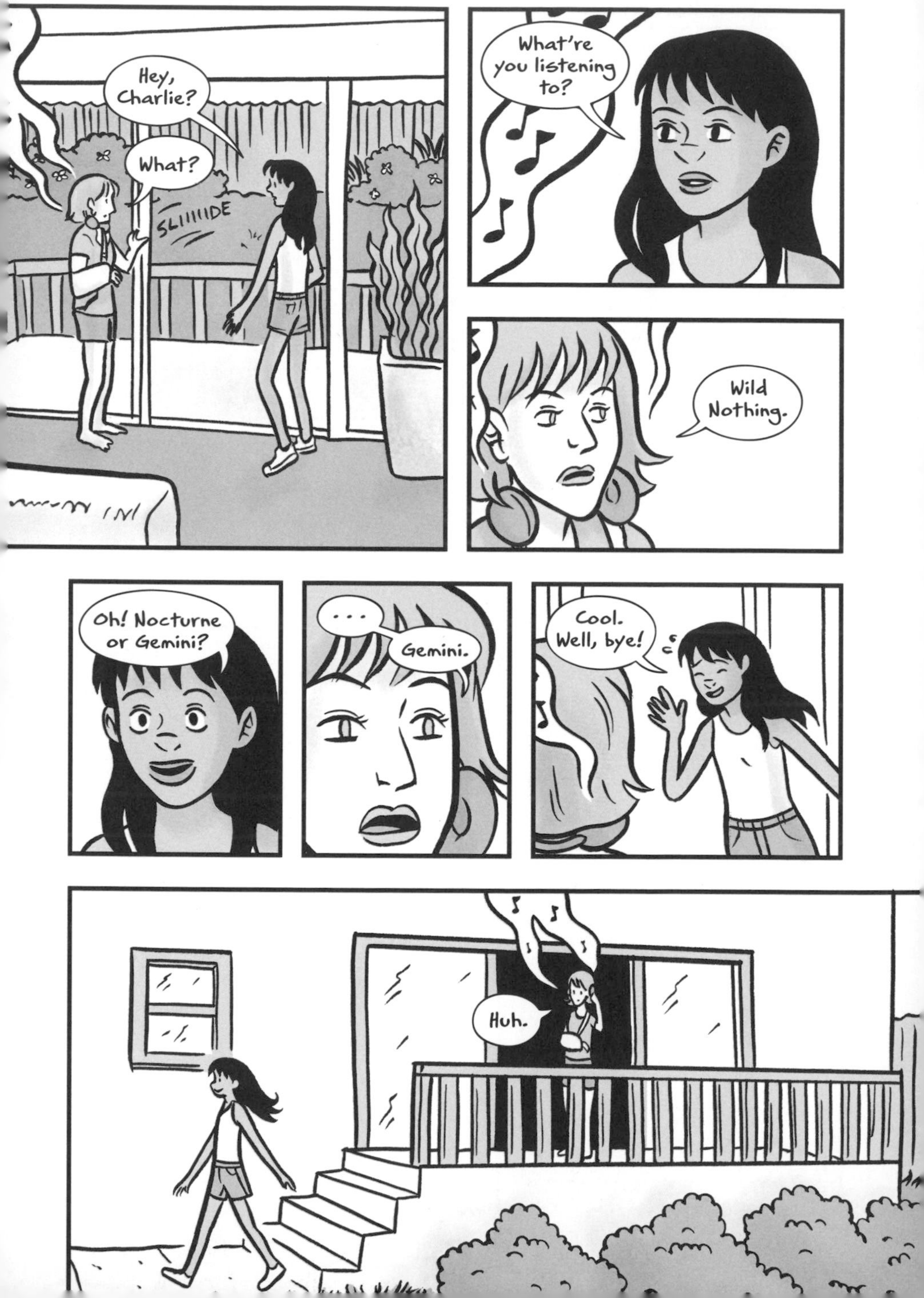
Hey, Charlie?
What?
SLIIIIIDE
What're you listening to?
Wild Nothing.
Oh! Nocturne or Gemini?
...
Gemini.
Cool. Well, bye!
Huh.

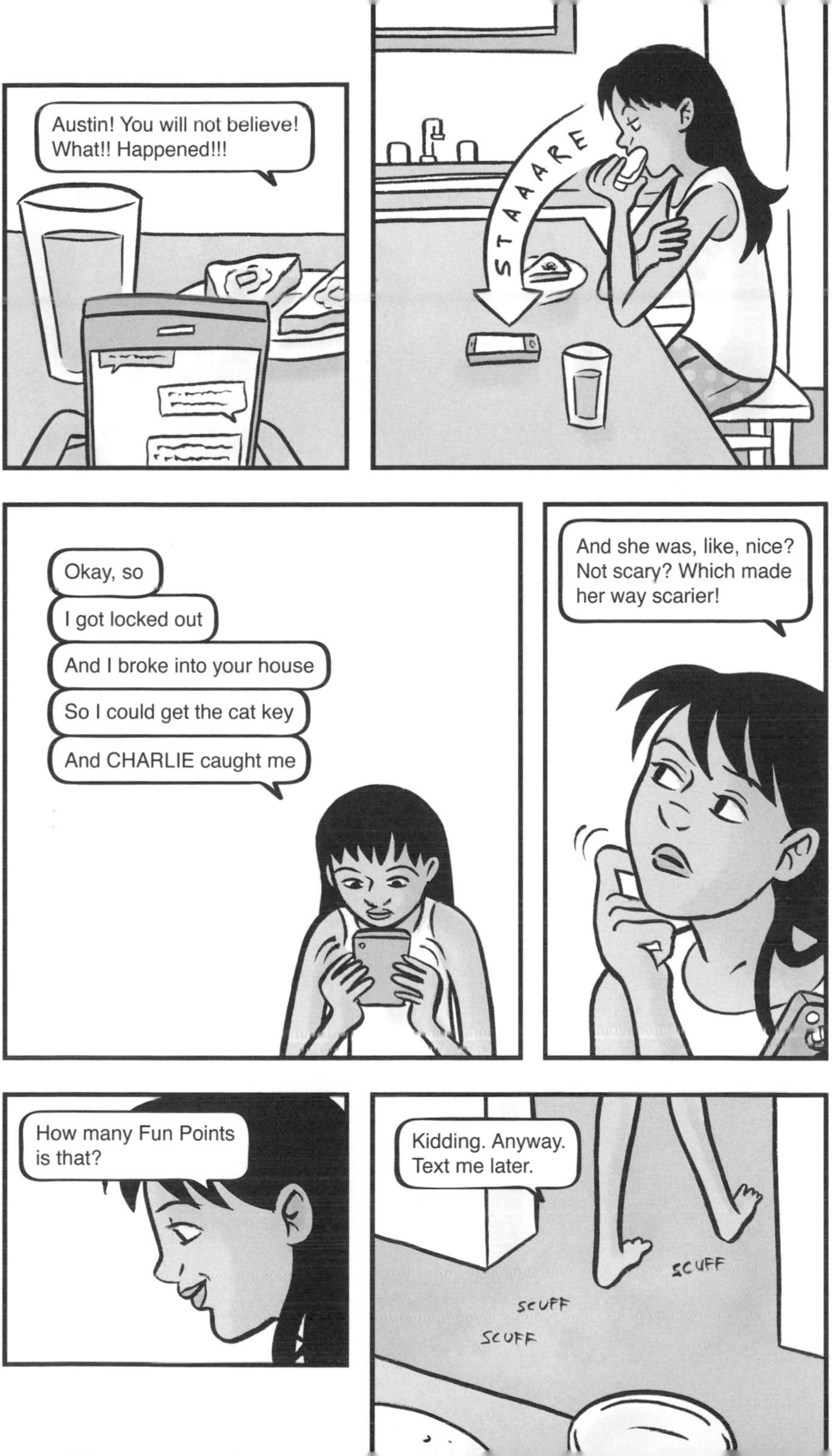
Austin! You will not believe! What!! Happened!!!
STAAARE
Okay, so
I got locked out
And I broke into your house
So I could get the cat key
And CHARLIE caught me
And she was, like, nice? Not scary? Which made her way scarier!
How many Fun Points is that?
Kidding. Anyway. Text me later.
SCUFF
SCUFF
SCUFF

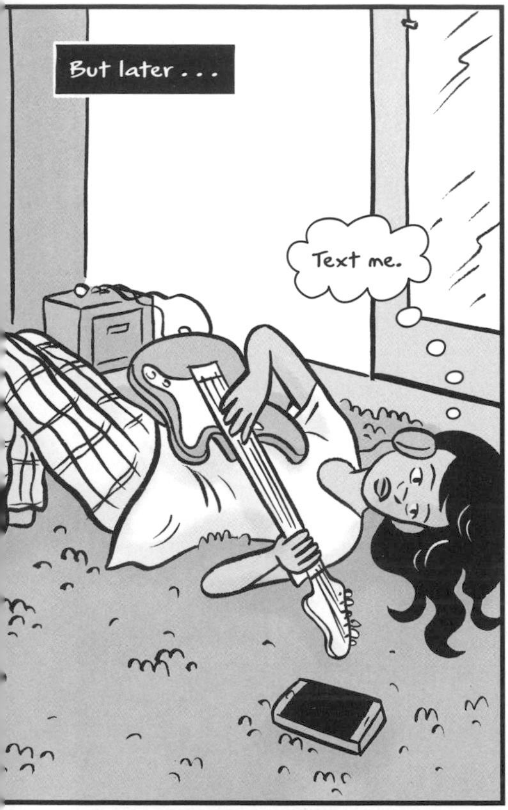
But later . . .
Text me.

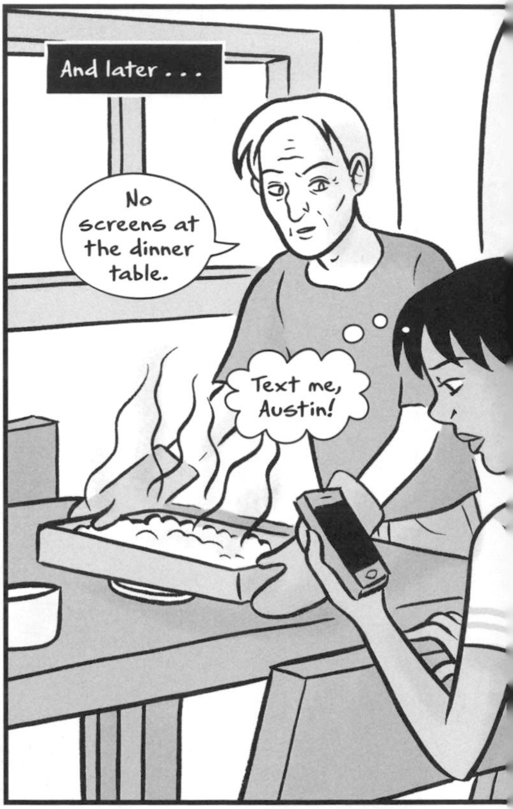
And later . . .
No screens at the dinner table.
Text me, Austin!

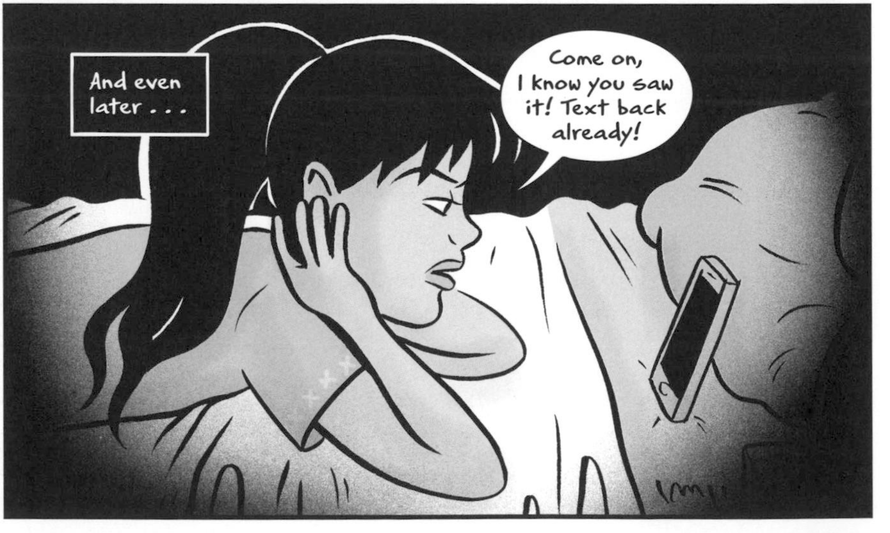
And even later . . .
Come on, I know you saw it! Text back already!

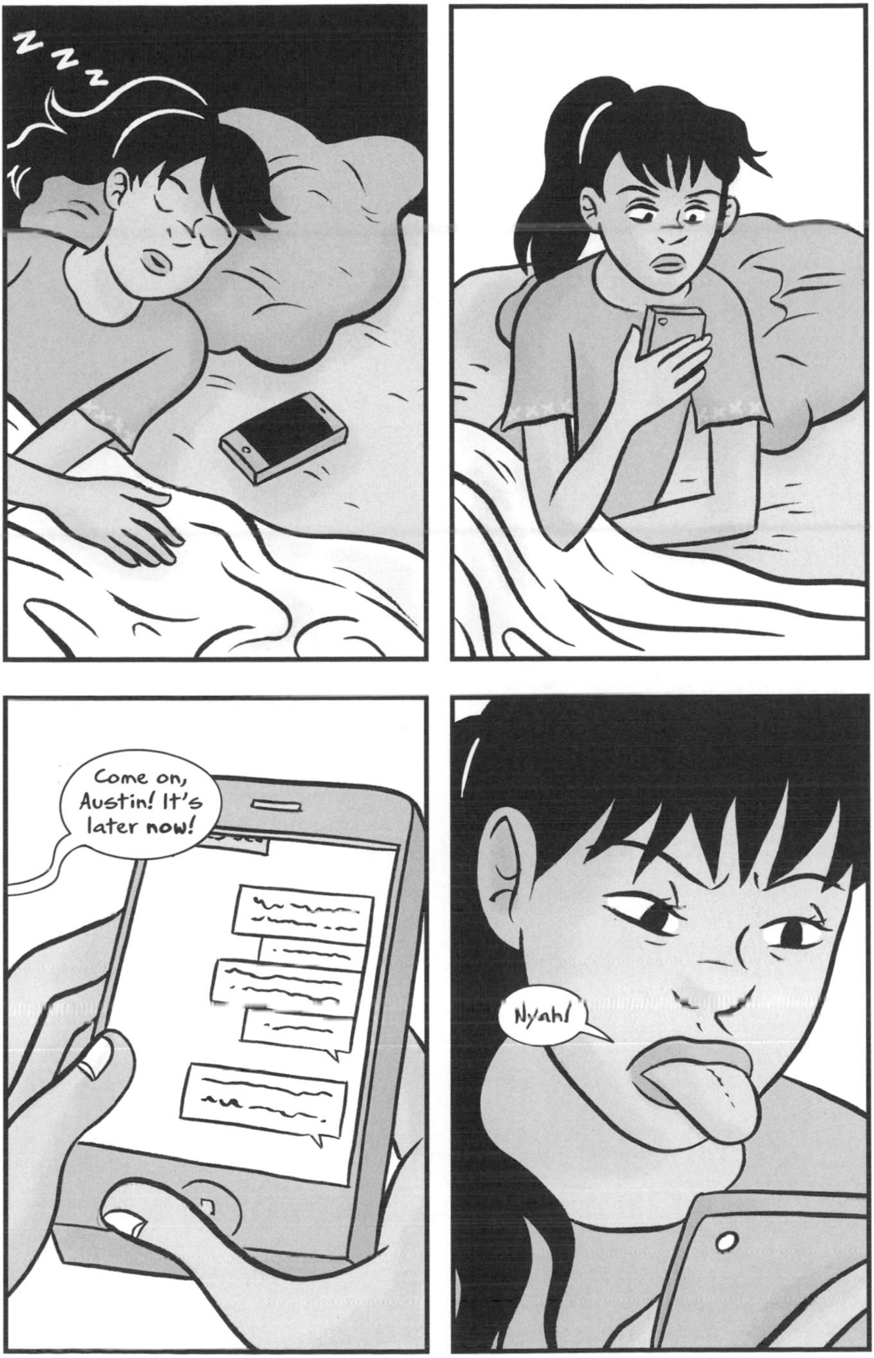
Z Z Z
Come on, Austin! It's later now!
Nyah!

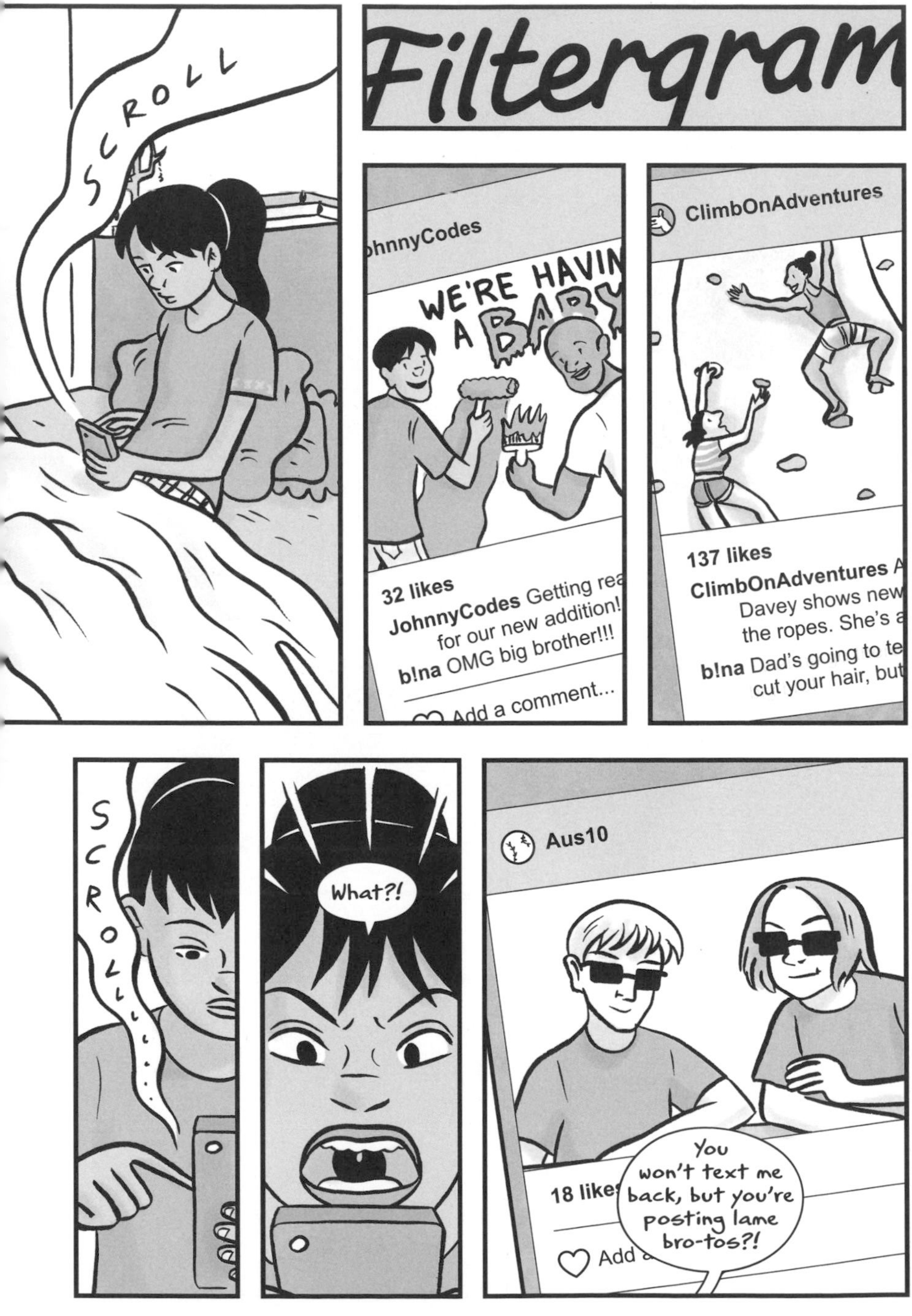

SCROLL
Filtergram
hnnyCodes
WE'RE HAVIN
A BABY
32 likes
JohnnyCodes Getting rea
for our new addition!
b!na OMG big brother!!!
Add a comment...
ClimbOnAdventures
137 likes
ClimbOnAdventures A
Davey shows new
the ropes. She's a
b!na Dad's going to te
cut your hair, but
SCROLL...
What?!
Aus10
18 likes
Add a
You won't text me back, but you're posting lame bro-tos?!

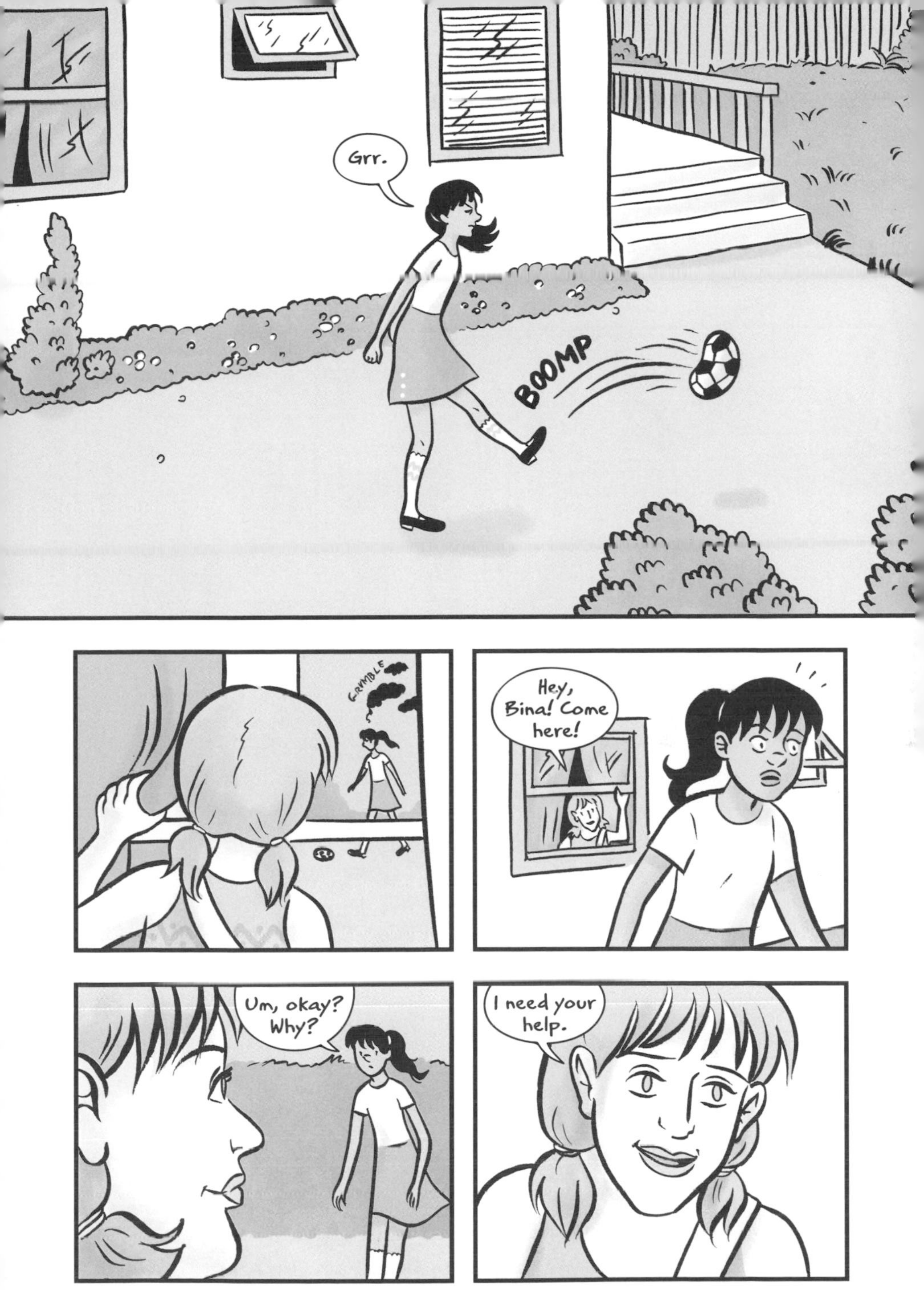
Grr.
BOOMP
GRUMBLE
Hey, Bina! Come here!
Um, okay? Why?
I need your help.

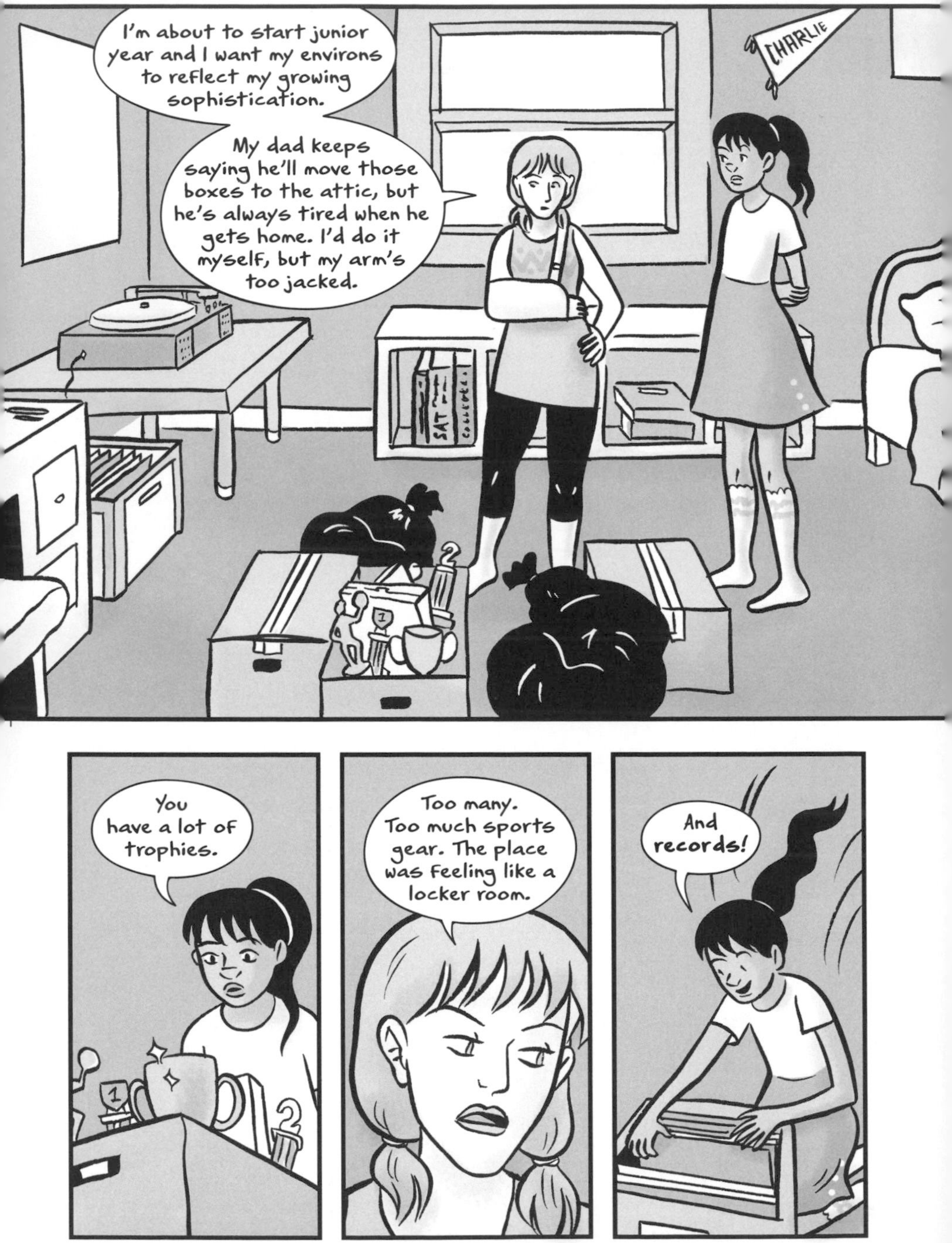
CHARLIE
I'm about to start junior year and I want my environs to reflect my growing sophistication.
My dad keeps saying he'll move those boxes to the attic, but he's always tired when he gets home. I'd do it myself, but my arm's too jacked.
SAT
COLLEGES
You have a lot of trophies.
Too many. Too much sports gear. The place was feeling like a locker room.
And records!

Austin never said you liked music.
BOWIE
BORY
UB BANDW
Yeah, well, he's the only one in the family who doesn't.
Ohmygosh! The new Junior Twins record!
You know them?
They're the **best**! I've been dying to hear this.
JUNIOR TWINS
Later. After you help me.
Think you can get this? I can handle the trash bags myself.
SHOVE

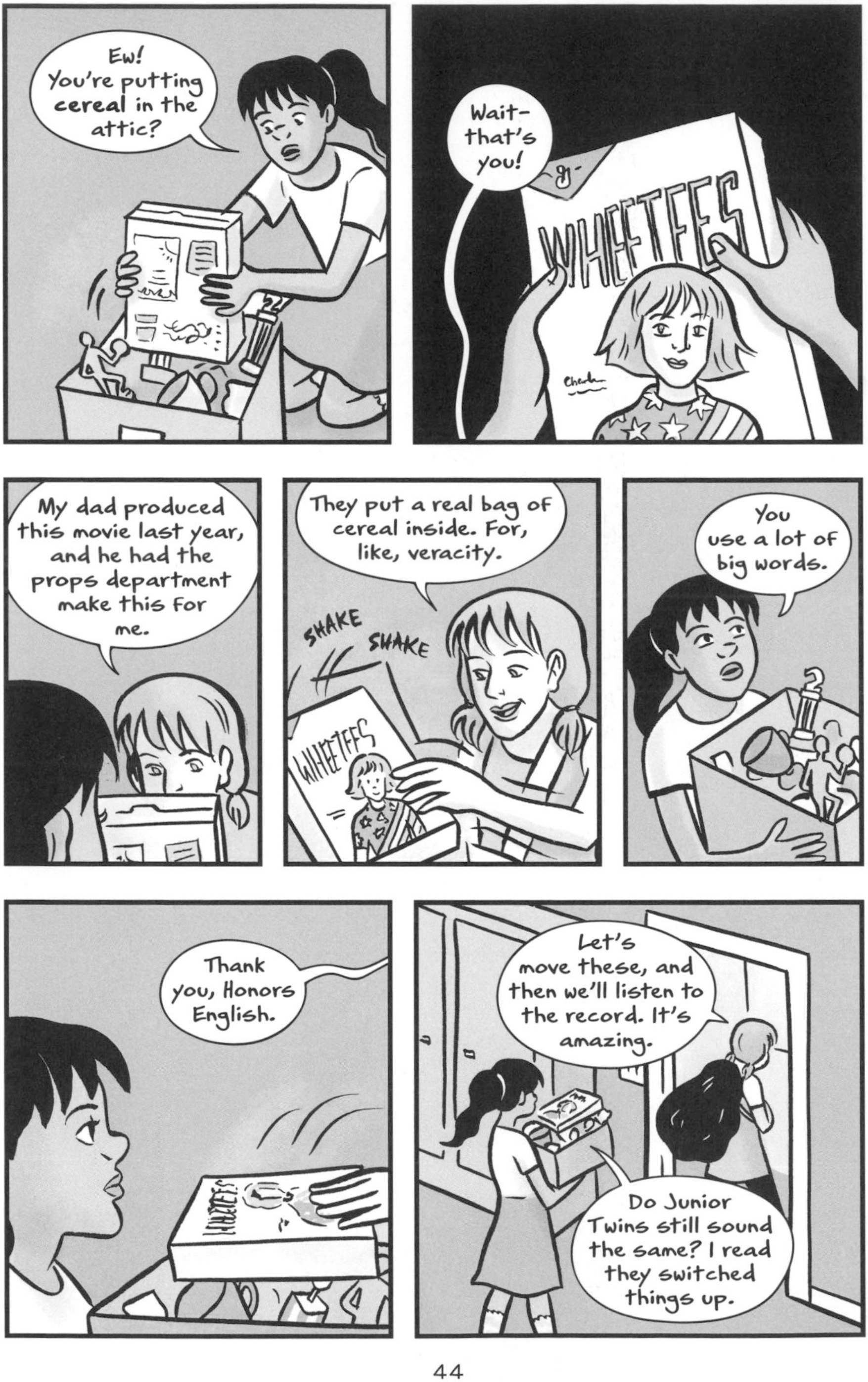

Ew! You're putting cereal in the attic?
Wait- that's you!
WHEETEES
My dad produced this movie last year, and he had the props department make this for me.
They put a real bag of cereal inside. For, like, veracity.
SHAKE
SHAKE
WHEETEES
You use a lot of big words.
Thank you, Honors English.
Let's move these, and then we'll listen to the record. It's amazing.
Do Junior Twins still sound the same? I read they switched things up.

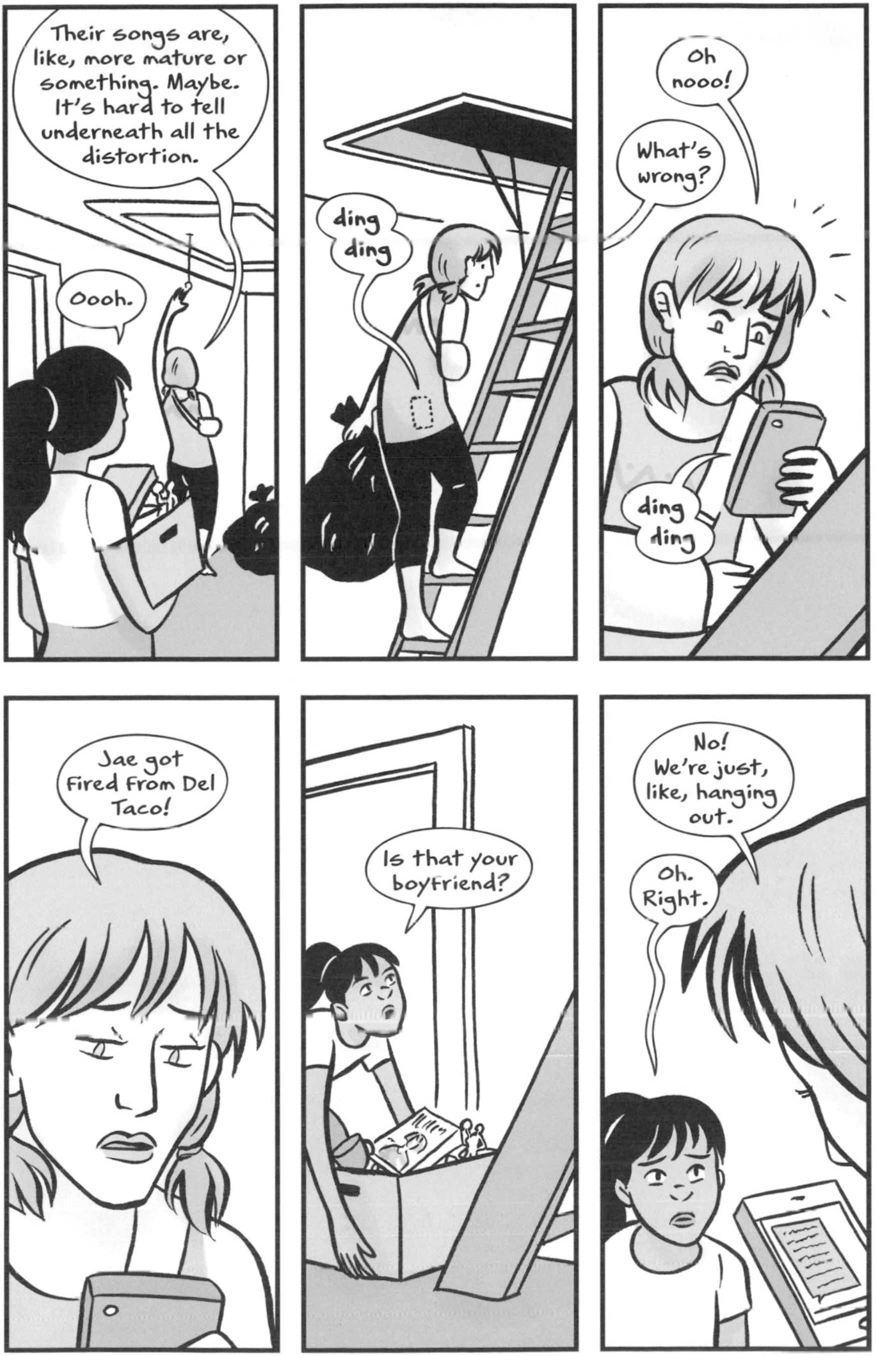
Their songs are, like, more mature or something. Maybe. It's hard to tell underneath all the distortion.
Oooh.
ding ding
Oh nooo!
What's wrong?
ding ding
Jae got fired from Del Taco!
Is that your boyfriend?
No! We're just, like, hanging out.
Oh. Right.

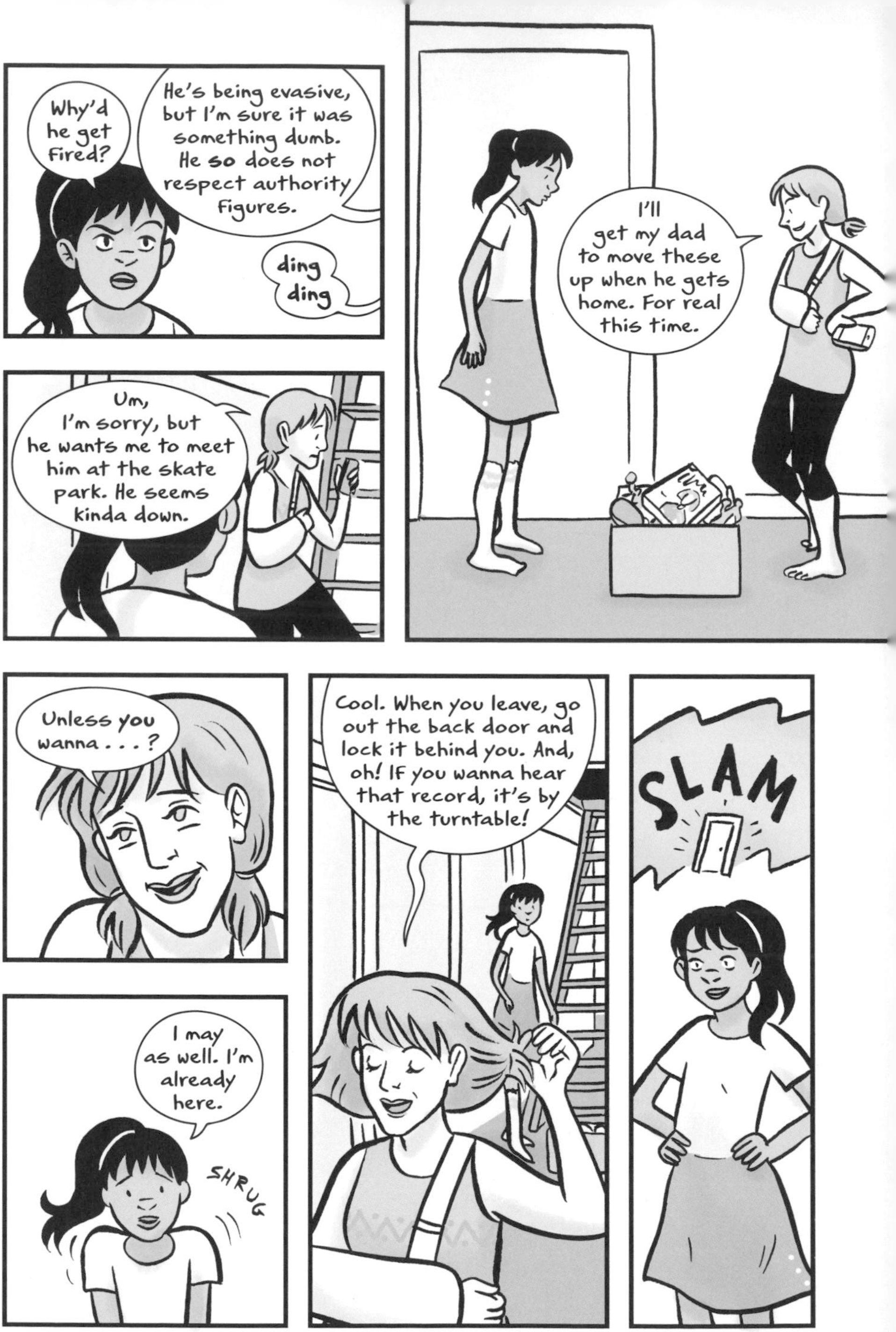
Why'd he get fired?
He's being evasive, but I'm sure it was something dumb. He so does not respect authority figures.
ding ding
Um, I'm sorry, but he wants me to meet him at the skate park. He seems kinda down.
I'll get my dad to move these up when he gets home. For real this time.
Unless you wanna . . . ?
I may as well. I'm already here.
SHRUG
Cool. When you leave, go out the back door and lock it behind you. And, oh! If you wanna hear that record, it's by the turntable!
SLAM

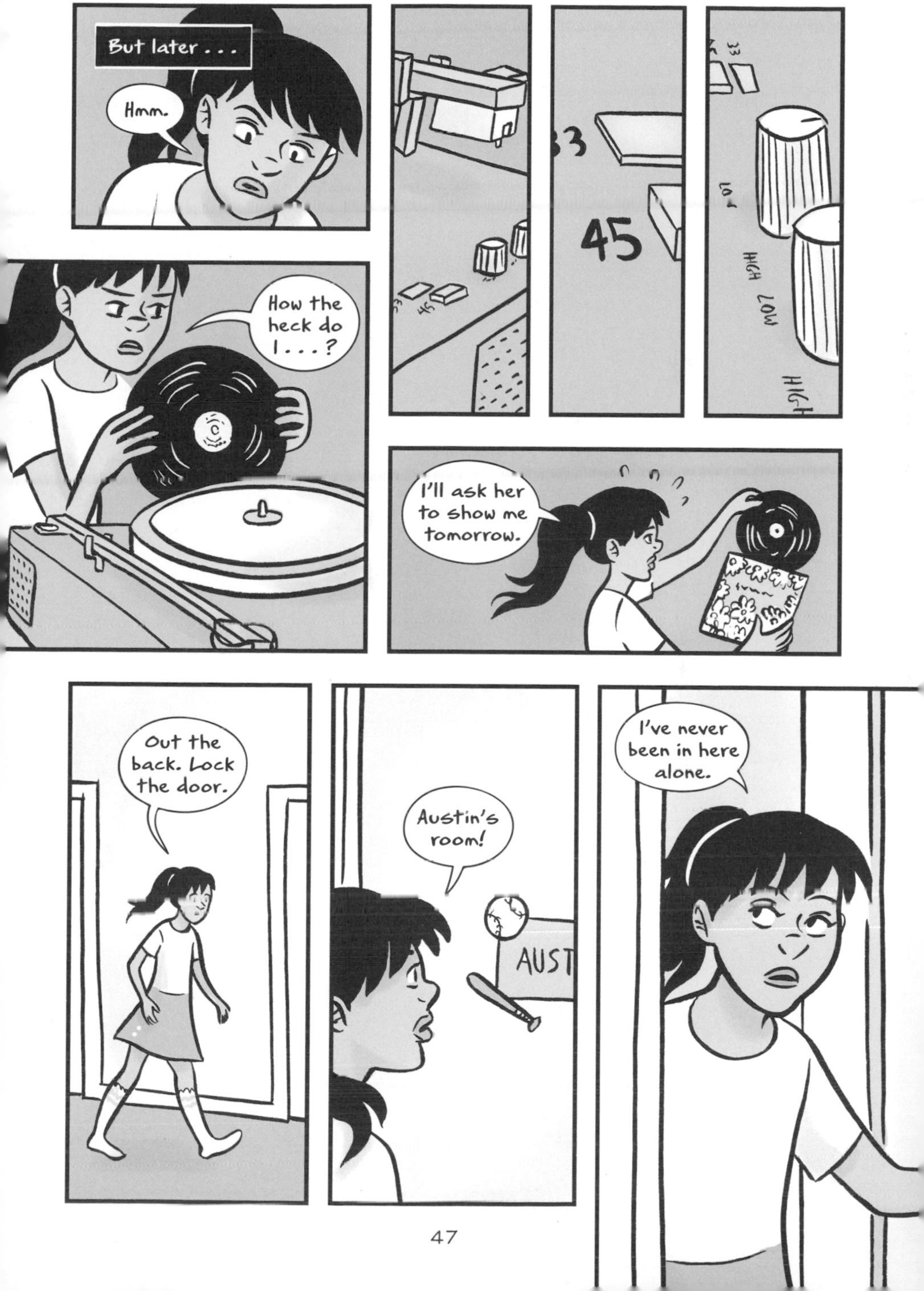
But later . . .
Hmm.
33
45
HIGH
LOW
How the heck do I . . . ?
I'll ask her to show me tomorrow.
Out the back. Lock the door.
Austin's room!
AUST
I've never been in here alone.

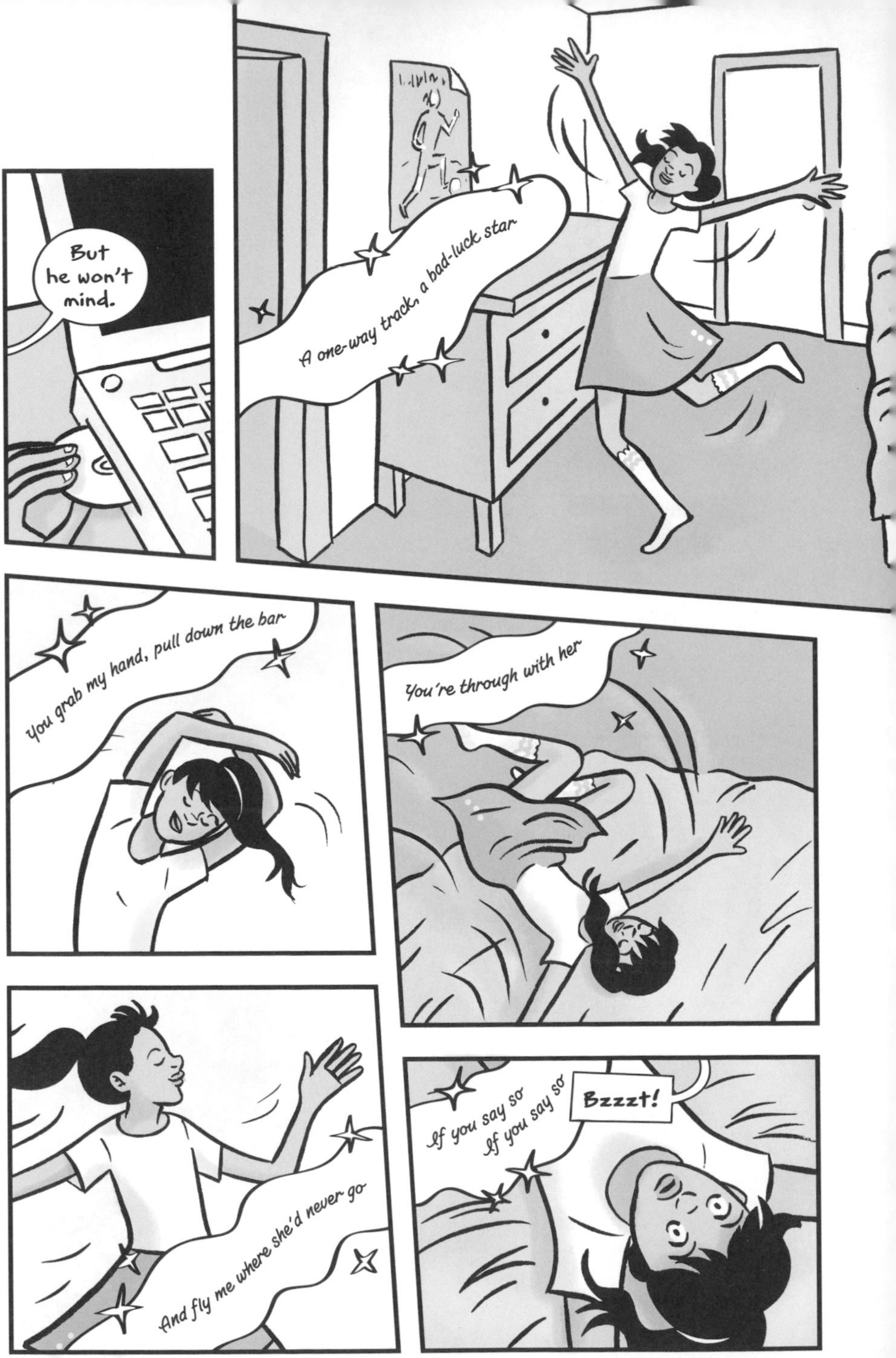
But he won't mind.
A one-way track, a bad-luck star
You grab my hand, pull down the bar
You're through with her
And fly me where she'd never go
If you say so
If you say so
Bzzzt!

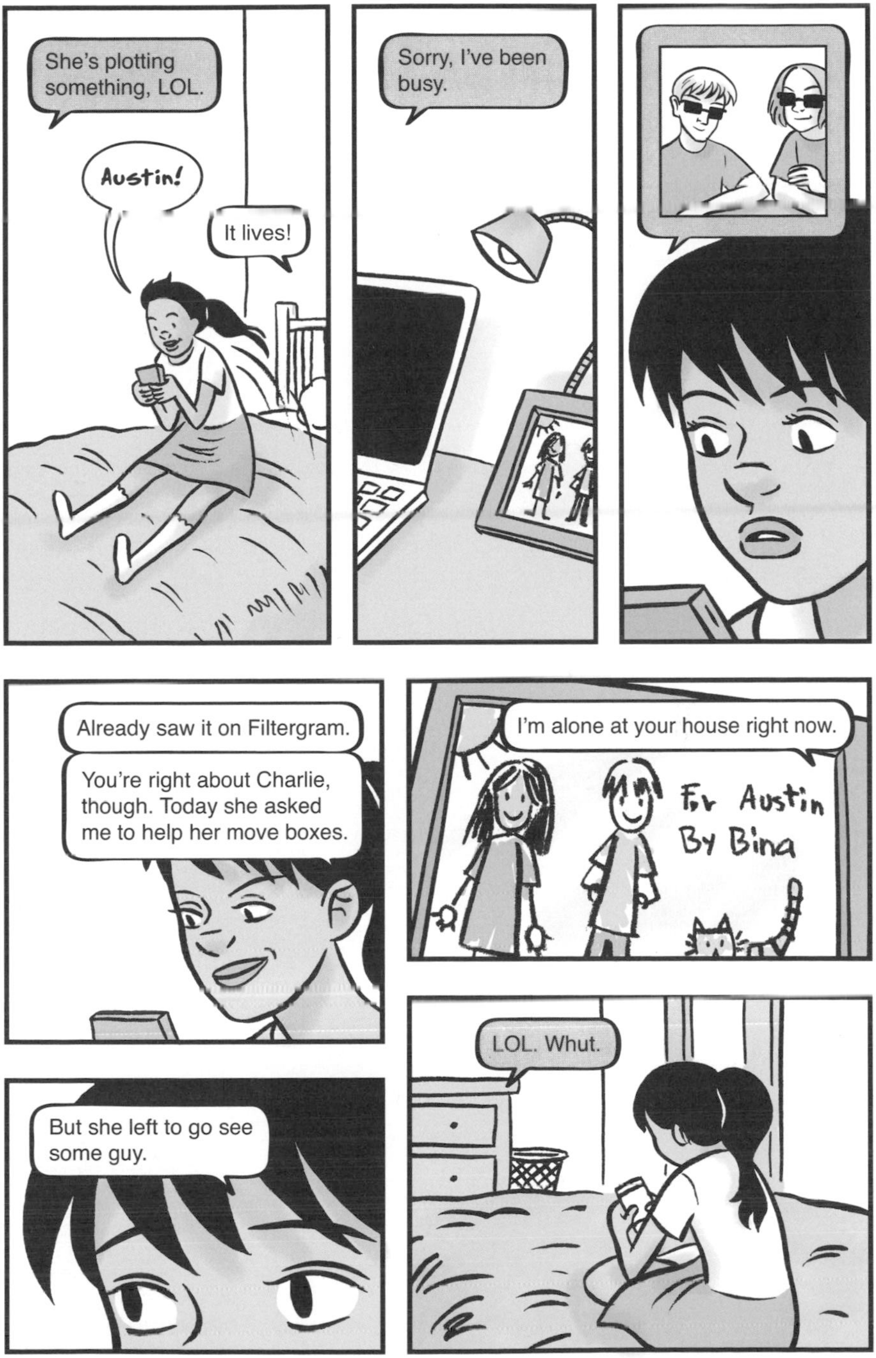
She's plotting something, LOL.
Austin!
It lives!
Sorry, I've been busy.
Already saw it on Filtergram.
You're right about Charlie, though. Today she asked me to help her move boxes.
I'm alone at your house right now.
For Austin By Bina
But she left to go see some guy.
LOL. Whut.

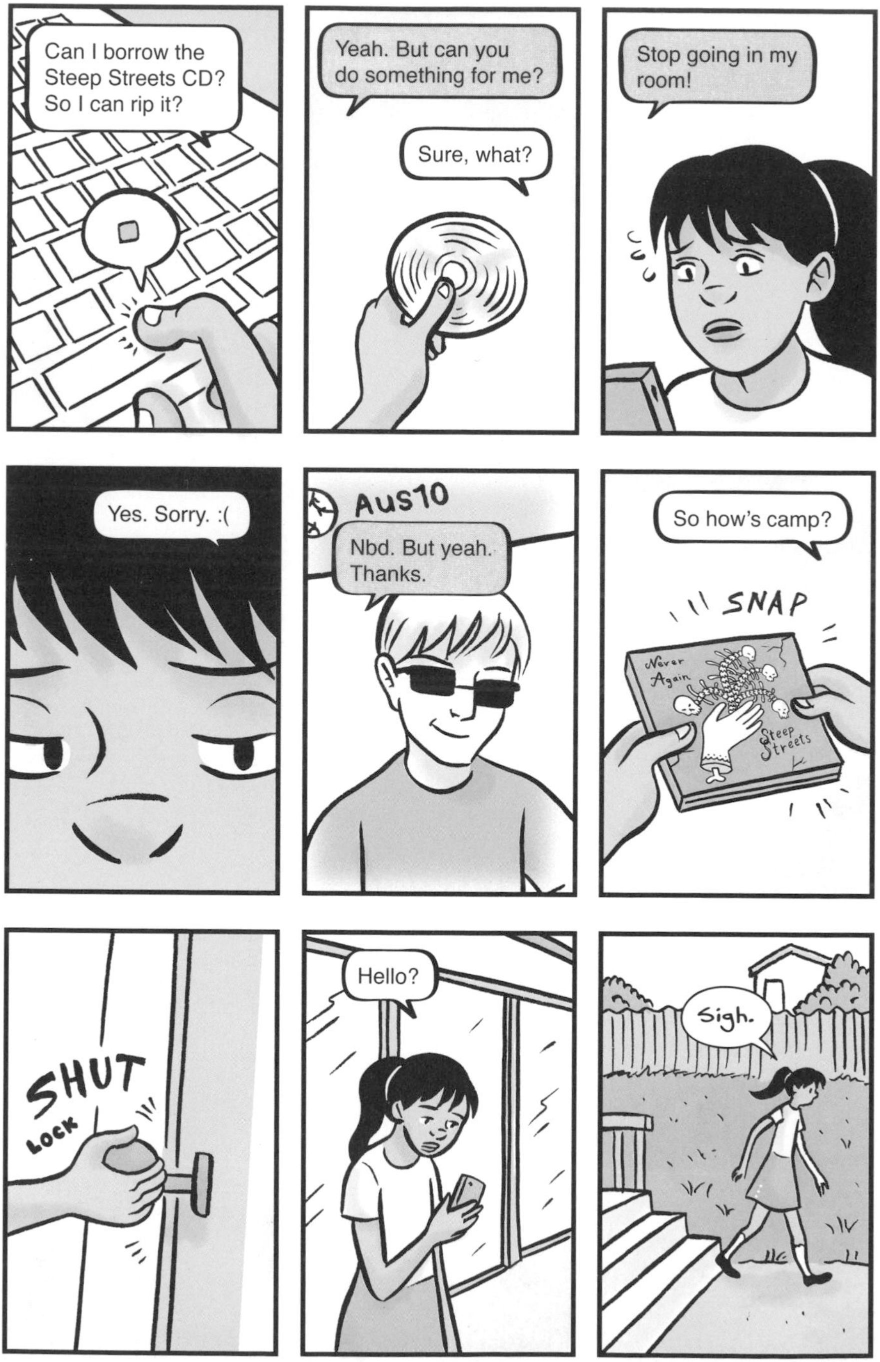
Can I borrow the Steep Streets CD? So I can rip it?
Yeah. But can you do something for me?
Sure, what?
Stop going in my room!
Yes. Sorry. :(
AUS10
Nbd. But yeah. Thanks.
So how's camp?
SNAP
Never Again
Steep Streets
SHUT
LOCK
Hello?
Sigh.

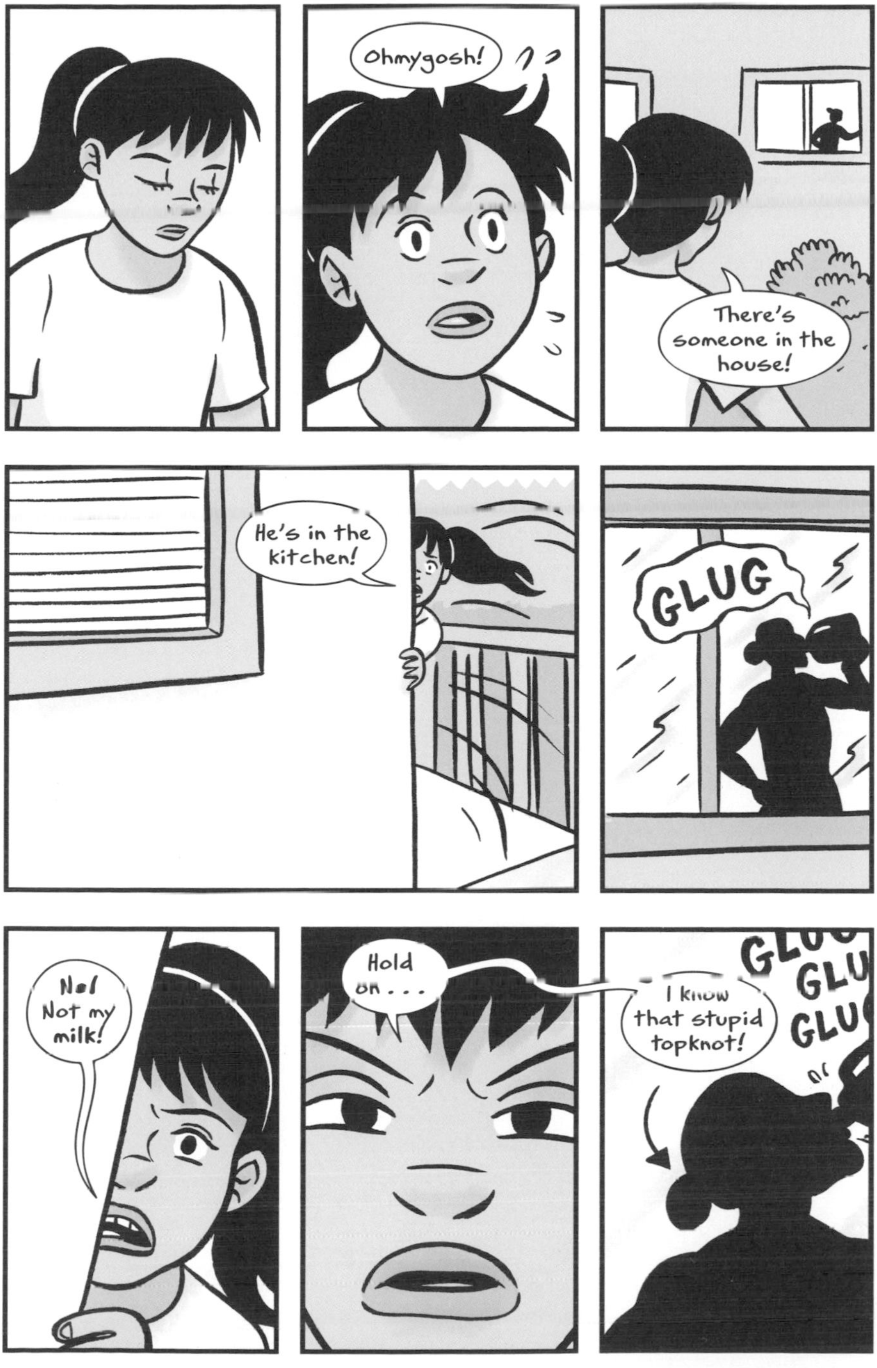
Ohmygosh!
There's someone in the house!
He's in the kitchen!
GLUG
No! Not my milk!
Hold on . . .
I know that stupid topknot!
GLUG GLU GLU

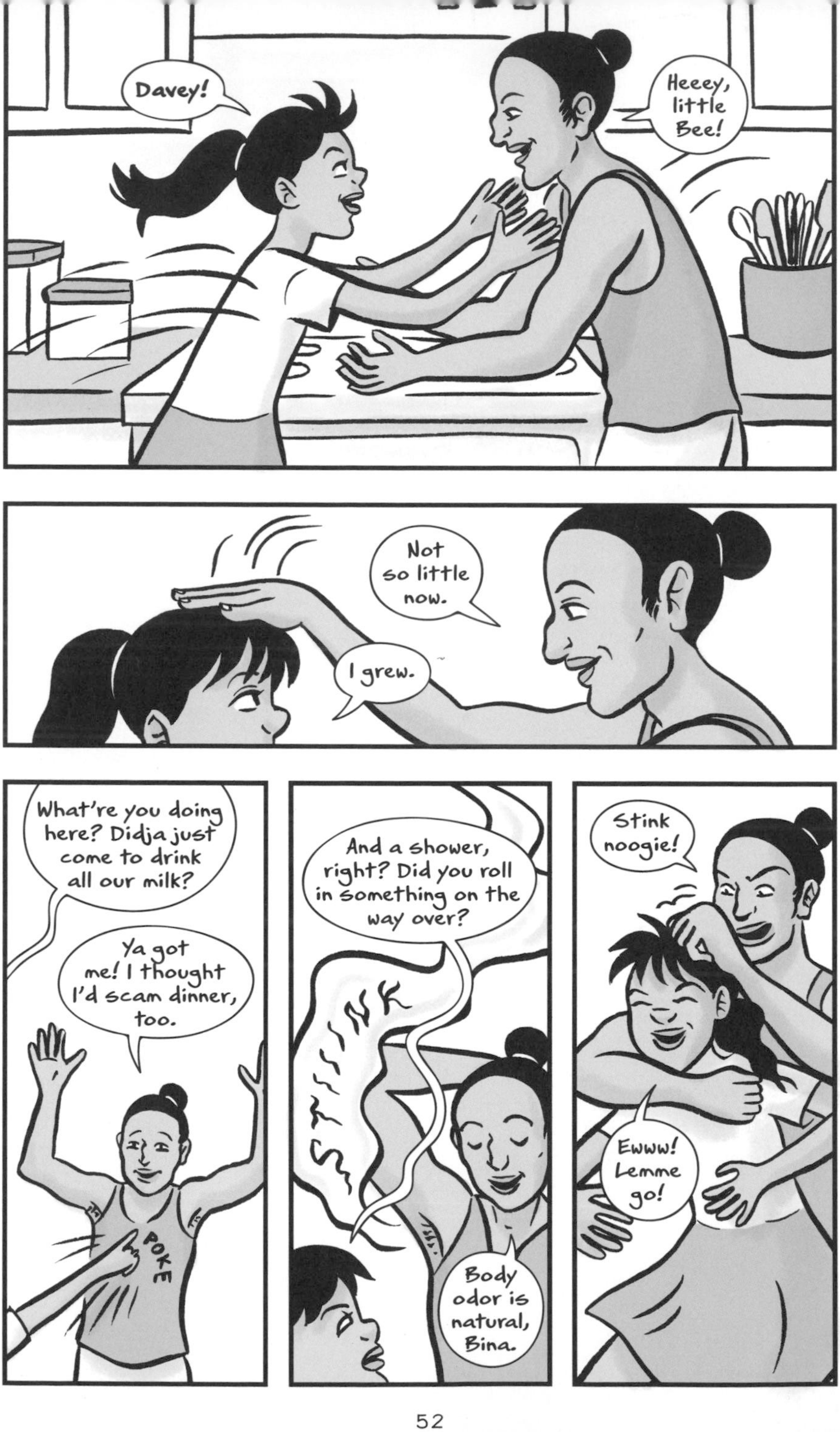
Davey!
Heeey, little Bee!
Not so little now.
I grew.
What're you doing here? Didja just come to drink all our milk?
Ya got me! I thought I'd scam dinner, too.
POKE
And a shower, right? Did you roll in something on the way over?
STIIINK
Body odor is natural, Bina.
Stink noogie!
Ewww! Lemme go!

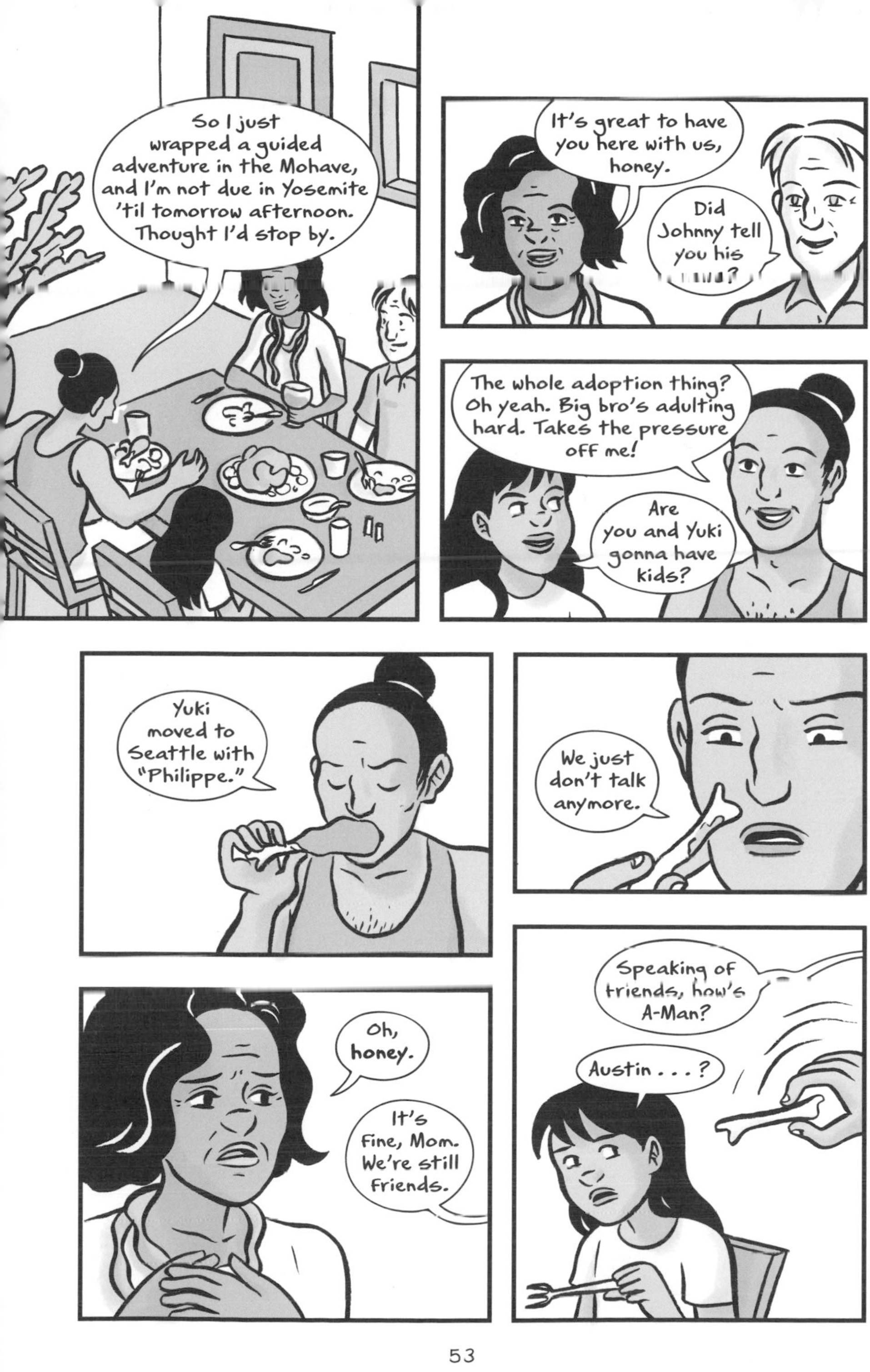
So I just wrapped a guided adventure in the Mohave, and I'm not due in Yosemite 'til tomorrow afternoon. Thought I'd stop by.
It's great to have you here with us, honey.
Did Johnny tell you his
The whole adoption thing? Oh yeah. Big bro's adulting hard. Takes the pressure off me!
Are you and Yuki gonna have kids?
Yuki moved to Seattle with "Philippe."
We just don't talk anymore.
Oh, honey.
It's fine, Mom. We're still friends.
Speaking of friends, how's A-Man?
Austin . . . ?

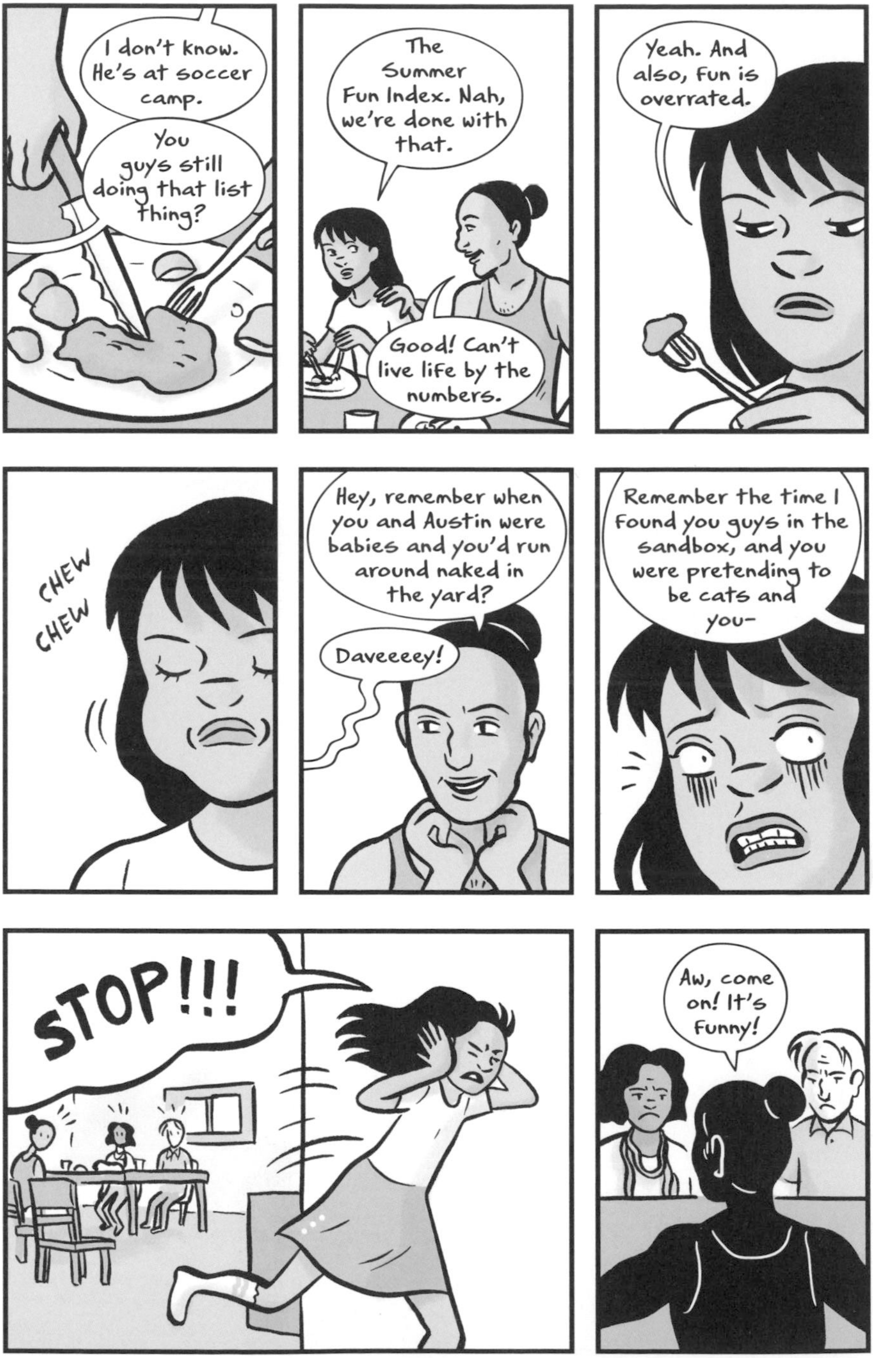

I don't know. He's at soccer camp.
You guys still doing that list thing?
The Summer Fun Index. Nah, we're done with that.
Good! Can't live life by the numbers.
Yeah. And also, fun is overrated.
CHEW CHEW
Hey, remember when you and Austin were babies and you'd run around naked in the yard?
Daveeeey!
Remember the time I found you guys in the sandbox, and you were pretending to be cats and you-
STOP!!!
Aw, come on! It's funny!

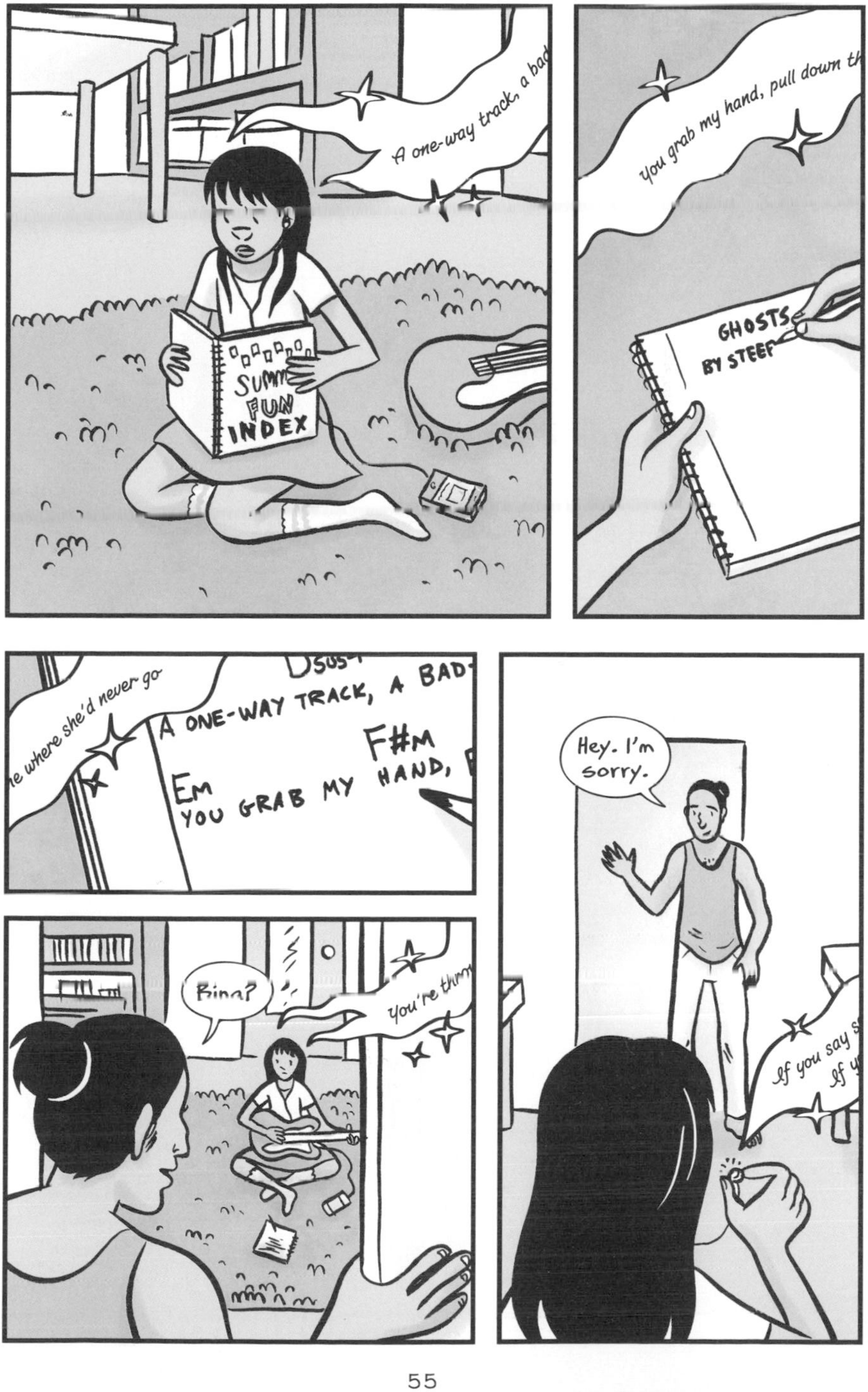

A one-way track, a bad
SUMM
FUN
INDEX
You grab my hand, pull down th
GHOSTS
BY STEEF
he where she'd never go
A ONE-WAY TRACK, A BAD-
F#M
EM
YOU GRAB MY HAND,
Hey. I'm sorry.
Bina?
You're thr
If you say
If y

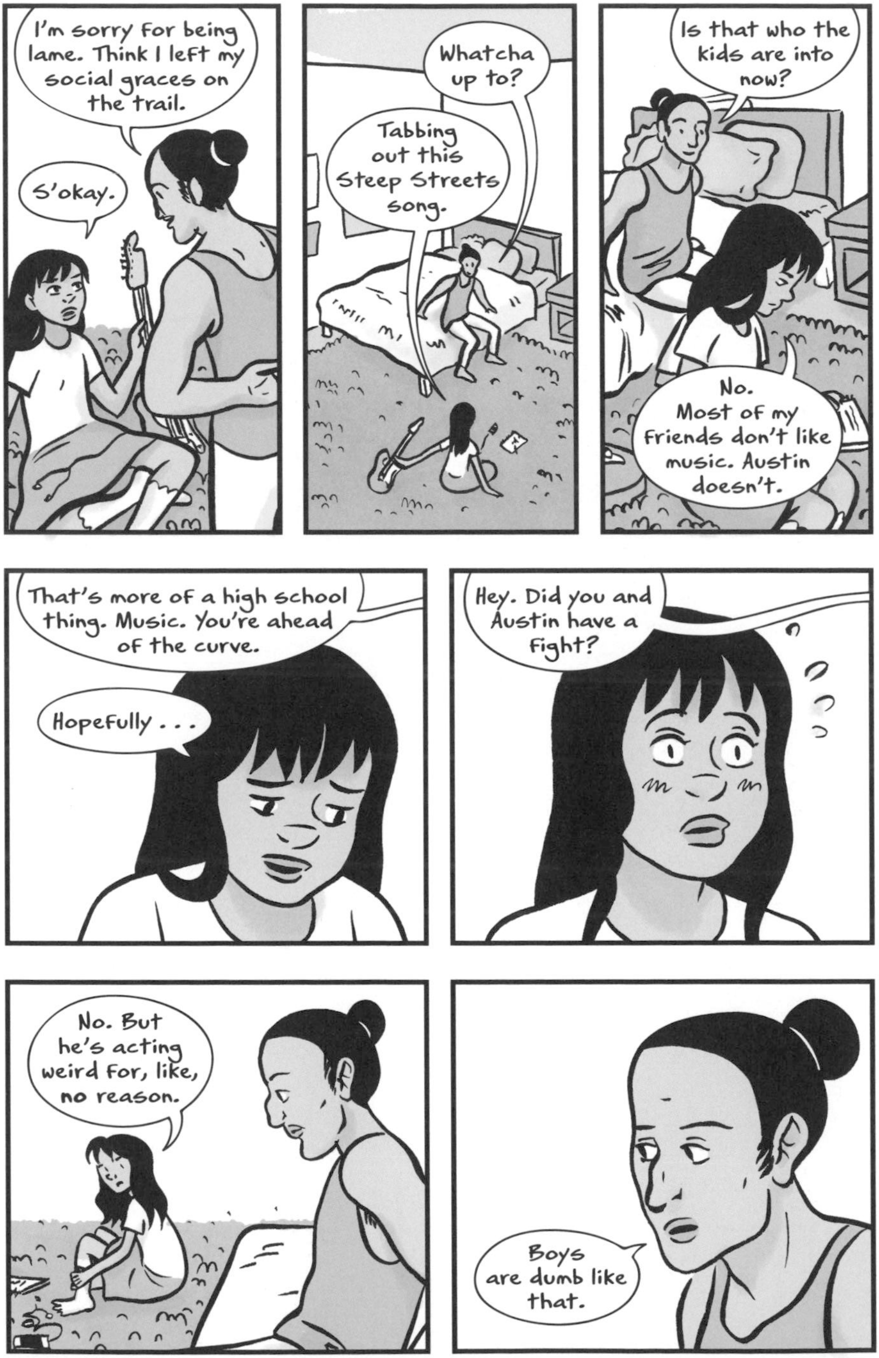
I'm sorry for being lame. Think I left my social graces on the trail.
S'okay.
Whatcha up to?
Tabbing out this Steep Streets song.
Is that who the kids are into now?
No. Most of my friends don't like music. Austin doesn't.
That's more of a high school thing. Music. You're ahead of the curve.
Hopefully . . .
Hey. Did you and Austin have a fight?
No. But he's acting weird for, like, no reason.
Boys are dumb like that.

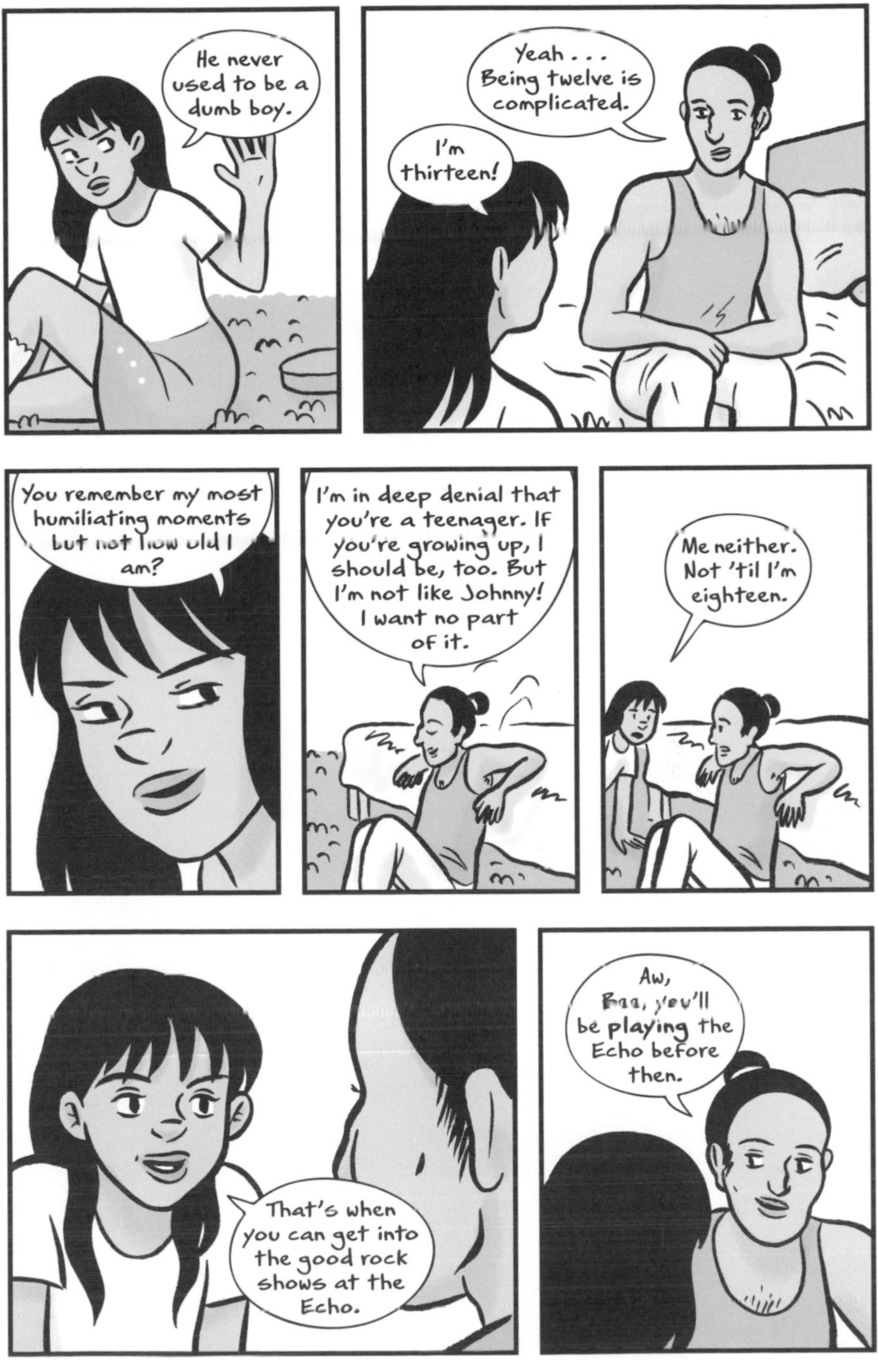
He never used to be a dumb boy.
Yeah . . . Being twelve is complicated.
I'm thirteen!
You remember my most humiliating moments but not how old I am?
I'm in deep denial that you're a teenager. If you're growing up, I should be, too. But I'm not like Johnny! I want no part of it.
Me neither. Not 'til I'm eighteen.
That's when you can get into the good rock shows at the Echo.
Aw, you'll be playing the Echo before then.

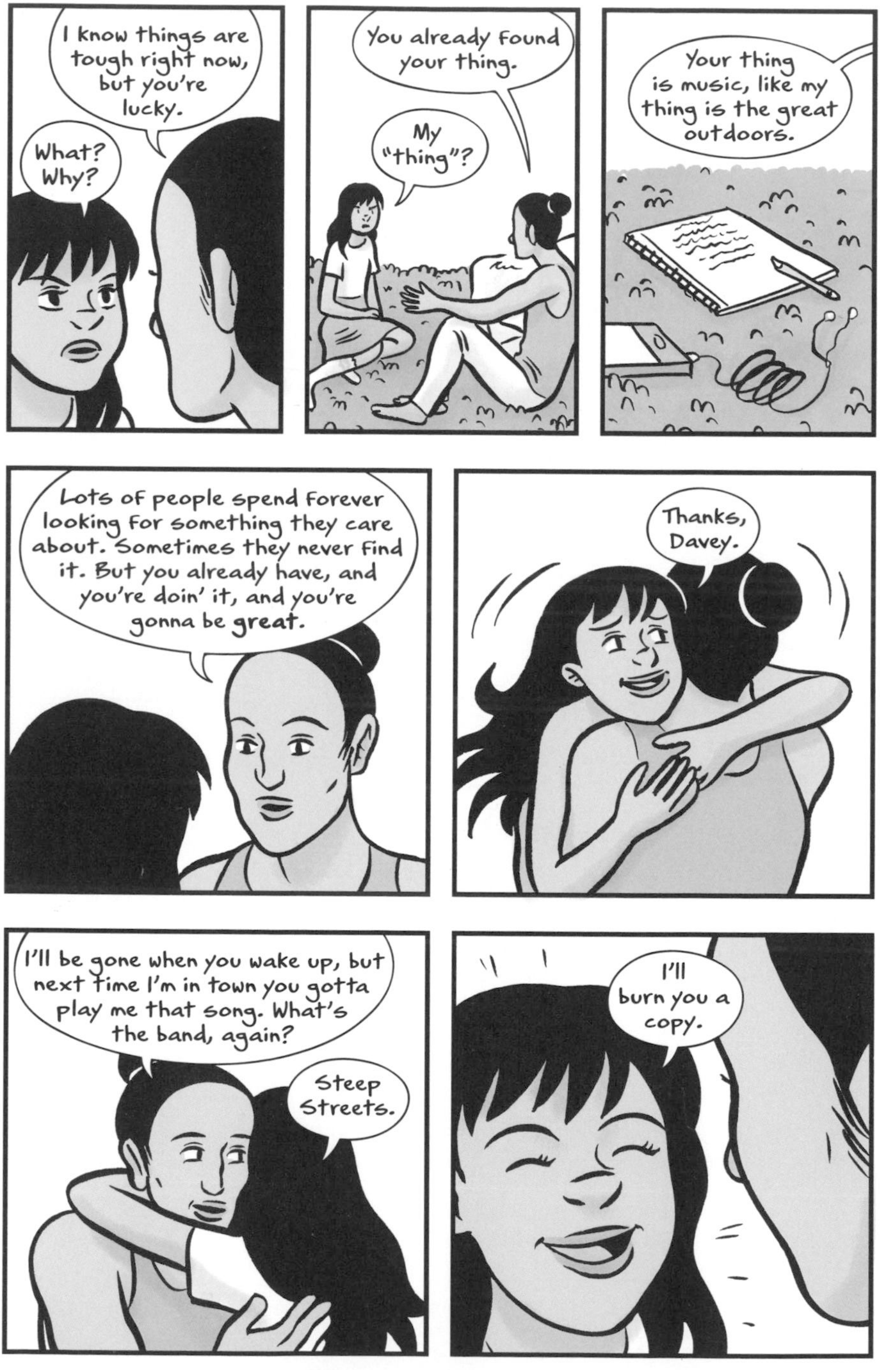
I know things are tough right now, but you're lucky.
What? Why?
You already found your thing.
My "thing"?
Your thing is music, like my thing is the great outdoors.
Lots of people spend forever looking for something they care about. Sometimes they never find it. But you already have, and you're doin' it, and you're gonna be great.
Thanks, Davey.
I'll be gone when you wake up, but next time I'm in town you gotta play me that song. What's the band, again?
Steep Streets.
I'll burn you a copy.

Week Three

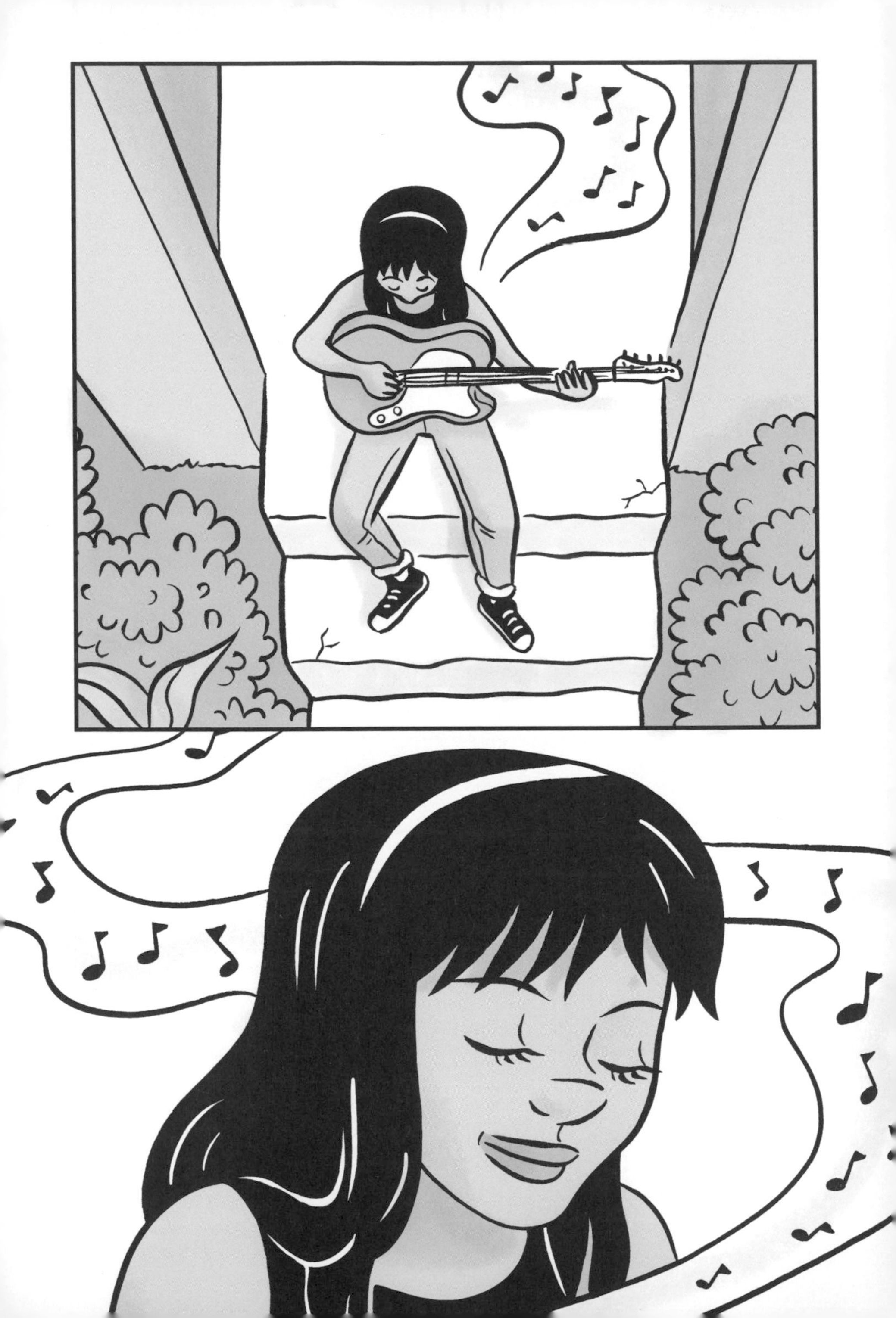

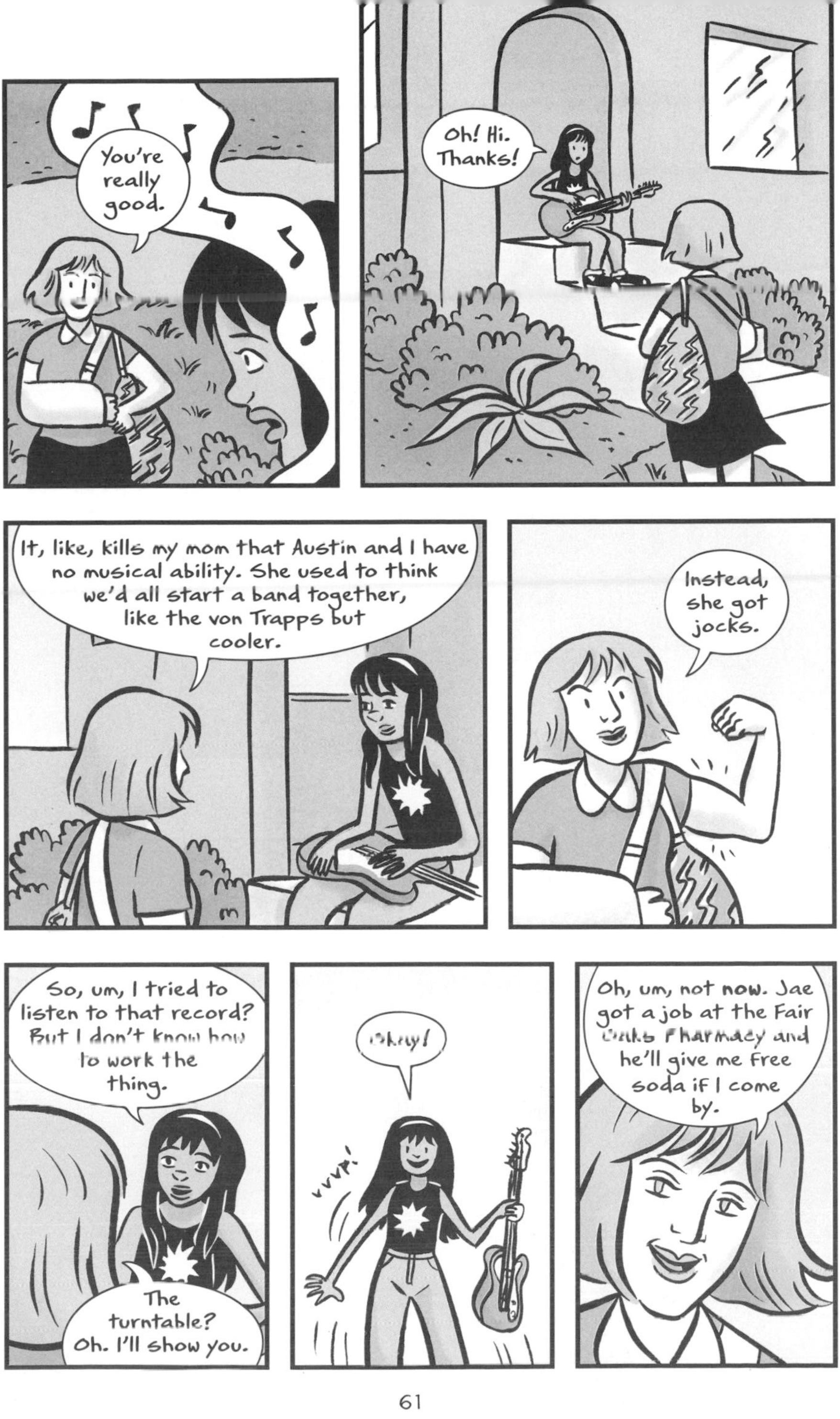
You're really good.
Oh! Hi. Thanks!
It, like, kills my mom that Austin and I have no musical ability. She used to think we'd all start a band together, like the von Trapps but cooler.
Instead, she got jocks.
So, um, I tried to listen to that record? But I don't know how to work the thing.
The turntable? Oh. I'll show you.
vvvp!
Okay!
Oh, um, not now. Jae got a job at the Fair Oaks Pharmacy and he'll give me free soda if I come by.

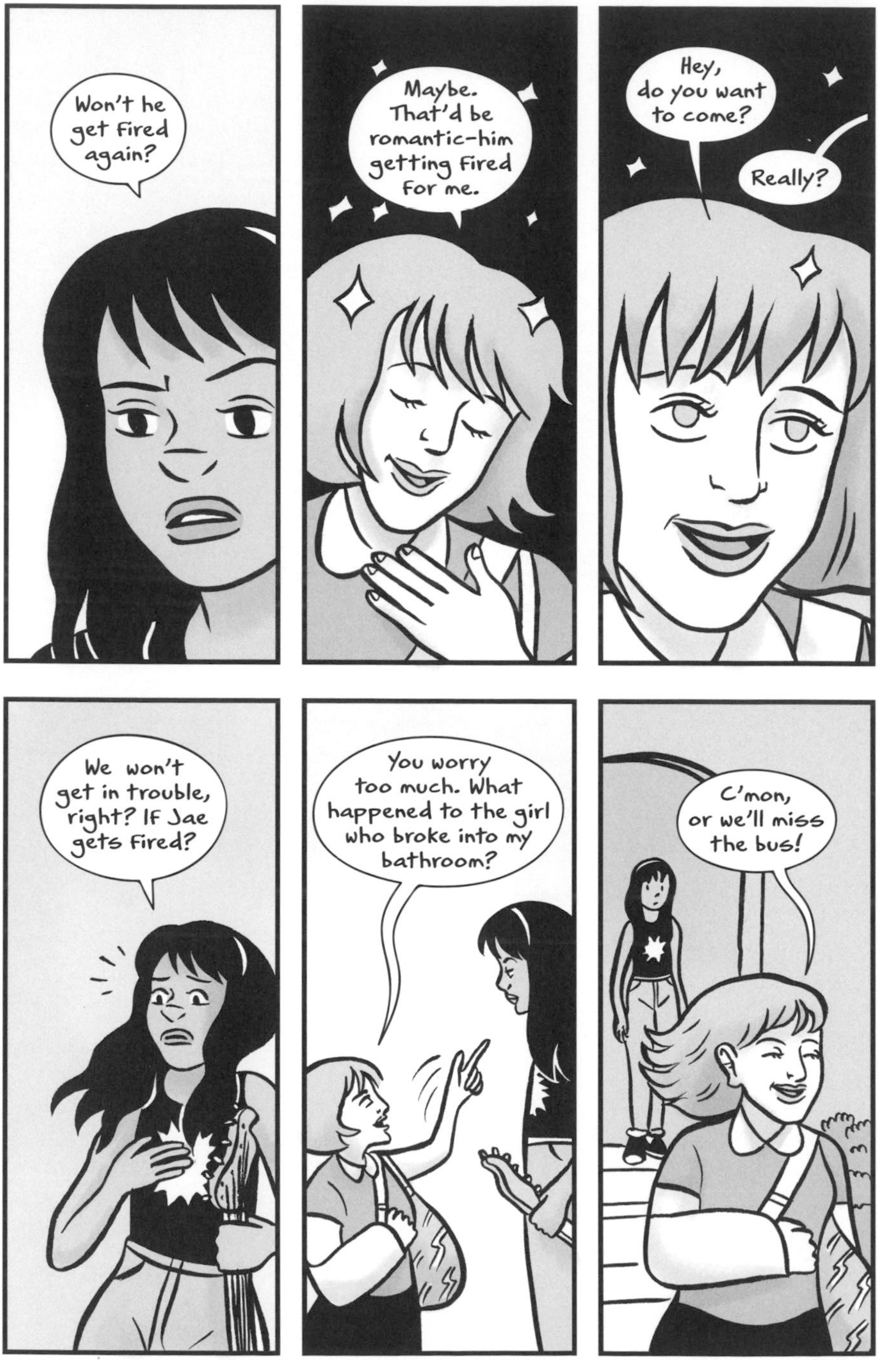
Won't he get fired again?
Maybe. That'd be romantic—him getting fired for me.
Hey, do you want to come?
Really?
We won't get in trouble, right? If Jae gets fired?
You worry too much. What happened to the girl who broke into my bathroom?
C'mon, or we'll miss the bus!

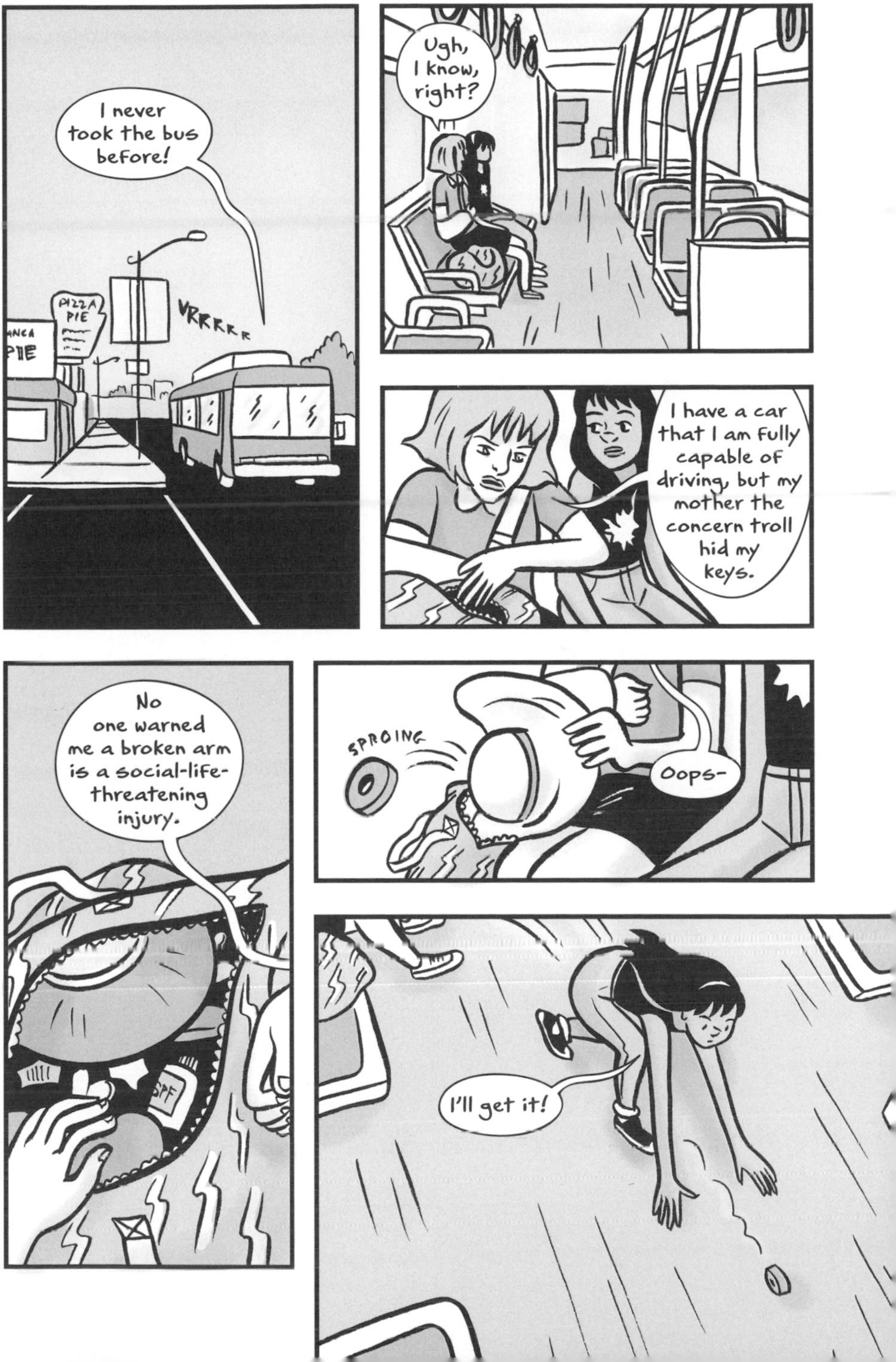
I never took the bus before!
PIZZA PIE
VRRRRRR
Ugh, I know, right?
I have a car that I am fully capable of driving, but my mother the concern troll hid my keys.
No one warned me a broken arm is a social-life-threatening injury.
SPF
SPROING
Oops-
I'll get it!

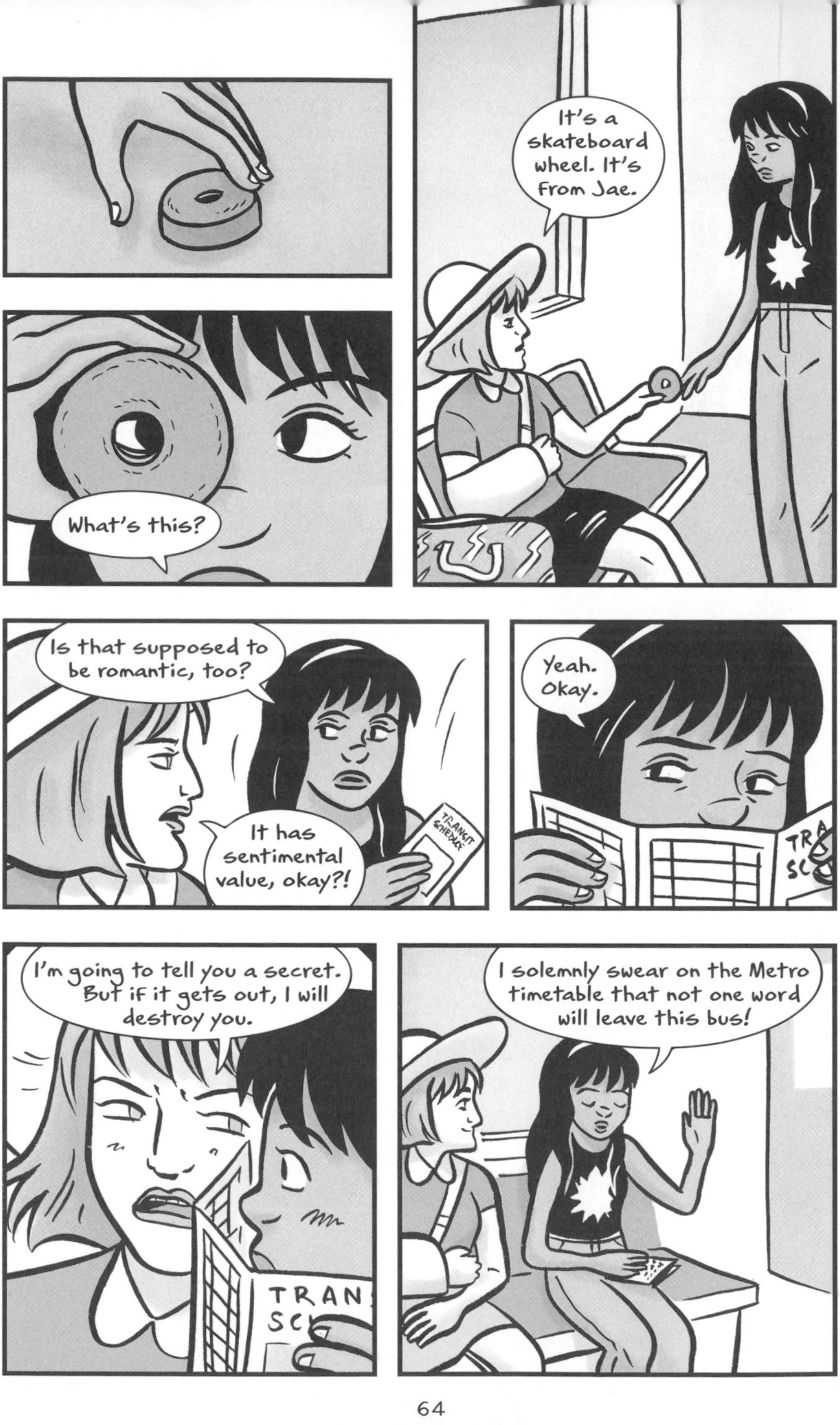

What's this?
It's a skateboard wheel. It's from Jae.
Is that supposed to be romantic, too?
It has sentimental value, okay?!
TRANSIT SCHEDULE
Yeah. Okay.
I'm going to tell you a secret. But if it gets out, I will destroy you.
I solemnly swear on the Metro timetable that not one word will leave this bus!

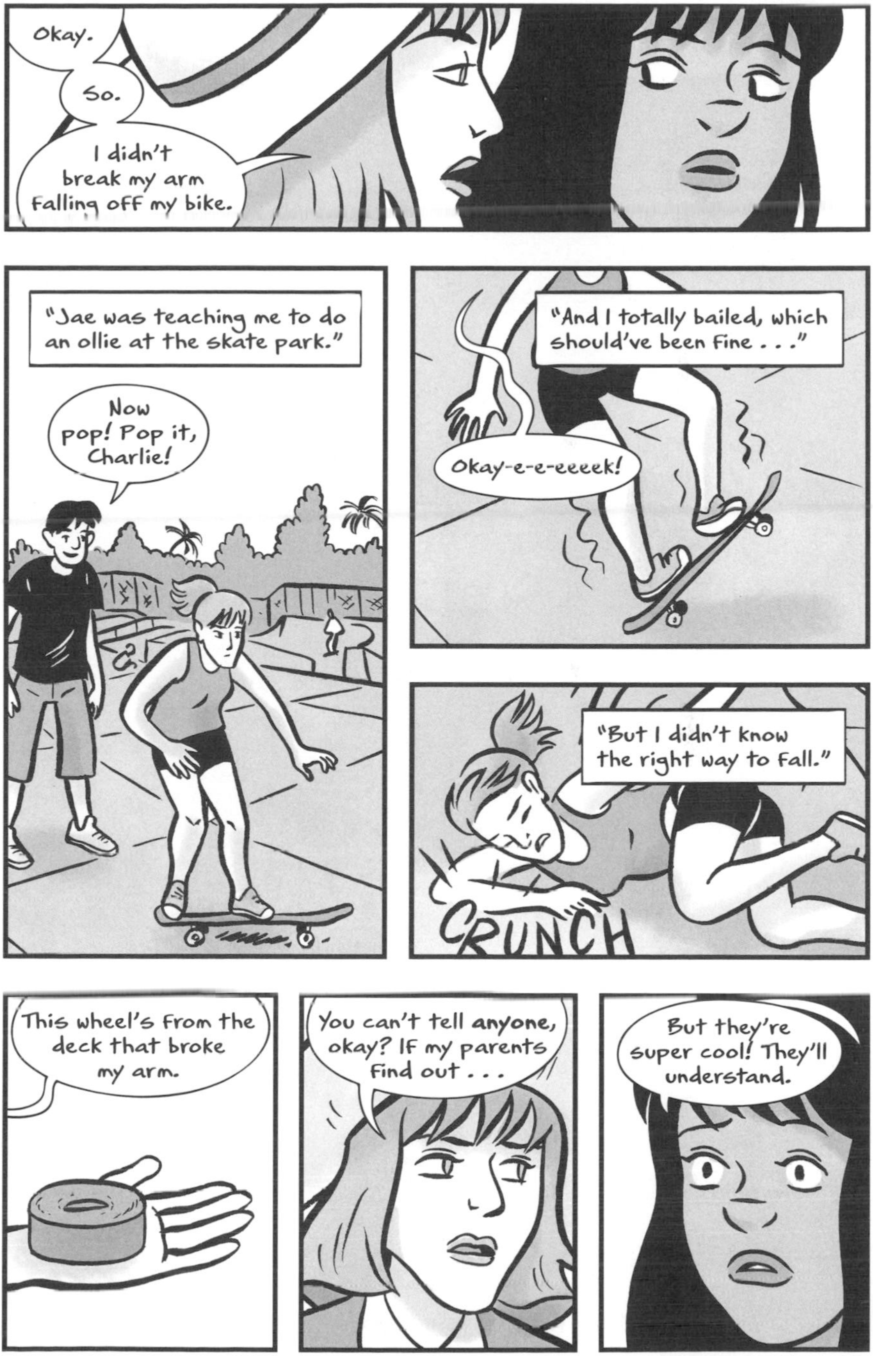
Okay.
So.
I didn't break my arm falling off my bike.
"Jae was teaching me to do an ollie at the skate park."
Now pop! Pop it, Charlie!
"And I totally bailed, which should've been fine . . ."
Okay-e-e-eeeek!
"But I didn't know the right way to fall."
CRUNCH
This wheel's from the deck that broke my arm.
You can't tell anyone, okay? If my parents find out . . .
But they're super cool! They'll understand.

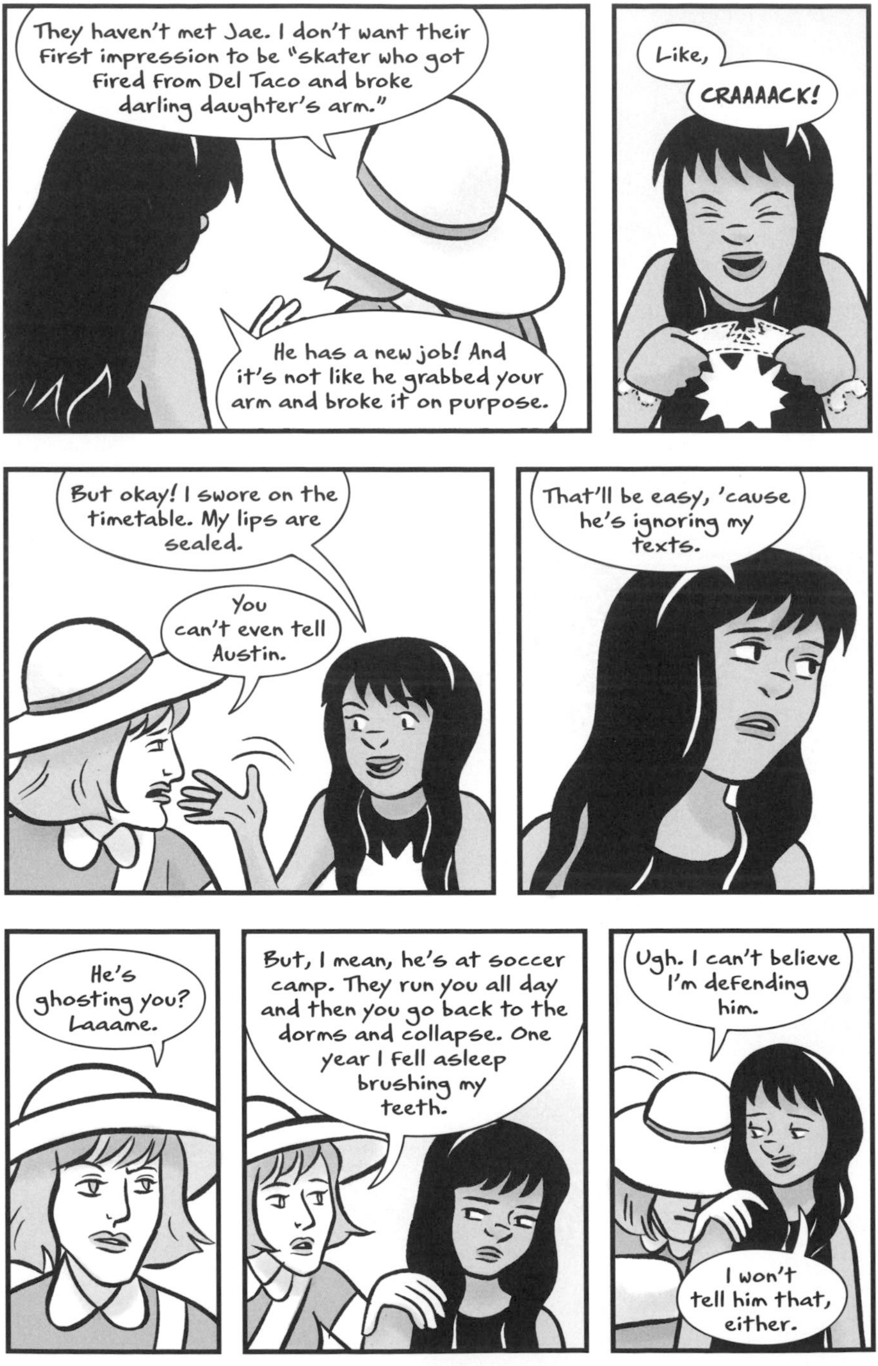
They haven't met Jae. I don't want their First impression to be "skater who got Fired From Del Taco and broke darling daughter's arm."
He has a new job! And it's not like he grabbed your arm and broke it on purpose.
Like,
CRAAAACK!
But okay! I swore on the timetable. My lips are sealed.
You can't even tell Austin.
That'll be easy, 'cause he's ignoring my texts.
He's ghosting you? Laaame.
But, I mean, he's at soccer camp. They run you all day and then you go back to the dorms and collapse. One year I Fell asleep brushing my teeth.
Ugh. I can't believe I'm defending him.
I won't tell him that, either.

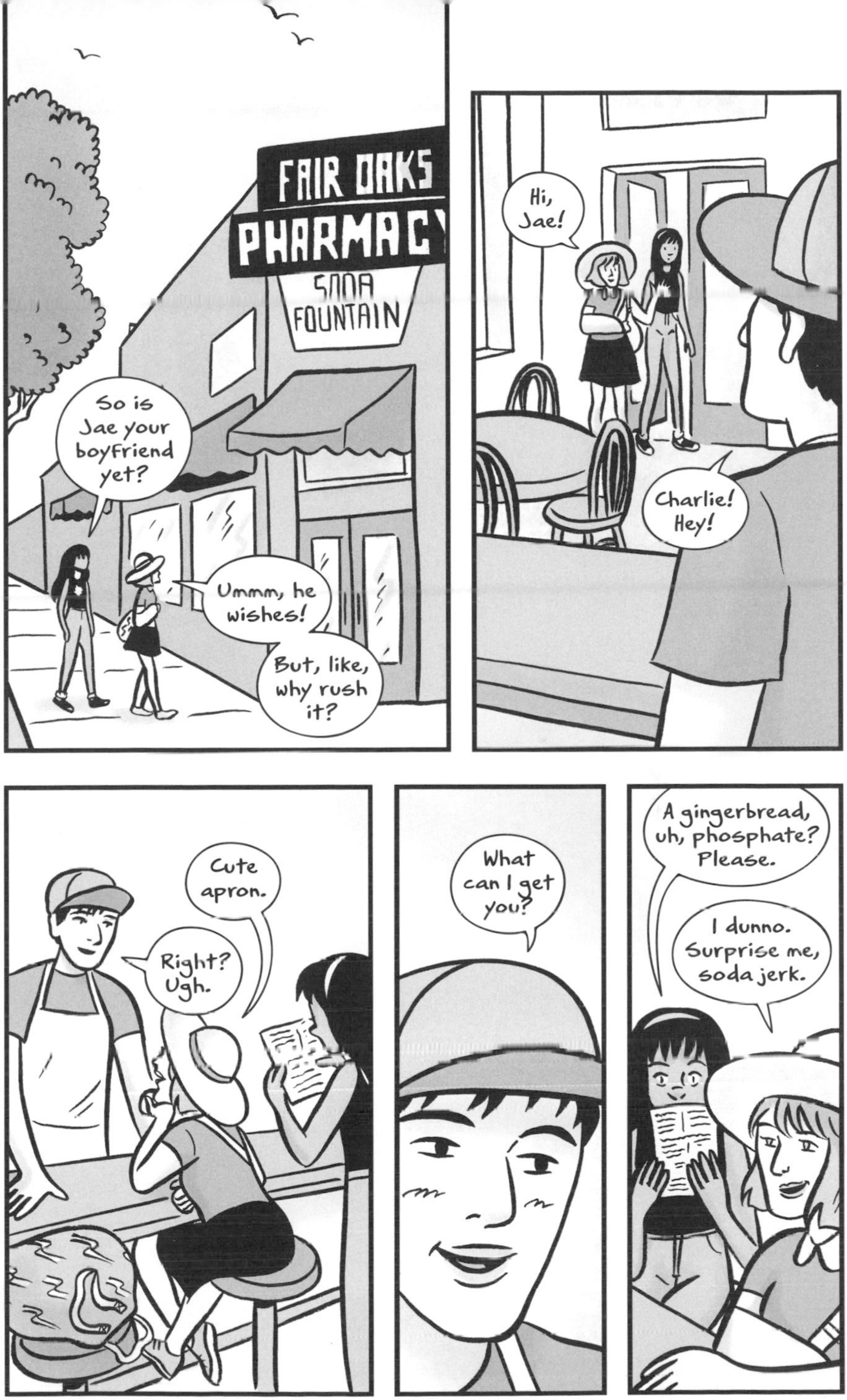
FAIR OAKS
PHARMACY
SODA
FOUNTAIN
So is Jae your boyfriend yet?
Ummm, he wishes!
But, like, why rush it?
Hi, Jae!
Charlie! Hey!
Cute apron.
Right? Ugh.
What can I get you?
A gingerbread, uh, phosphate? Please.
I dunno. Surprise me, soda jerk.

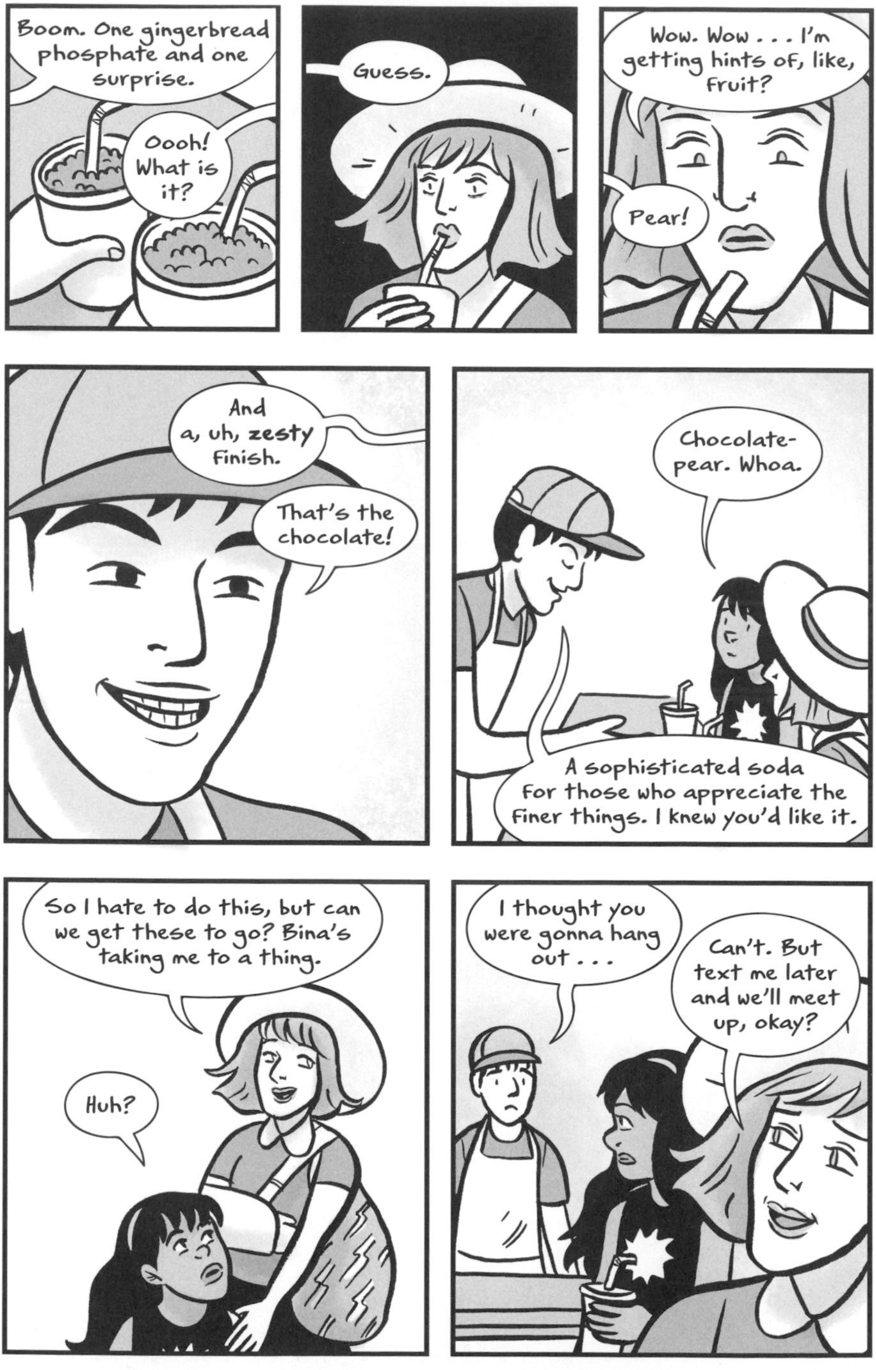
Boom. One gingerbread phosphate and one surprise.
Oooh! What is it?
Guess.
Wow. Wow . . . I'm getting hints of, like, fruit?
Pear!
And a, uh, zesty finish.
That's the chocolate!
Chocolate-pear. Whoa.
A sophisticated soda for those who appreciate the finer things. I knew you'd like it.
So I hate to do this, but can we get these to go? Bina's taking me to a thing.
Huh?
I thought you were gonna hang out . . .
Can't. But text me later and we'll meet up, okay?

So we came all this way to see that dude for, like, two seconds? I don't get it!
Bina, I can't drink this! It's beyond vile. And he was so proud! What was I supposed to do?
Can I try it?
Slurp
Ewww.
See?!
It sounded good, but-
There's a plant. Dump it in there.
NO! I'm gonna drink it!
What?! Why?
I feel sorry for it.
It's a soda. It doesn't have feelings!
Charlie?

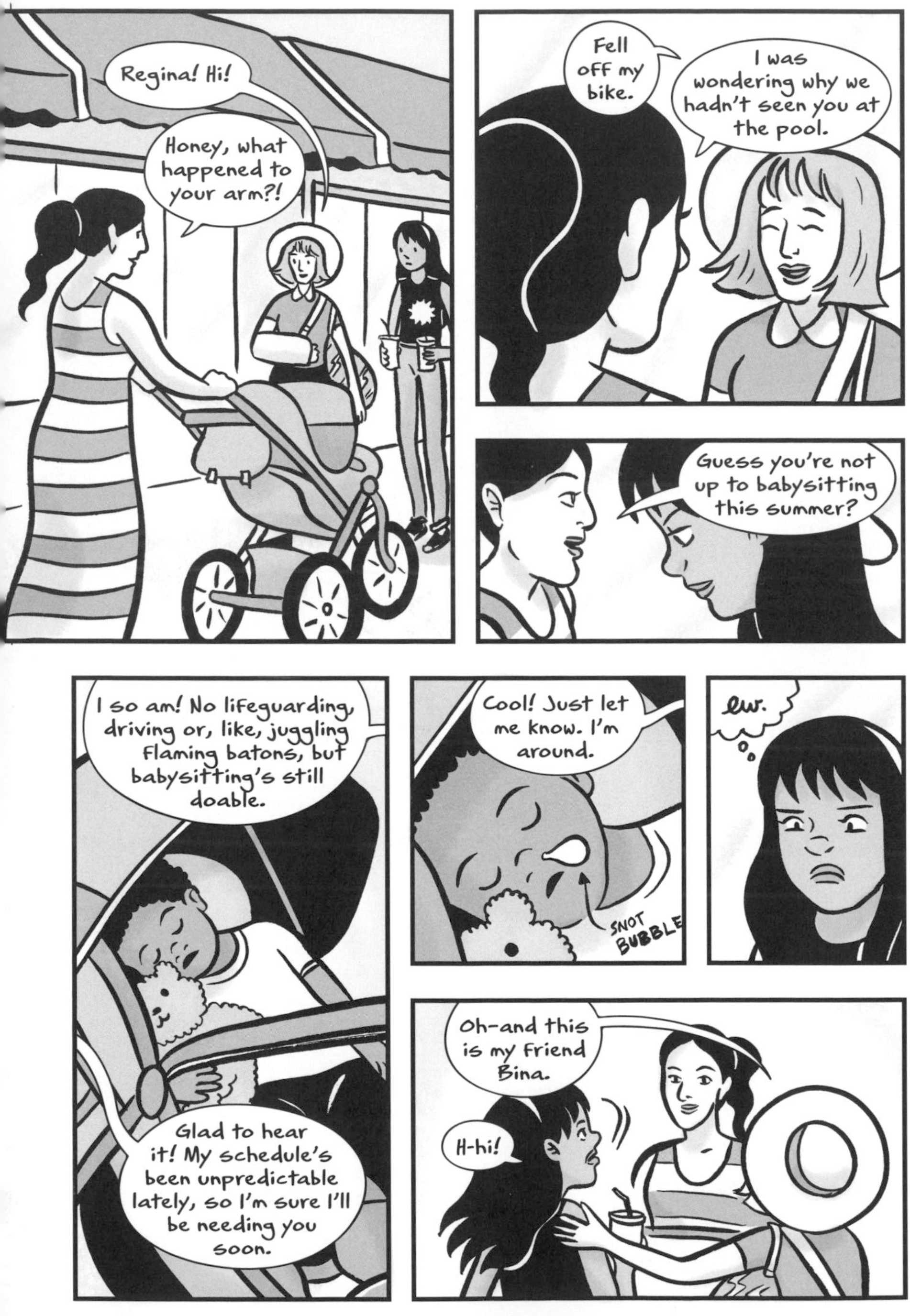
Regina! Hi!
Honey, what happened to your arm?!
Fell off my bike.
I was wondering why we hadn't seen you at the pool.
Guess you're not up to babysitting this summer?
I so am! No lifeguarding, driving or, like, juggling flaming batons, but babysitting's still doable.
Glad to hear it! My schedule's been unpredictable lately, so I'm sure I'll be needing you soon.
Cool! Just let me know. I'm around.
SNOT BUBBLE
ew.
Oh—and this is my friend Bina.
H-hi!

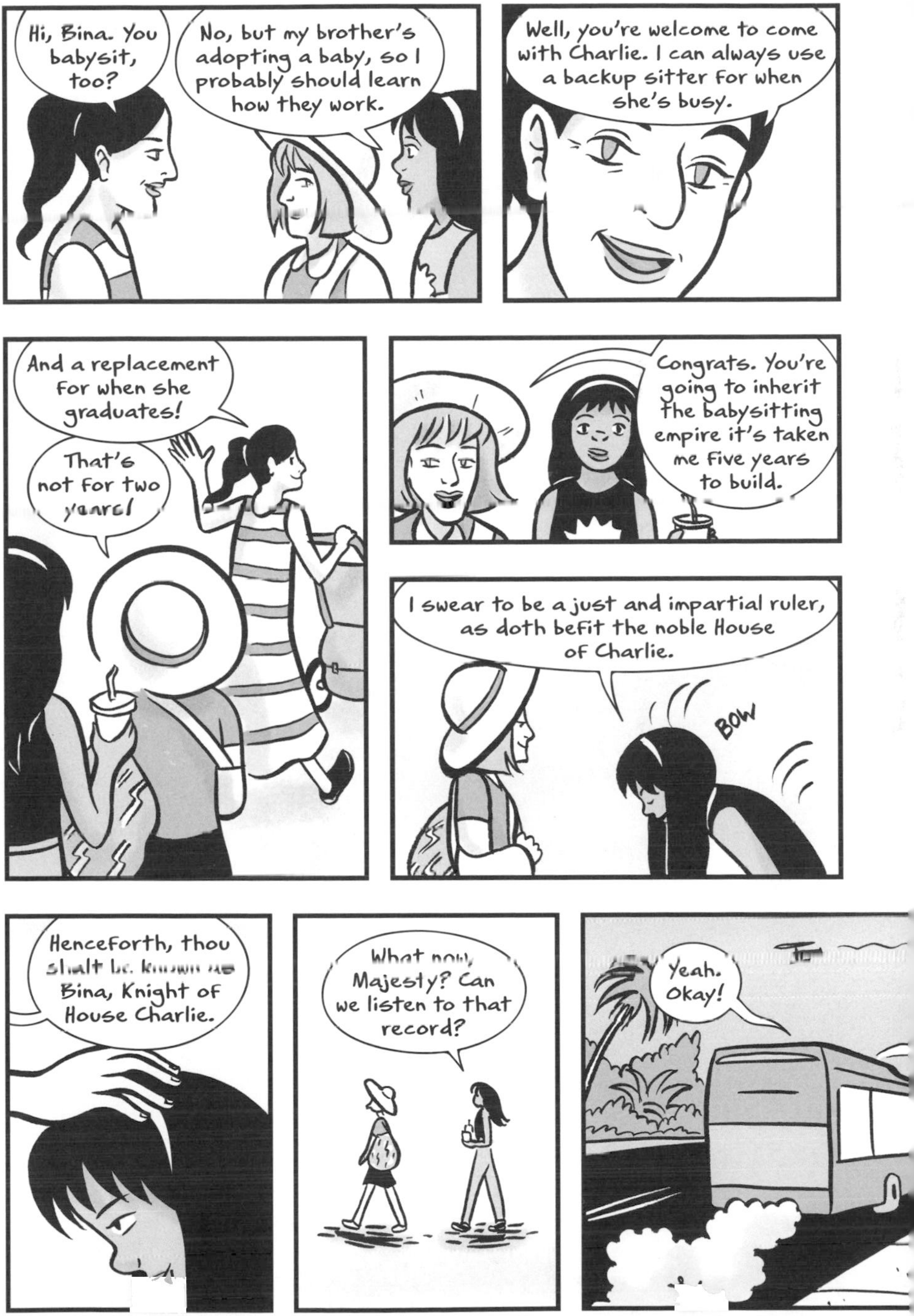
Hi, Bina. You babysit, too?
No, but my brother's adopting a baby, so I probably should learn how they work.
Well, you're welcome to come with Charlie. I can always use a backup sitter for when she's busy.
And a replacement for when she graduates!
That's not for two years!
Congrats. You're going to inherit the babysitting empire it's taken me five years to build.
I swear to be a just and impartial ruler, as doth befit the noble House of Charlie.
BOW
Henceforth, thou
Bina, Knight of House Charlie.
What now, Majesty? Can we listen to that record?
Yeah. Okay!

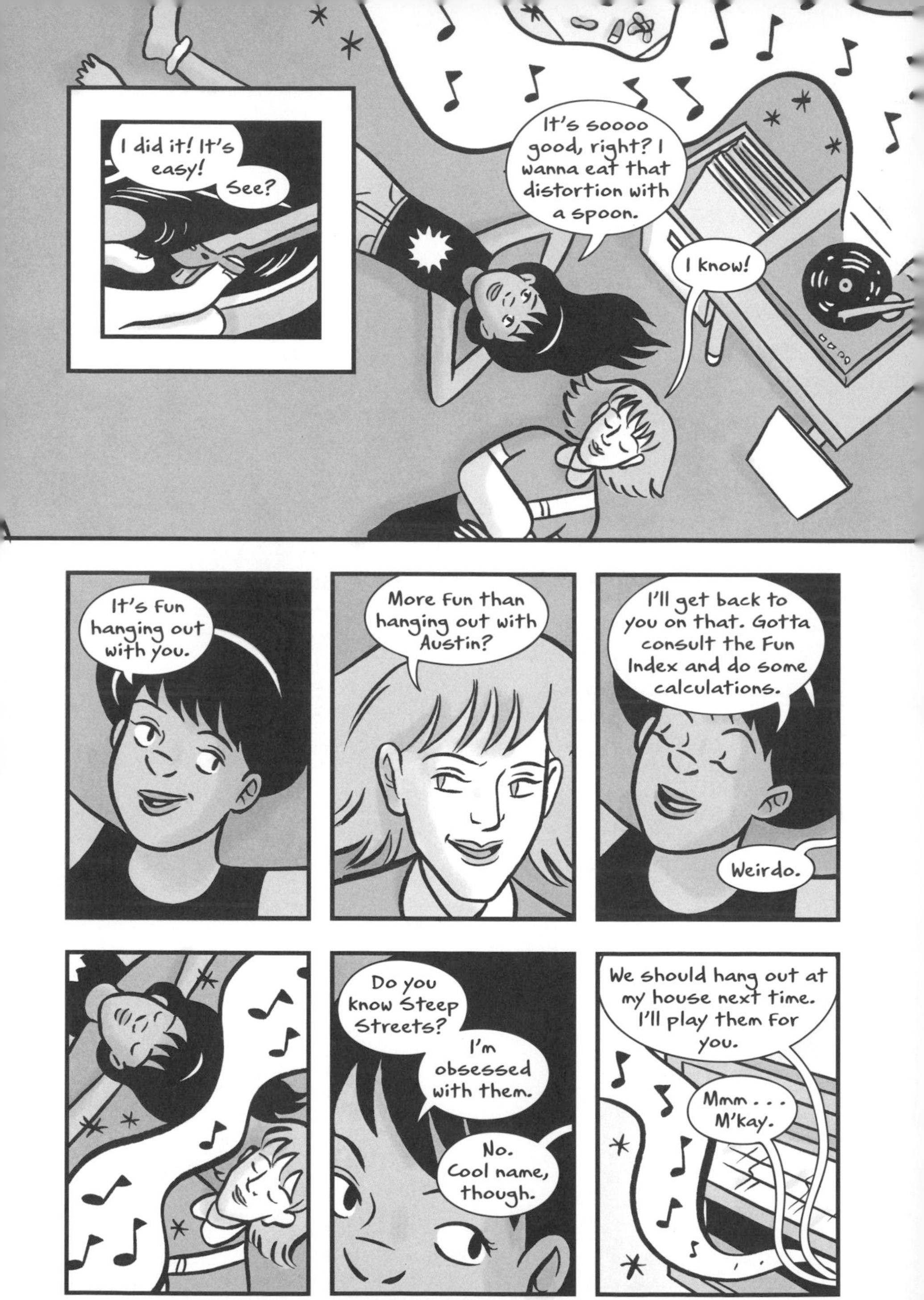
I did it! It's easy!
See?
It's soooo good, right? I wanna eat that distortion with a spoon.
I know!
It's fun hanging out with you.
More fun than hanging out with Austin?
I'll get back to you on that. Gotta consult the Fun Index and do some calculations.
Weirdo.
Do you know Steep Streets?
I'm obsessed with them.
No. Cool name, though.
We should hang out at my house next time. I'll play them for you.
Mmm . . . M'kay.

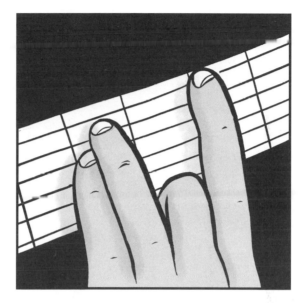

Week Four

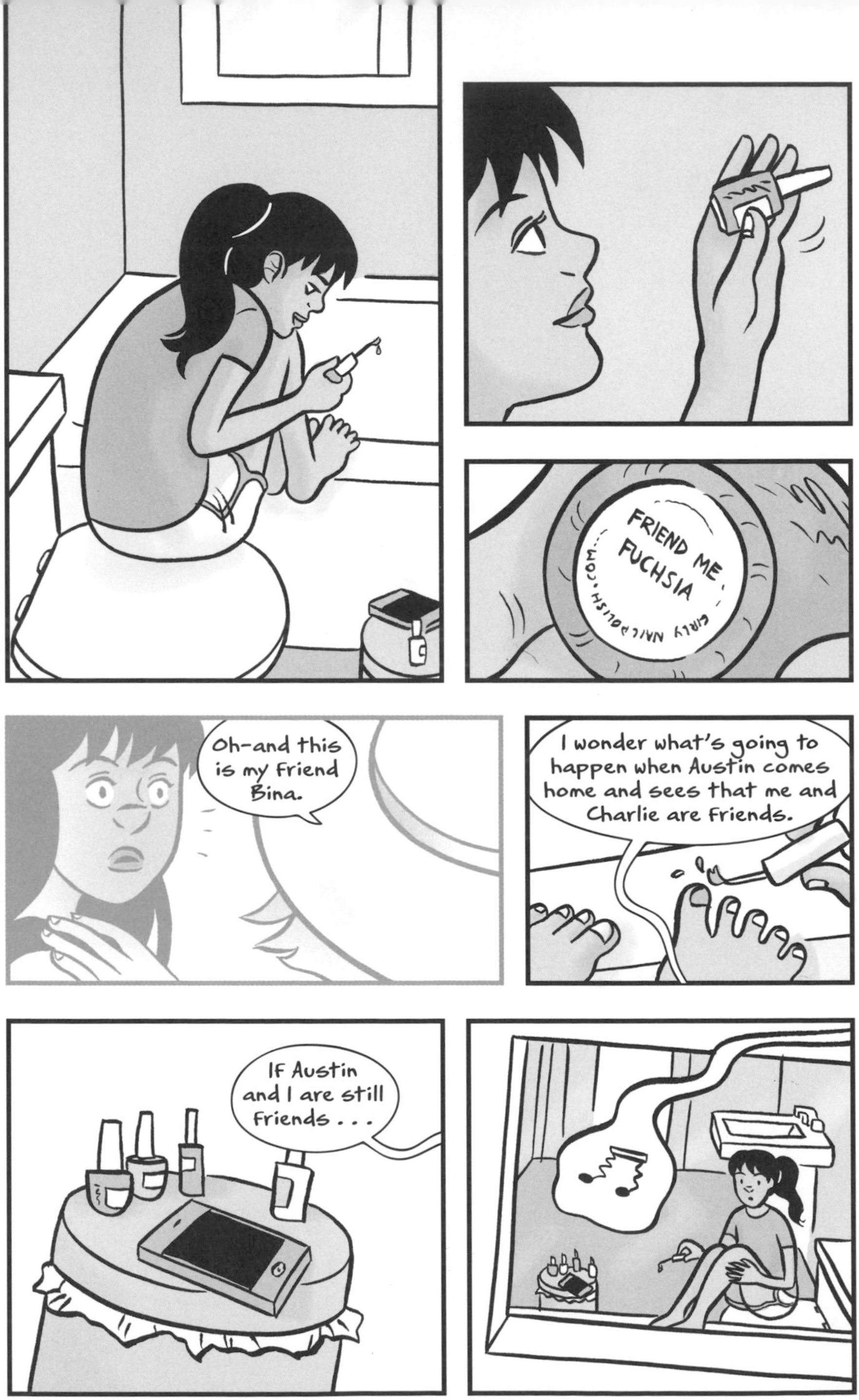
FRIEND ME FUCHSIA
GIRLY NAILPOLISH.COM
Oh—and this is my friend Bina.
I wonder what's going to happen when Austin comes home and sees that me and Charlie are friends.
If Austin and I are still friends . . .

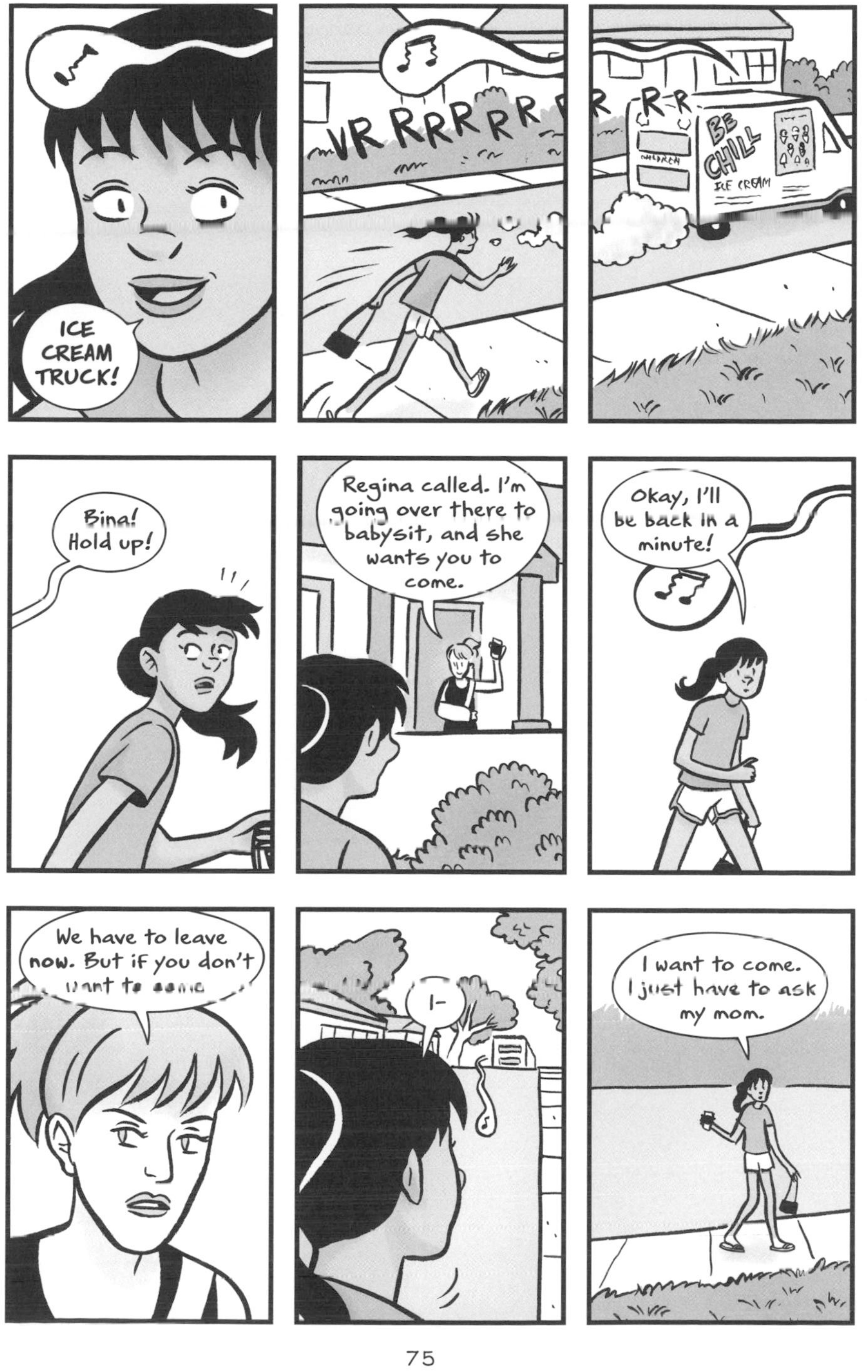
ICE CREAM TRUCK!
VRRRRRRR
BE CHILL
ICE CREAM
Bina! Hold up!
Regina called. I'm going over there to babysit, and she wants you to come.
Okay, I'll be back in a minute!
We have to leave now. But if you don't
I-
I want to come. I just have to ask my mom.

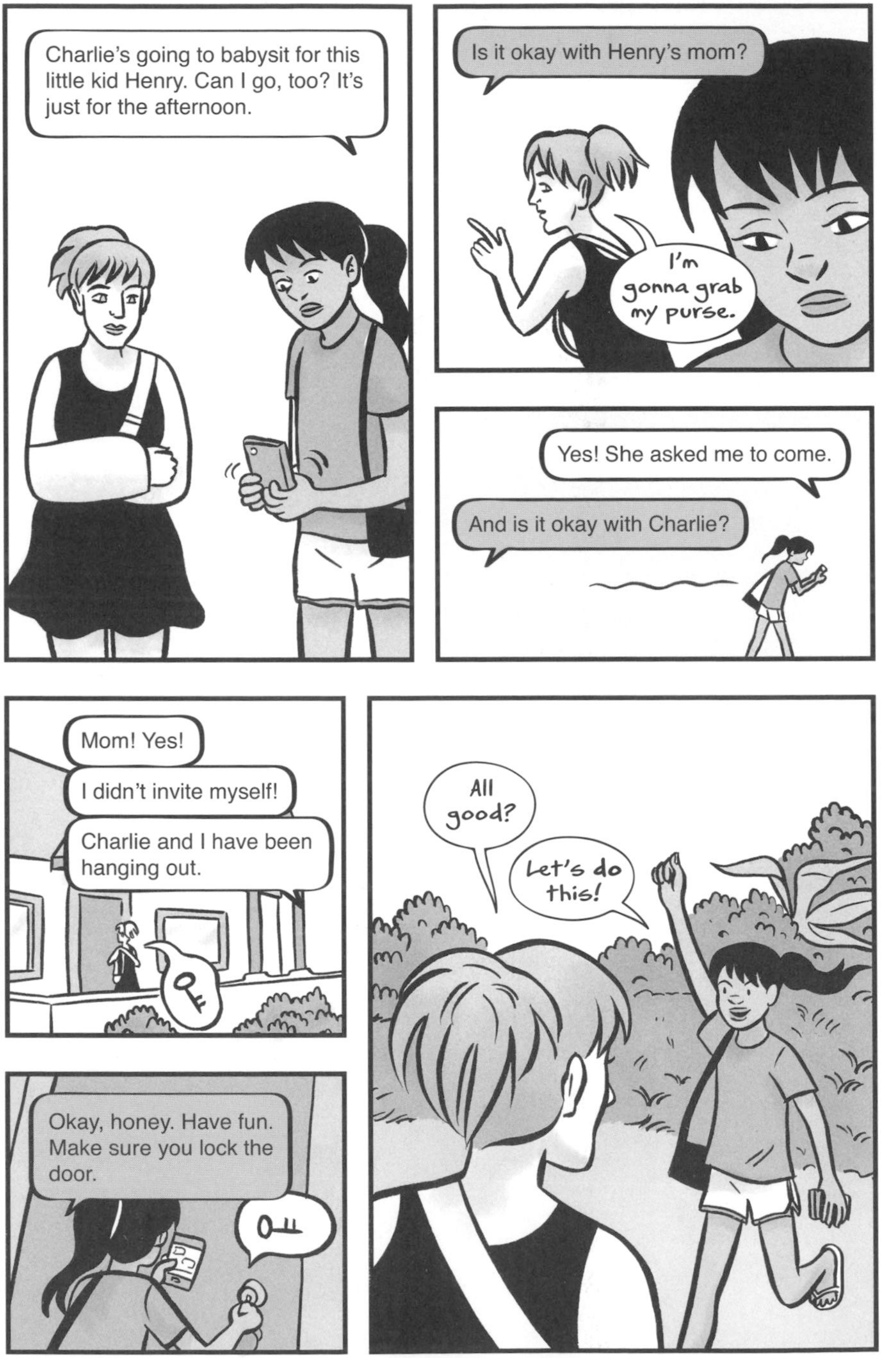
Charlie's going to babysit for this little kid Henry. Can I go, too? It's just for the afternoon.
Is it okay with Henry's mom?
I'm gonna grab my purse.
Yes! She asked me to come.
And is it okay with Charlie?
Mom! Yes!
I didn't invite myself!
Charlie and I have been hanging out.
Okay, honey. Have fun. Make sure you lock the door.
All good?
Let's do this!

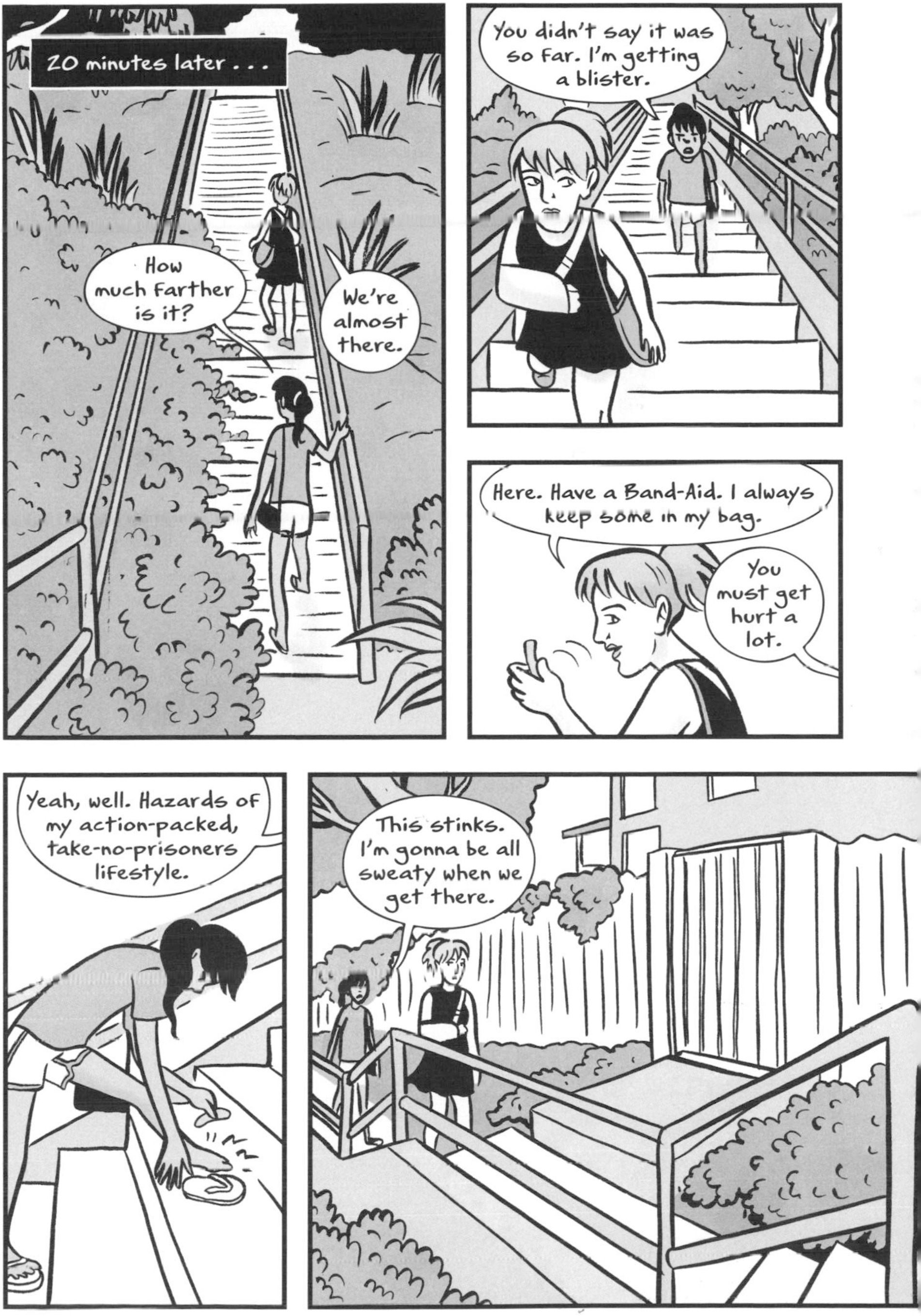
20 minutes later . . .
How much farther is it?
We're almost there.
You didn't say it was so far. I'm getting a blister.
Here. Have a Band-Aid. I always keep some in my bag.
You must get hurt a lot.
Yeah, well. Hazards of my action-packed, take-no-prisoners lifestyle.
This stinks. I'm gonna be all sweaty when we get there.

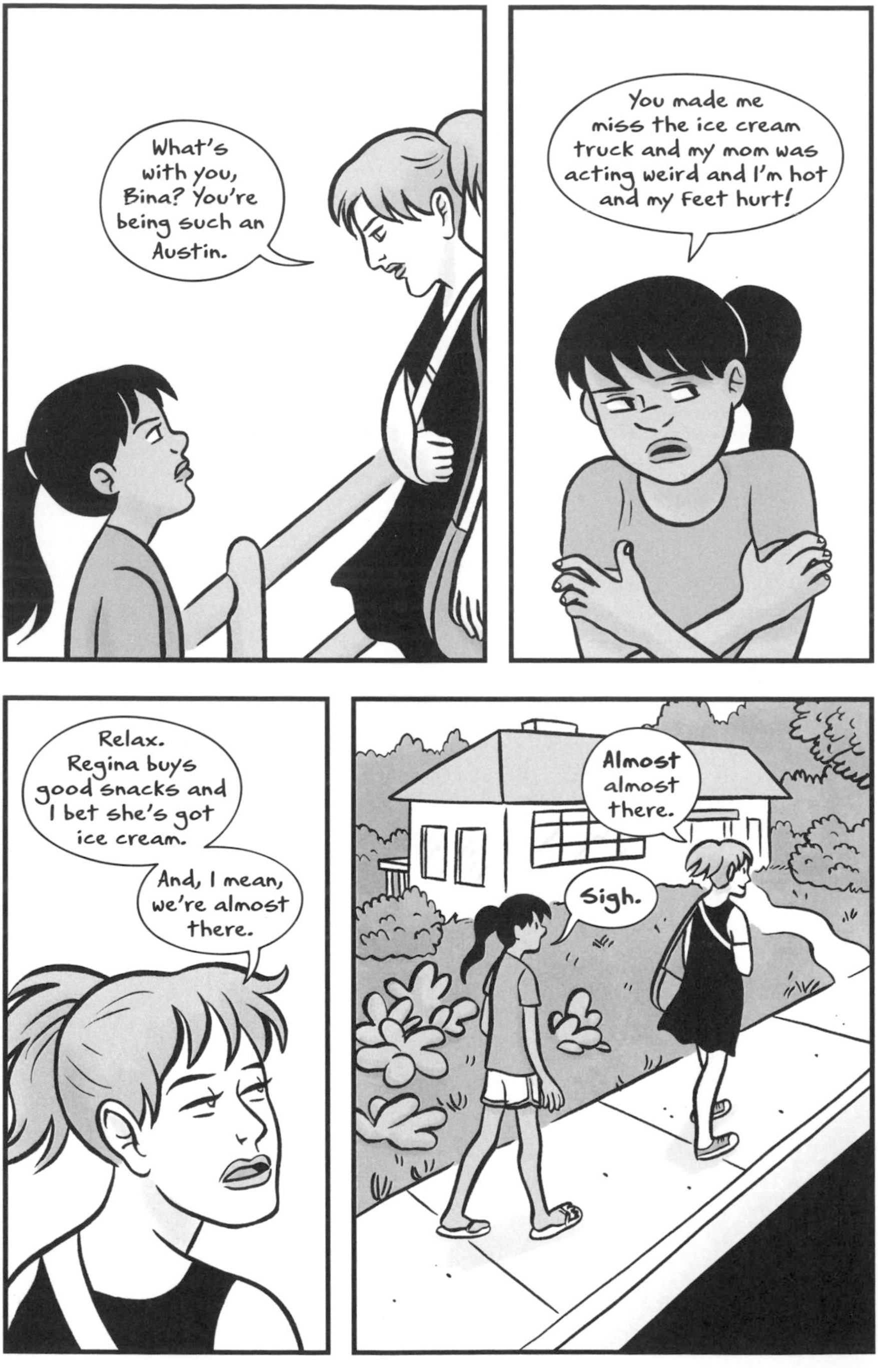
What's with you, Bina? You're being such an Austin.
You made me miss the ice cream truck and my mom was acting weird and I'm hot and my feet hurt!
Relax. Regina buys good snacks and I bet she's got ice cream.
And, I mean, we're almost there.
Almost almost there.
Sigh.

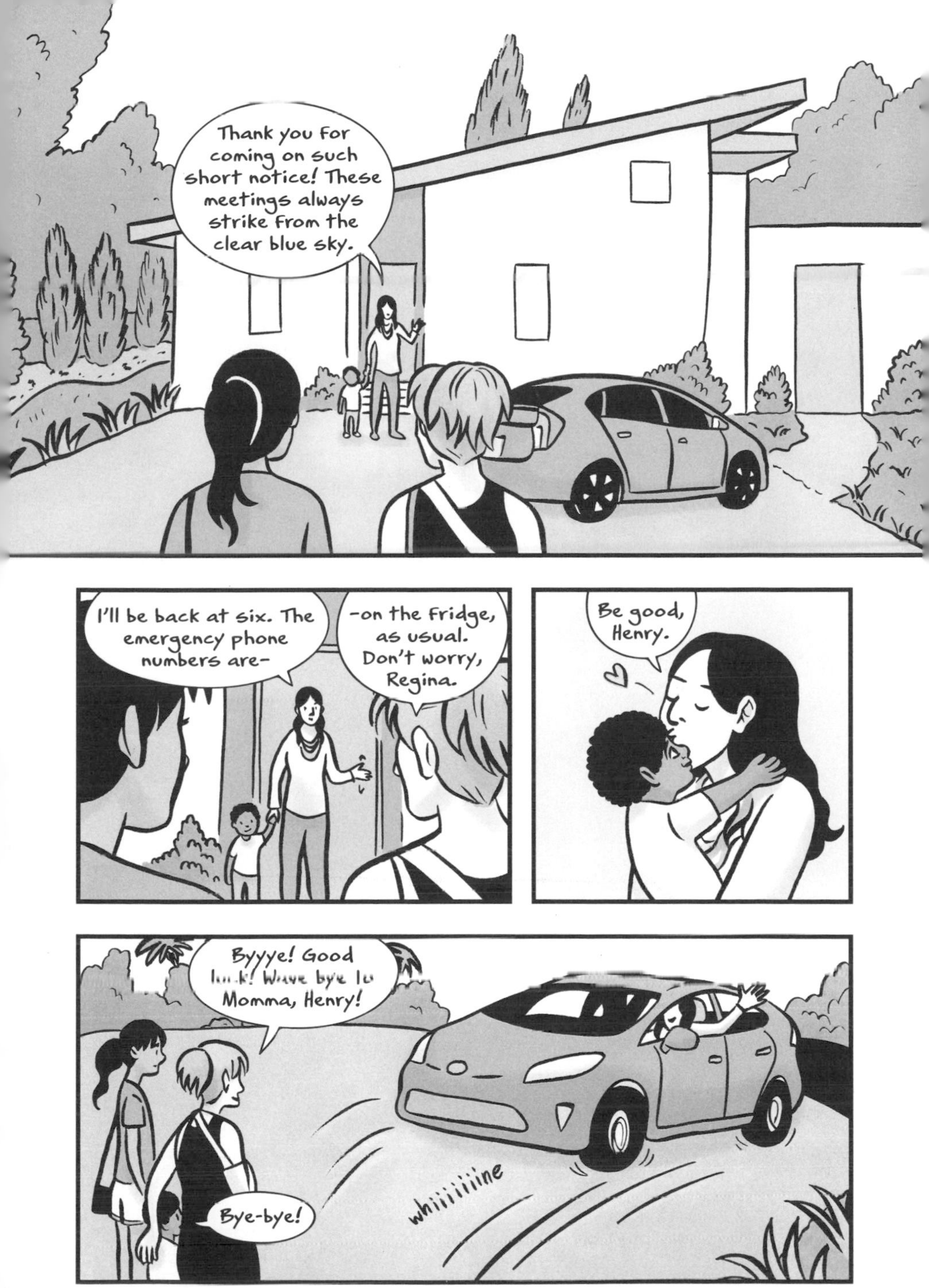
Thank you for coming on such short notice! These meetings always strike from the clear blue sky.
I'll be back at six. The emergency phone numbers are-
-on the fridge, as usual. Don't worry, Regina.
Be good, Henry.
Byyye! Good luck! Wave bye to Momma, Henry!
whiiiiiiine
Bye-bye!

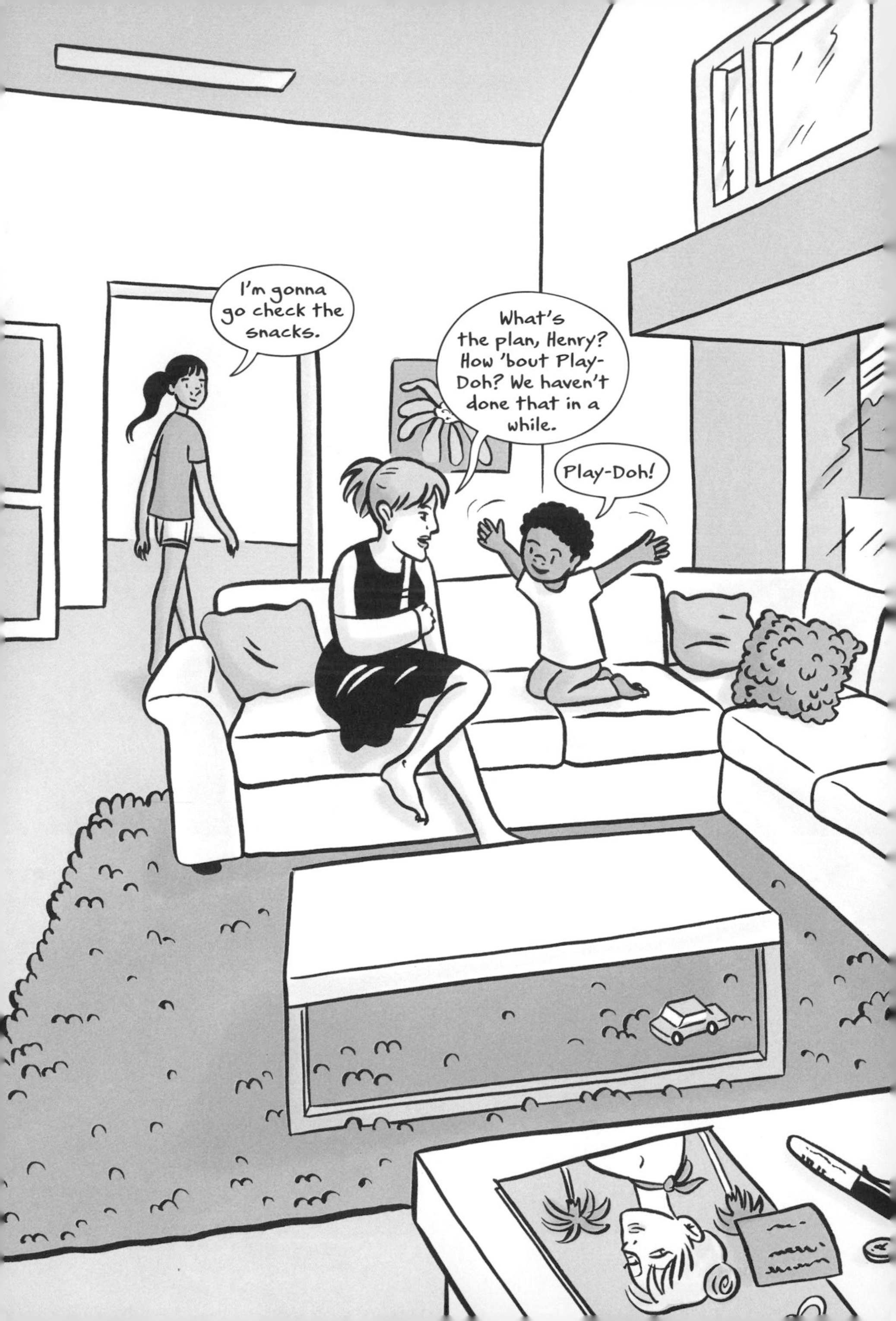
I'm gonna go check the snacks.
What's the plan, Henry? How 'bout Play-Doh? We haven't done that in a while.
Play-Doh!

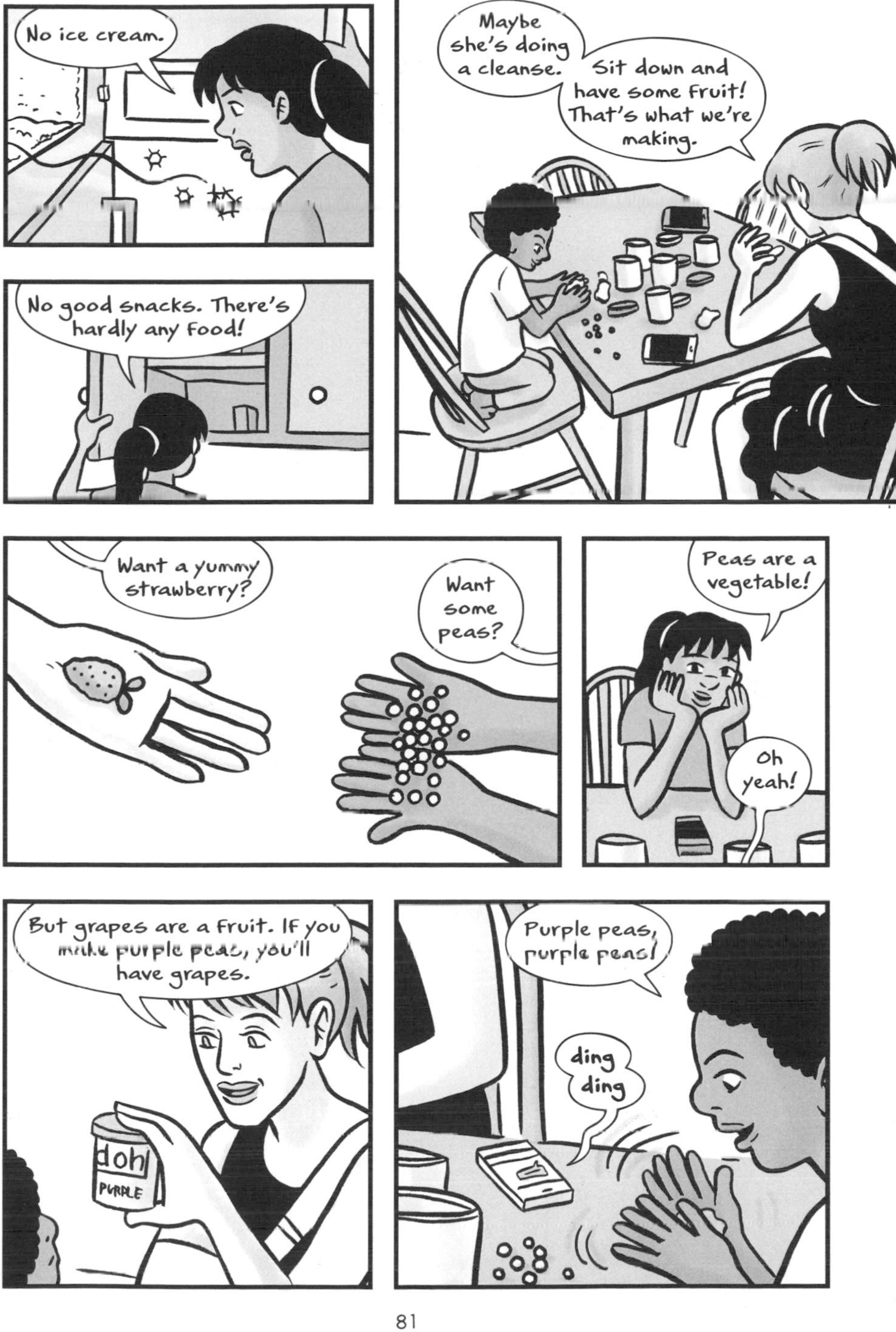
No ice cream.
No good snacks. There's hardly any food!
Maybe she's doing a cleanse.
Sit down and have some fruit! That's what we're making.
Want a yummy strawberry?
Want some peas?
Peas are a vegetable!
Oh yeah!
But grapes are a fruit. If you make purple peas, you'll have grapes.
doh
PURPLE
Purple peas, purple peas!
ding ding

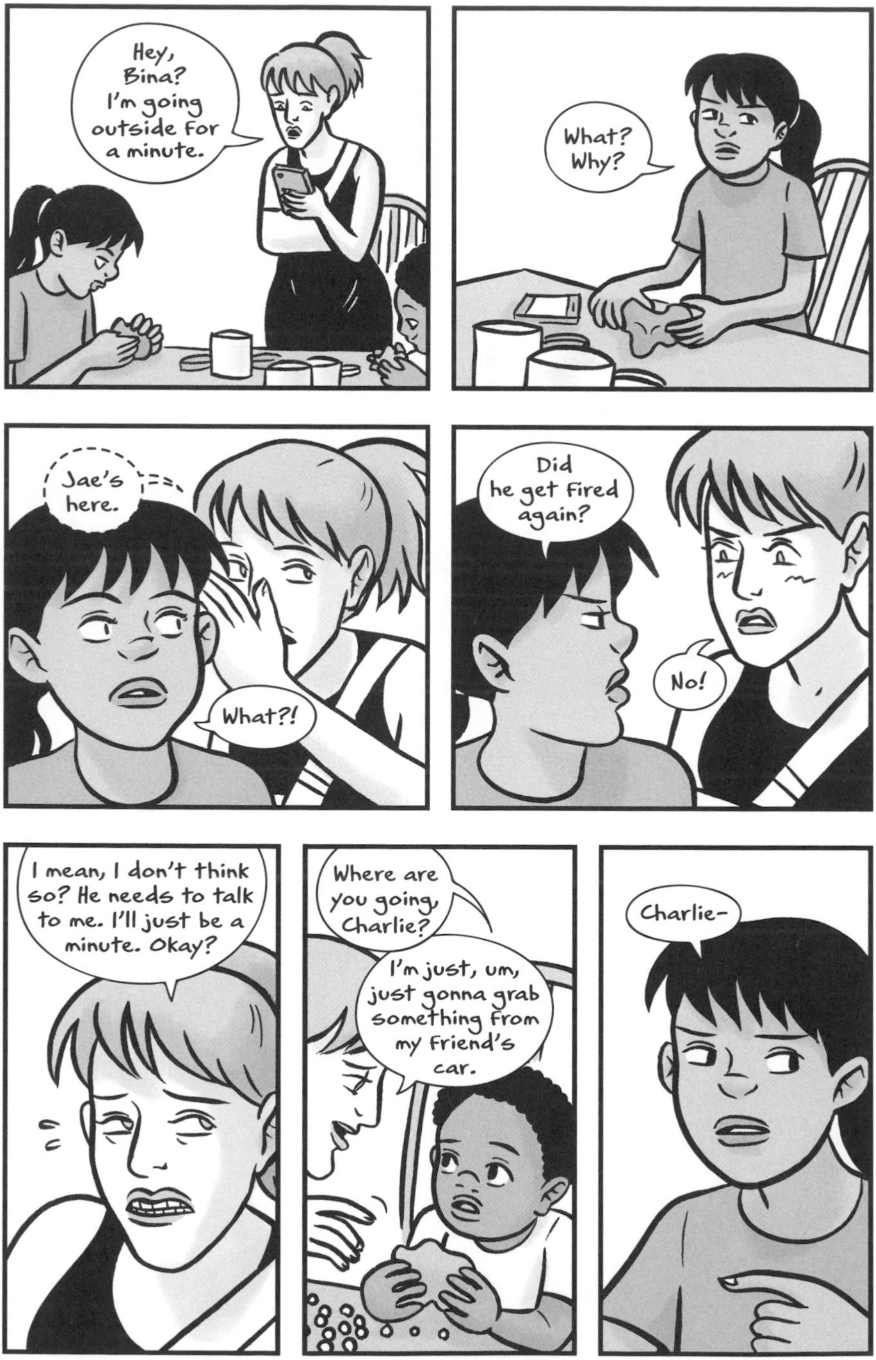
Hey, Bina? I'm going outside for a minute.
What? Why?
Jae's here.
What?!
Did he get fired again?
No!
I mean, I don't think so? He needs to talk to me. I'll just be a minute. Okay?
Where are you going, Charlie?
I'm just, um, just gonna grab something from my friend's car.
Charlie-

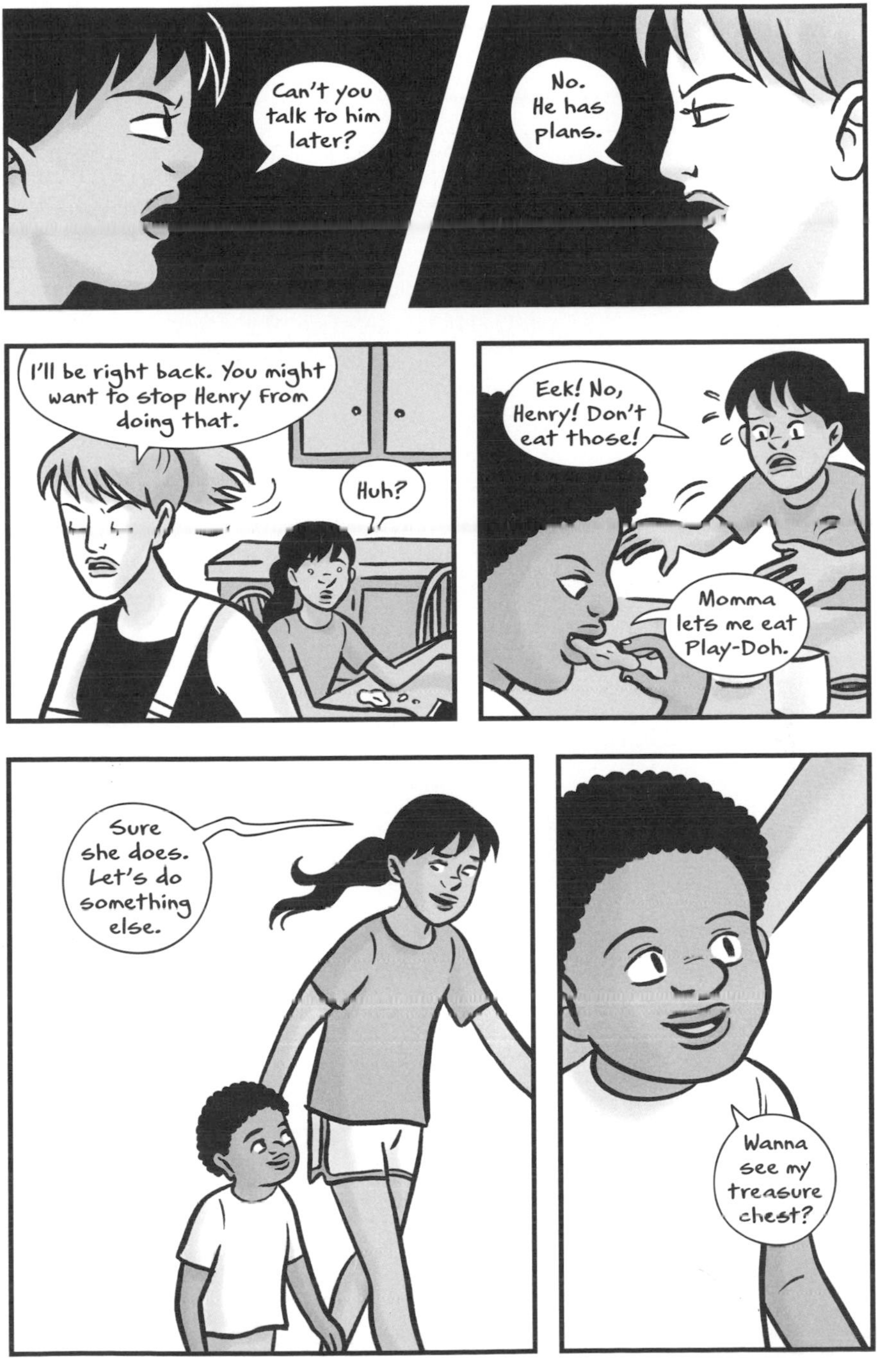
Can't you talk to him later?
No. He has plans.
I'll be right back. You might want to stop Henry from doing that.
Huh?
Eek! No, Henry! Don't eat those!
Momma lets me eat Play-Doh.
Sure she does. Let's do something else.
Wanna see my treasure chest?

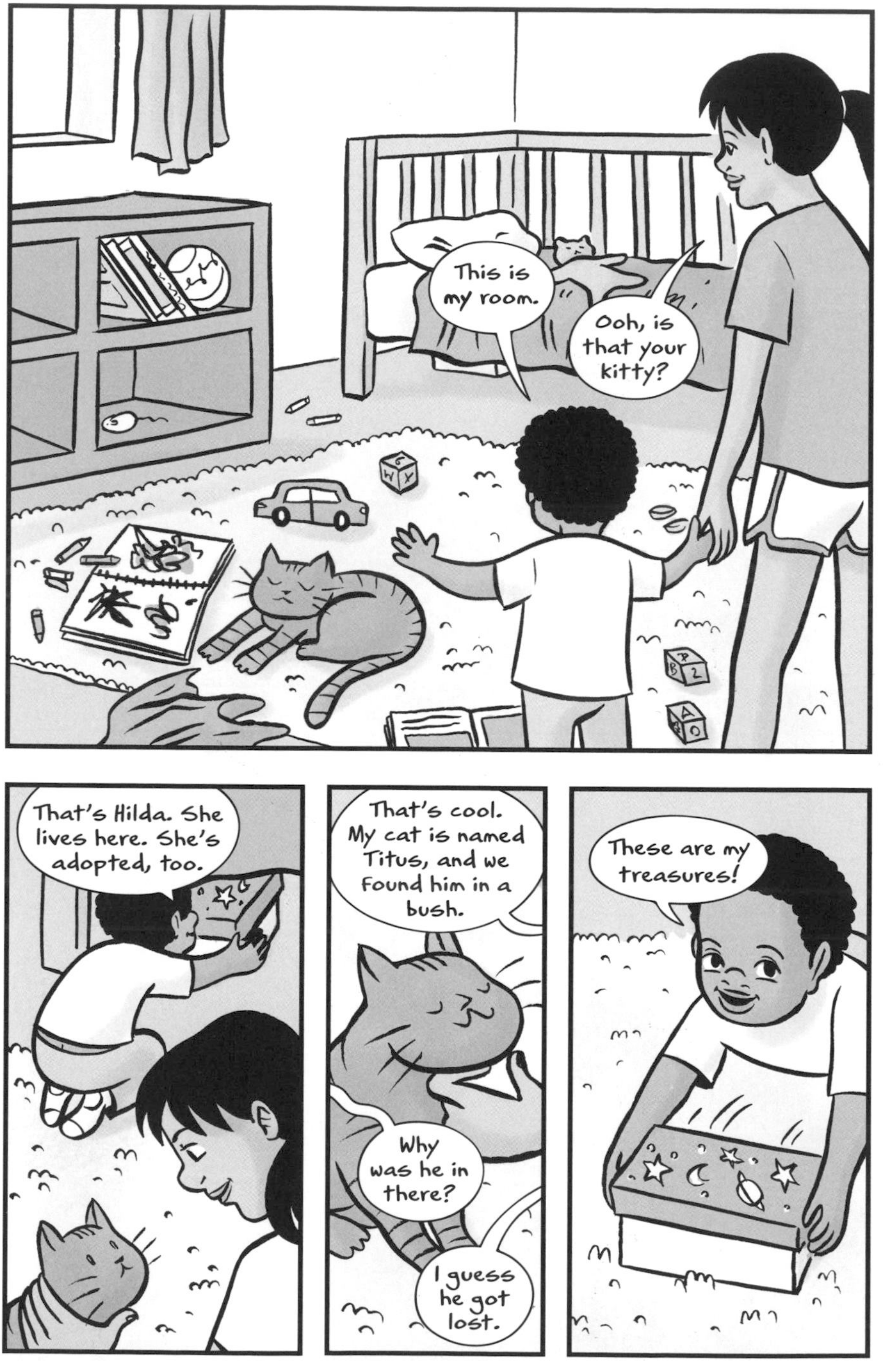
This is my room.
Ooh, is that your kitty?
That's Hilda. She lives here. She's adopted, too.
That's cool. My cat is named Titus, and we found him in a bush.
Why was he in there?
I guess he got lost.
These are my treasures!

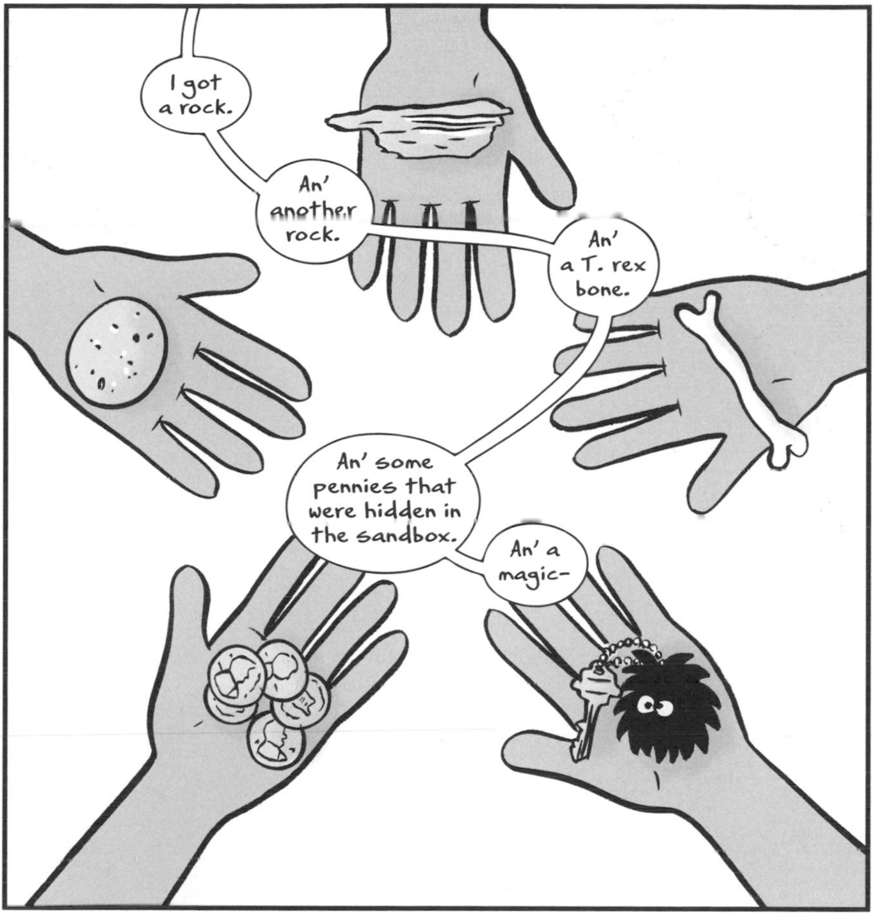
I got a rock.
An' another rock.
An' a T. rex bone.
An' some pennies that were hidden in the sandbox.
An' a magic-

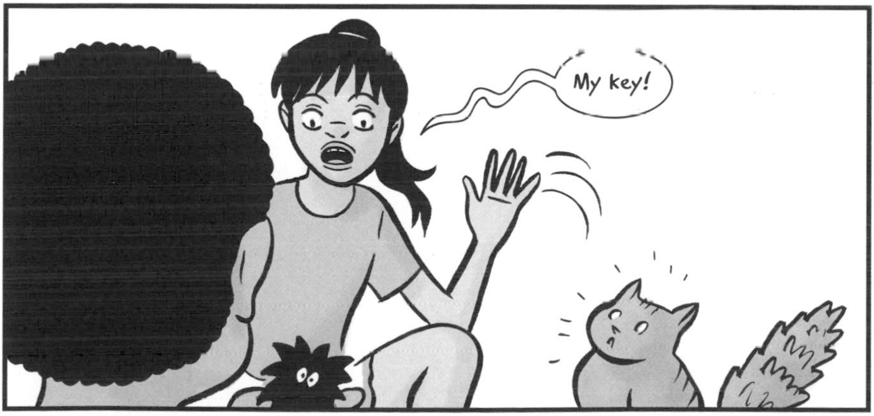
My key!

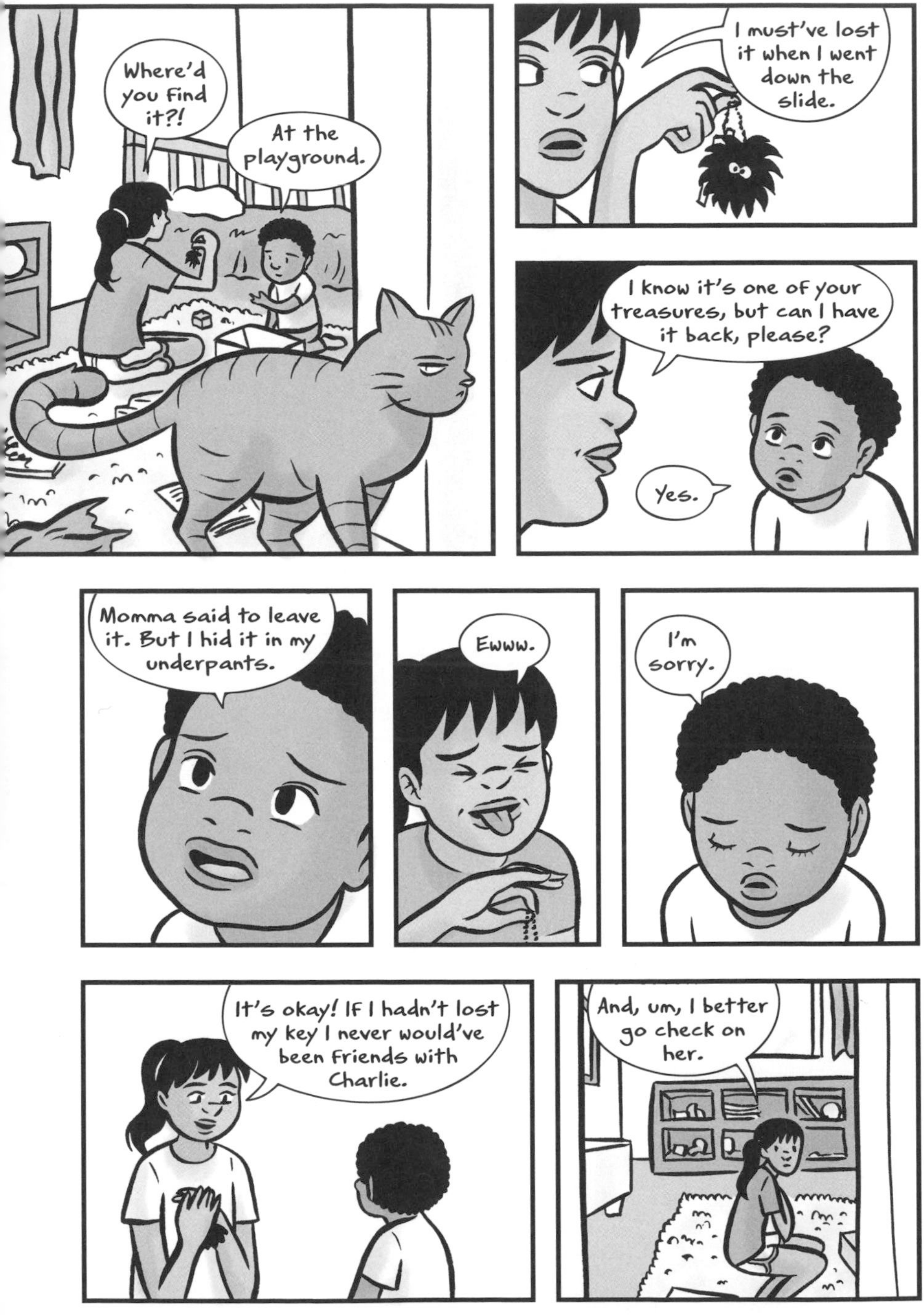
Where'd you find it?!
At the playground.
I must've lost it when I went down the slide.
I know it's one of your treasures, but can I have it back, please?
Yes.
Momma said to leave it. But I hid it in my underpants.
Ewww.
I'm sorry.
It's okay! If I hadn't lost my key I never would've been friends with Charlie.
And, um, I better go check on her.

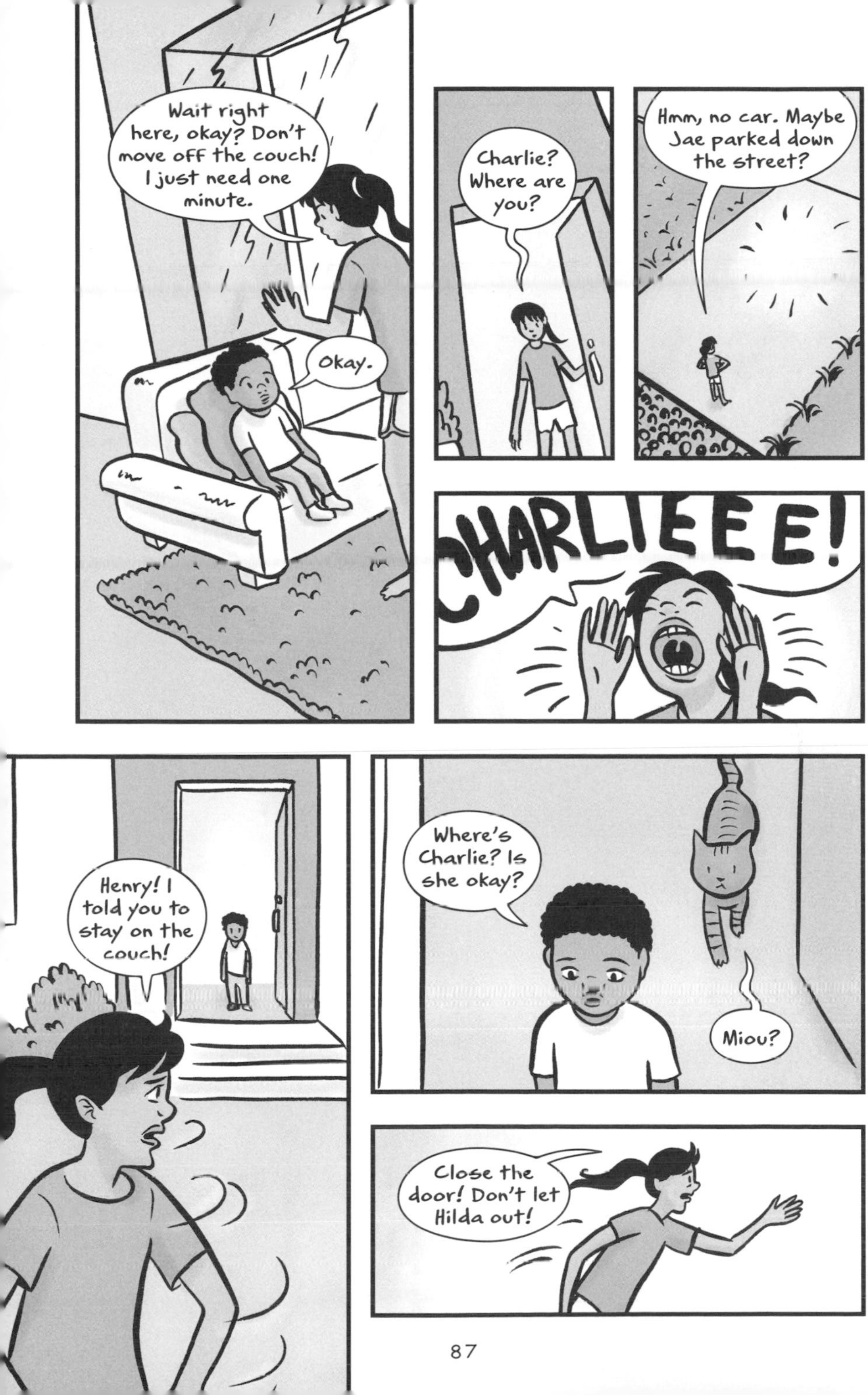
Wait right here, okay? Don't move off the couch! I just need one minute.
Okay.
Charlie? Where are you?
Hmm, no car. Maybe Jae parked down the street?
CHARLIEEE!
Henry! I told you to stay on the couch!
Where's Charlie? Is she okay?
Miou?
Close the door! Don't let Hilda out!

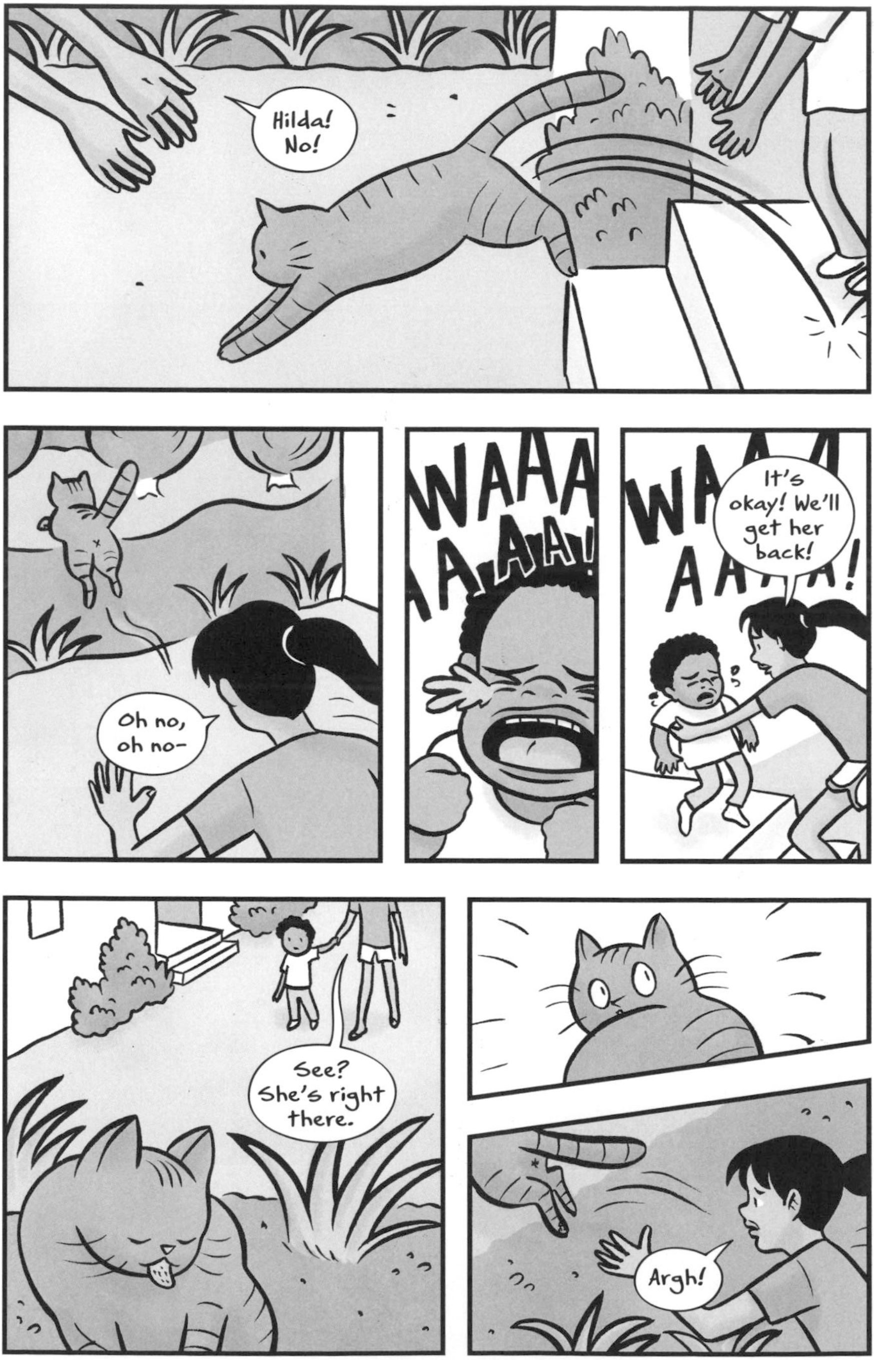
Hilda! No!
Oh no, oh no-
WAAAAAA!
WAAAAAA!
It's okay! We'll get her back!
See? She's right there.
Argh!

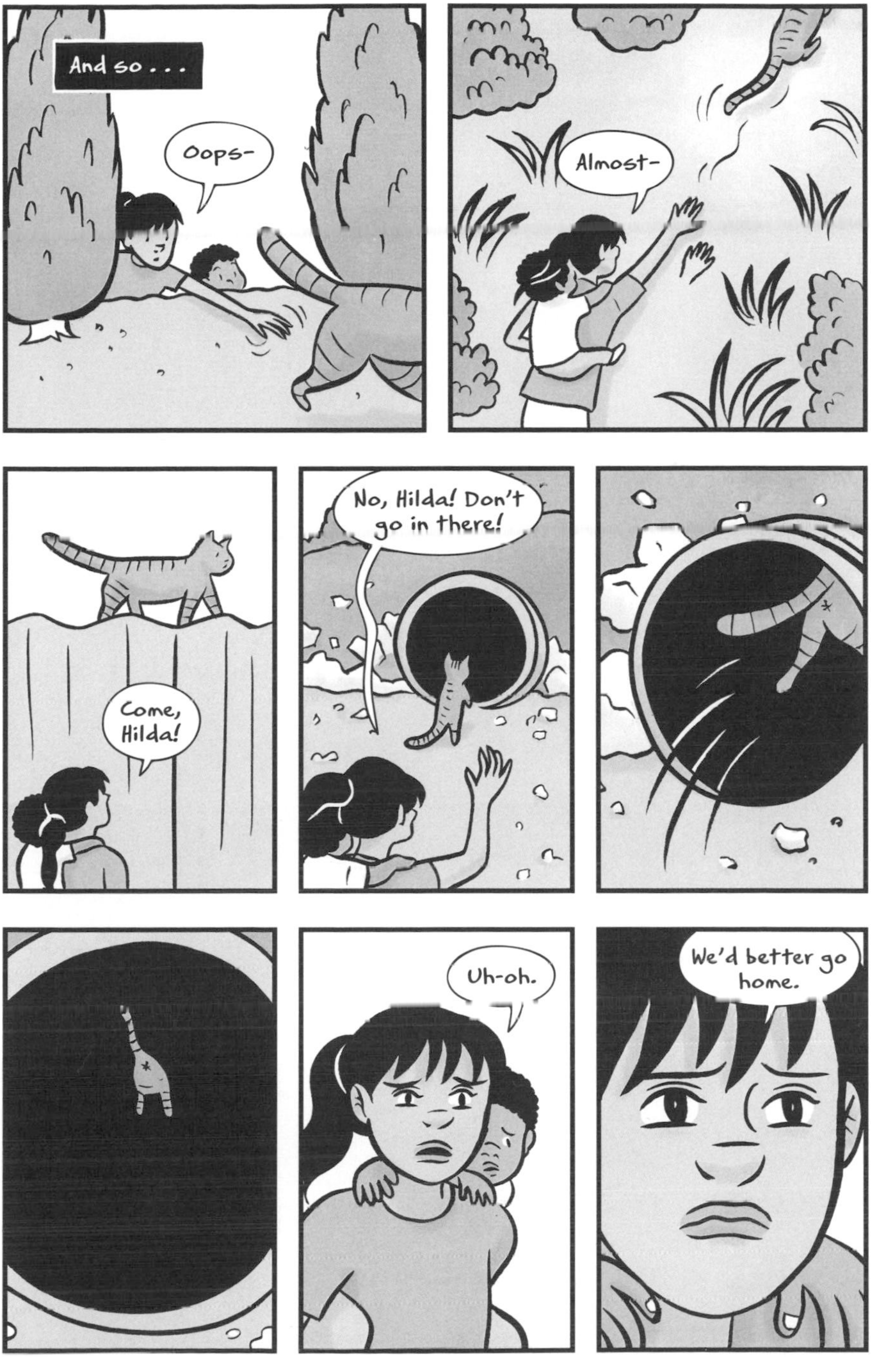
And so . . .
Oops-
Almost-
Come, Hilda!
No, Hilda! Don't go in there!
Uh-oh.
We'd better go home.

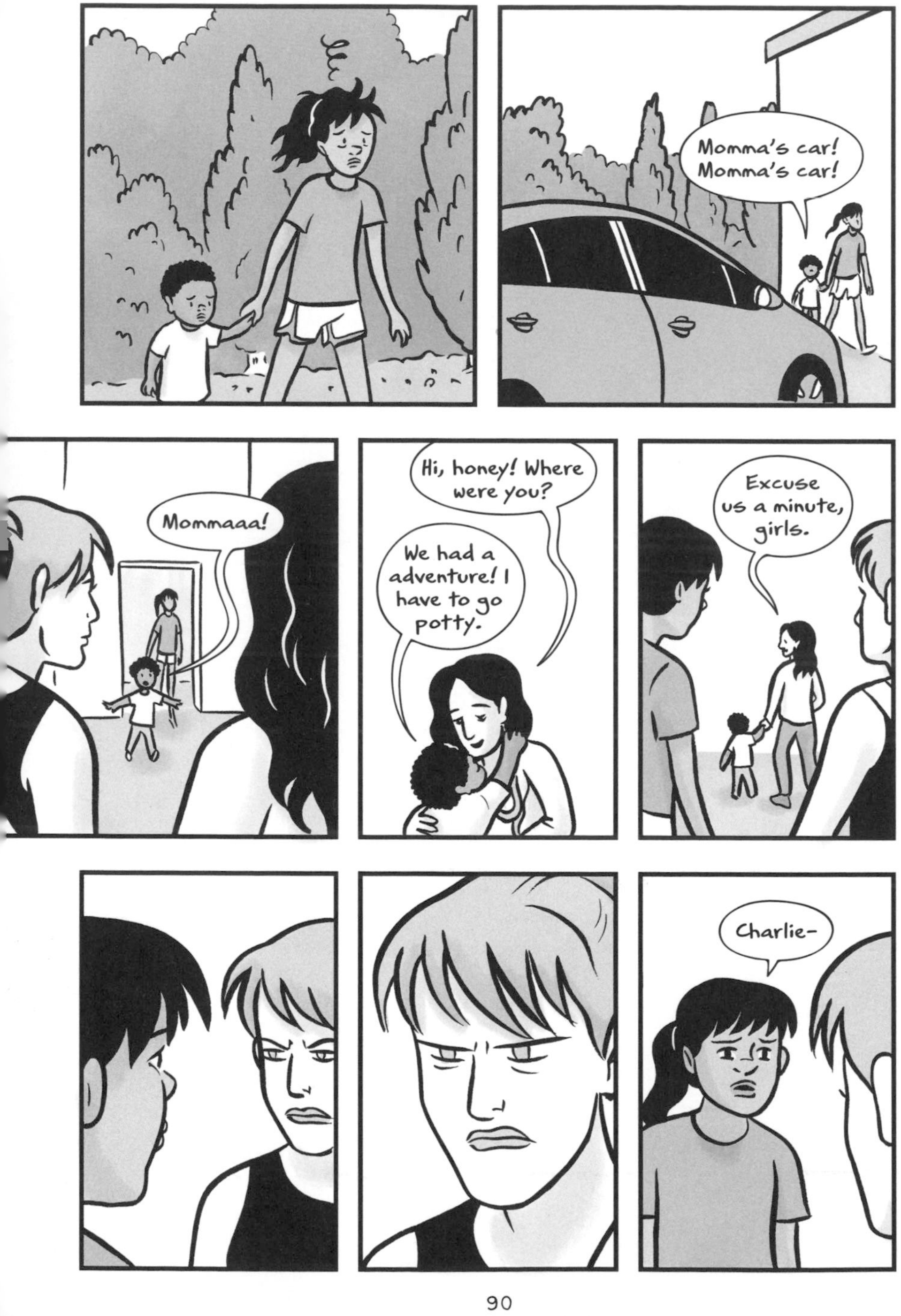
Momma's car! Momma's car!
Mommaaa!
Hi, honey! Where were you?
We had a adventure! I have to go potty.
Excuse us a minute, girls.
Charlie-

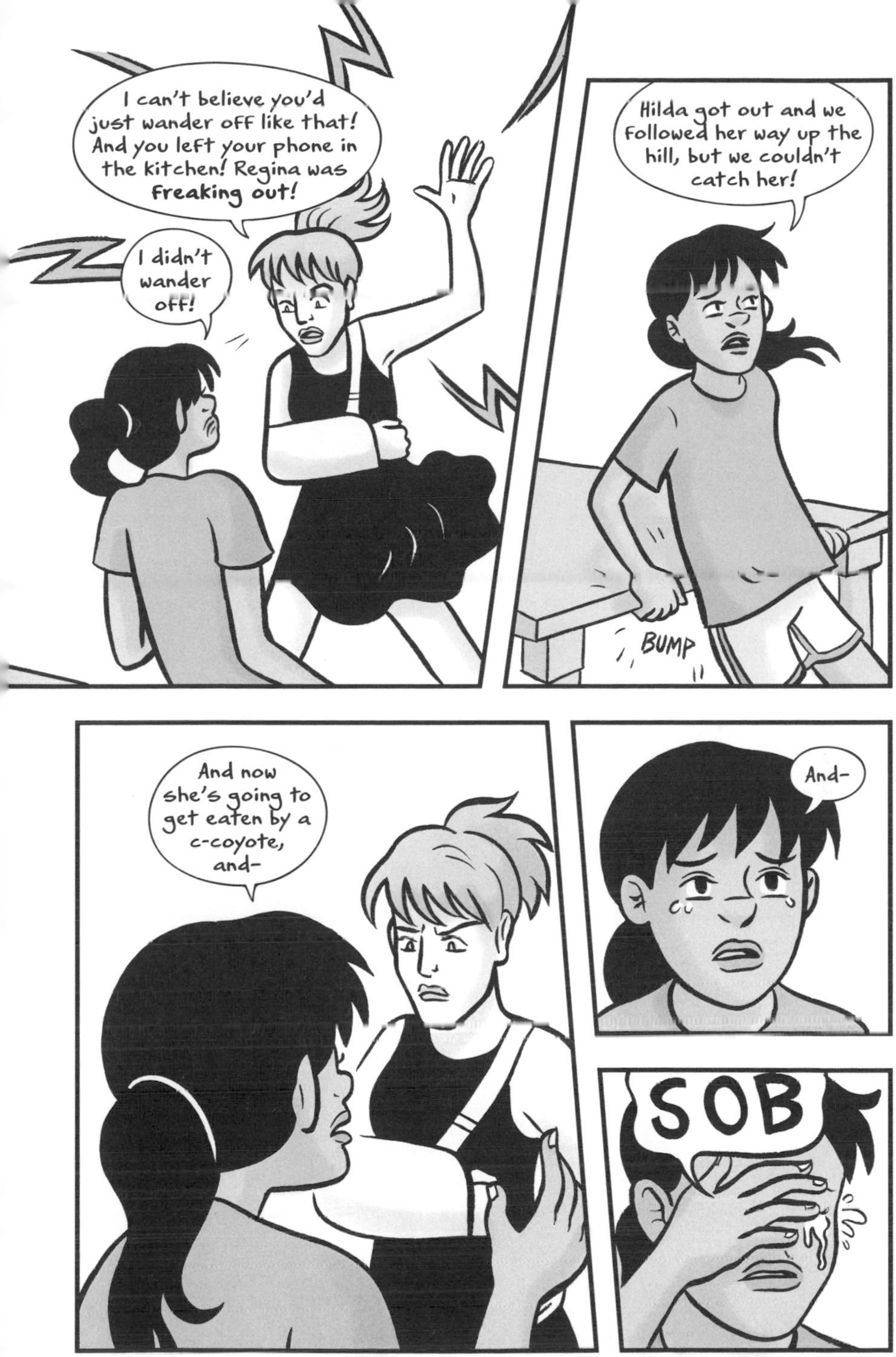
I can't believe you'd just wander off like that! And you left your phone in the kitchen! Regina was freaking out!
I didn't wander off!
Hilda got out and we followed her way up the hill, but we couldn't catch her!
BUMP
And now she's going to get eaten by a c-coyote, and-
And-
SOB

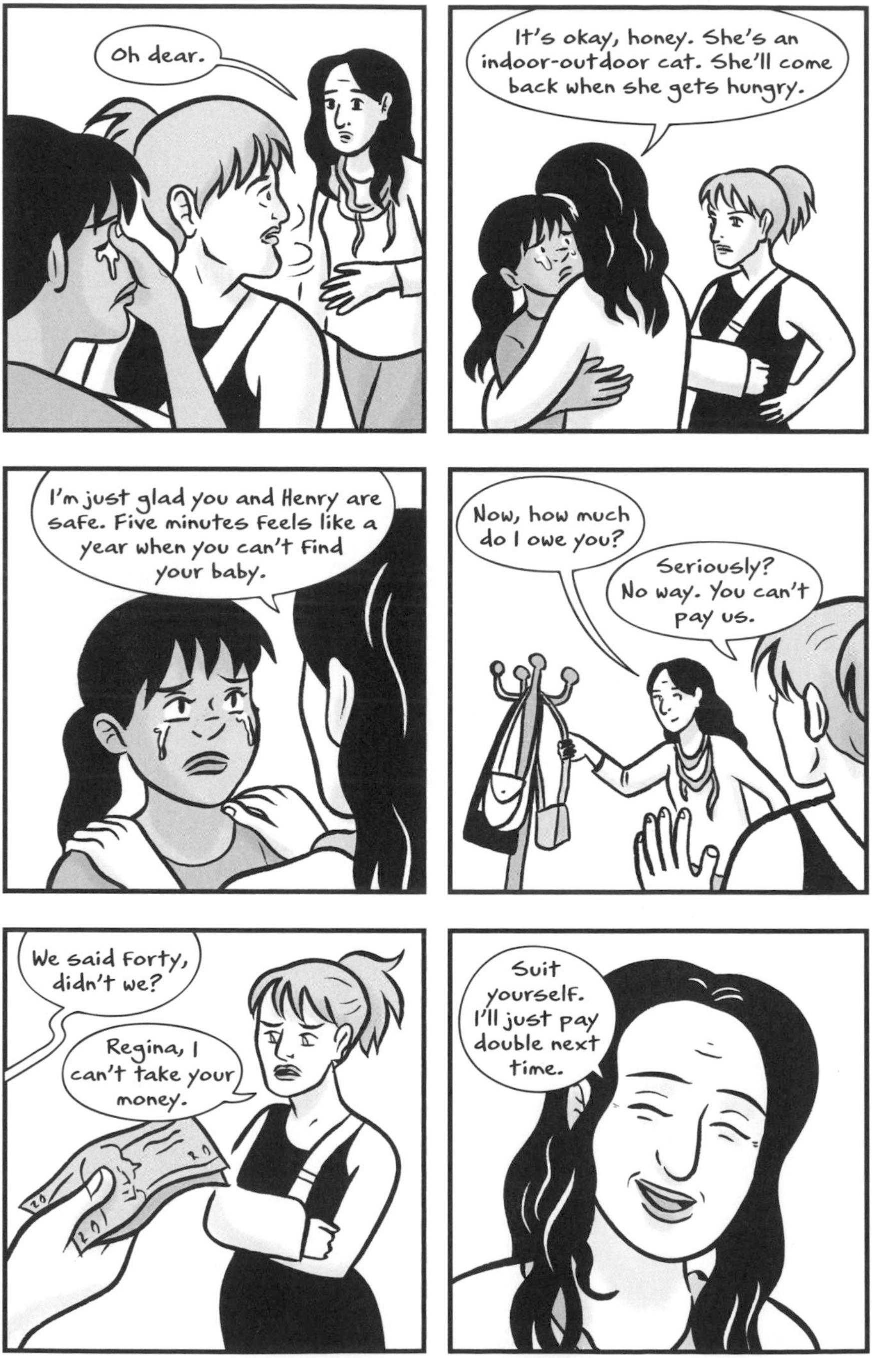
Oh dear.
It's okay, honey. She's an indoor-outdoor cat. She'll come back when she gets hungry.
I'm just glad you and Henry are safe. Five minutes feels like a year when you can't find your baby.
Now, how much do I owe you?
Seriously? No way. You can't pay us.
We said forty, didn't we?
Regina, I can't take your money.
Suit yourself. I'll just pay double next time.

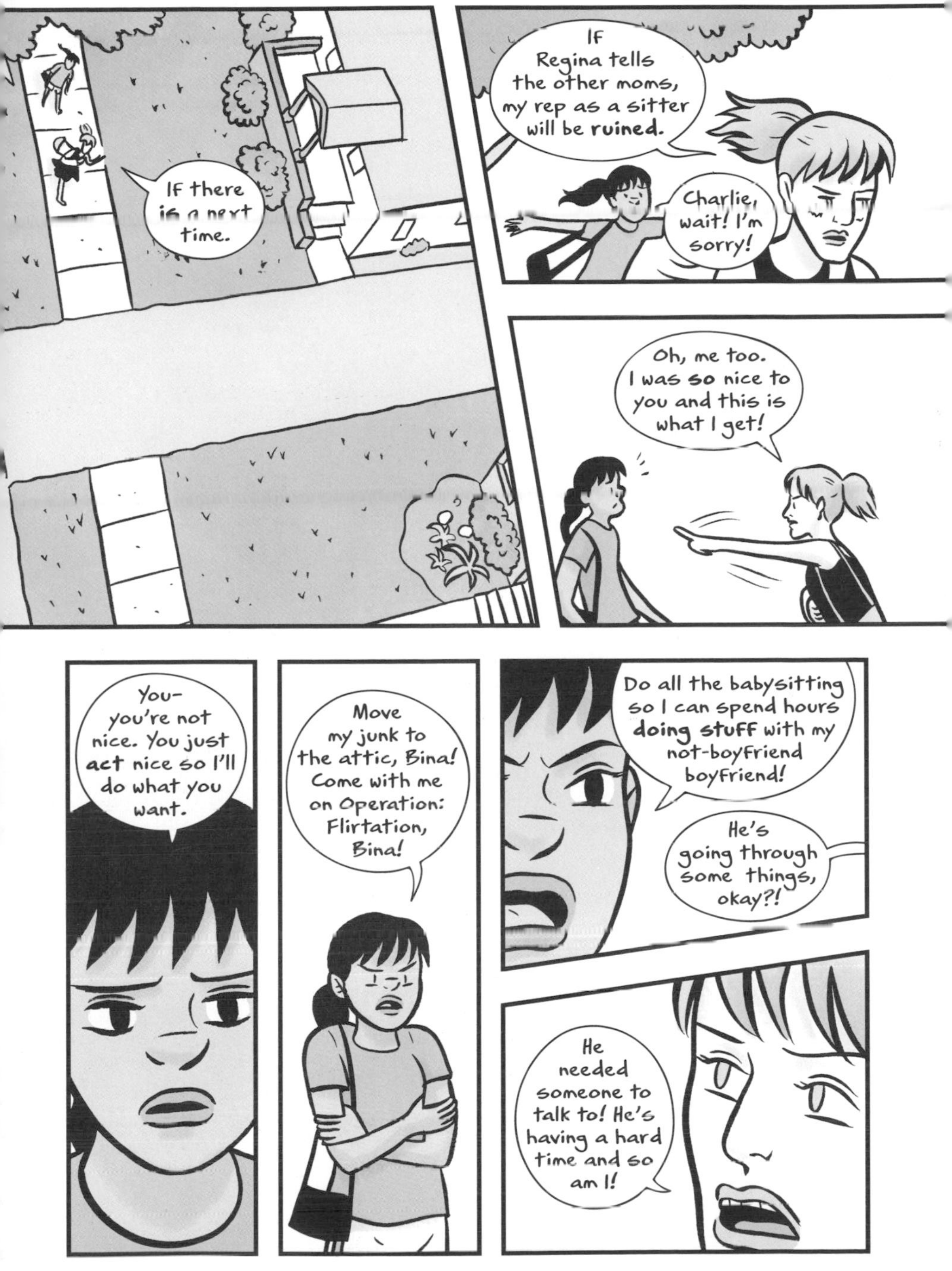
If there is a next time.
If Regina tells the other moms, my rep as a sitter will be **ruined.**
Charlie, wait! I'm sorry!
Oh, me too. I was **so** nice to you and this is what I get!
You— you're not nice. You just **act** nice so I'll do what you want.
Move my junk to the attic, Bina! Come with me on Operation: Flirtation, Bina!
Do all the babysitting so I can spend hours **doing stuff** with my not-boyfriend boyfriend!
He's going through some things, okay?!
He needed someone to talk to! He's having a hard time and so am I!

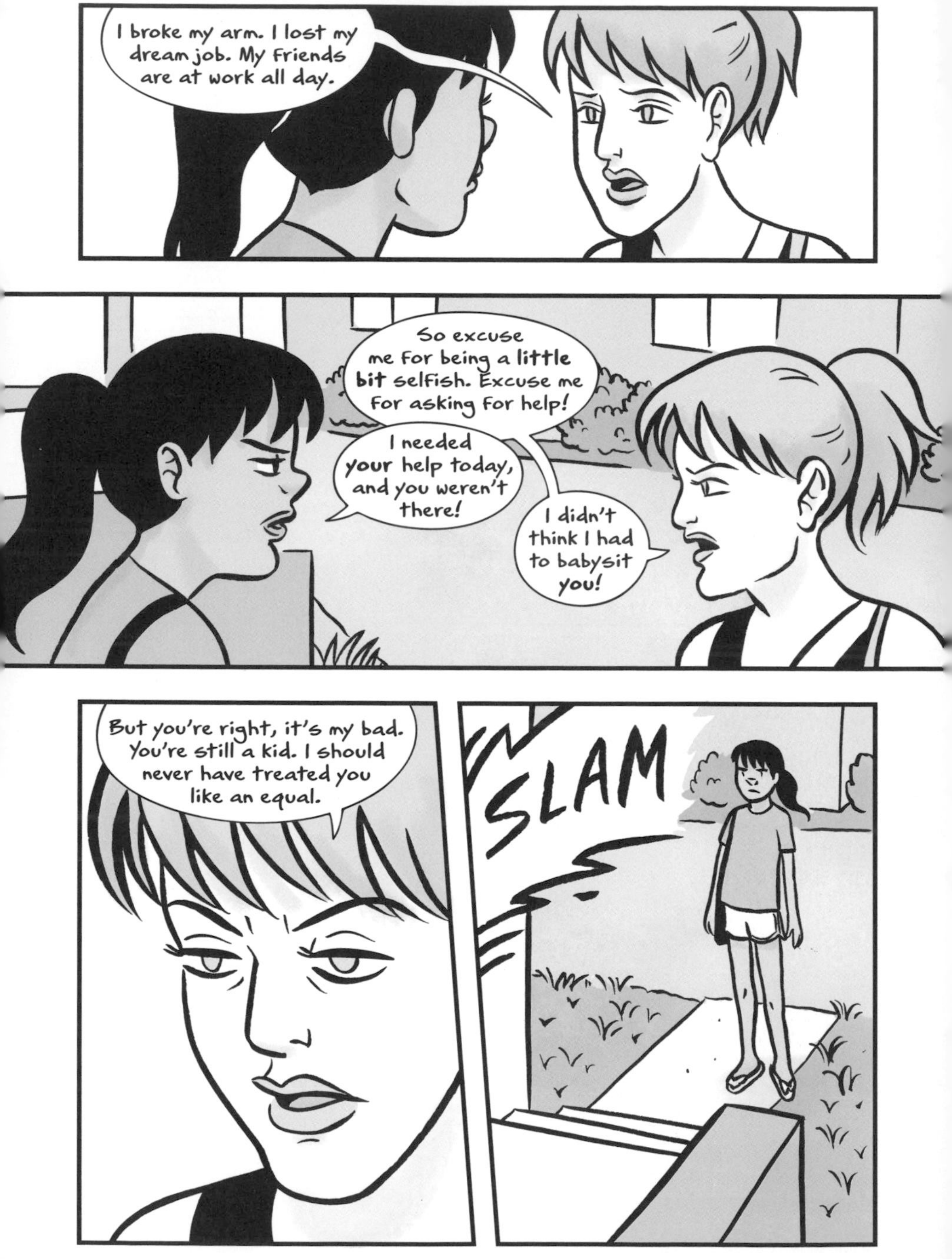
I broke my arm. I lost my dream job. My friends are at work all day.
So excuse me for being a little bit selfish. Excuse me for asking for help!
I needed your help today, and you weren't there!
I didn't think I had to babysit you!
But you're right, it's my bad. You're still a kid. I should never have treated you like an equal.
SLAM

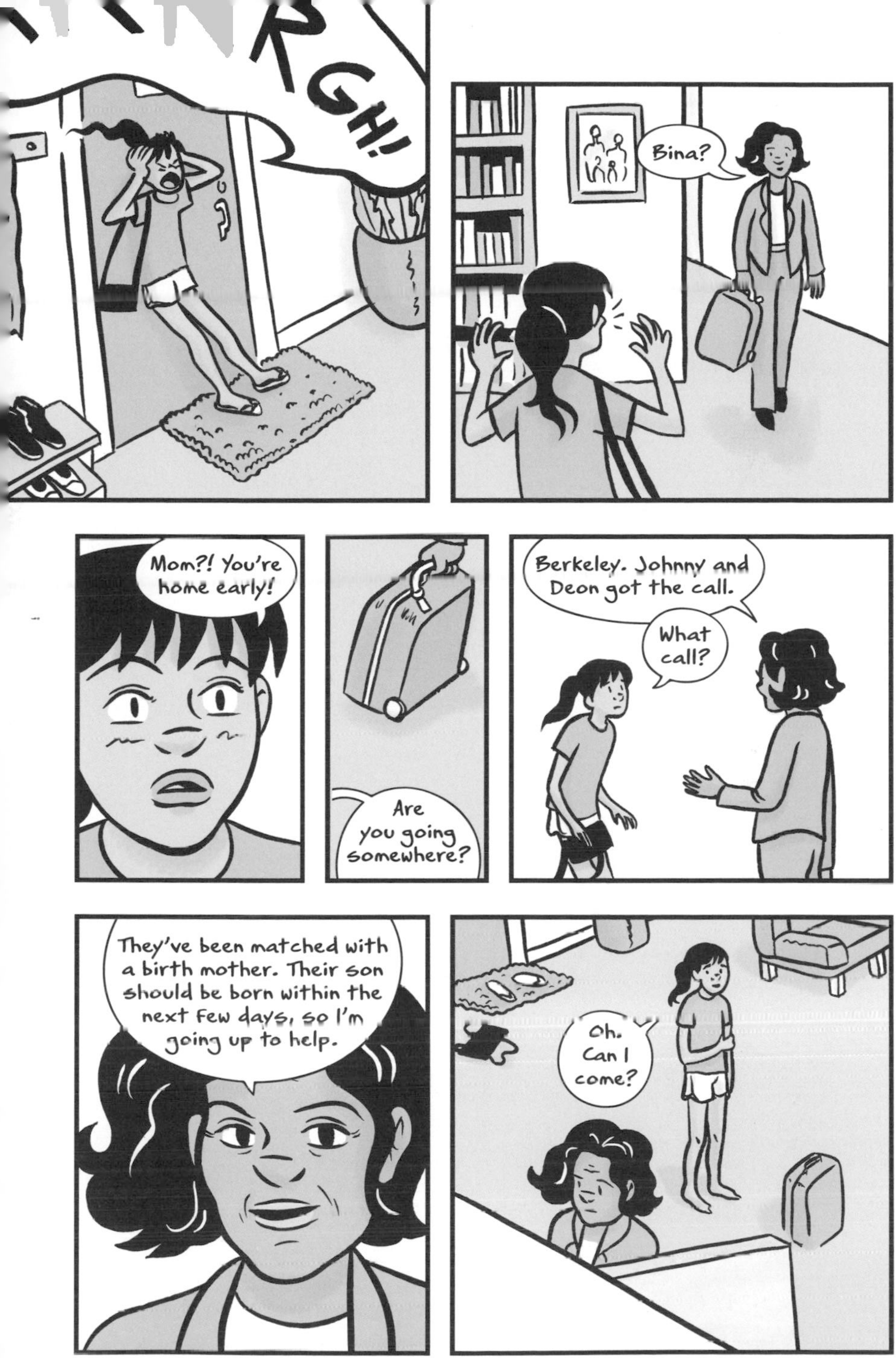
RRGH!
Bina?
Mom?! You're home early!
Are you going somewhere?
Berkeley. Johnny and Deon got the call.
What call?
They've been matched with a birth mother. Their son should be born within the next few days, so I'm going up to help.
Oh. Can I come?

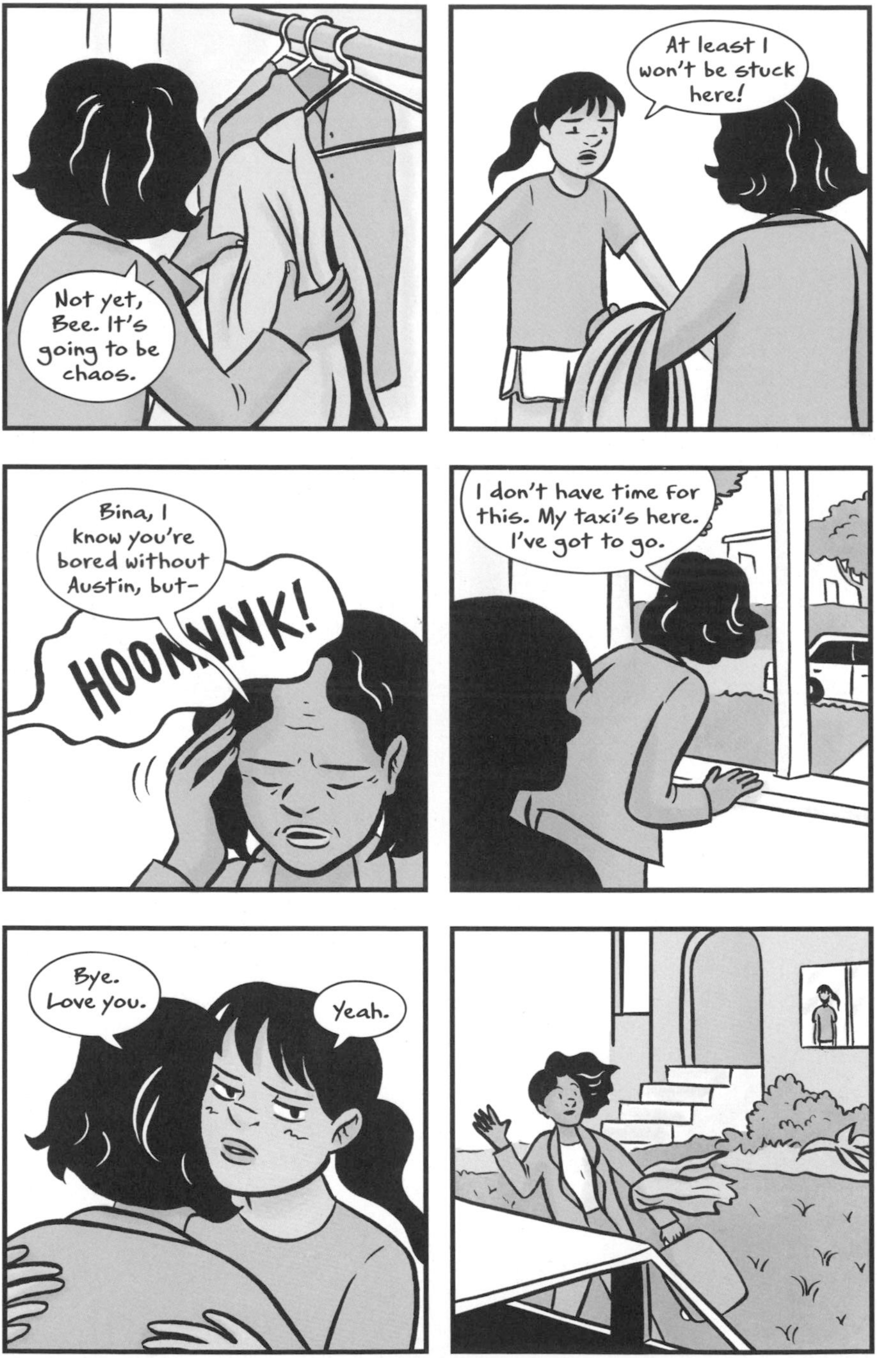
Not yet, Bee. It's going to be chaos.
At least I won't be stuck here!
Bina, I know you're bored without Austin, but-
HOONNNK!
I don't have time for this. My taxi's here. I've got to go.
Bye. Love you.
Yeah.

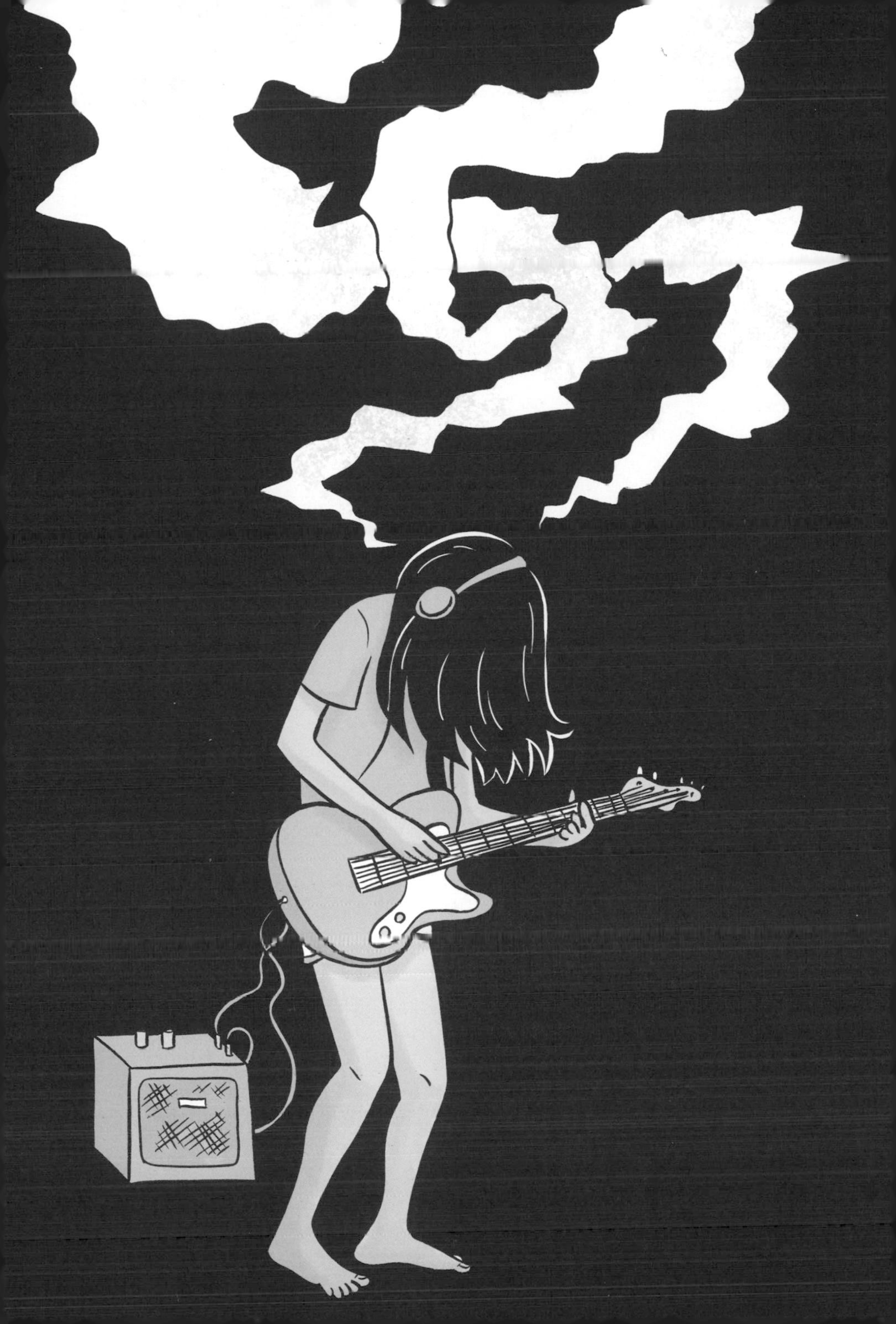

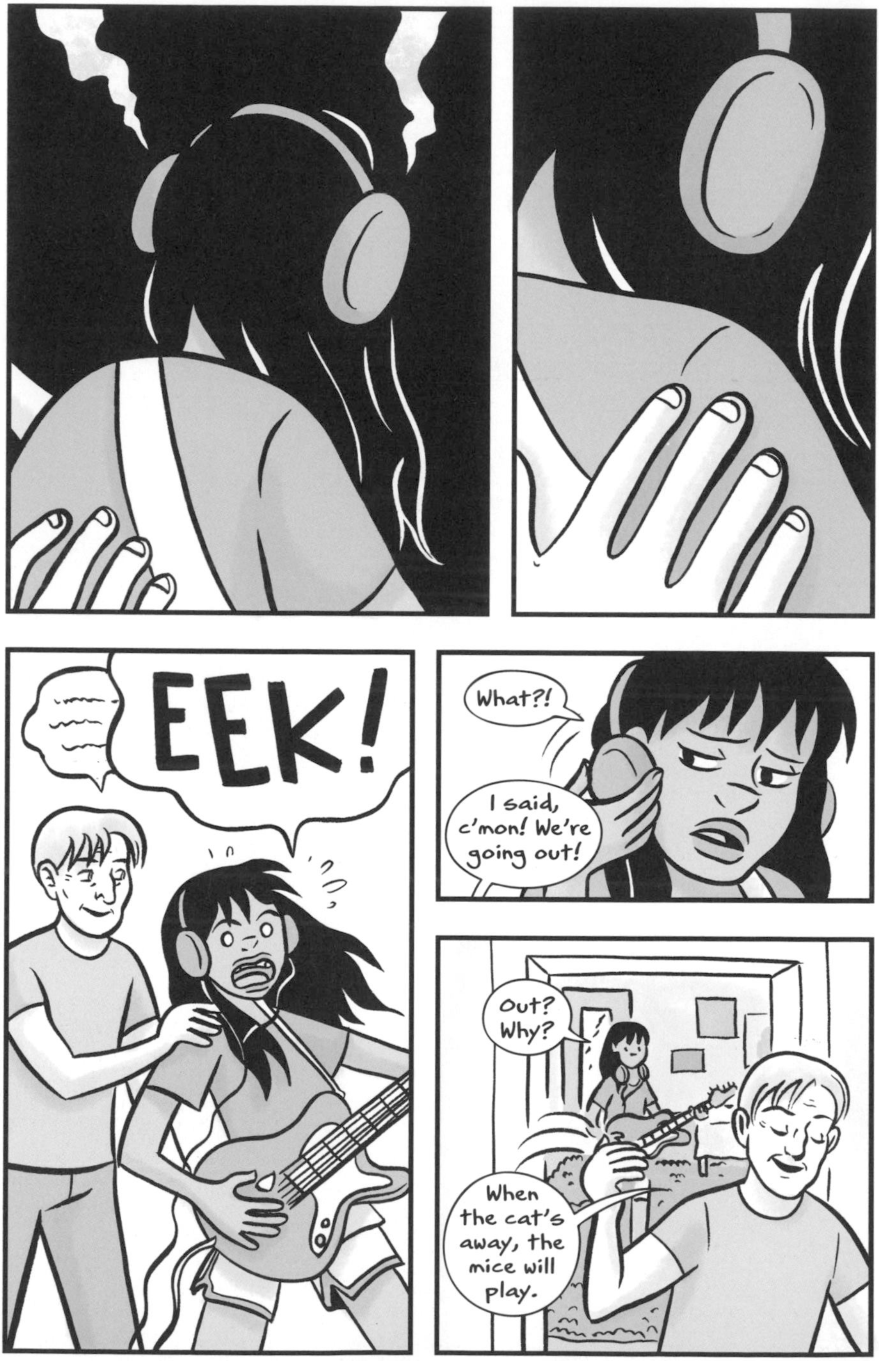
EEK!
What?!
I said, c'mon! We're going out!
Out? Why?
When the cat's away, the mice will play.

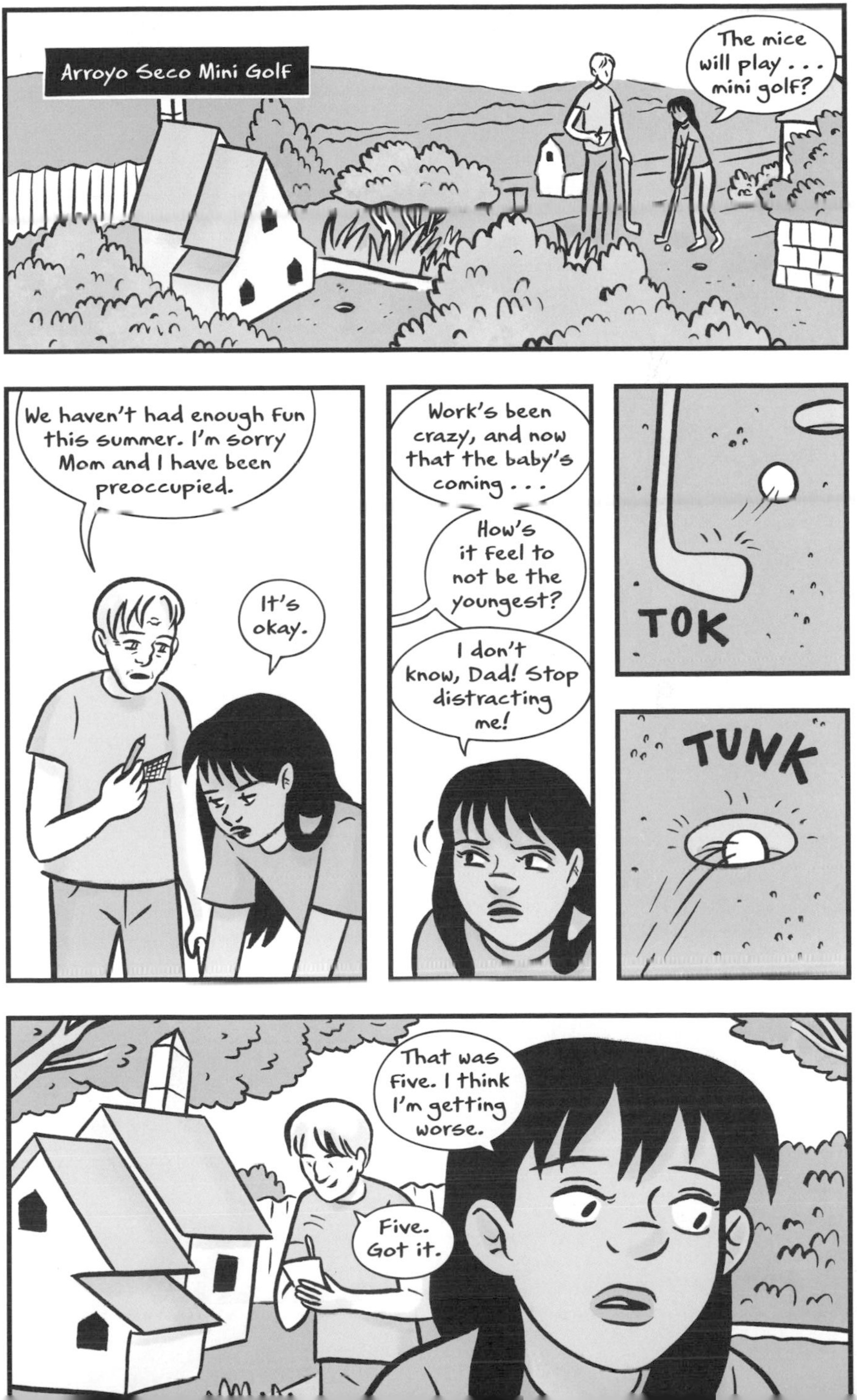
Arroyo Seco Mini Golf
The mice will play . . . mini golf?
We haven't had enough fun this summer. I'm sorry Mom and I have been preoccupied.
It's okay.
Work's been crazy, and now that the baby's coming . . .
How's it feel to not be the youngest?
I don't know, Dad! Stop distracting me!
TOK
TUNK
That was five. I think I'm getting worse.
Five. Got it.

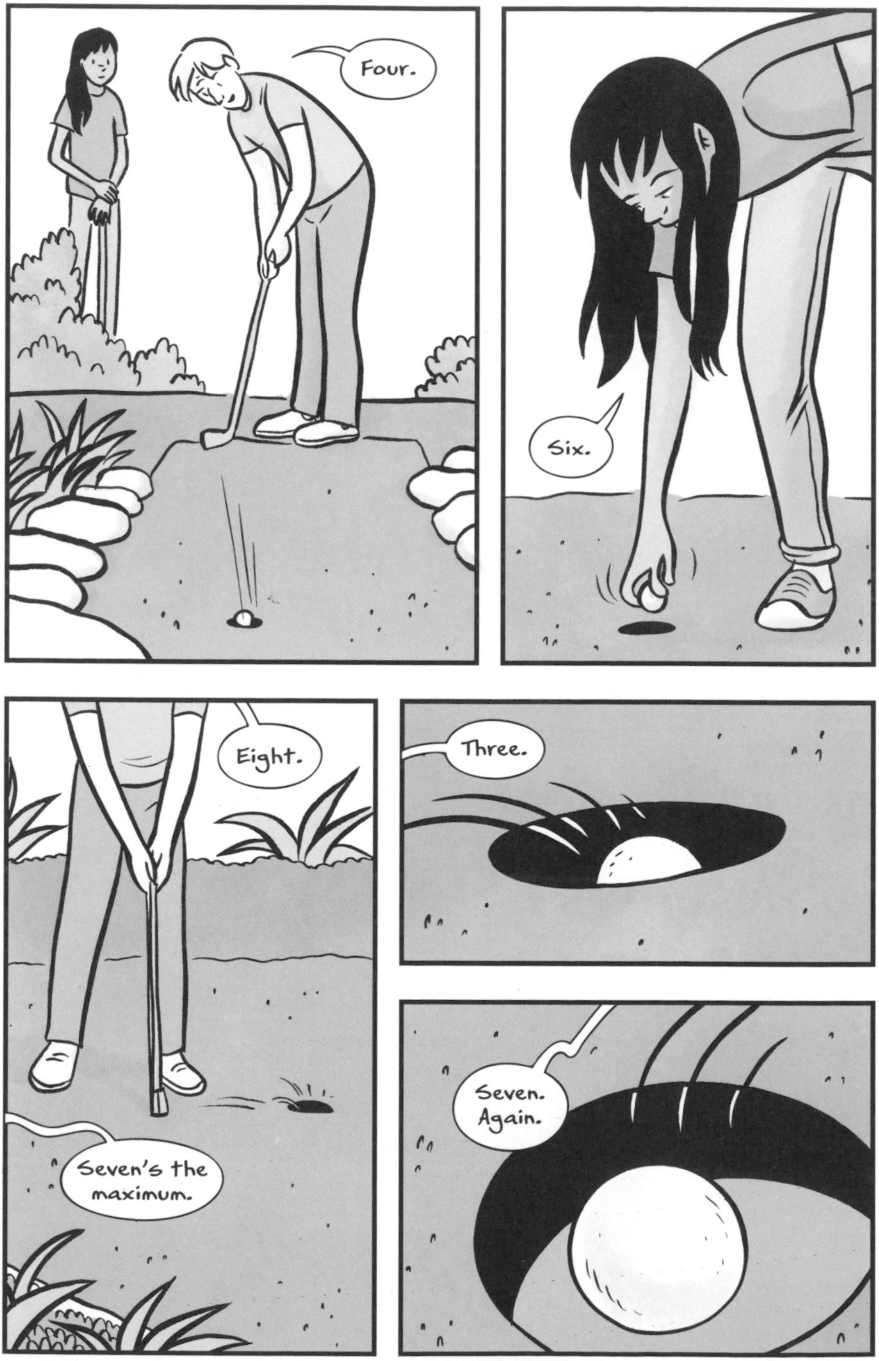
Four.
Six.
Eight.
Seven's the maximum.
Three.
Seven. Again.

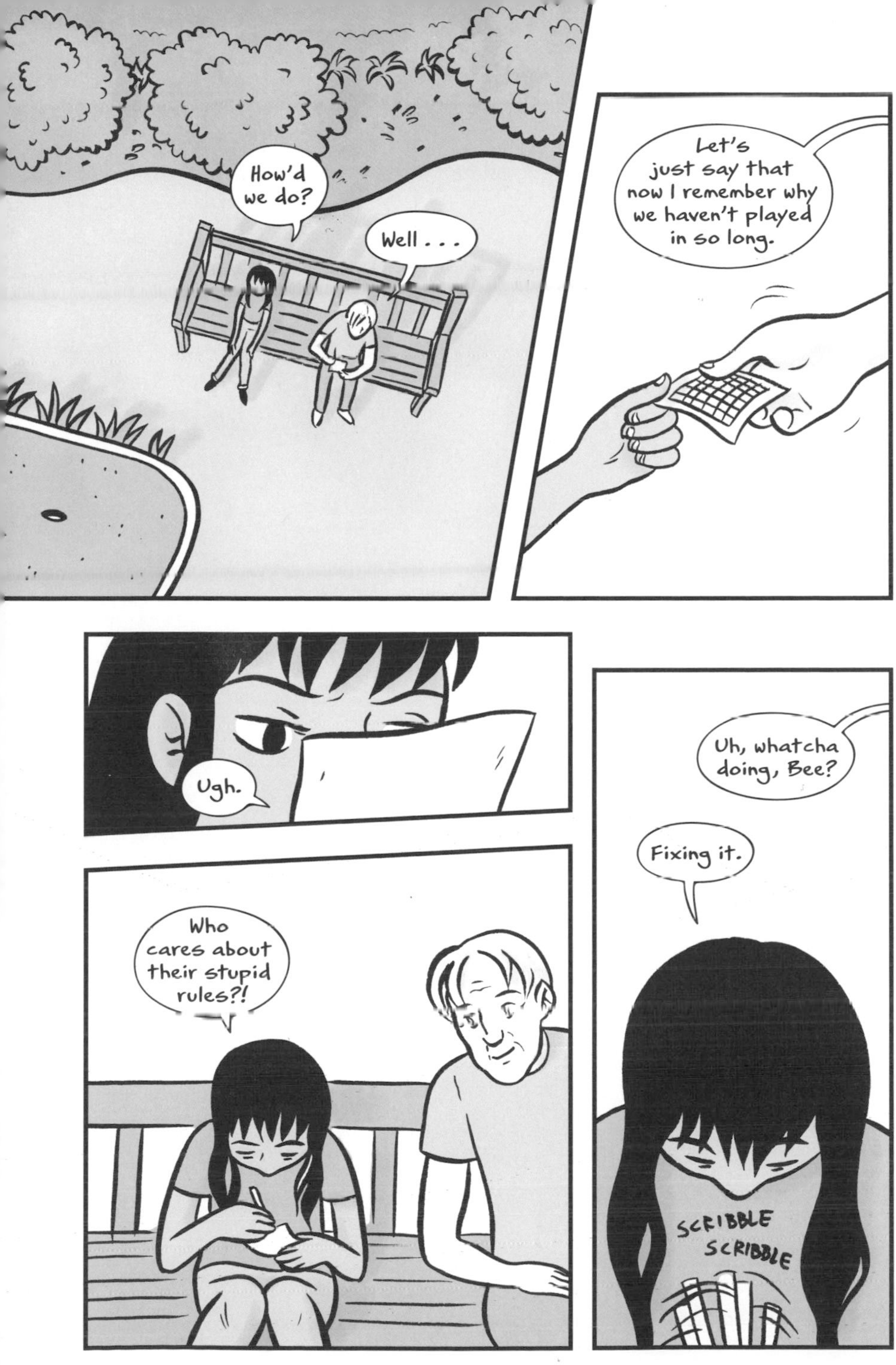
How'd we do?
Well . . .
Let's just say that now I remember why we haven't played in so long.
Ugh.
Uh, whatcha doing, Bee?
Fixing it.
Who cares about their stupid rules?!
SCRIBBLE
SCRIBBLE

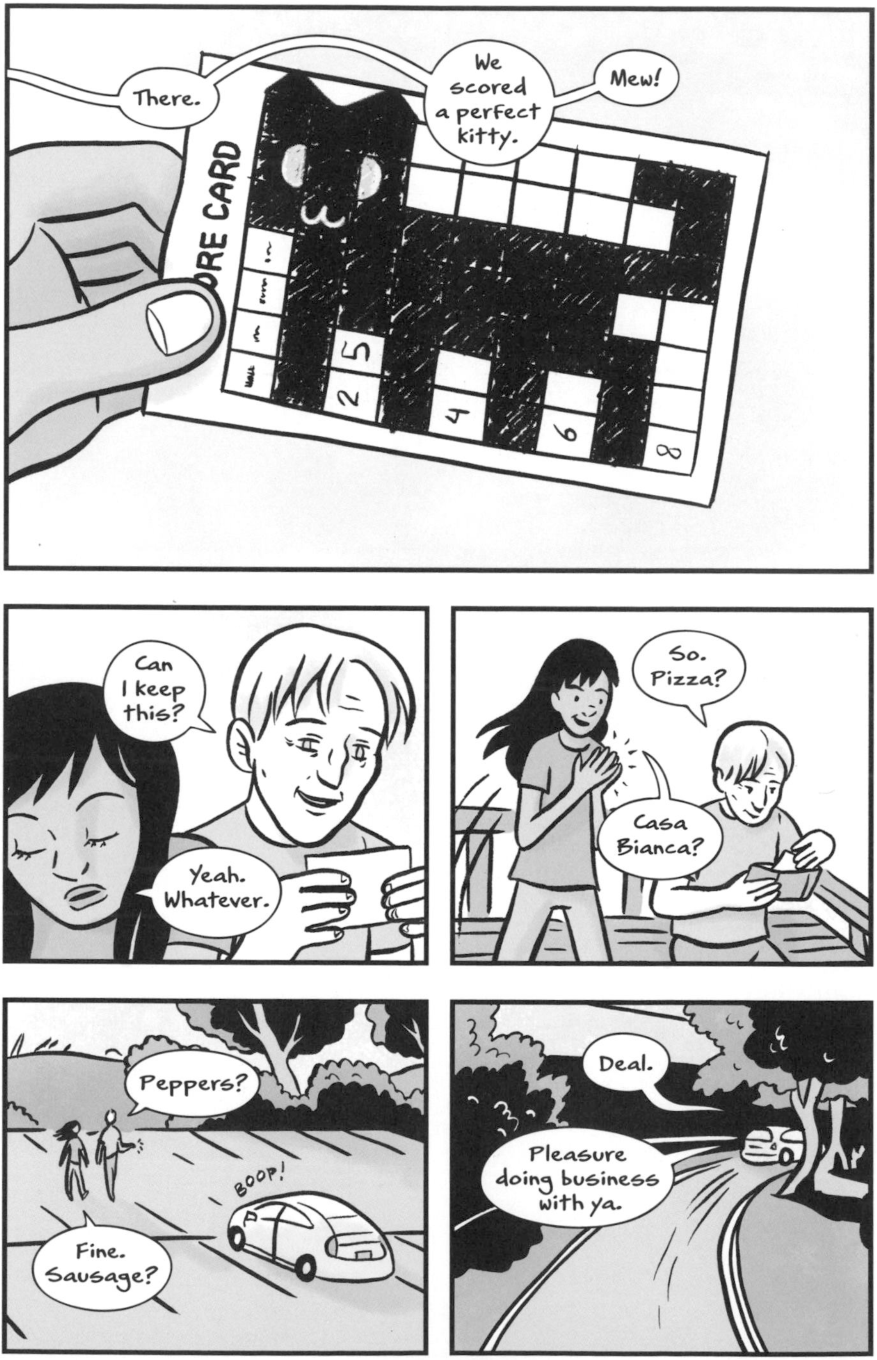
There.
We scored a perfect kitty.
Mew!
ORE CARD
5
2
4
6
8
Can I keep this?
Yeah. Whatever.
So. Pizza?
Casa Bianca?
Peppers?
Fine. Sausage?
BOOP!
Deal.
Pleasure doing business with ya.

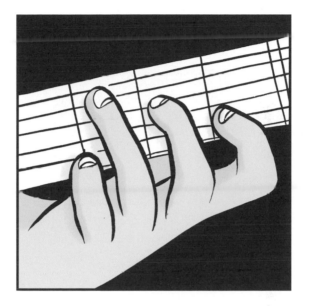

Week Five

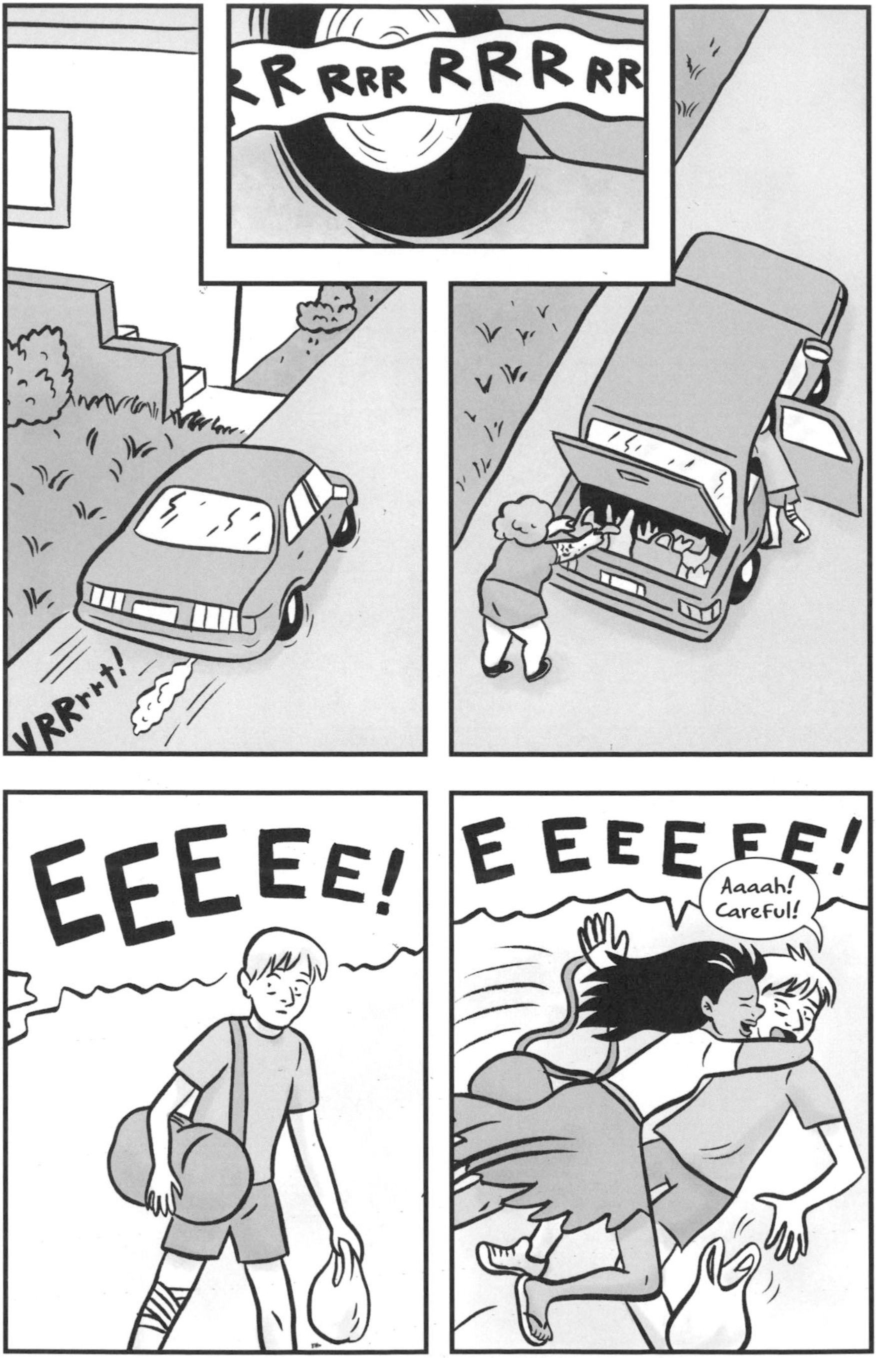
RRRRRRRRR
VRRrrrt!
EEEEEE!
EEEEEE!
Aaaah! Careful!

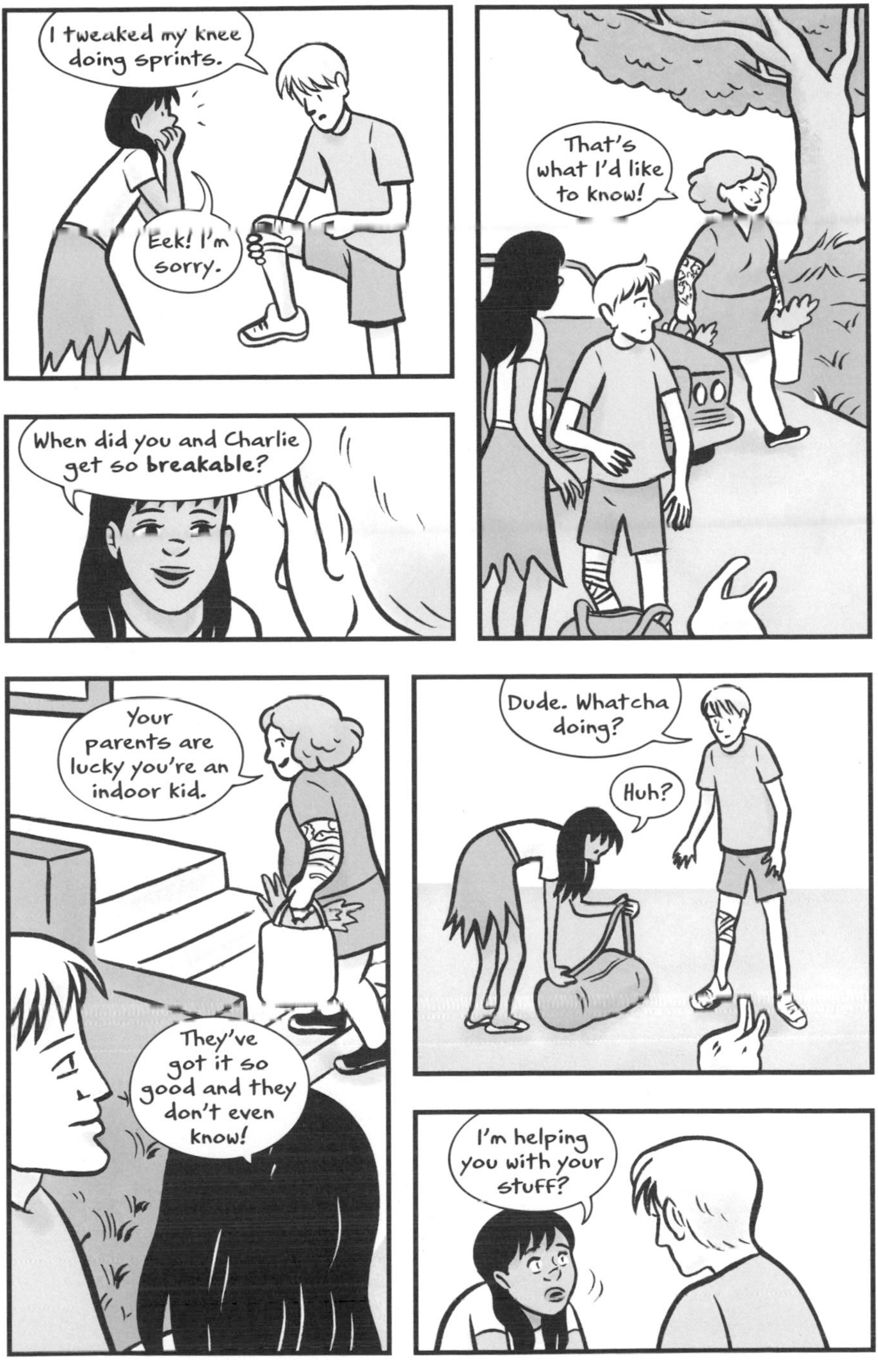
I tweaked my knee doing sprints.
Eek! I'm sorry.
When did you and Charlie get so breakable?
That's what I'd like to know!
Your parents are lucky you're an indoor kid.
They've got it so good and they don't even know!
Dude. Whatcha doing?
Huh?
I'm helping you with your stuff?

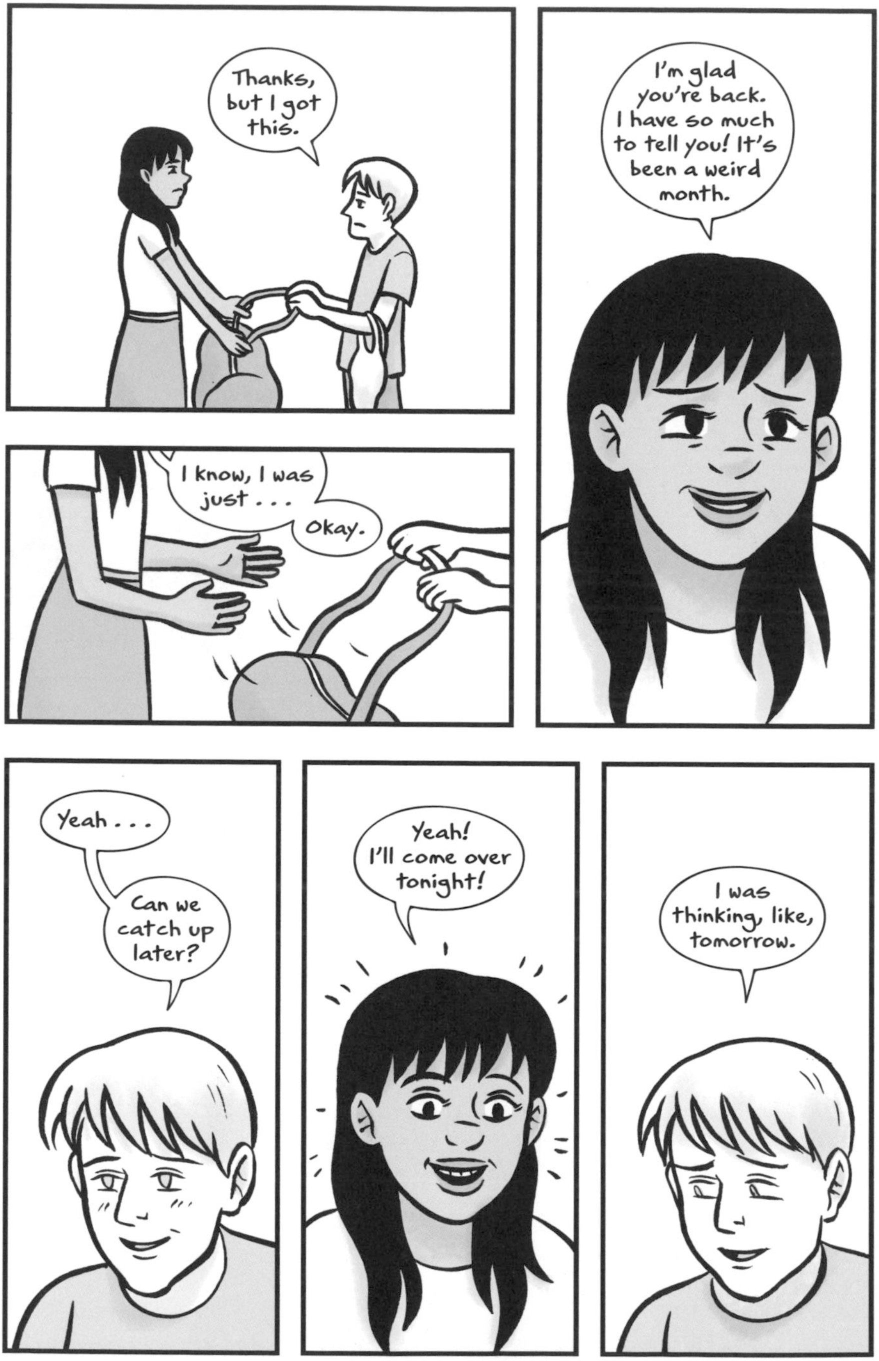
Thanks, but I got this.
I'm glad you're back. I have so much to tell you! It's been a weird month.
I know, I was just . . .
Okay.
Yeah . . .
Can we catch up later?
Yeah! I'll come over tonight!
I was thinking, like, tomorrow.

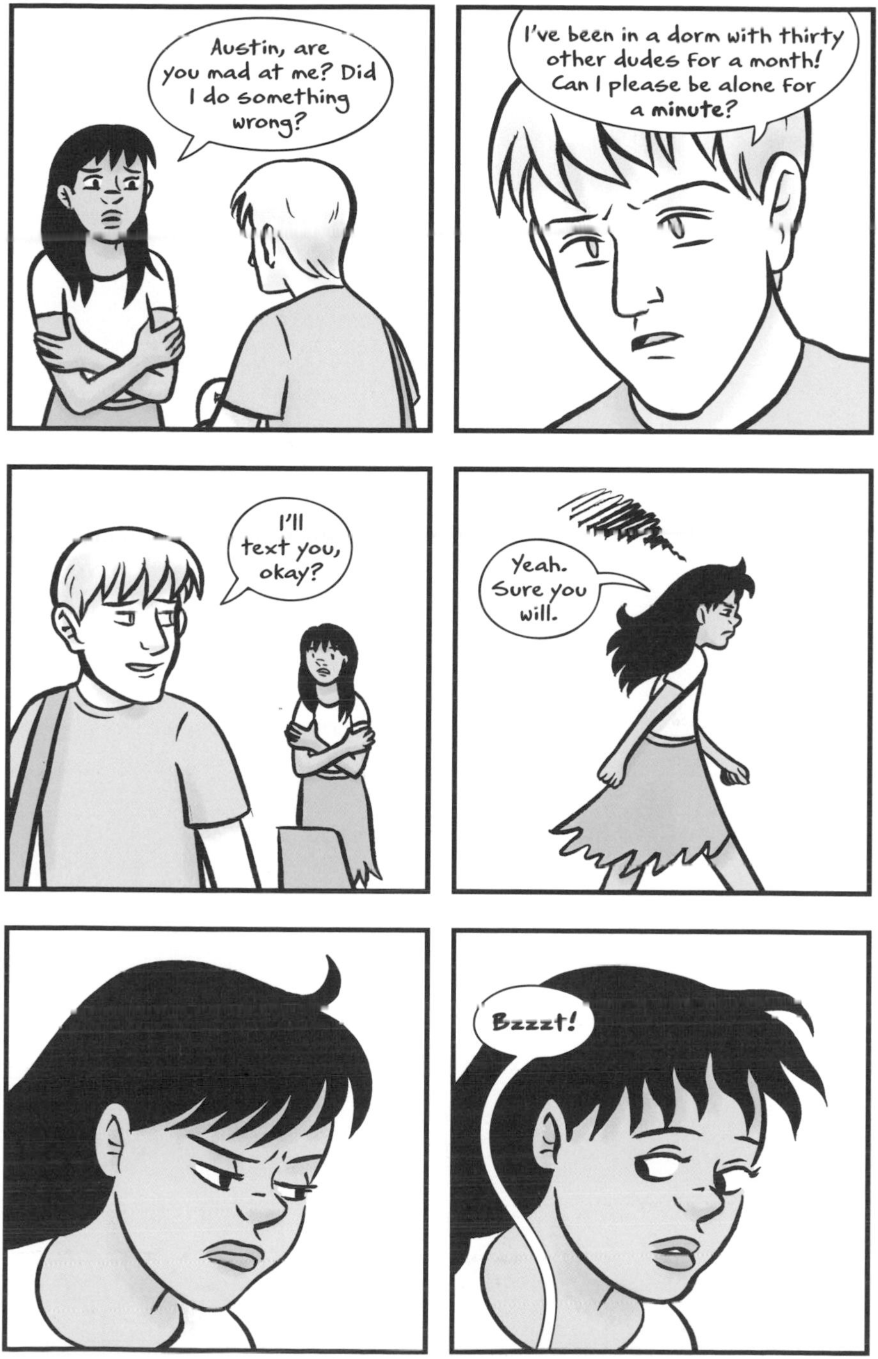
Austin, are you mad at me? Did I do something wrong?
I've been in a dorm with thirty other dudes for a month! Can I please be alone for a minute?
I'll text you, okay?
Yeah. Sure you will.
Bzzzt!

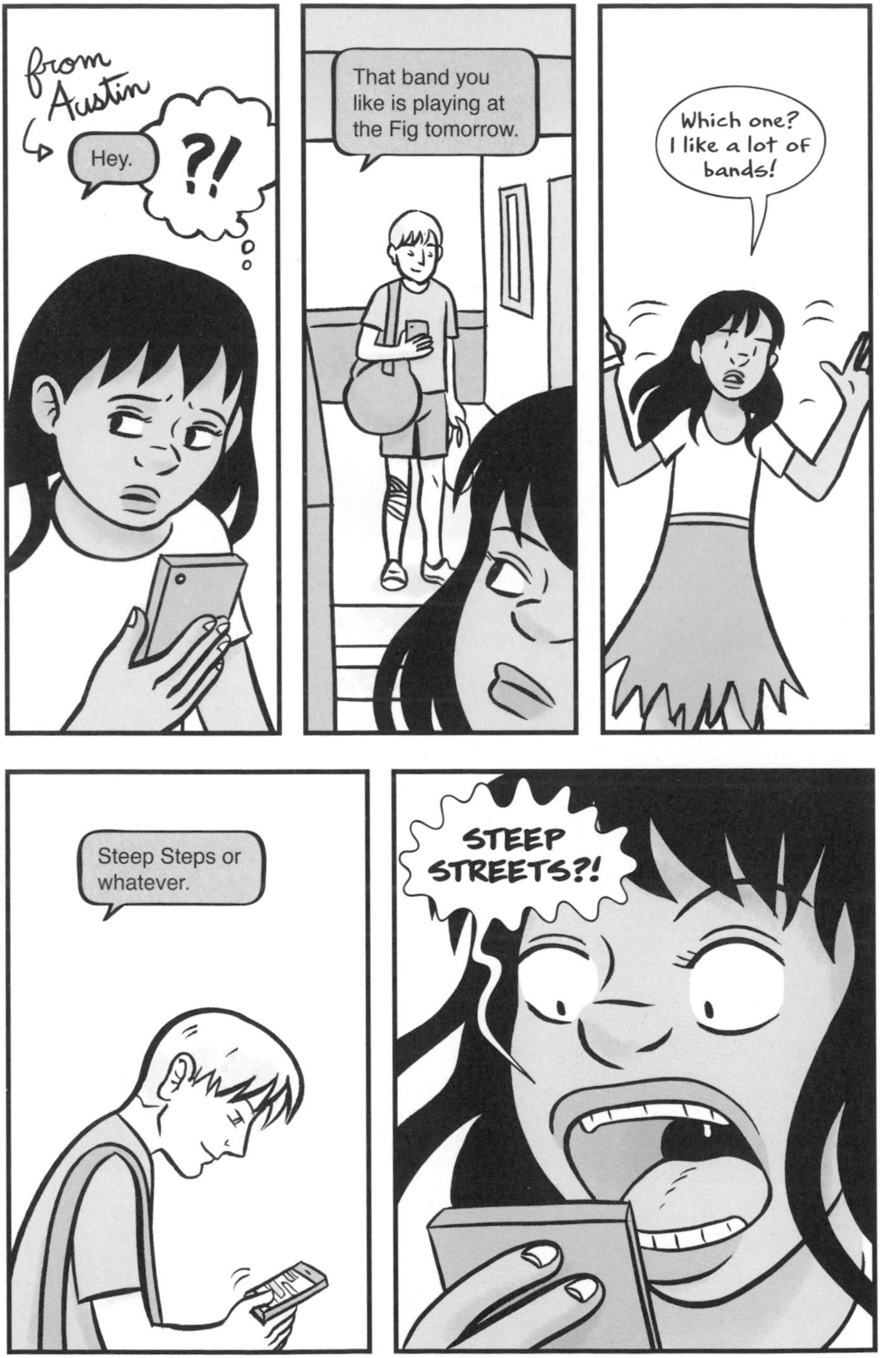
from Austin
Hey.
?!
That band you like is playing at the Fig tomorrow.
Which one? I like a lot of bands!
Steep Steps or whatever.
STEEP STREETS?!

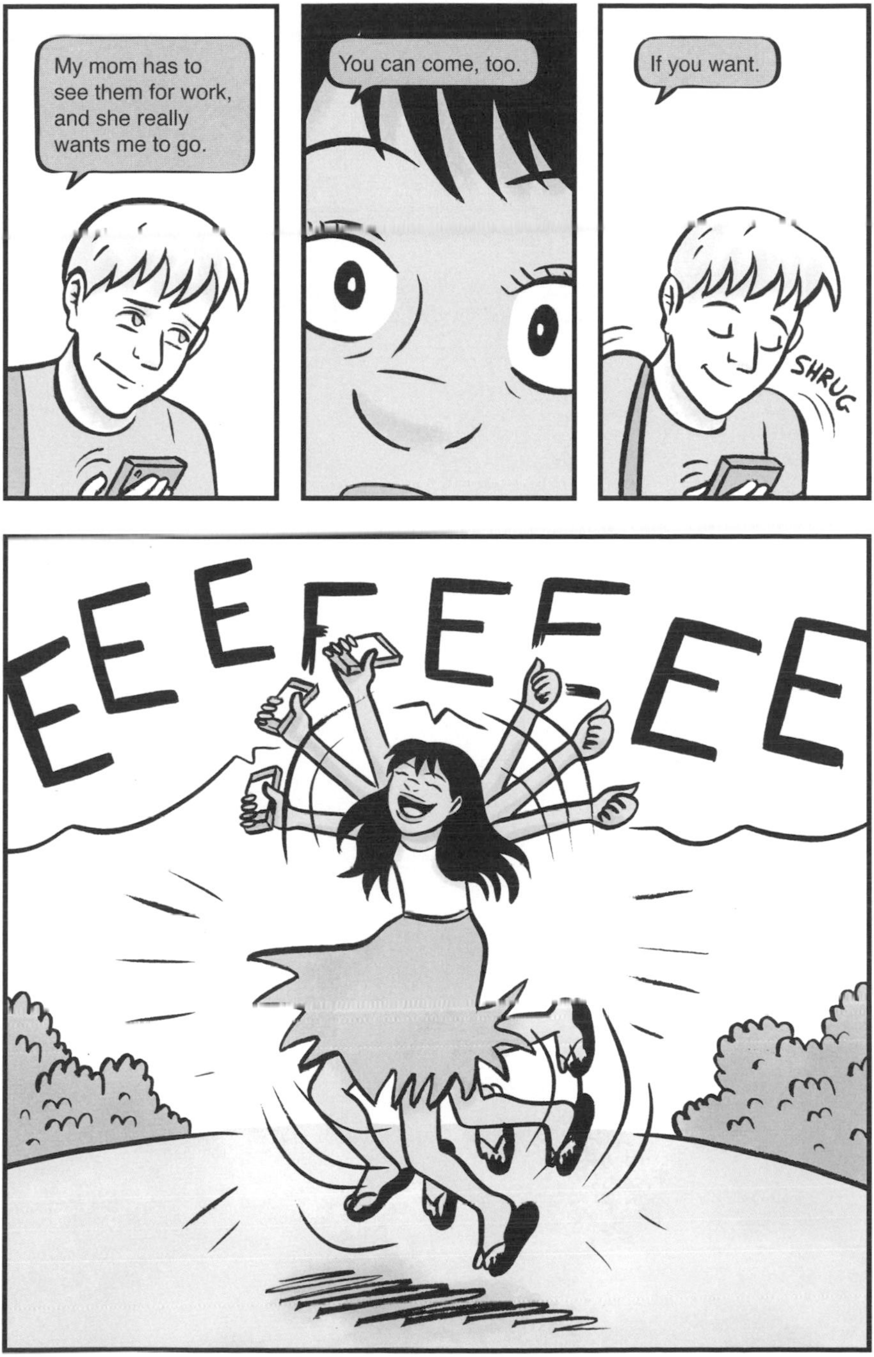
My mom has to see them for work, and she really wants me to go.
You can come, too.
If you want.
SHRUG
EEEEEEEE

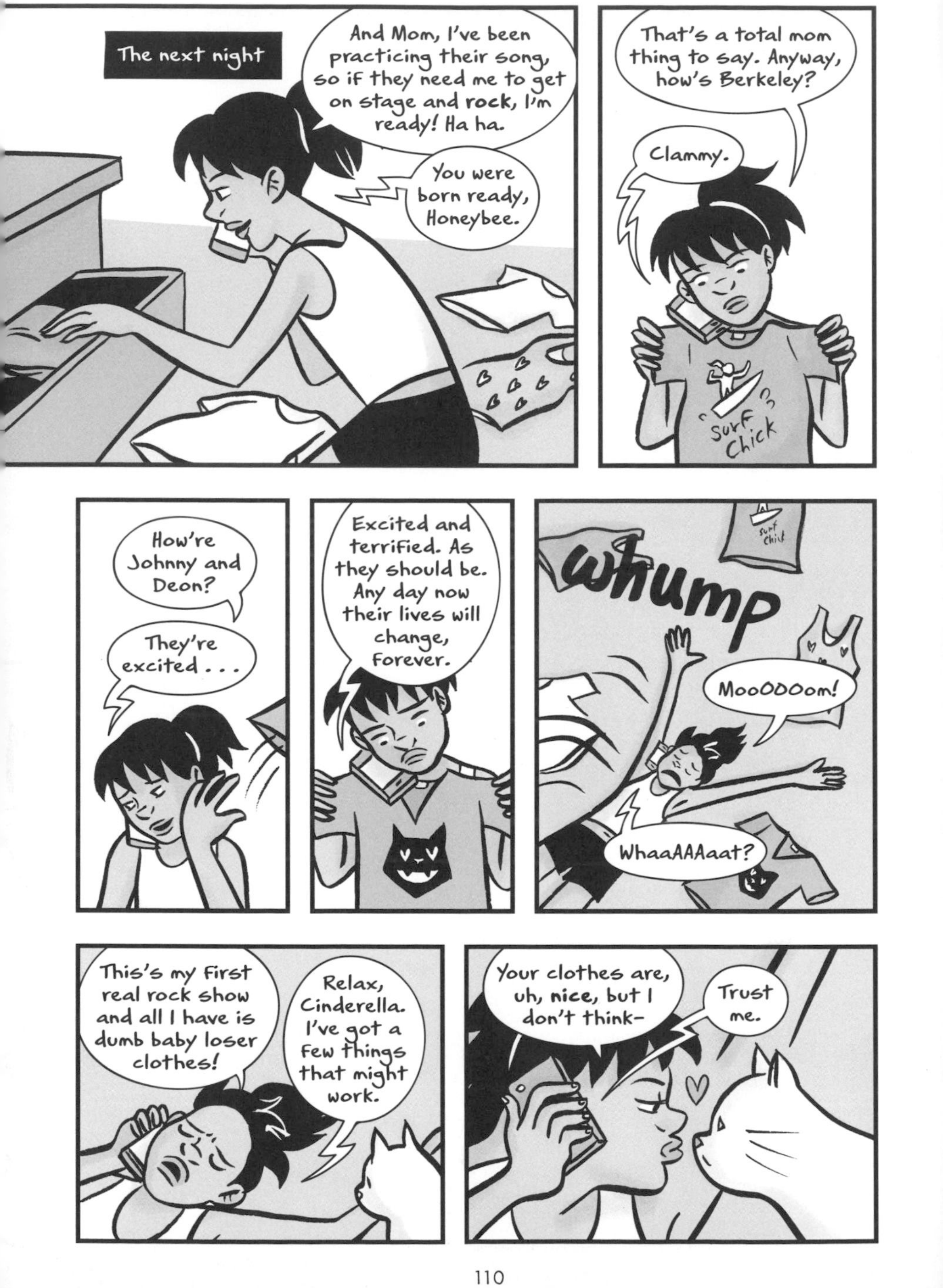
The next night
And Mom, I've been practicing their song, so if they need me to get on stage and rock, I'm ready! Ha ha.
You were born ready, Honeybee.
That's a total mom thing to say. Anyway, how's Berkeley?
Clammy.
Surf Chick
How're Johnny and Deon?
They're excited . . .
Excited and terrified. As they should be. Any day now their lives will change, Forever.
whump
MooOOOom!
WhaaAAAaat?
This's my first real rock show and all I have is dumb baby loser clothes!
Relax, Cinderella. I've got a few things that might work.
Your clothes are, uh, nice, but I don't think-
Trust me.

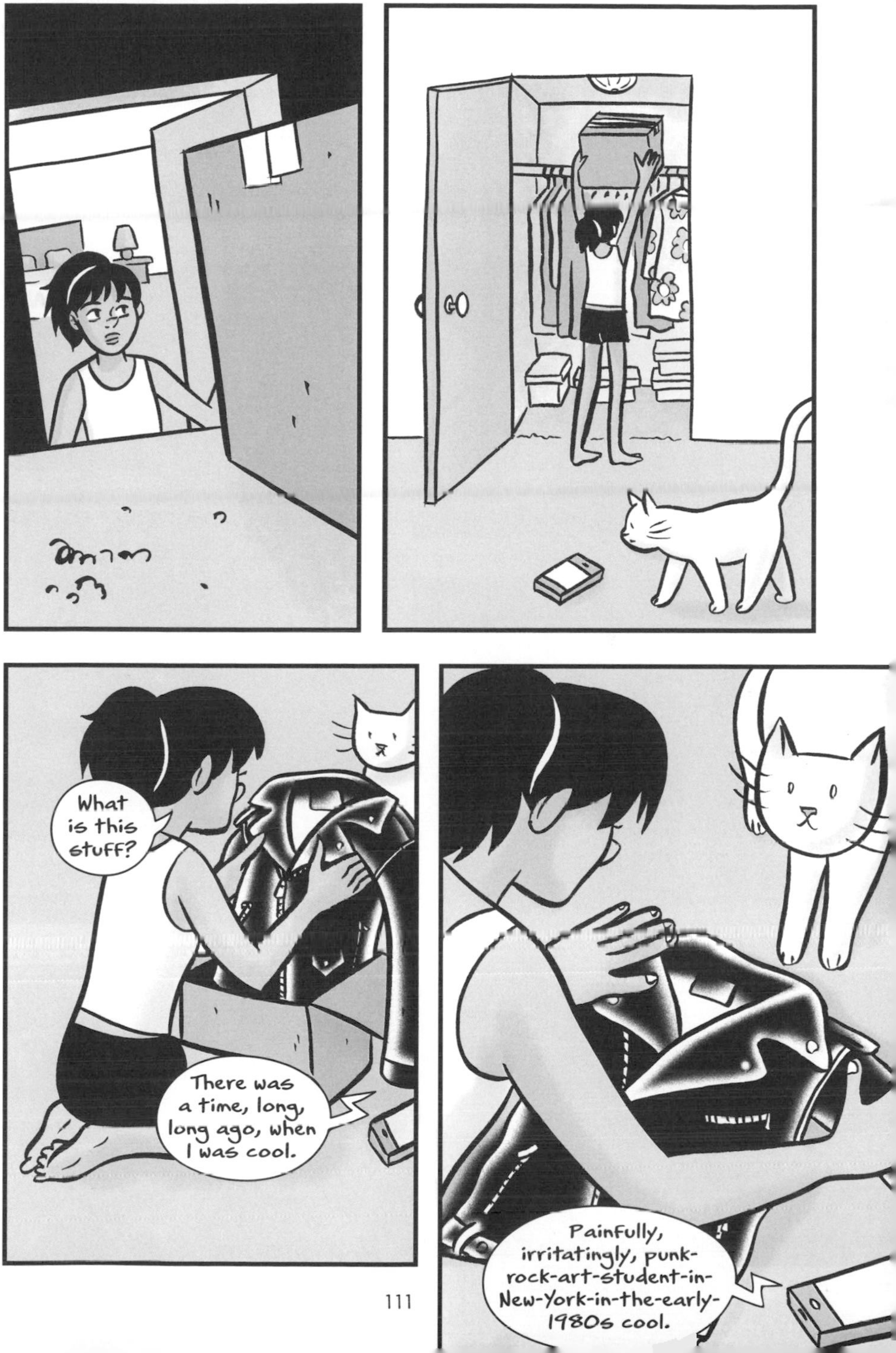
What is this stuff?
There was a time, long, long ago, when I was cool.
Painfully, irritatingly, punk-rock-art-student-in-New-York-in-the-early-1980s cool.

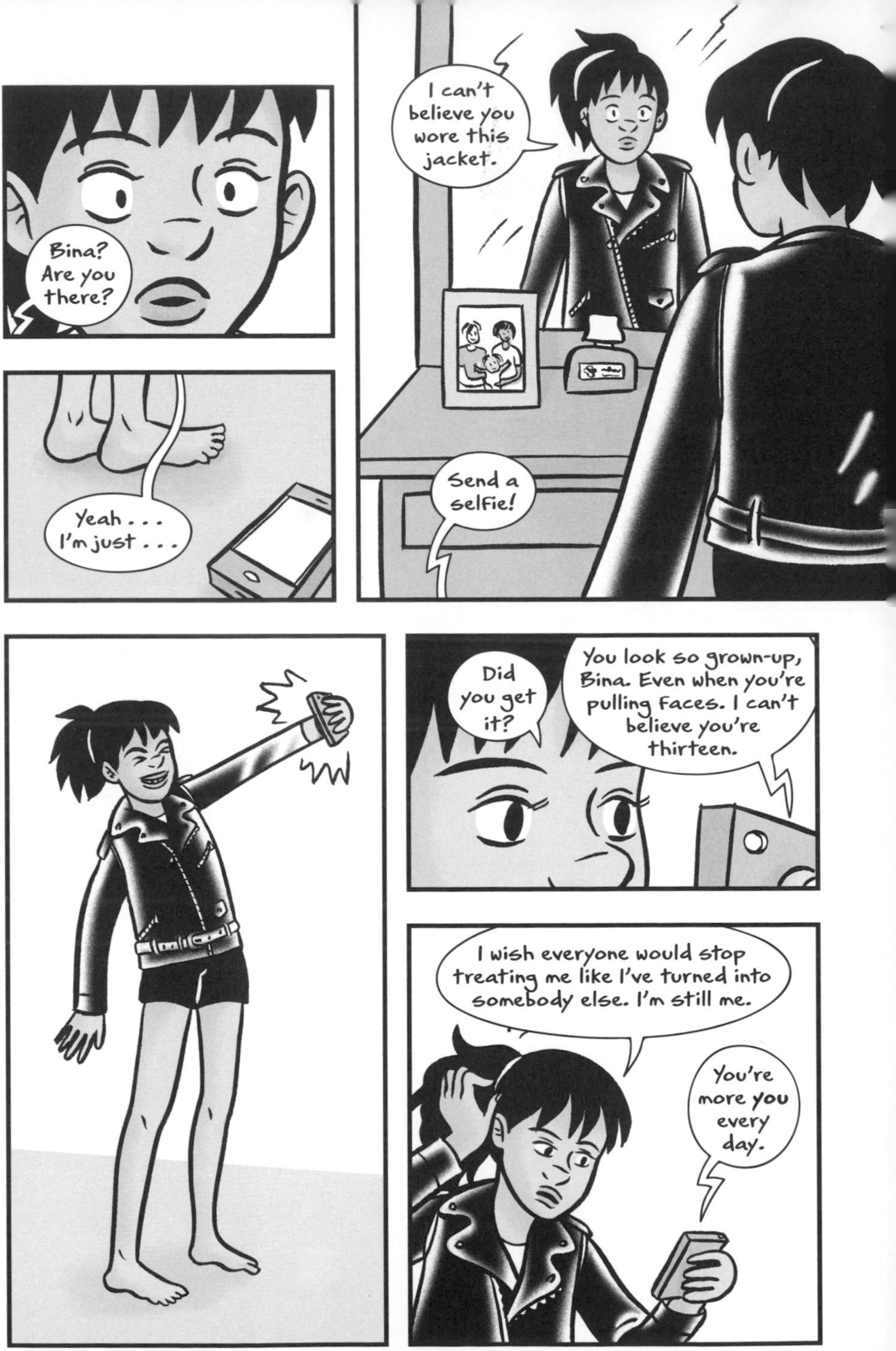
Bina? Are you there?
I can't believe you wore this jacket.
Yeah . . . I'm just . . .
Send a selfie!
Did you get it?
You look so grown-up, Bina. Even when you're pulling faces. I can't believe you're thirteen.
I wish everyone would stop treating me like I've turned into somebody else. I'm still me.
You're more you every day.

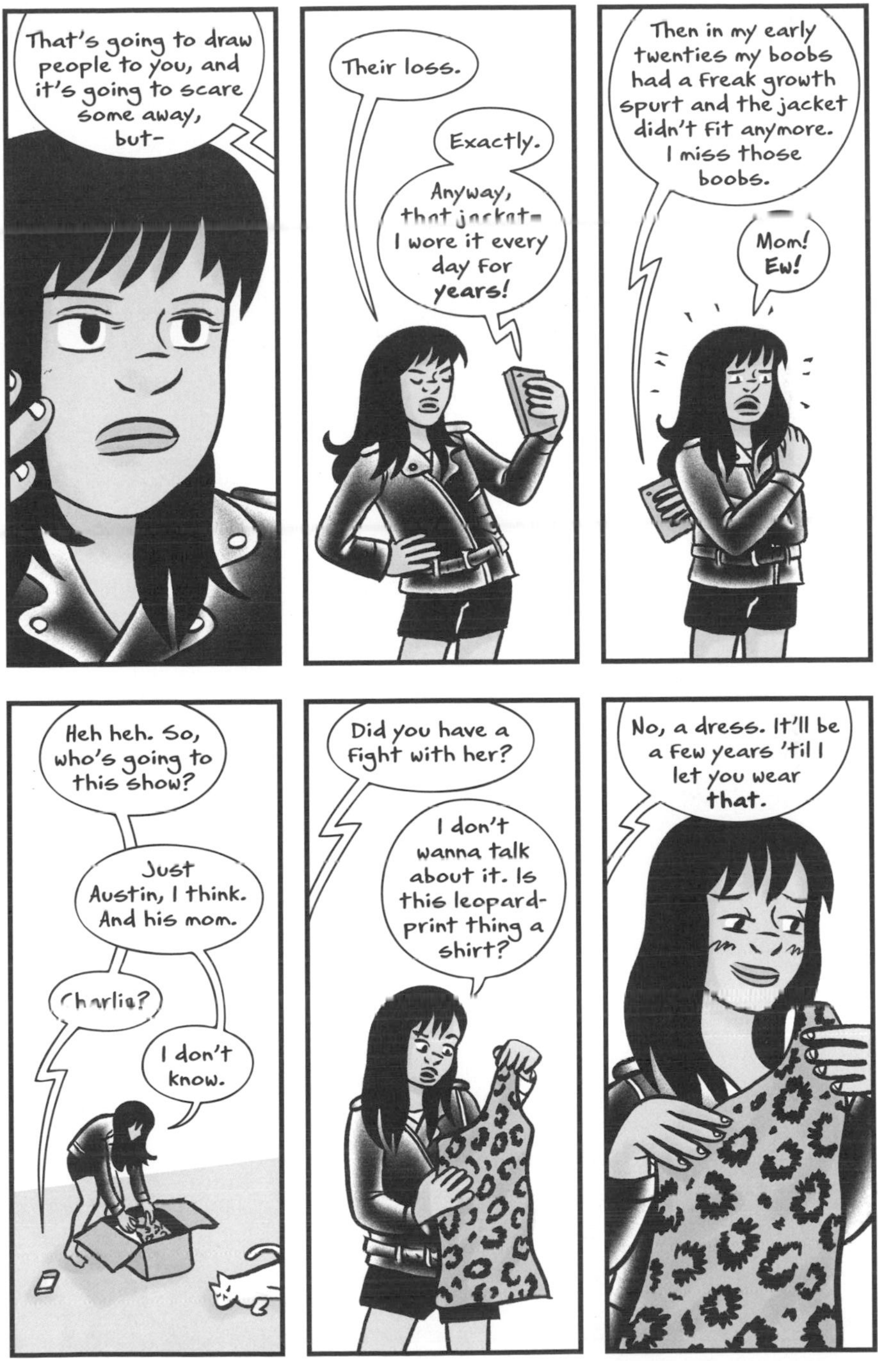
That's going to draw people to you, and it's going to scare some away, but-
Their loss.
Exactly.
Anyway, that jacket- I wore it every day for years!
Then in my early twenties my boobs had a freak growth spurt and the jacket didn't fit anymore. I miss those boobs.
Mom! Ew!
Heh heh. So, who's going to this show?
Just Austin, I think. And his mom.
Charlie?
I don't know.
Did you have a fight with her?
I don't wanna talk about it. Is this leopard-print thing a shirt?
No, a dress. It'll be a few years 'til I let you wear that.

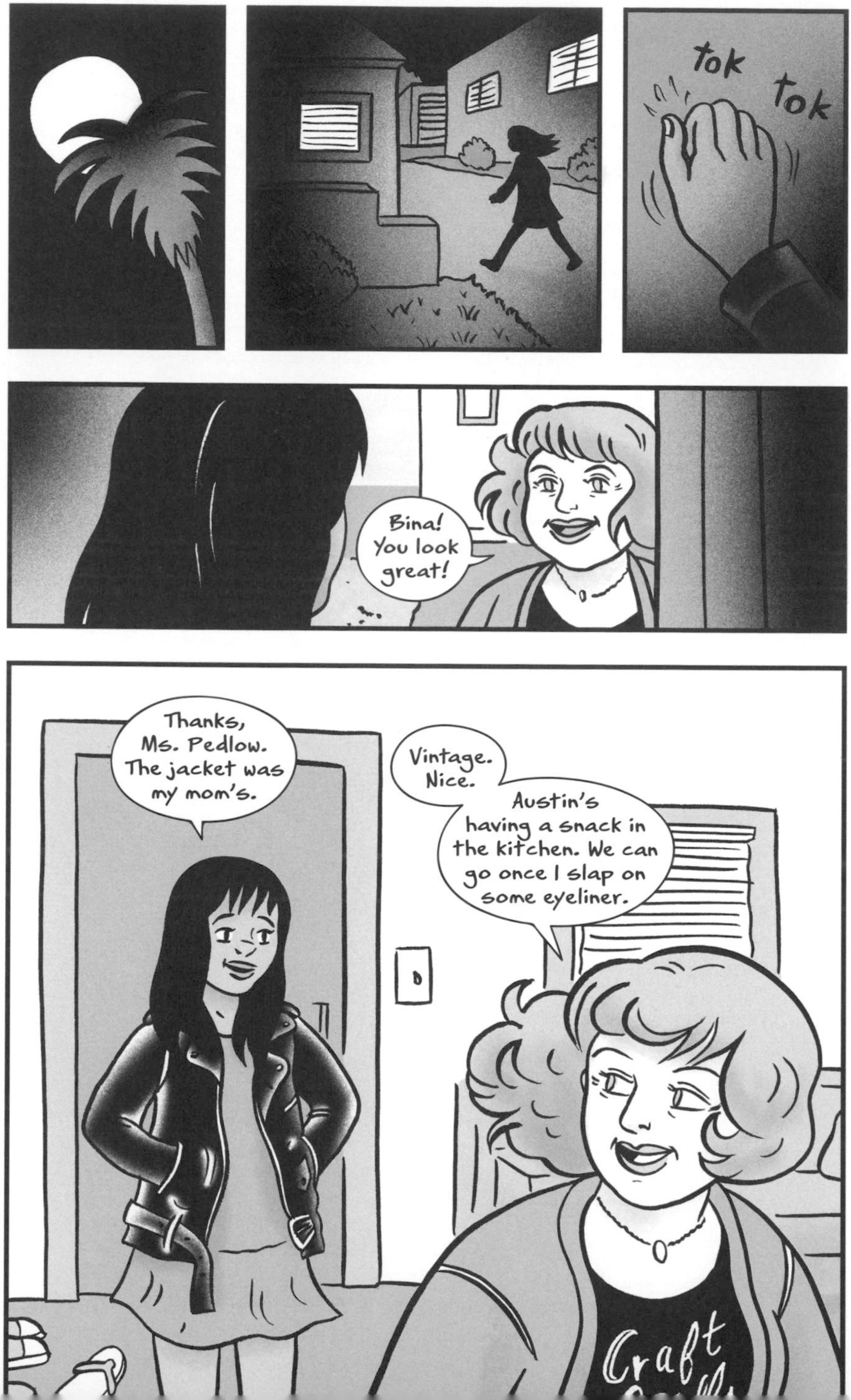
tok
tok
Bina! You look great!
Thanks, Ms. Pedlow. The jacket was my mom's.
Vintage. Nice.
Austin's having a snack in the kitchen. We can go once I slap on some eyeliner.
Craft

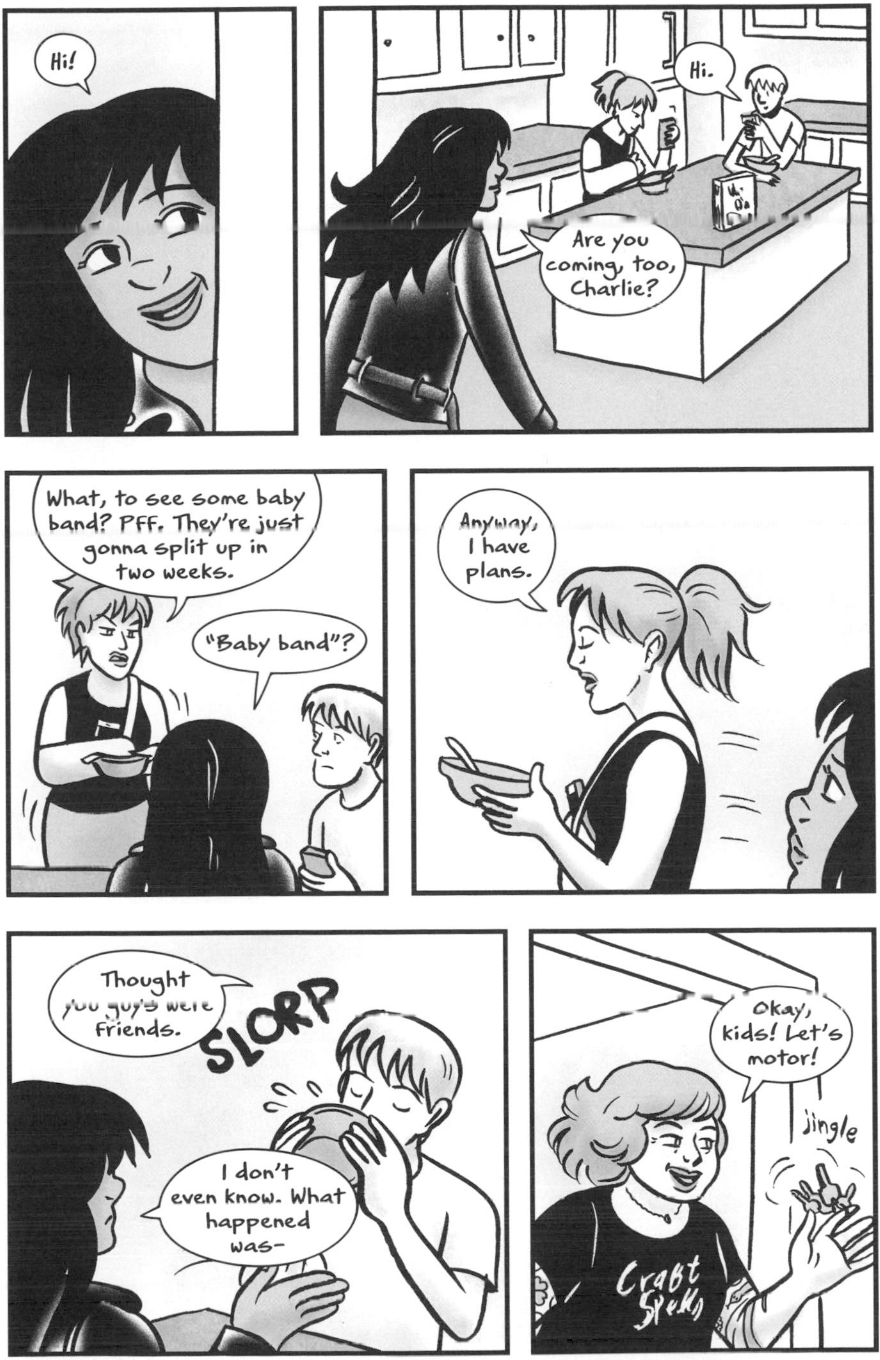
Hi!
Hi.
Are you coming, too, Charlie?
What, to see some baby band? PFF. They're just gonna split up in two weeks.
"Baby band"?
Anyway, I have plans.
Thought you guys were friends.
SLORP
I don't even know. What happened was-
Okay, kids! Let's motor!
jingle

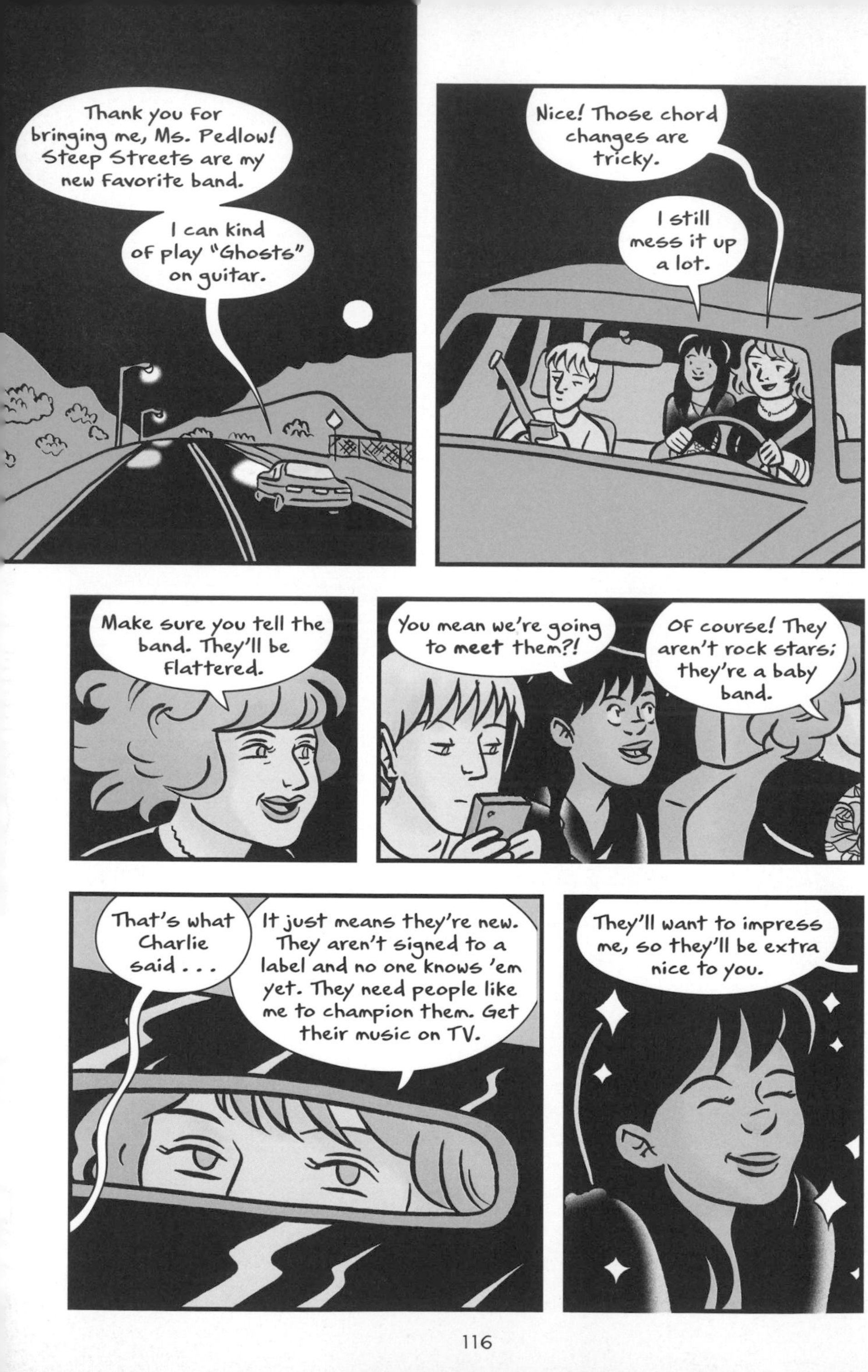
Thank you for bringing me, Ms. Pedlow! Steep Streets are my new favorite band.
I can kind of play "Ghosts" on guitar.
Nice! Those chord changes are tricky.
I still mess it up a lot.
Make sure you tell the band. They'll be flattered.
You mean we're going to meet them?!
Of course! They aren't rock stars; they're a baby band.
That's what Charlie said . . .
It just means they're new. They aren't signed to a label and no one knows 'em yet. They need people like me to champion them. Get their music on TV.
They'll want to impress me, so they'll be extra nice to you.

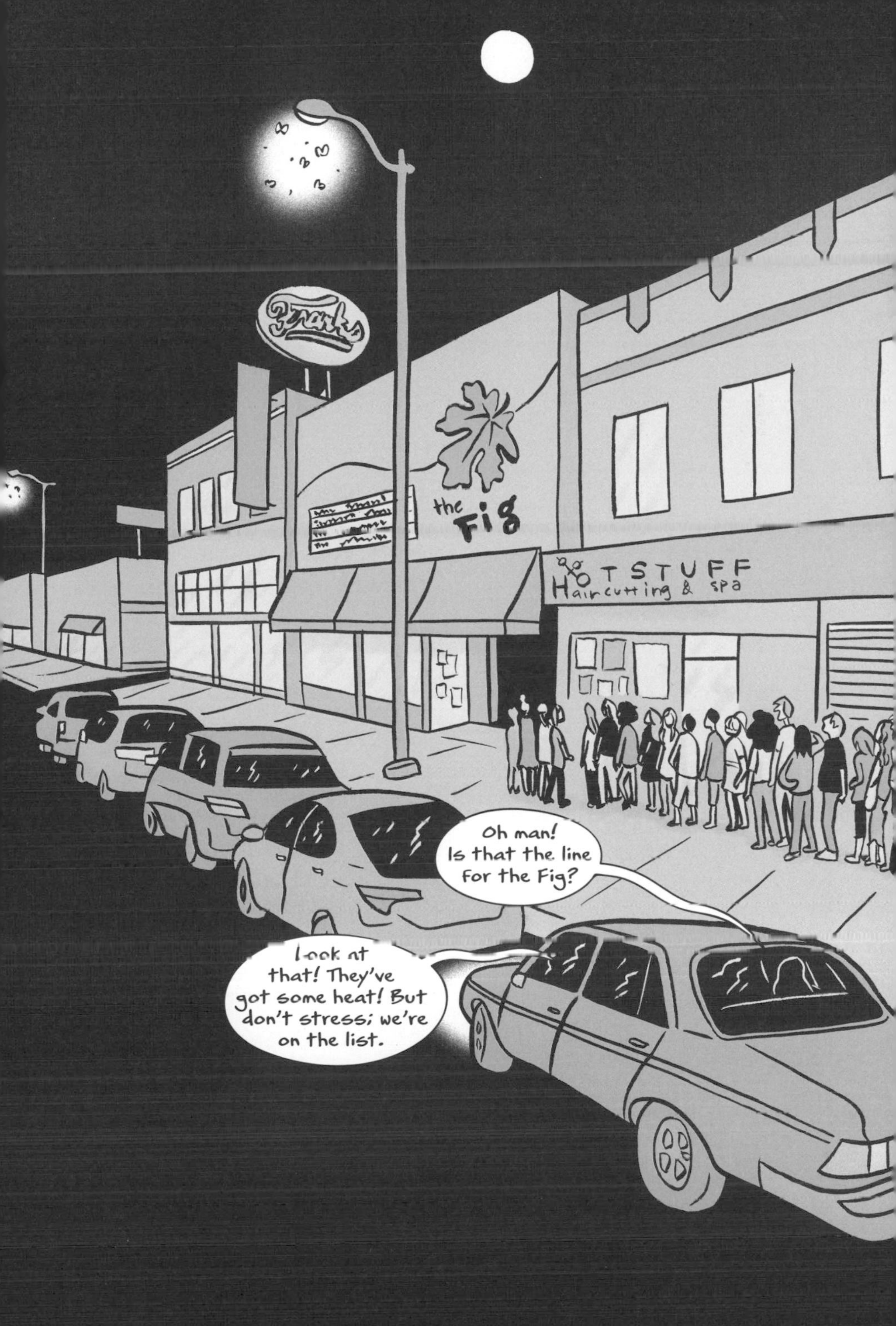
the Fig
HOT STUFF
Haircutting & spa
Oh man! Is that the line for the Fig?
Look at that! They've got some heat! But don't stress; we're on the list.

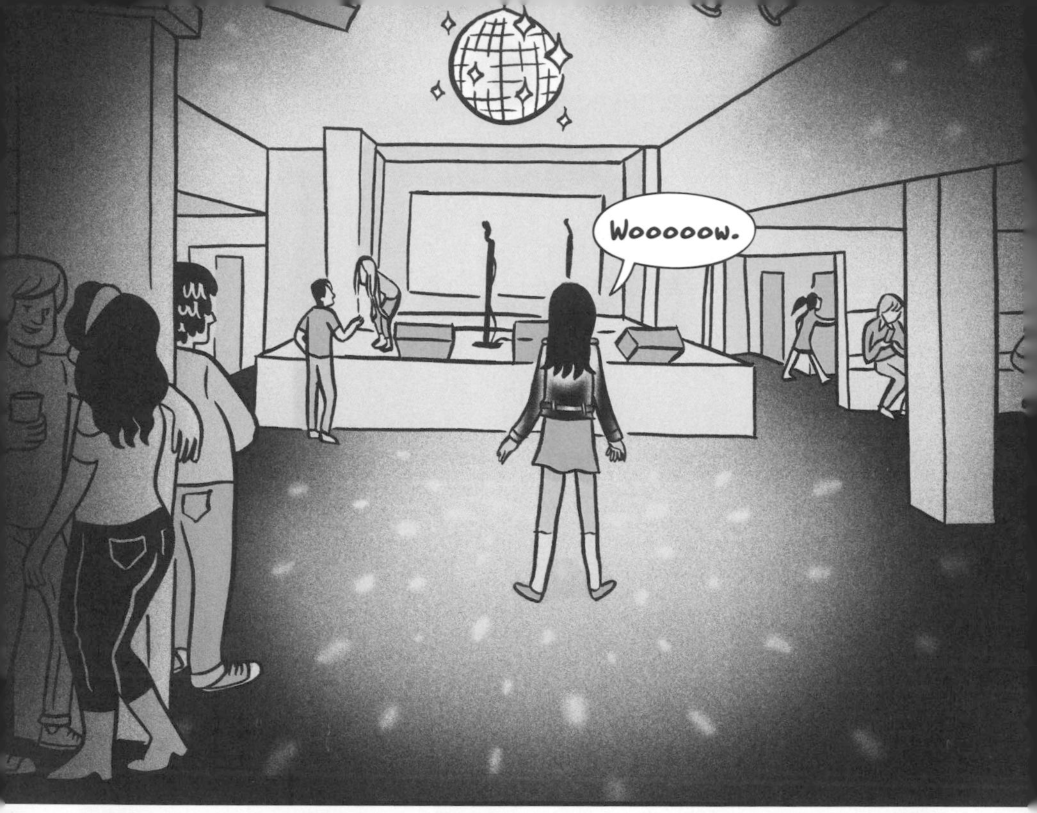
Woooooow.

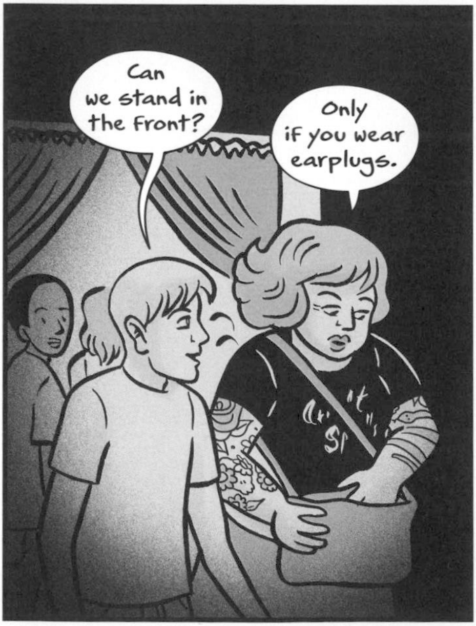
Can we stand in the front?
Only if you wear earplugs.

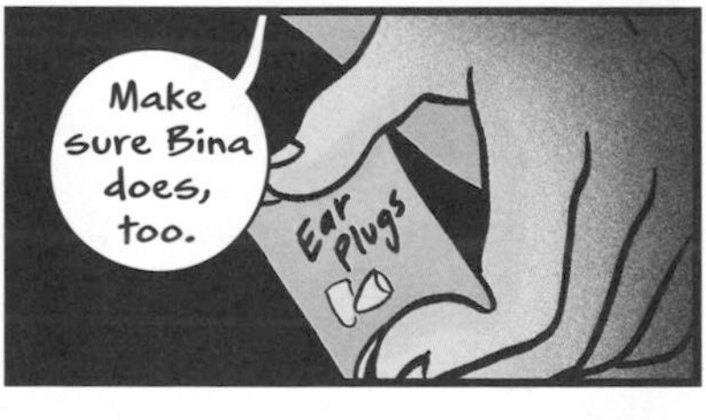
Make sure Bina does, too.
Ear plugs

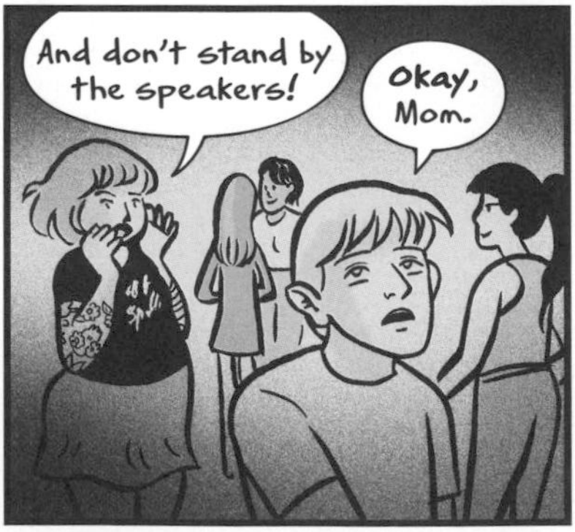
And don't stand by the speakers!
Okay, Mom.

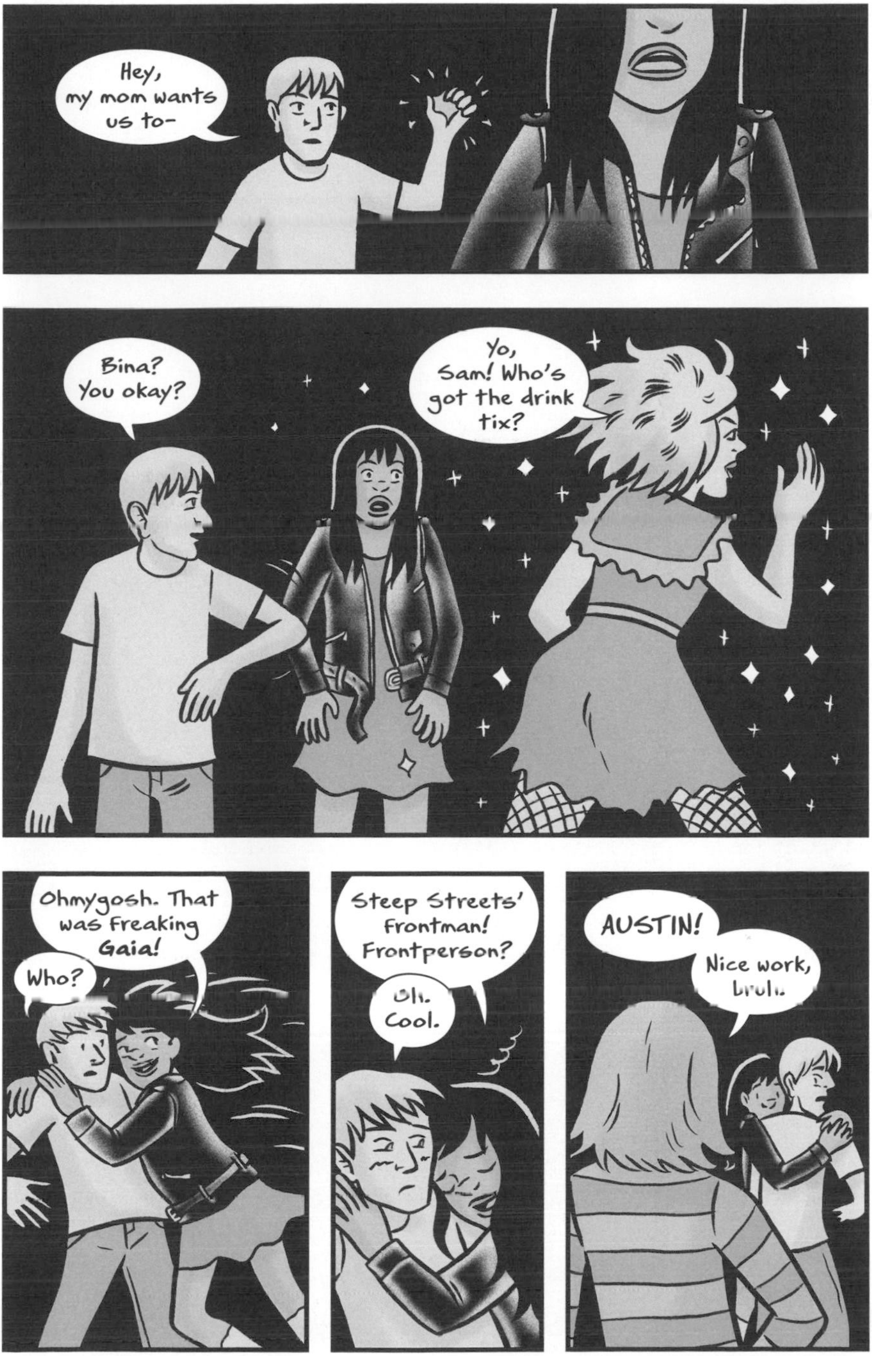
Hey, my mom wants us to-
Bina? You okay?
Yo, Sam! Who's got the drink tix?
Ohmygosh. That was Freaking Gaia!
Who?
Steep Streets' Frontman! Frontperson?
Cool.
AUSTIN!
Nice work,

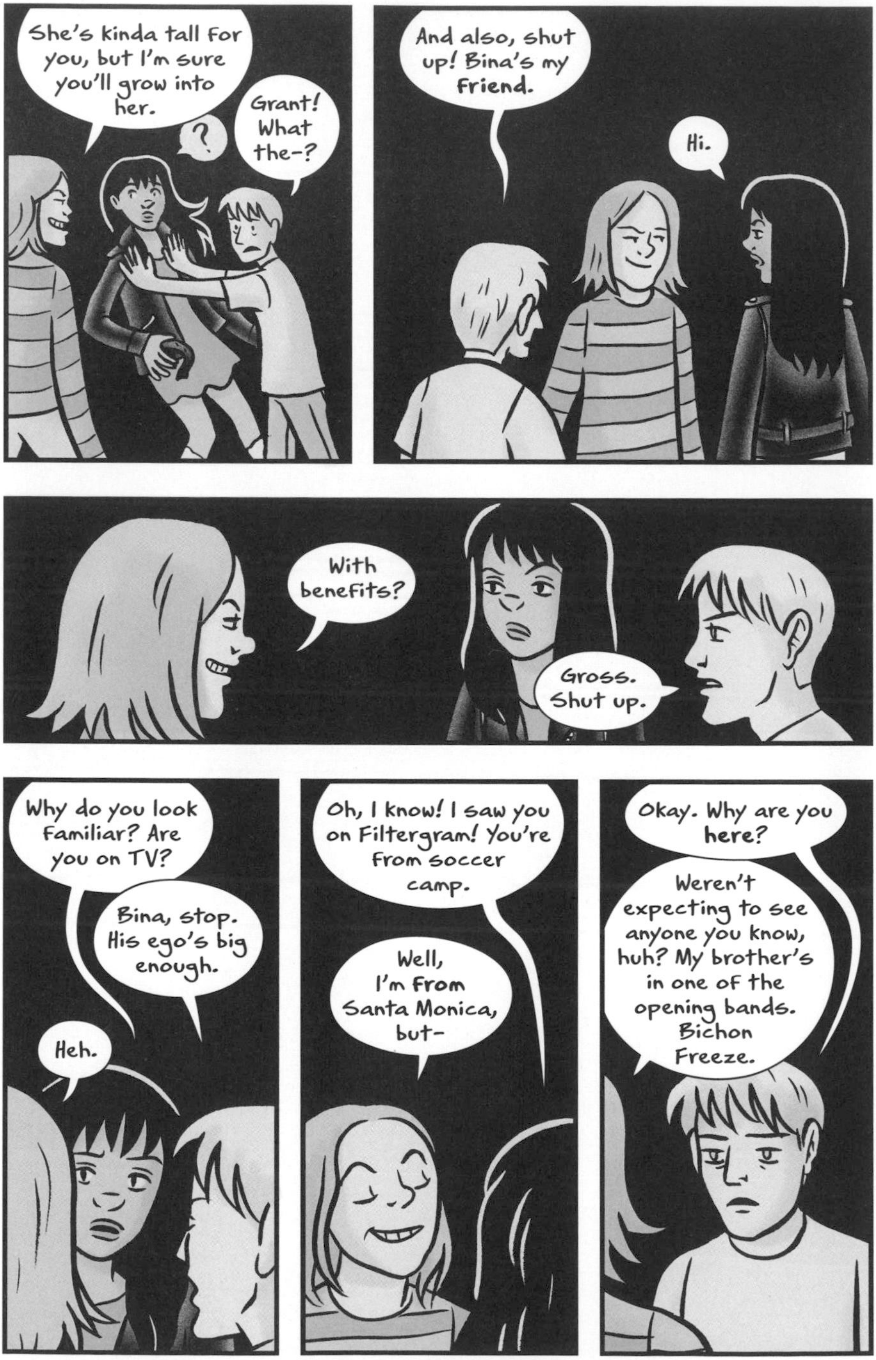
She's kinda tall for you, but I'm sure you'll grow into her.
?
Grant! What the-?
And also, shut up! Bina's my friend.
Hi.
With benefits?
Gross. Shut up.
Why do you look familiar? Are you on TV?
Bina, stop. His ego's big enough.
Heh.
Oh, I know! I saw you on Filtergram! You're from soccer camp.
Well, I'm from Santa Monica, but-
Okay. Why are you here?
Weren't expecting to see anyone you know, huh? My brother's in one of the opening bands. Bichon Freeze.

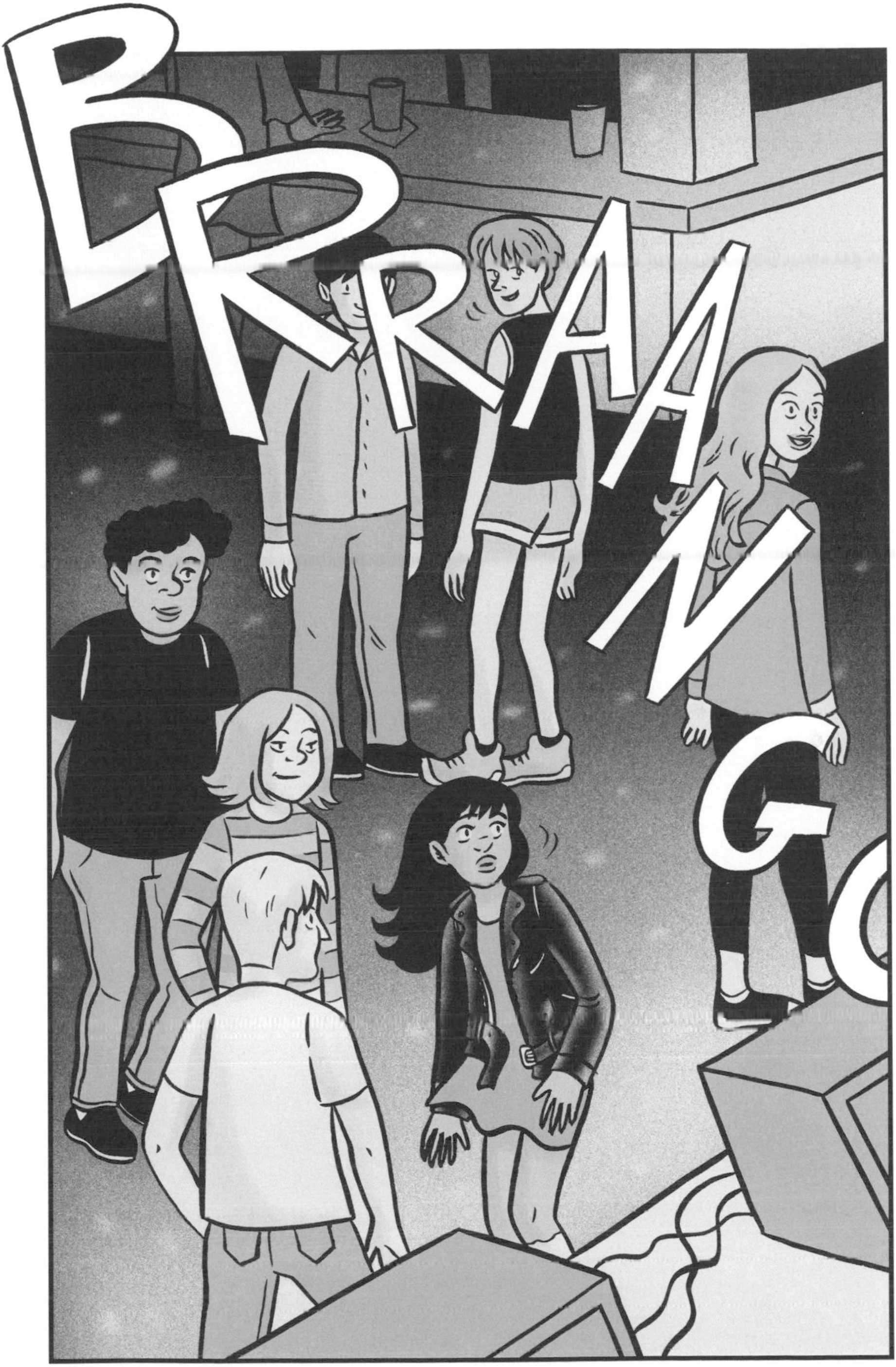
BRRAANGG

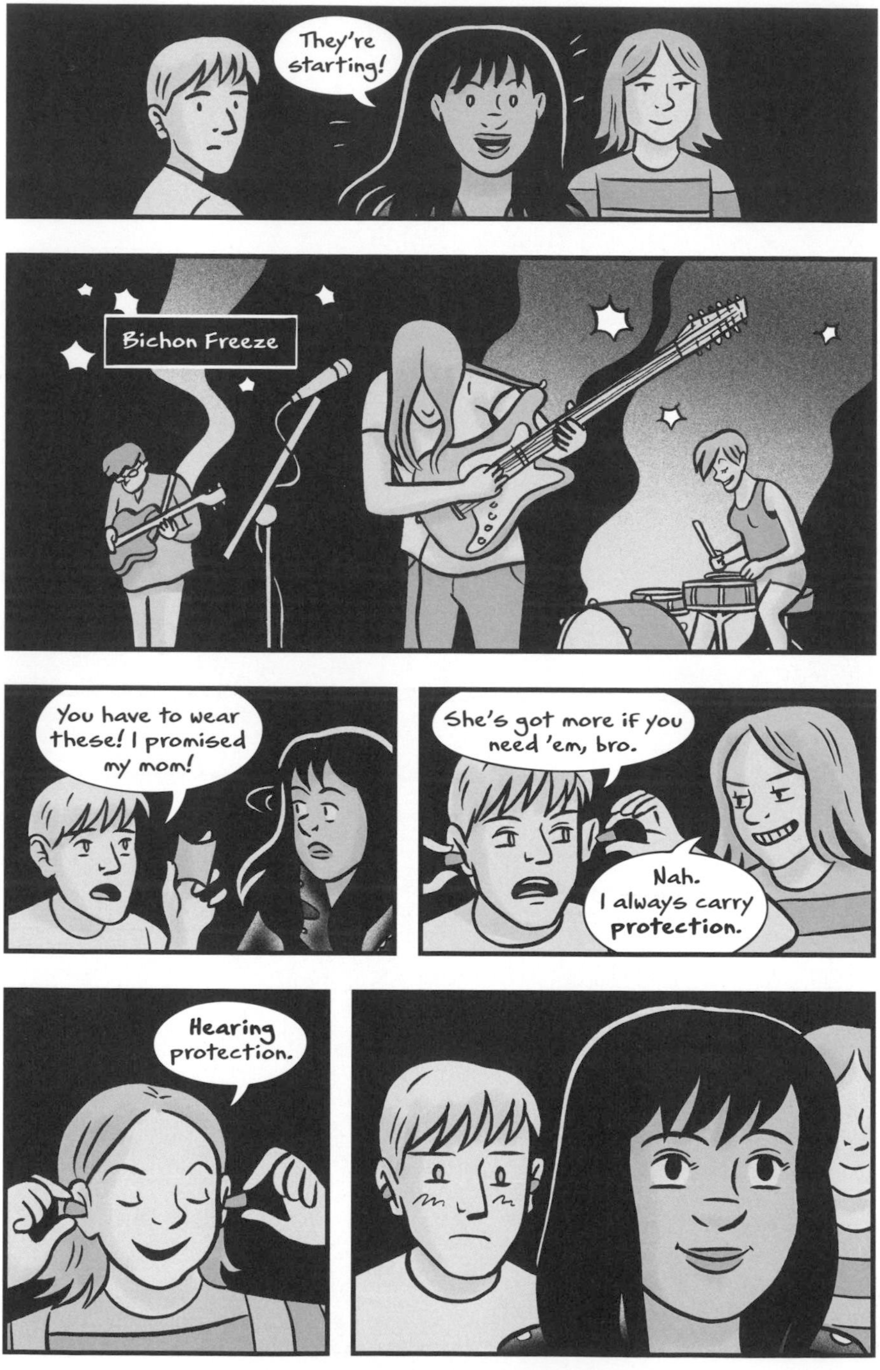
They're starting!
Bichon Freeze
You have to wear these! I promised my mom!
She's got more if you need 'em, bro.
Nah. I always carry protection.
Hearing protection.

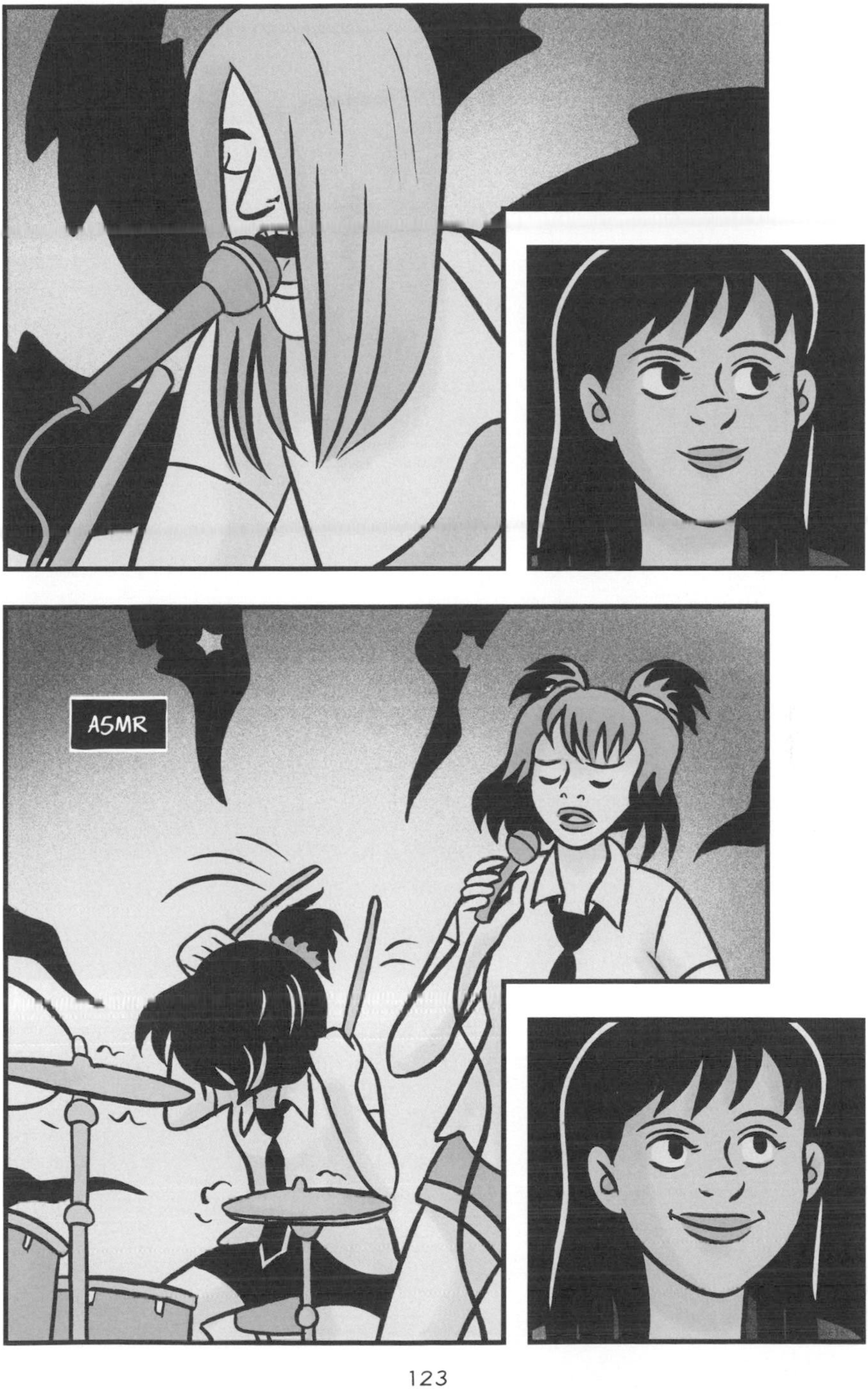
ASMR

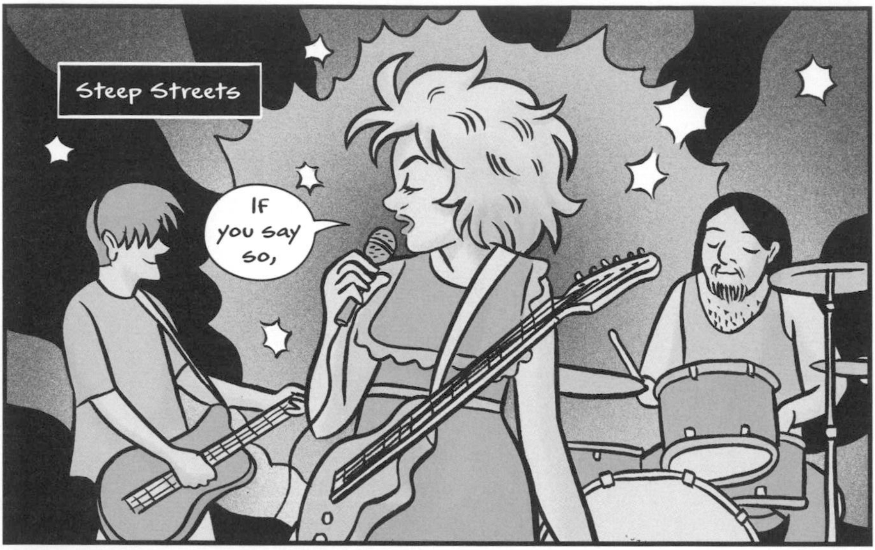
Steep Streets
If you say so,

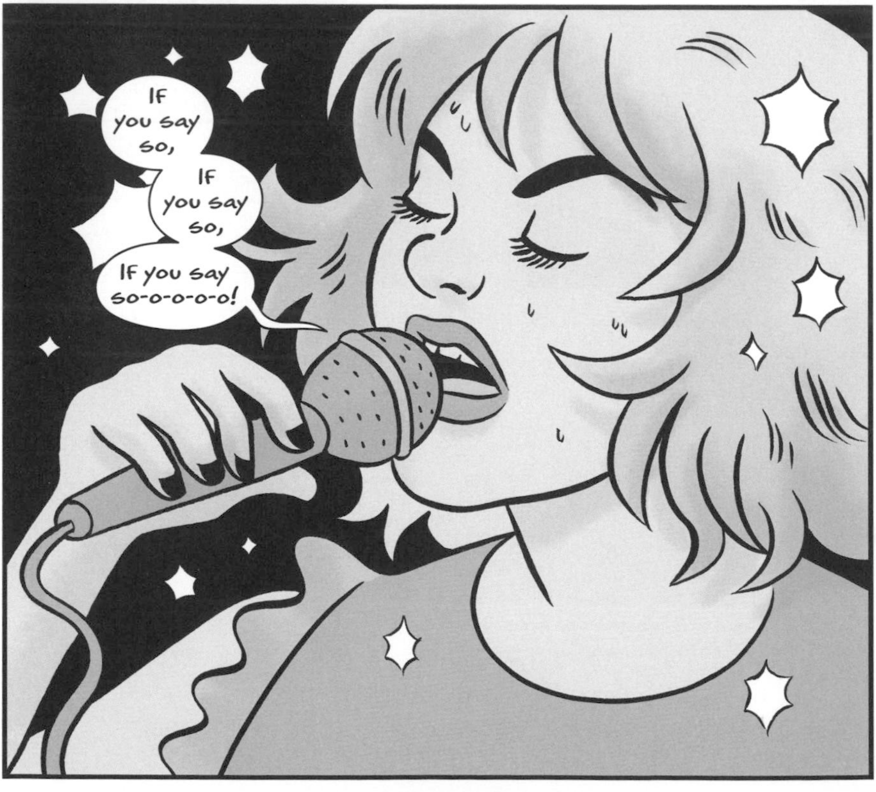
If you say so,
If you say so,
If you say so-o-o-o-o!

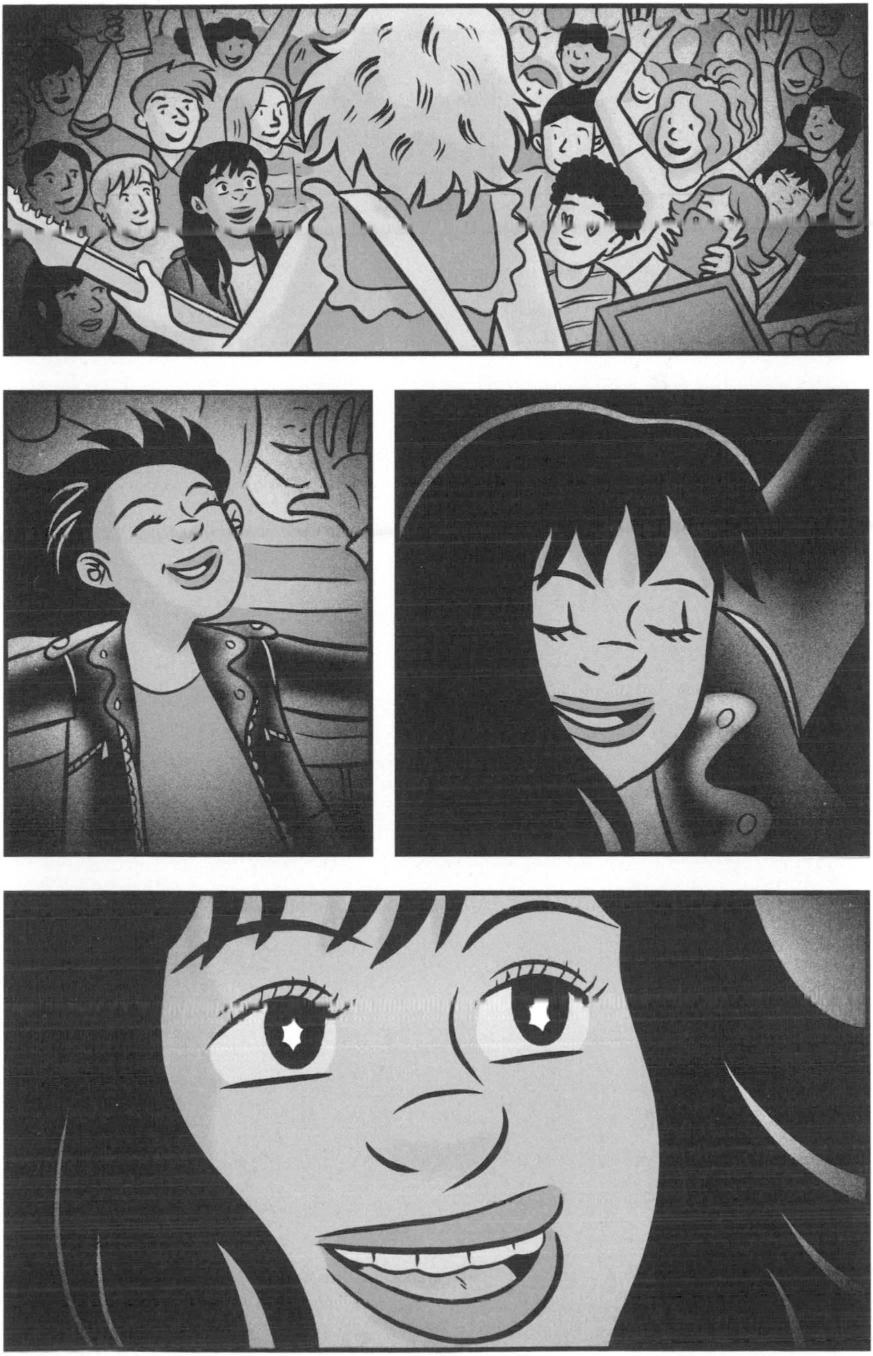

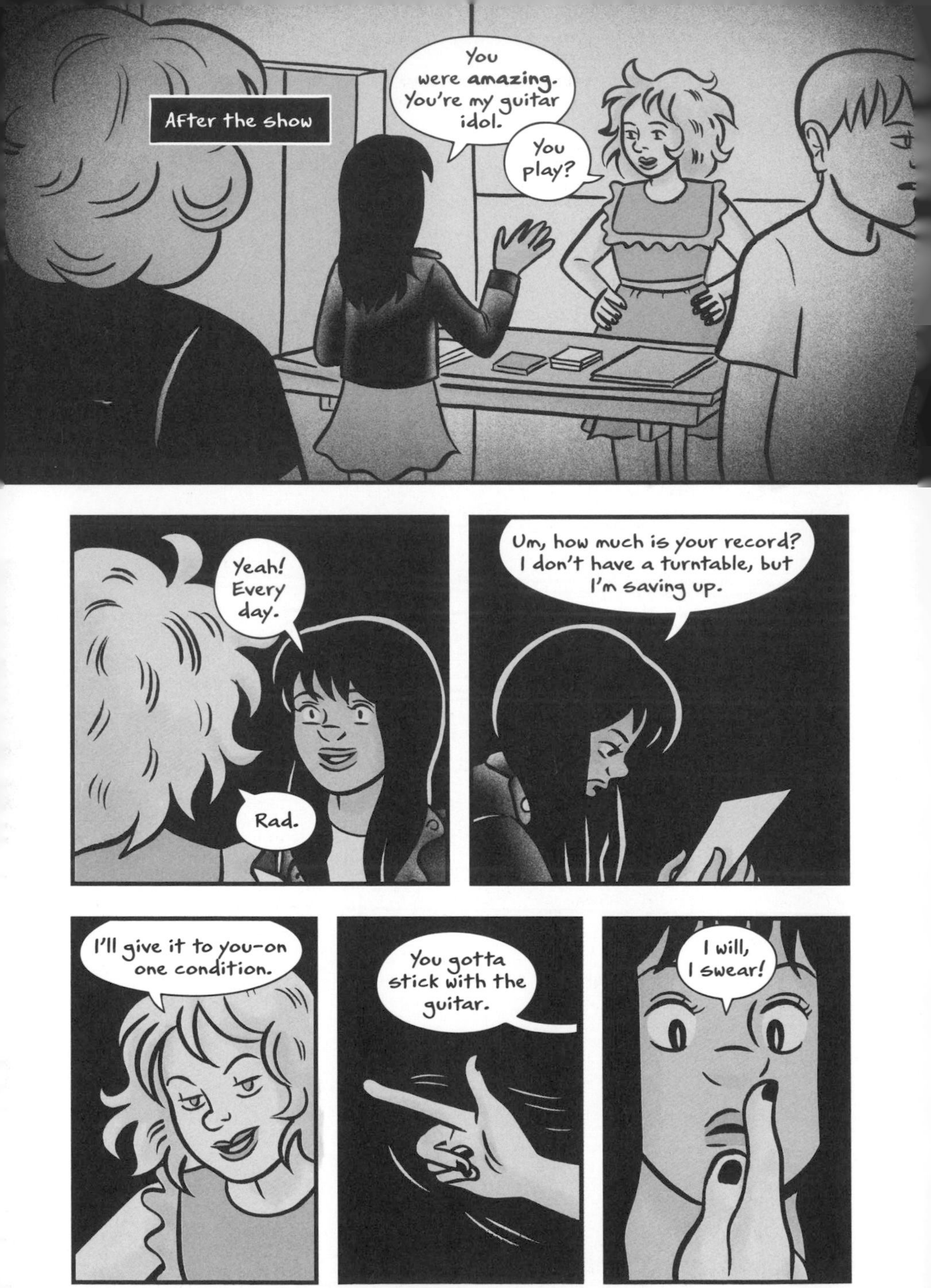
After the show
You were amazing. You're my guitar idol.
You play?
Yeah! Every day.
Rad.
Um, how much is your record? I don't have a turntable, but I'm saving up.
I'll give it to you-on one condition.
You gotta stick with the guitar.
I will, I swear!

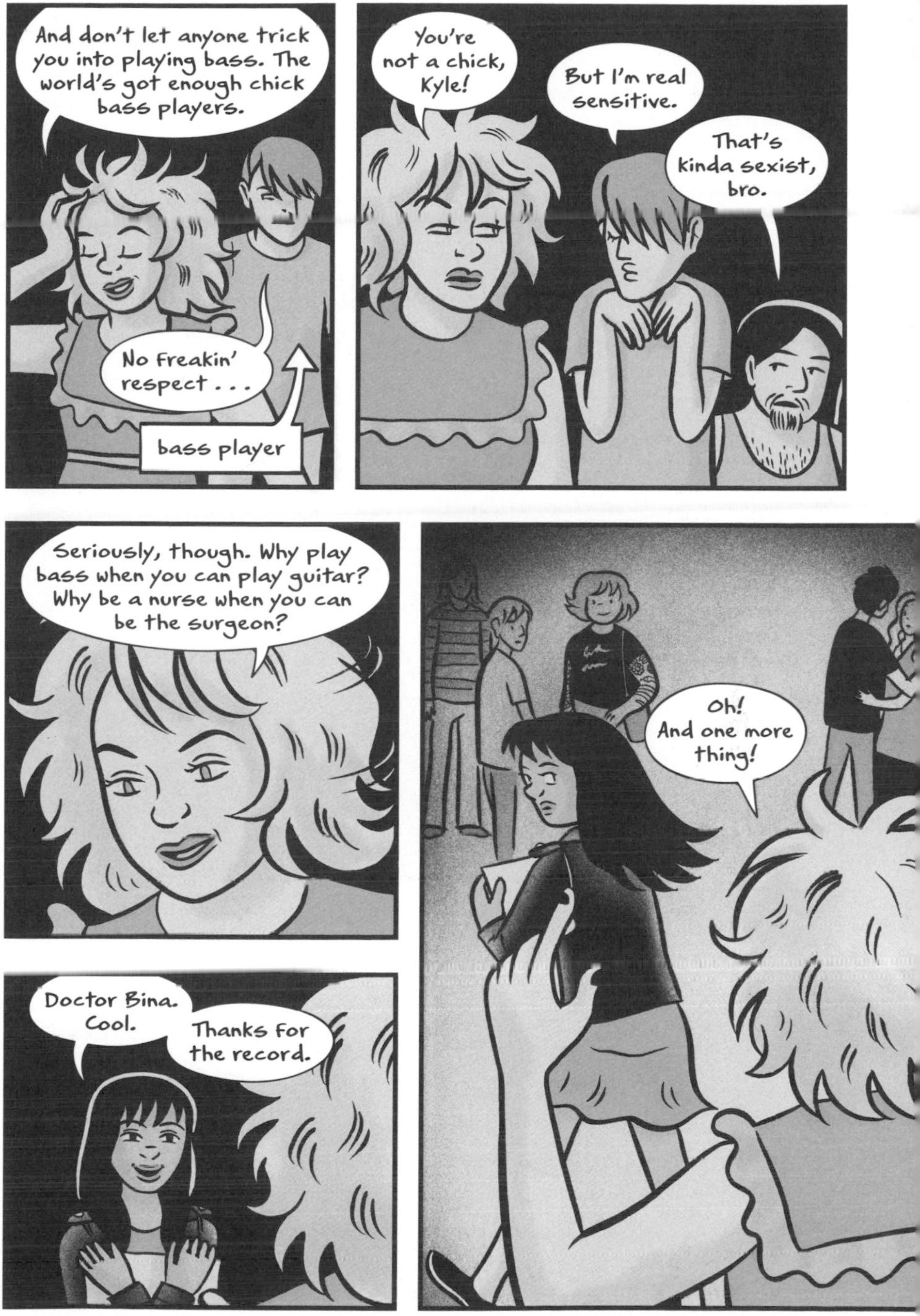
And don't let anyone trick you into playing bass. The world's got enough chick bass players.
No freakin' respect . . .
bass player
You're not a chick, Kyle!
But I'm real sensitive.
That's kinda sexist, bro.
Seriously, though. Why play bass when you can play guitar? Why be a nurse when you can be the surgeon?
Doctor Bina. Cool.
Thanks for the record.
Oh! And one more thing!

You gotta start a band!
I will, when I'm good enough!
Starting a band is the only way you'll get good enough to start a band.
Okay! I . . . I will!

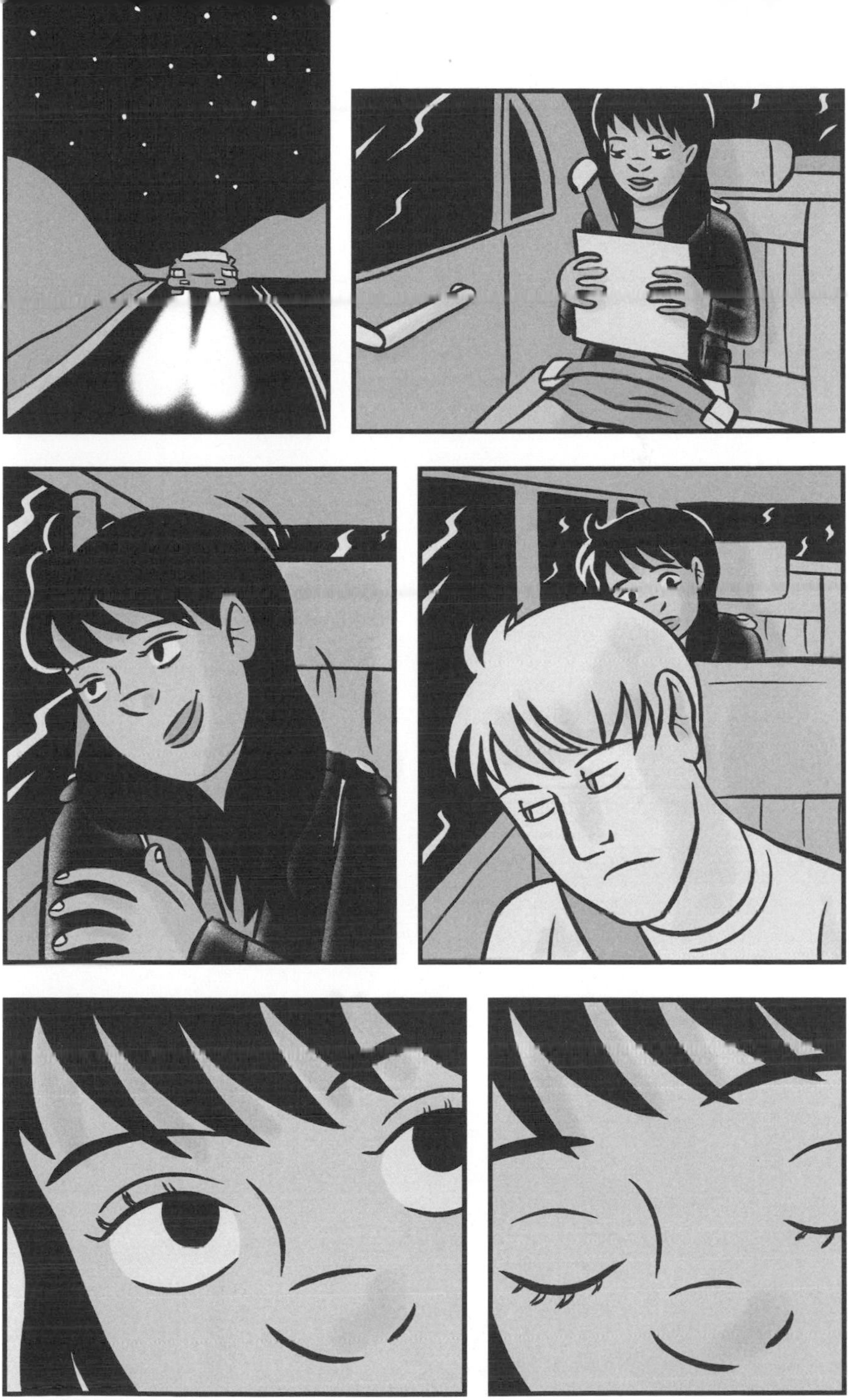

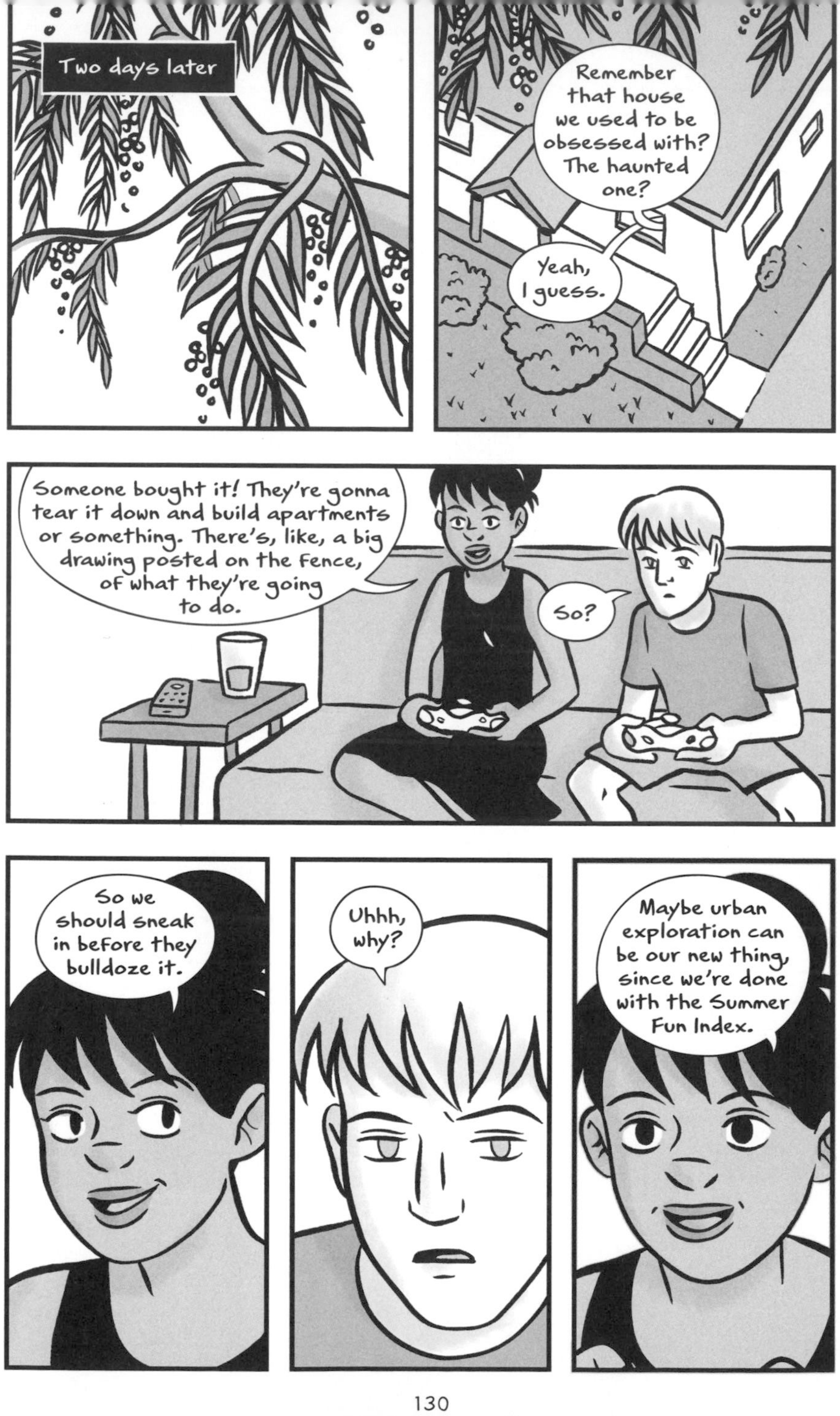

Two days later
Remember that house we used to be obsessed with? The haunted one?
Yeah, I guess.
Someone bought it! They're gonna tear it down and build apartments or something. There's, like, a big drawing posted on the fence, of what they're going to do.
So?
So we should sneak in before they bulldoze it.
Uhhh, why?
Maybe urban exploration can be our new thing, since we're done with the Summer Fun Index.

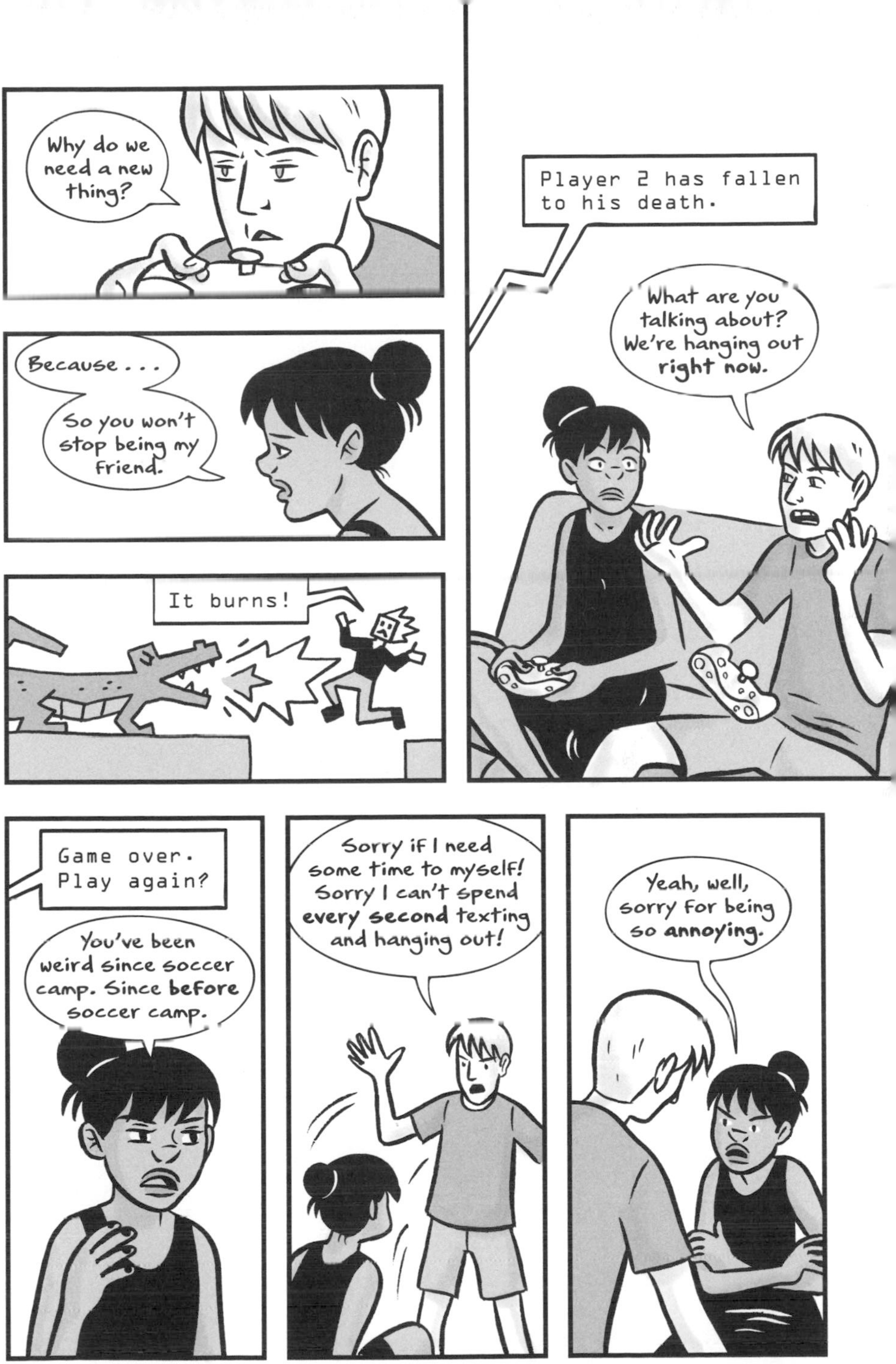

Why do we need a new thing?
Because . . .
So you won't stop being my friend.
It burns!
Player 2 has fallen to his death.
What are you talking about? We're hanging out **right now.**
Game over. Play again?
You've been weird since soccer camp. Since **before** soccer camp.
Sorry if I need some time to myself! Sorry I can't spend **every second** texting and hanging out!
Yeah, well, sorry for being so **annoying.**

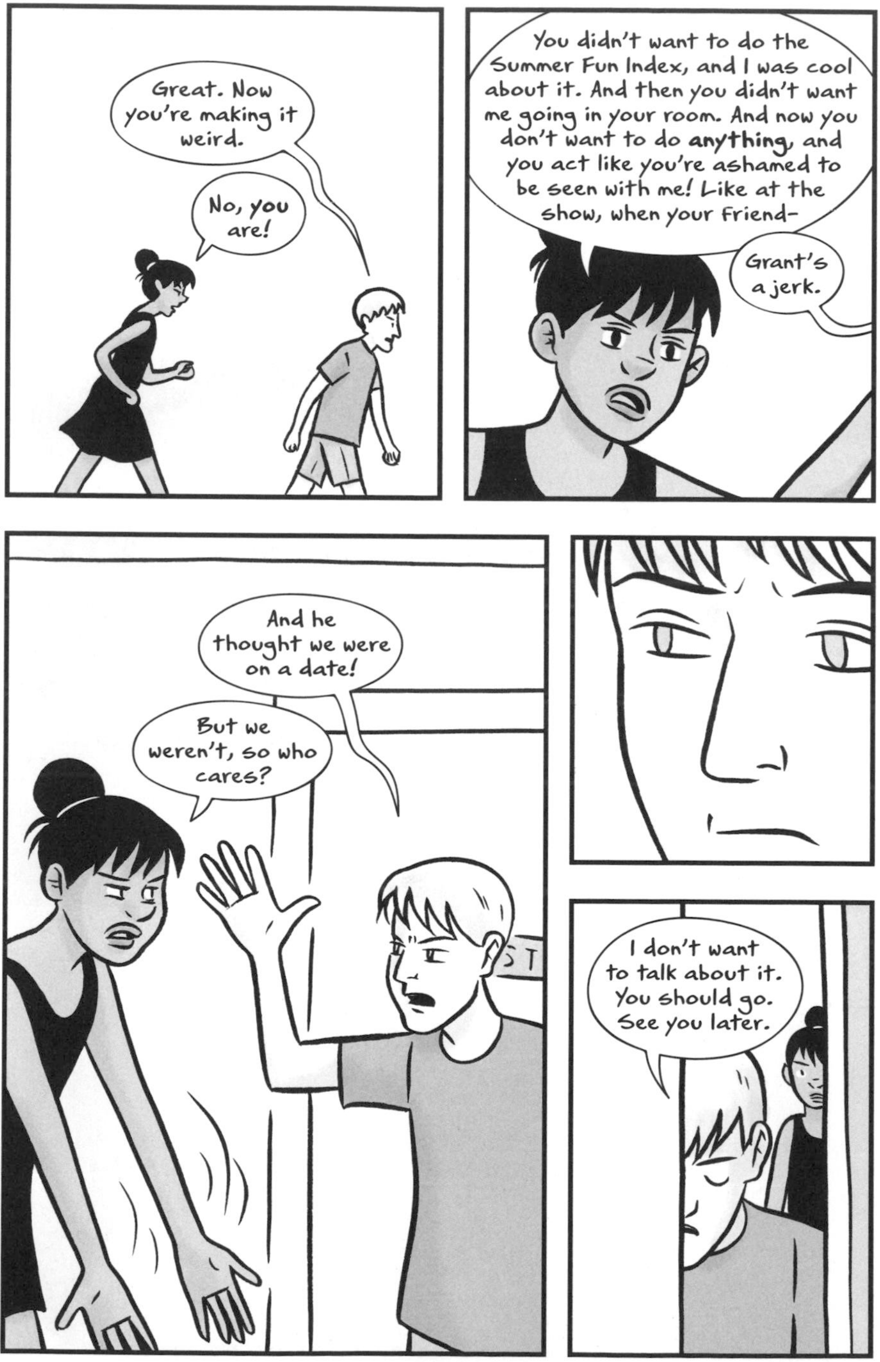
Great. Now you're making it weird.
No, you are!
You didn't want to do the Summer Fun Index, and I was cool about it. And then you didn't want me going in your room. And now you don't want to do **anything**, and you act like you're ashamed to be seen with me! Like at the show, when your friend–
Grant's a jerk.
And he thought we were on a date!
But we weren't, so who cares?
I don't want to talk about it. You should go. See you later.

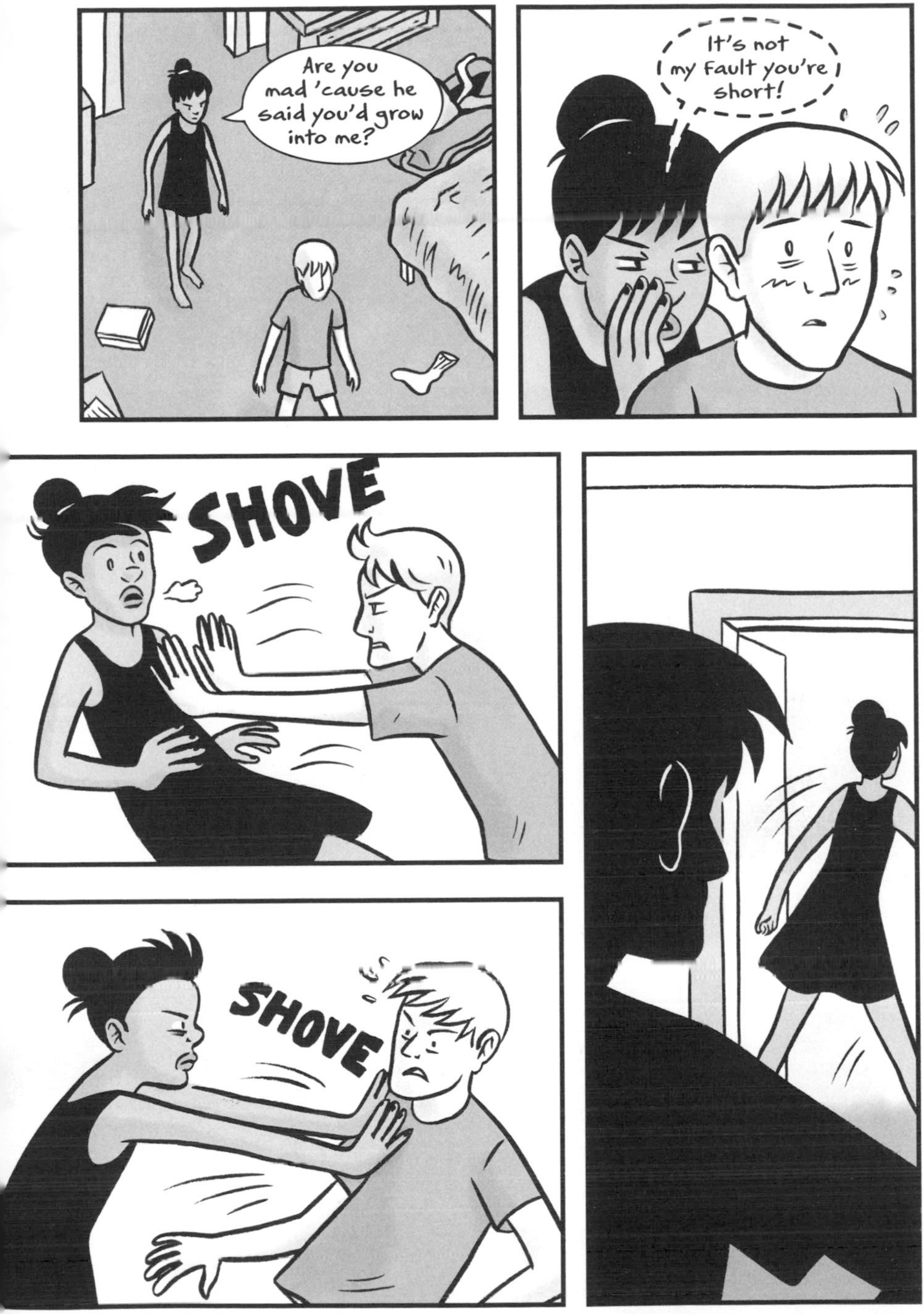
Are you mad 'cause he said you'd grow into me?
It's not my fault you're short!
SHOVE
SHOVE

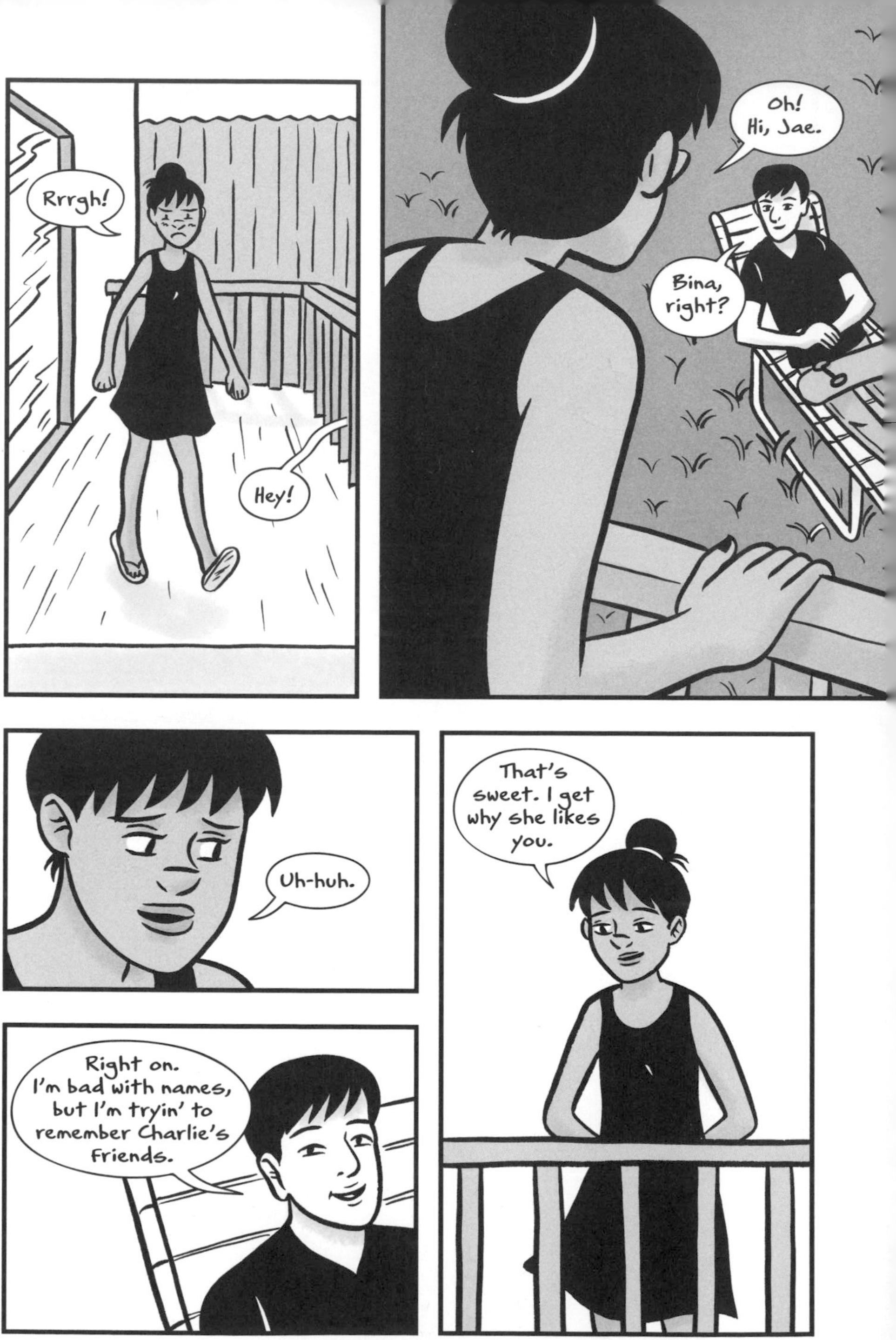
Rrrgh!
Hey!
Oh! Hi, Jae.
Bina, right?
Uh-huh.
Right on. I'm bad with names, but I'm tryin' to remember Charlie's friends.
That's sweet. I get why she likes you.

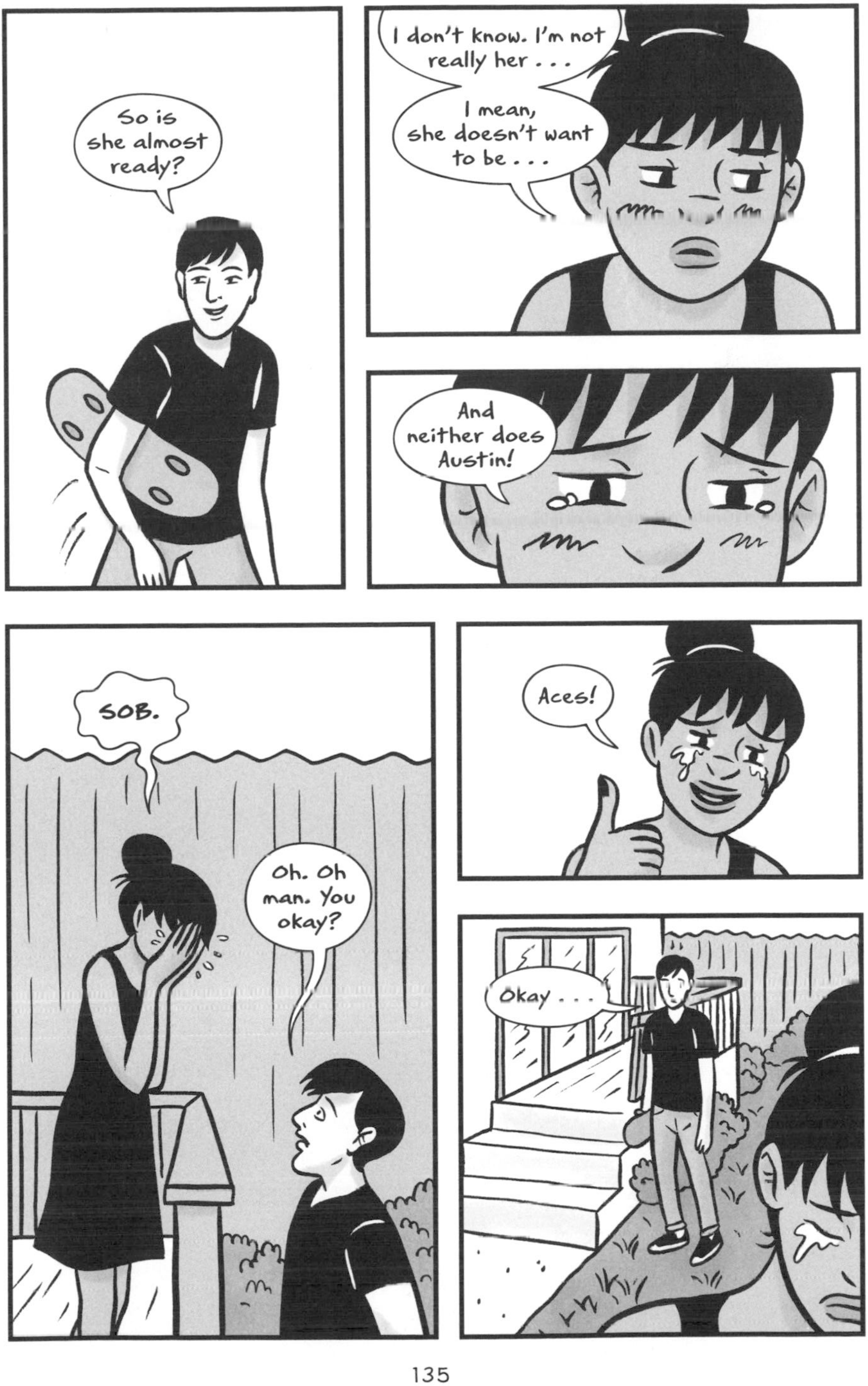
So is she almost ready?
I don't know. I'm not really her . . .
I mean, she doesn't want to be . . .
And neither does Austin!
SOB.
Oh. Oh man. You okay?
Aces!
Okay . . .

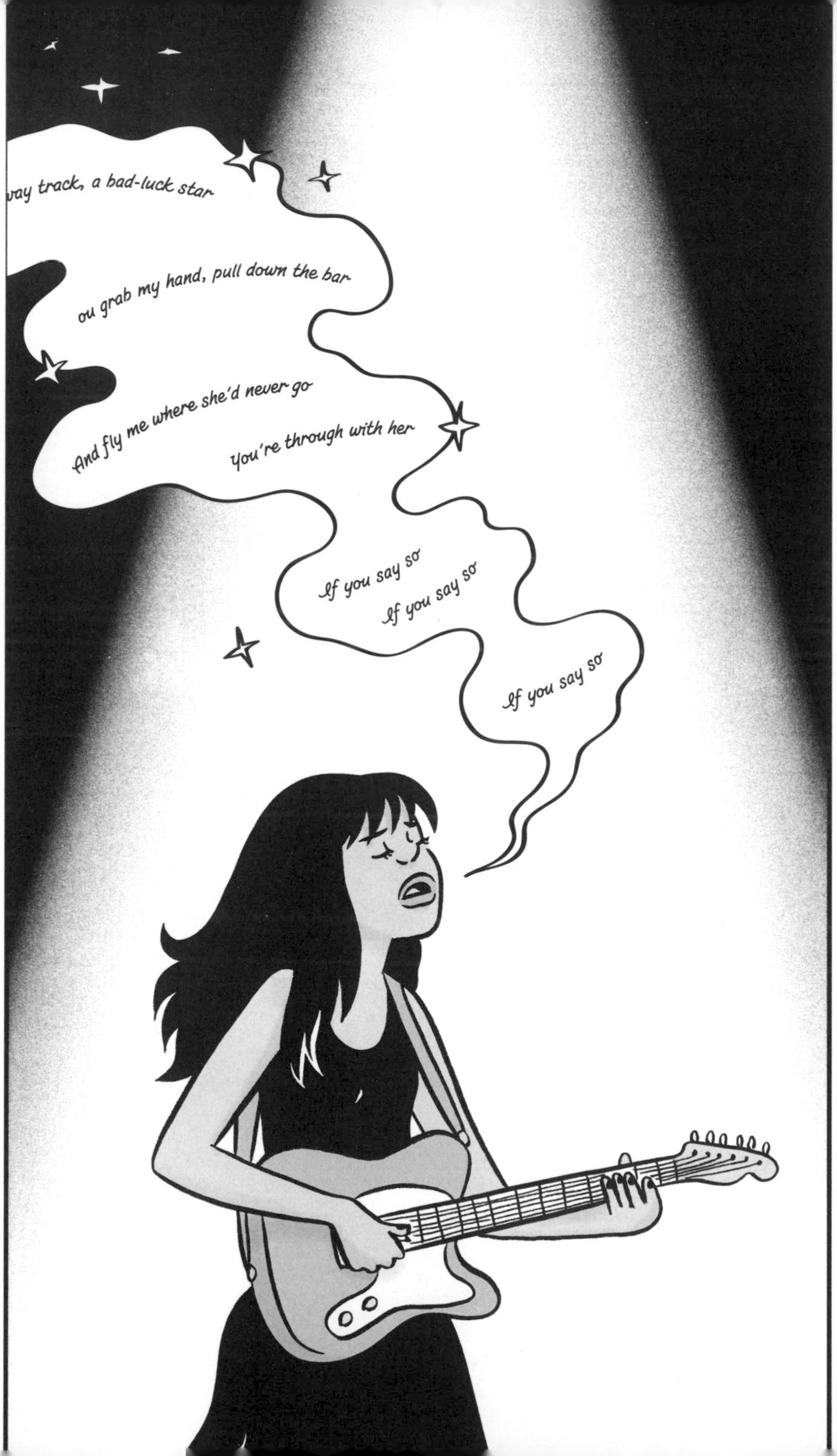
way track, a bad-luck star
ou grab my hand, pull down the bar
And fly me where she'd never go
You're through with her
If you say so
If you say so
If you say so

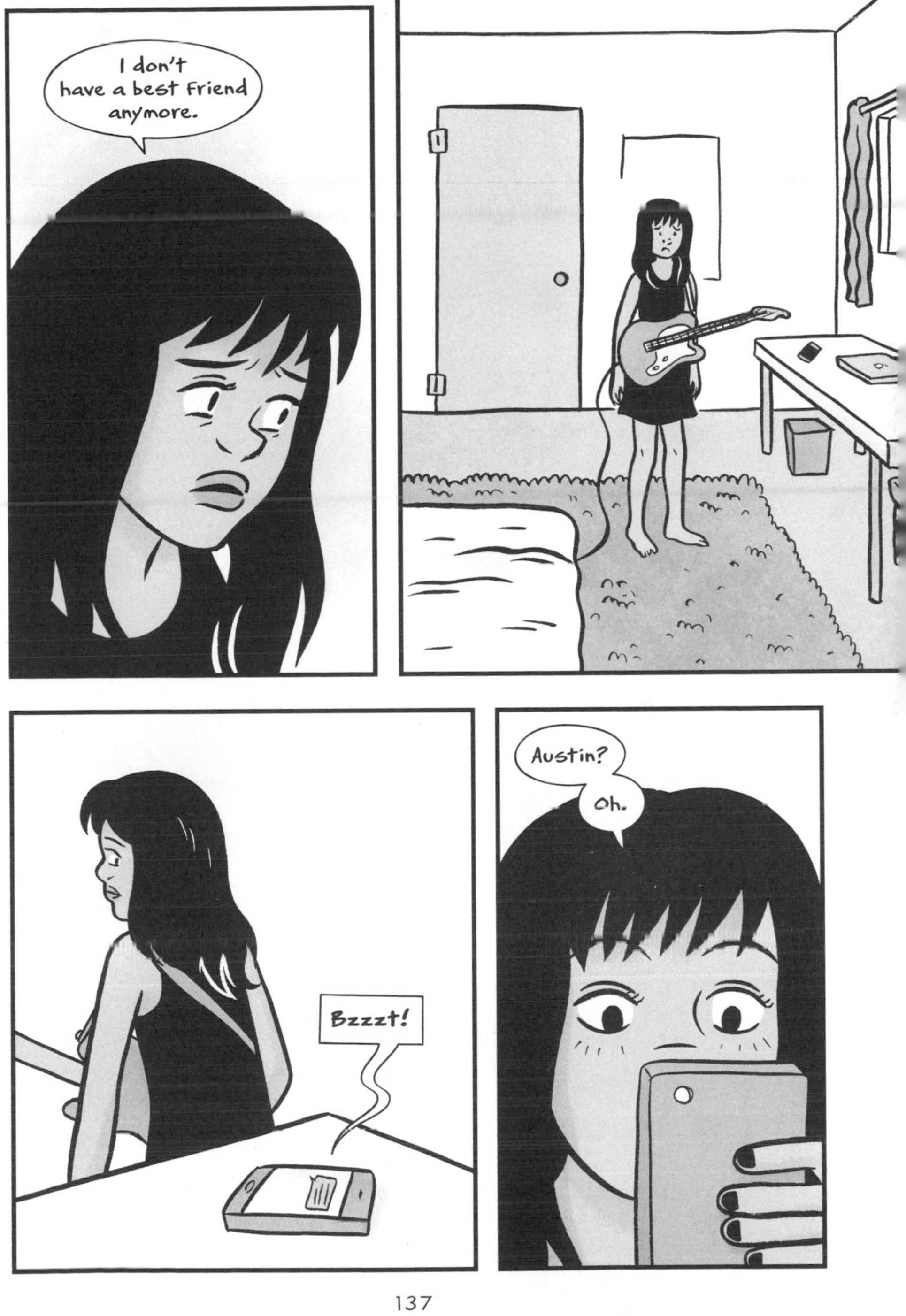
I don't have a best friend anymore.
Bzzzt!
Austin?
Oh.

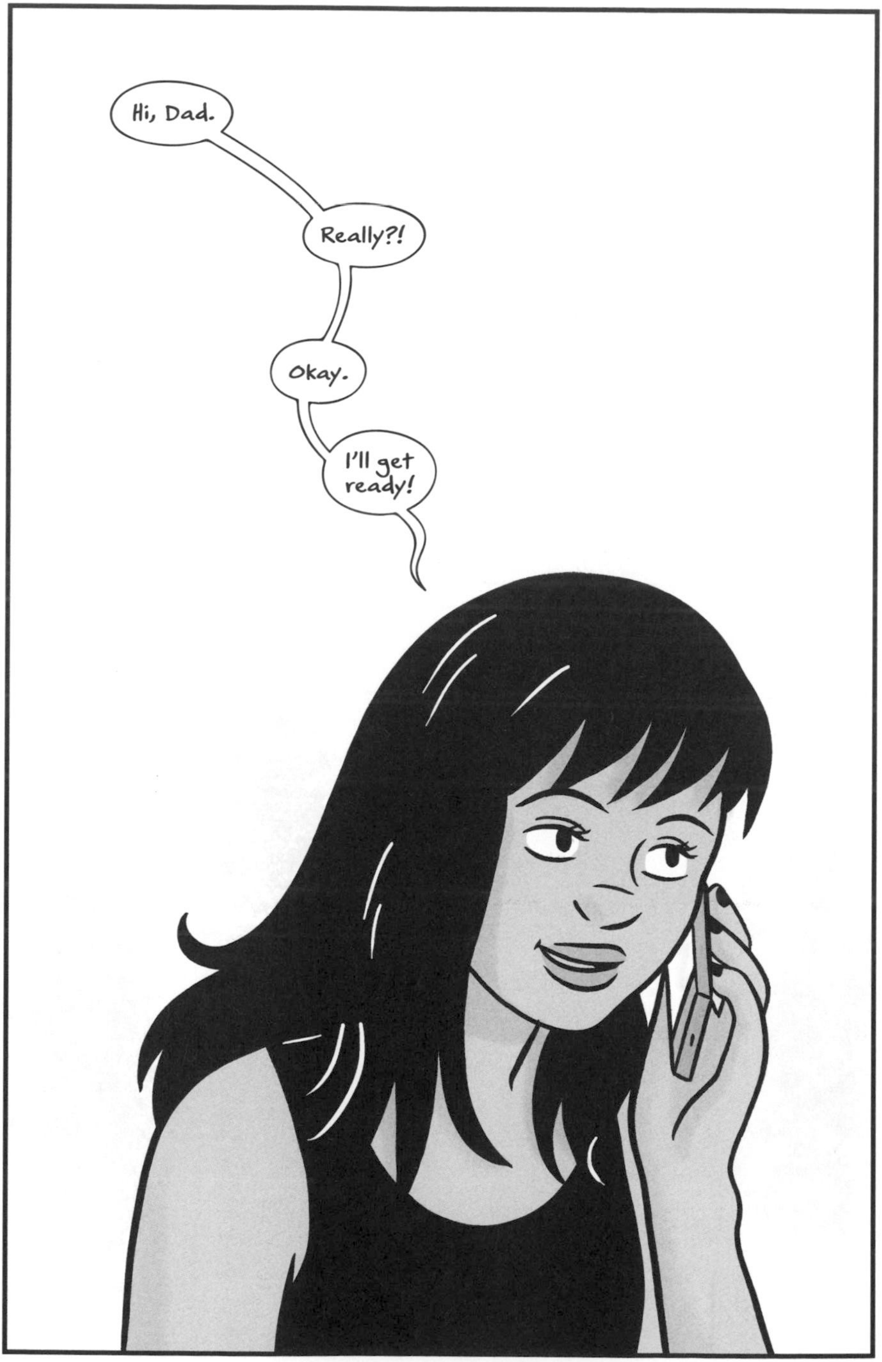
Hi, Dad.
Really?!
Okay.
I'll get ready!

CheapShuttle
to San Francisco
GATE
98

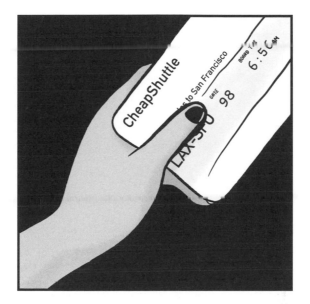

Week Six

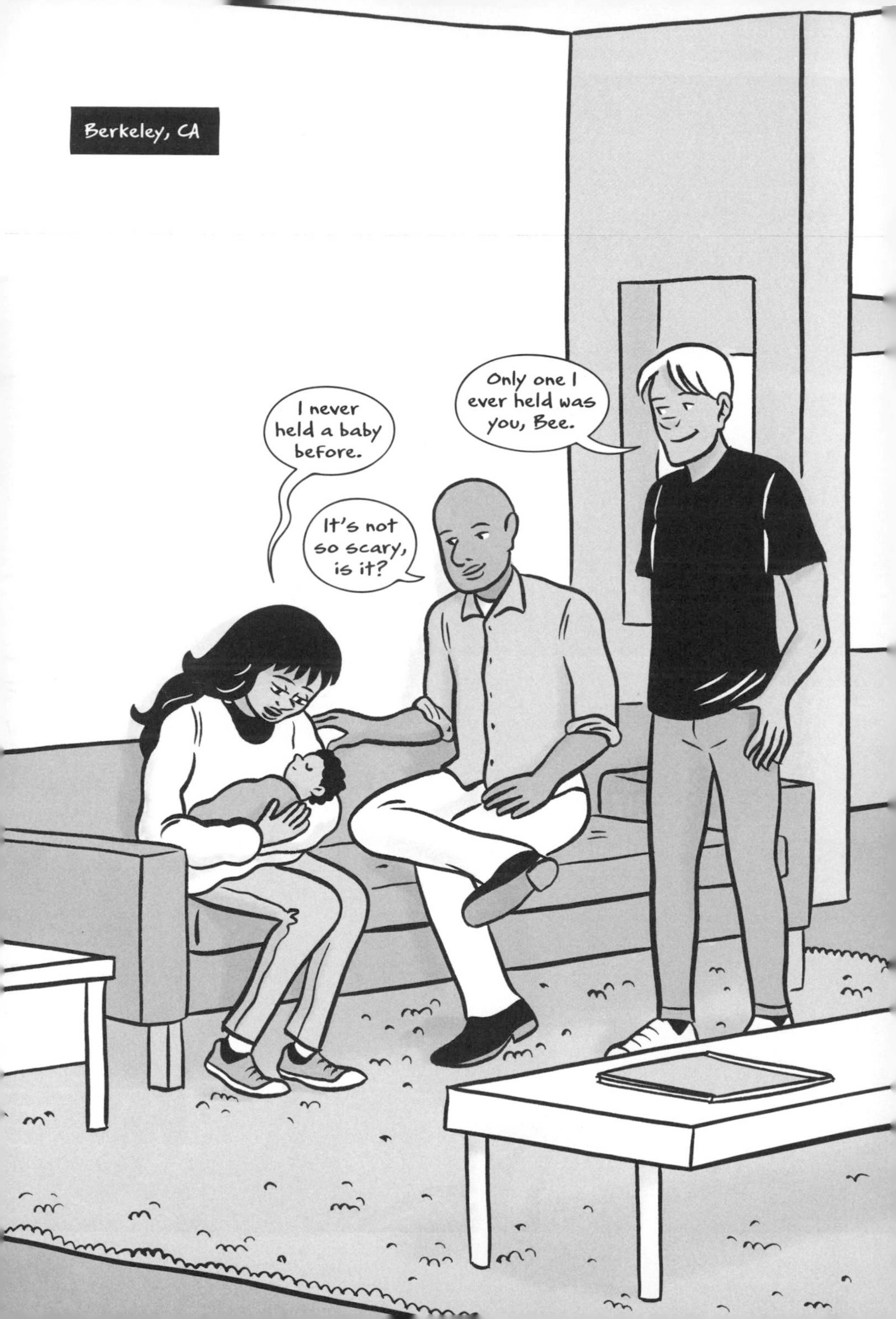

Berkeley, CA
I never held a baby before.
It's not so scary, is it?
Only one I ever held was you, Bee.

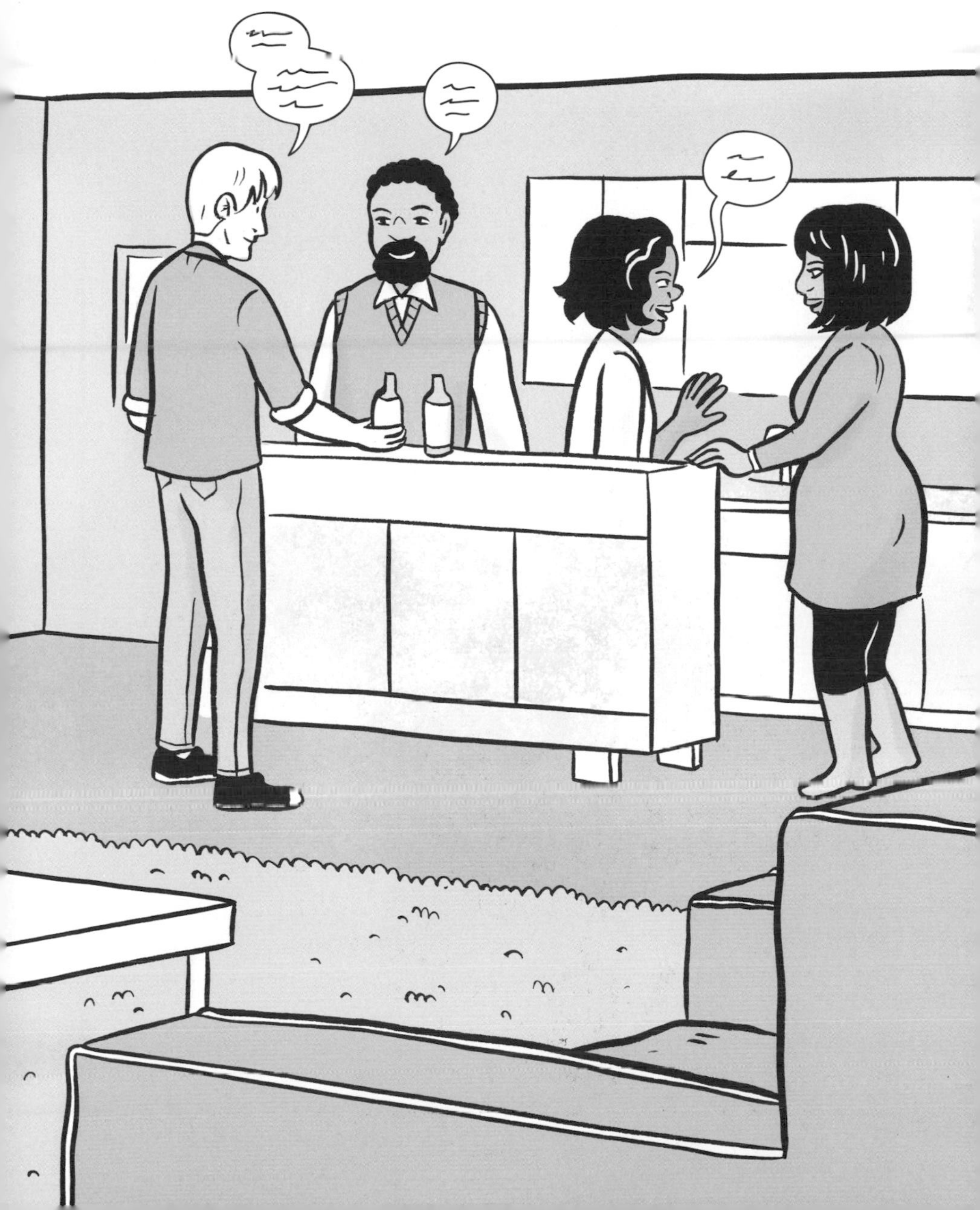

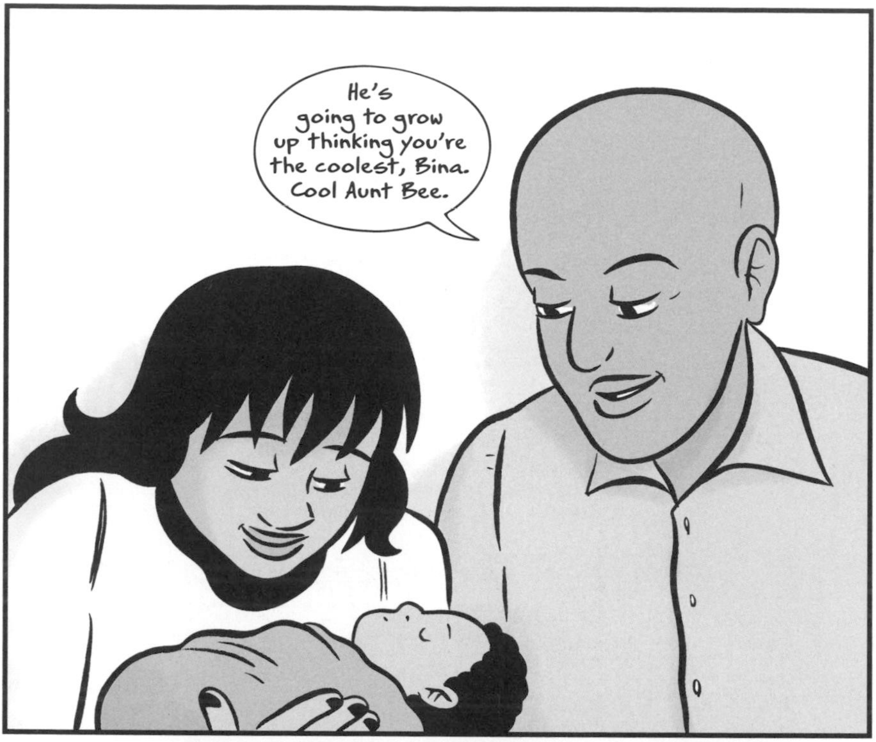
He's going to grow up thinking you're the coolest, Bina. Cool Aunt Bee.

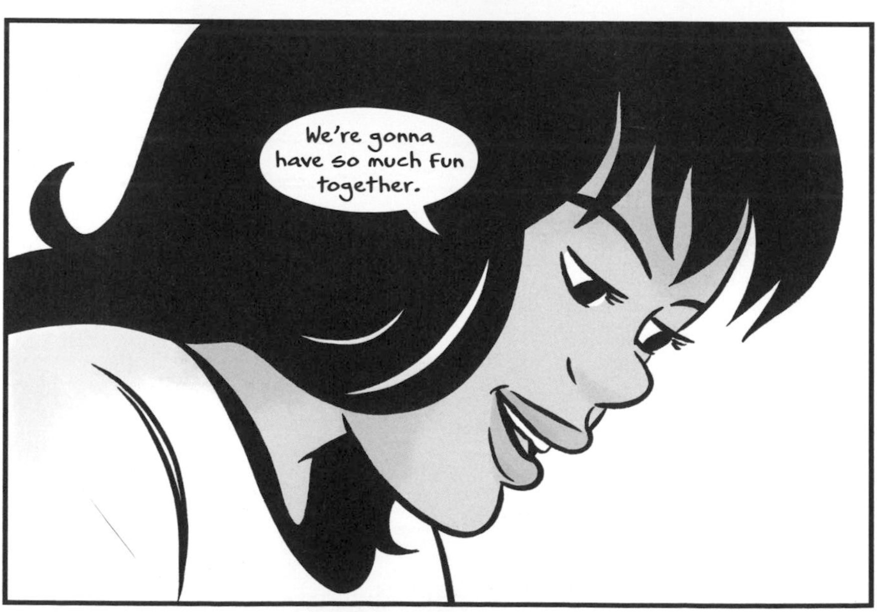
We're gonna have so much fun together.

CheapShuttle
Bina Loc

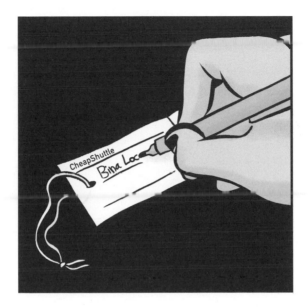

Week Seven

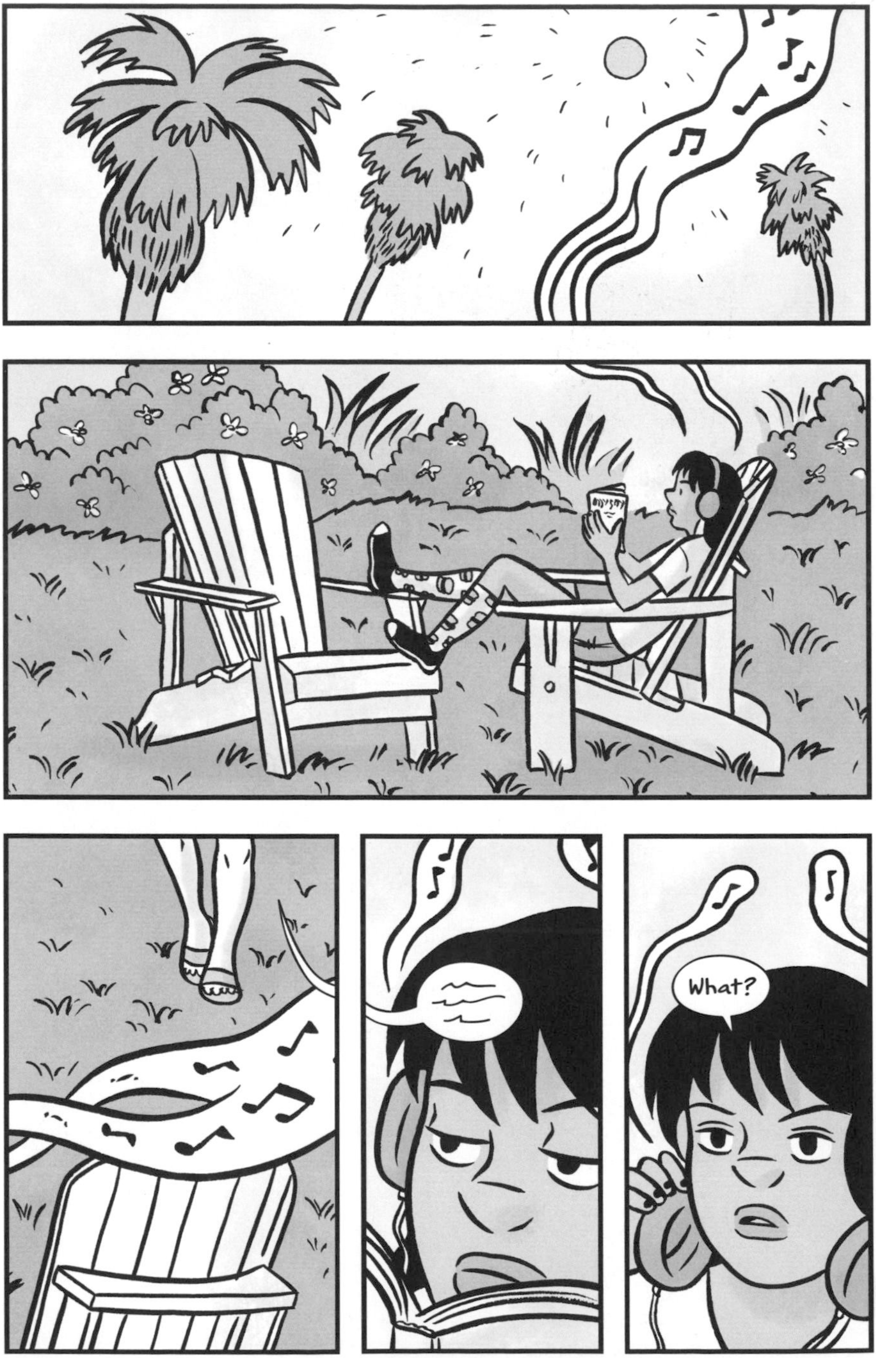
What?

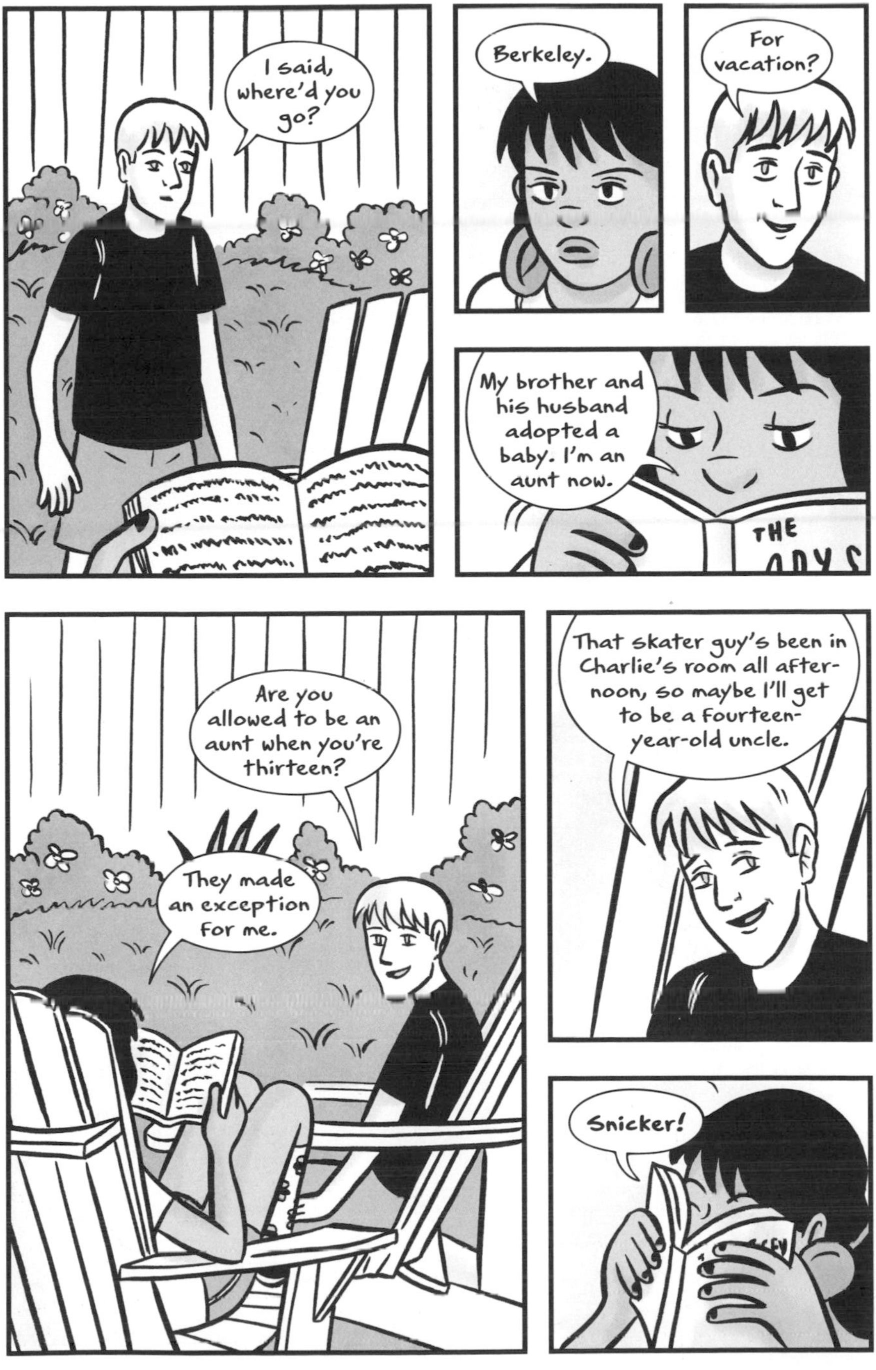
I said, where'd you go?
Berkeley.
For vacation?
My brother and his husband adopted a baby. I'm an aunt now.
THE
Are you allowed to be an aunt when you're thirteen?
They made an exception for me.
That skater guy's been in Charlie's room all afternoon, so maybe I'll get to be a fourteen-year-old uncle.
Snicker!

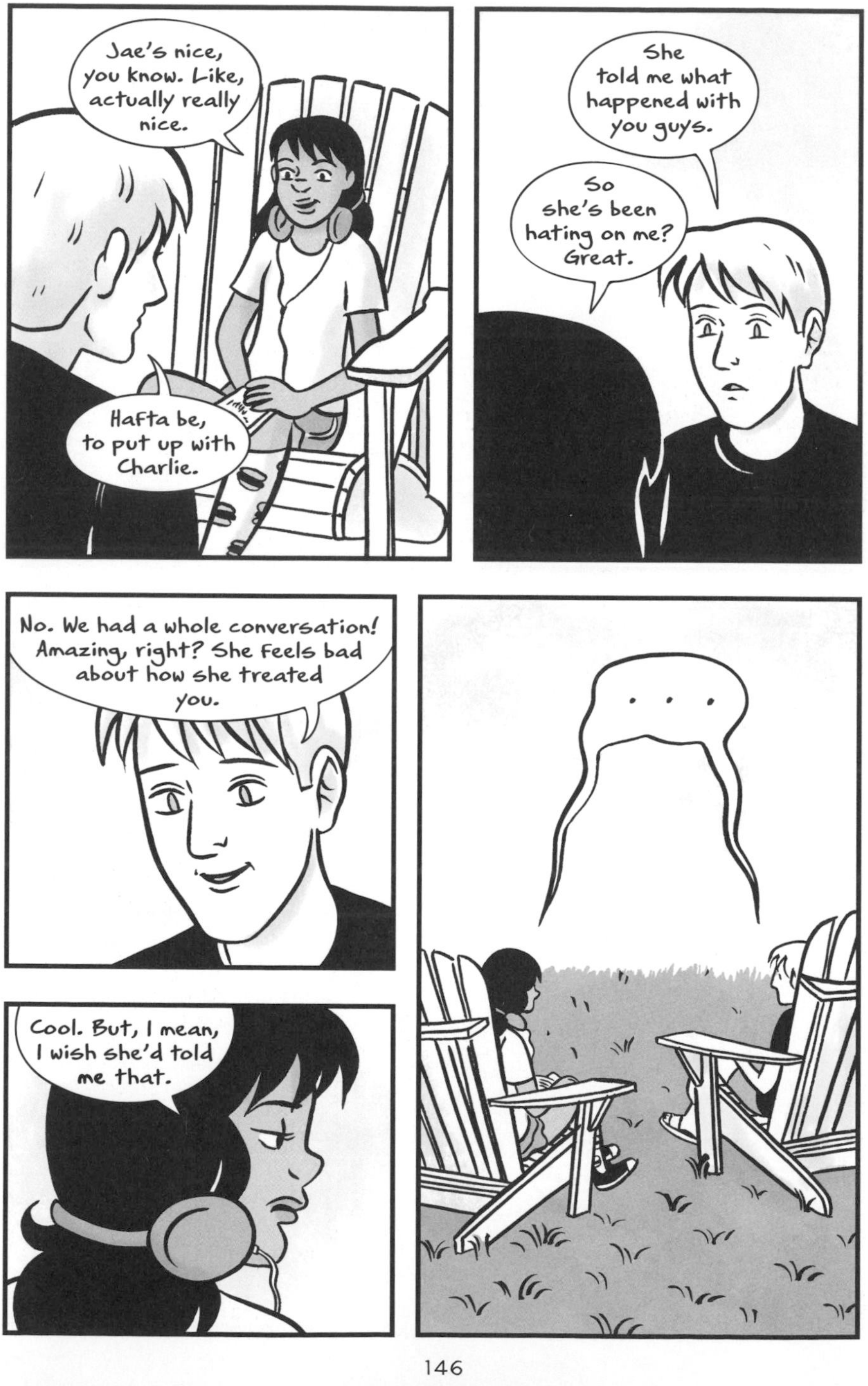
Jae's nice, you know. Like, actually really nice.
Hafta be, to put up with Charlie.
She told me what happened with you guys.
So she's been hating on me? Great.
No. We had a whole conversation! Amazing, right? She feels bad about how she treated you.
Cool. But, I mean, I wish she'd told me that.
. . .

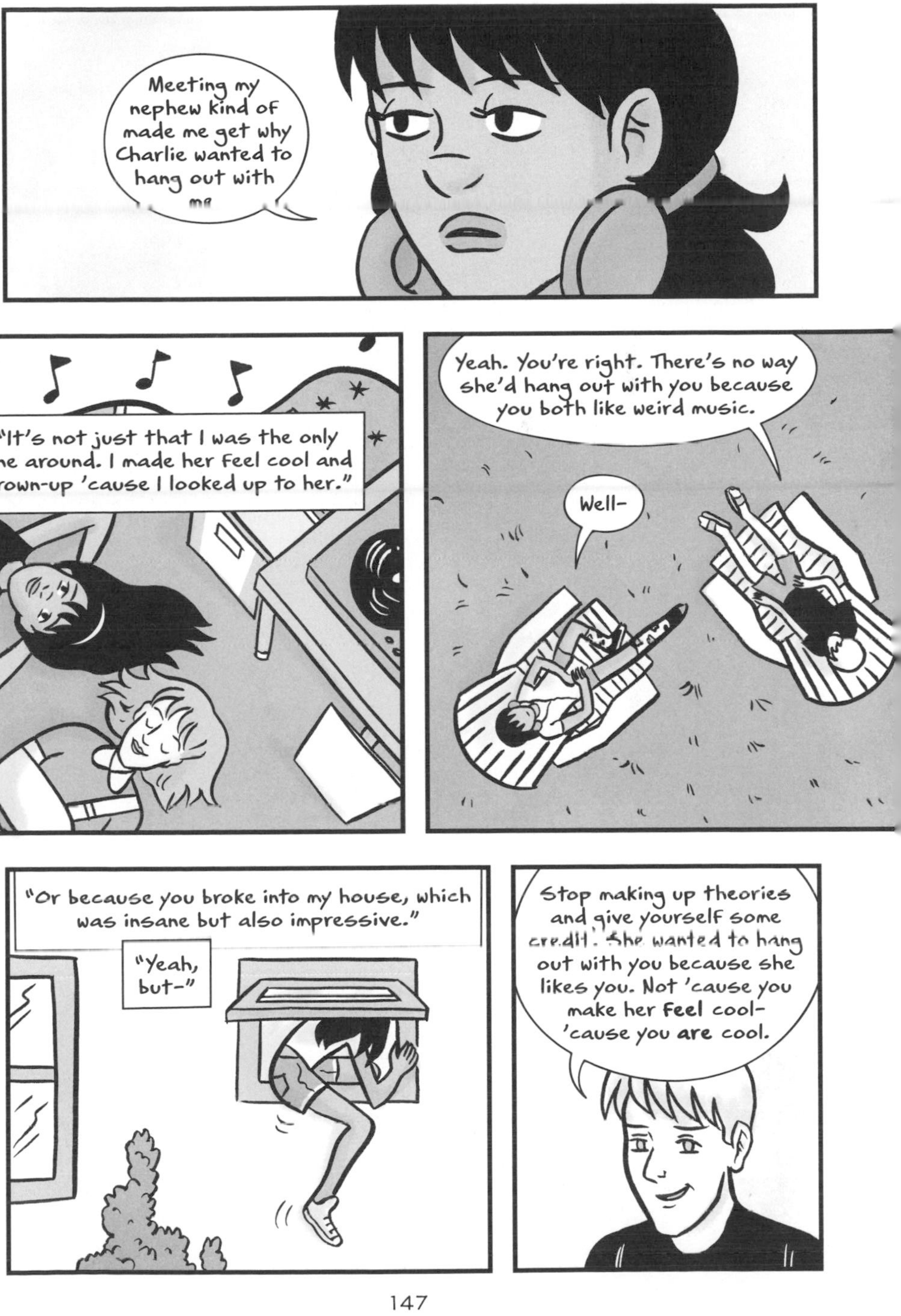
Meeting my nephew kind of made me get why Charlie wanted to hang out with me
"It's not just that I was the only one around. I made her feel cool and grown-up 'cause I looked up to her."
Yeah. You're right. There's no way she'd hang out with you because you both like weird music.
Well-
"Or because you broke into my house, which was insane but also impressive."
"Yeah, but-"
Stop making up theories and give yourself some credit. She wanted to hang out with you because she likes you. Not 'cause you make her feel cool- 'cause you are cool.

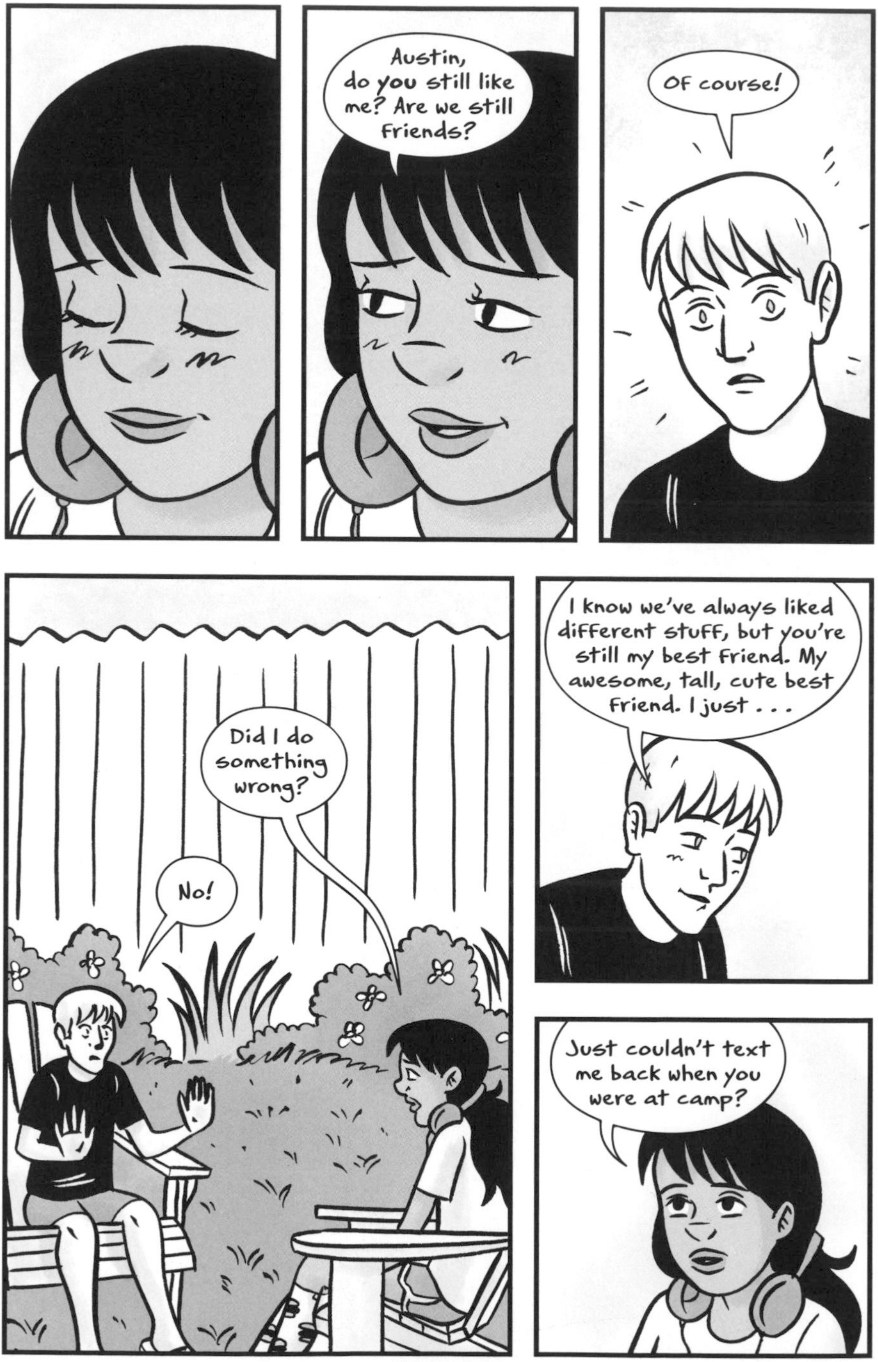
Austin, do you still like me? Are we still friends?
Of course!
Did I do something wrong?
No!
I know we've always liked different stuff, but you're still my best friend. My awesome, tall, cute best friend. I just . . .
Just couldn't text me back when you were at camp?

I don't know any other guys with girl best friends.
Girlfriends—yeah. There was this one guy at camp who texted his girlfriend every night, and the whole team made fun of him.
Grant said he was whipped.
I didn't want them saying that about me.

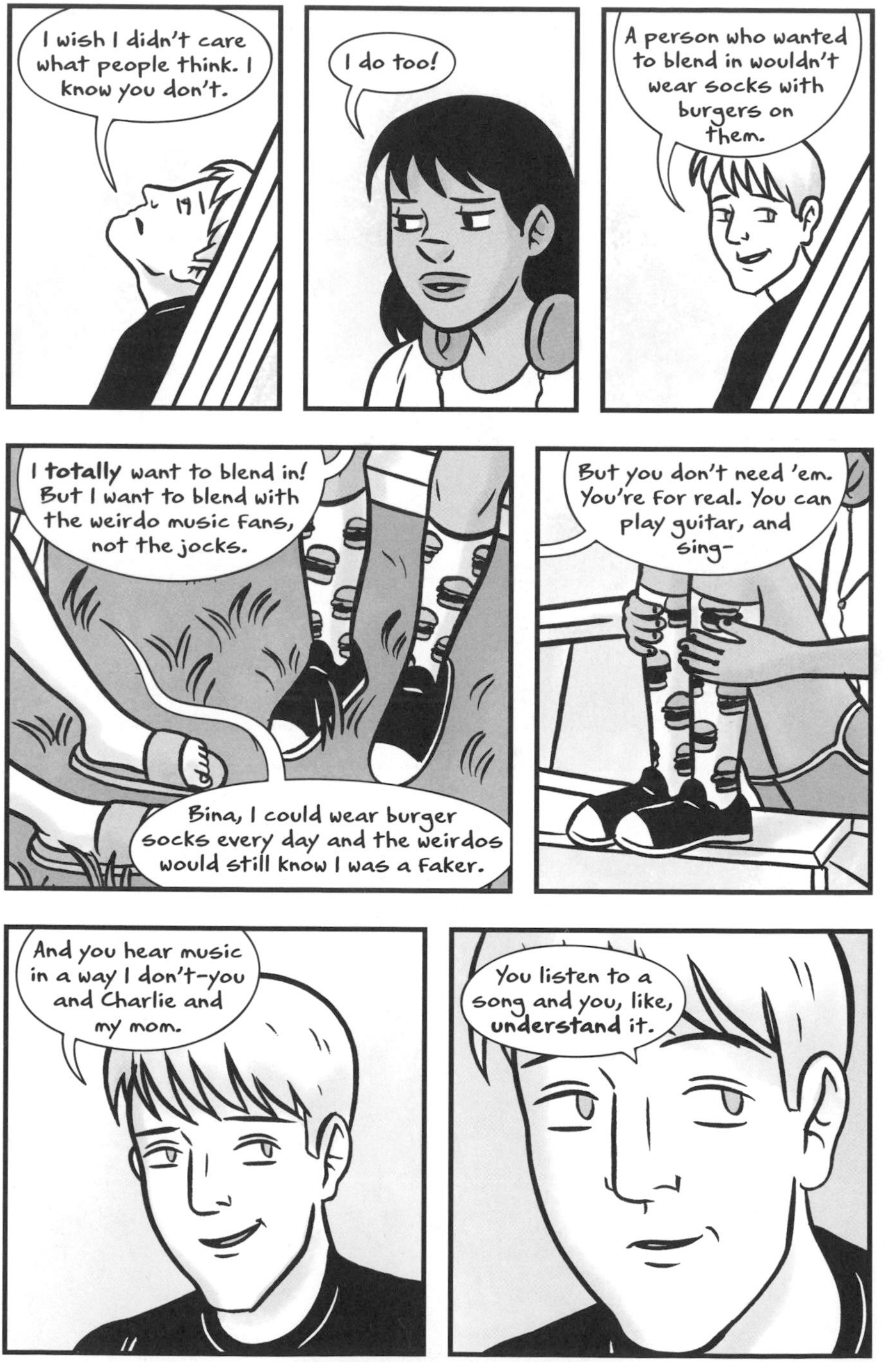
I wish I didn't care what people think. I know you don't.
I do too!
A person who wanted to blend in wouldn't wear socks with burgers on them.
I **totally** want to blend in! But I want to blend with the weirdo music fans, not the jocks.
Bina, I could wear burger socks every day and the weirdos would still know I was a faker.
But you don't need 'em. You're for real. You can play guitar, and sing-
And you hear music in a way I don't-you and Charlie and my mom.
You listen to a song and you, like, **understand** it.

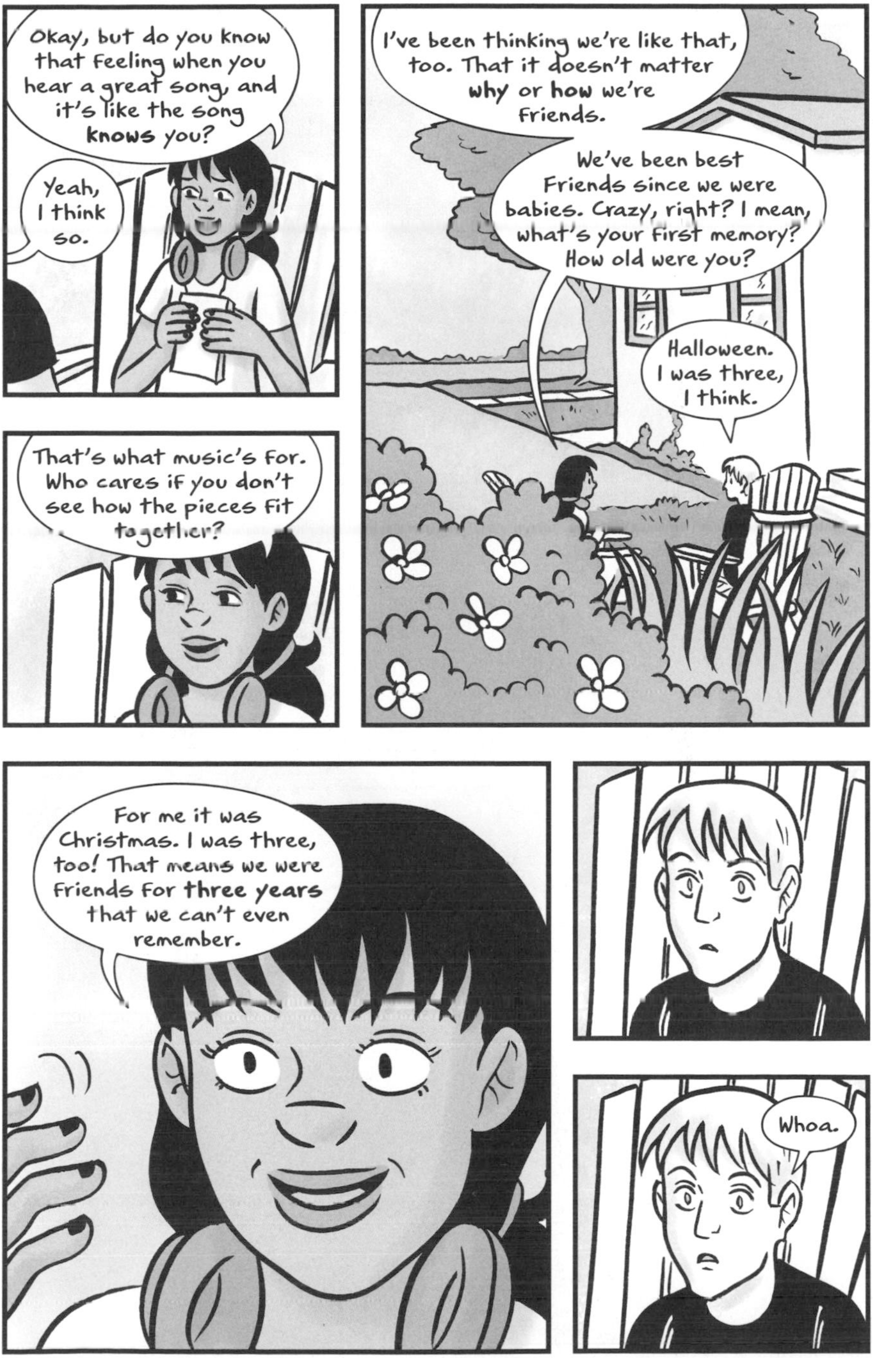

Okay, but do you know that feeling when you hear a great song, and it's like the song **knows** you?
Yeah, I think so.
I've been thinking we're like that, too. That it doesn't matter **why** or **how** we're friends.
We've been best friends since we were babies. Crazy, right? I mean, what's your first memory? How old were you?
Halloween. I was three, I think.
That's what music's for. Who cares if you don't see how the pieces fit together?
For me it was Christmas. I was three, too! That means we were friends for **three years** that we can't even remember.
Whoa.

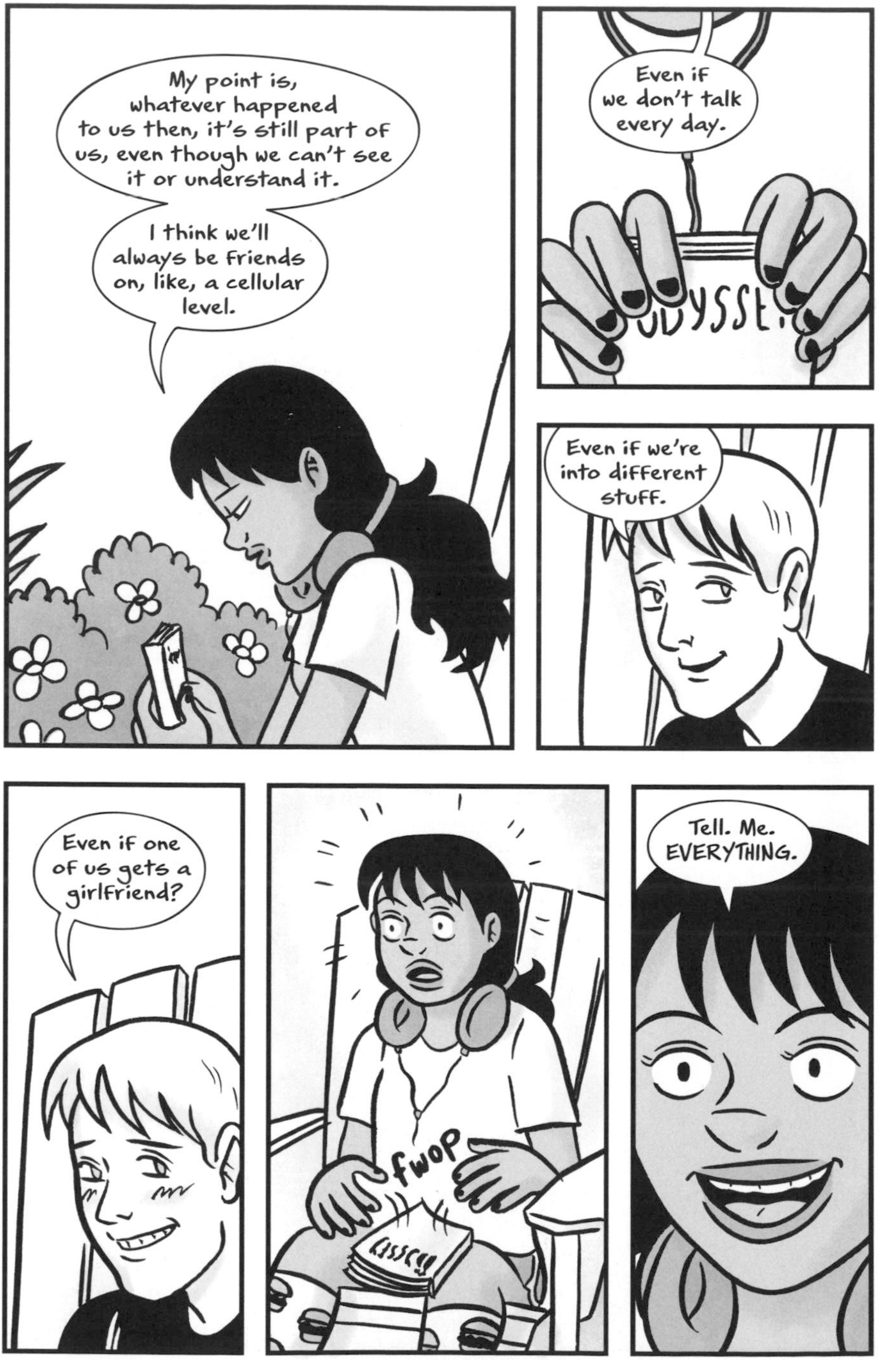
My point is, whatever happened to us then, it's still part of us, even though we can't see it or understand it.
I think we'll always be friends on, like, a cellular level.
Even if we don't talk every day.
ODYSSEY
Even if we're into different stuff.
Even if one of us gets a girlfriend?
fwop
Tell. Me. EVERYTHING.

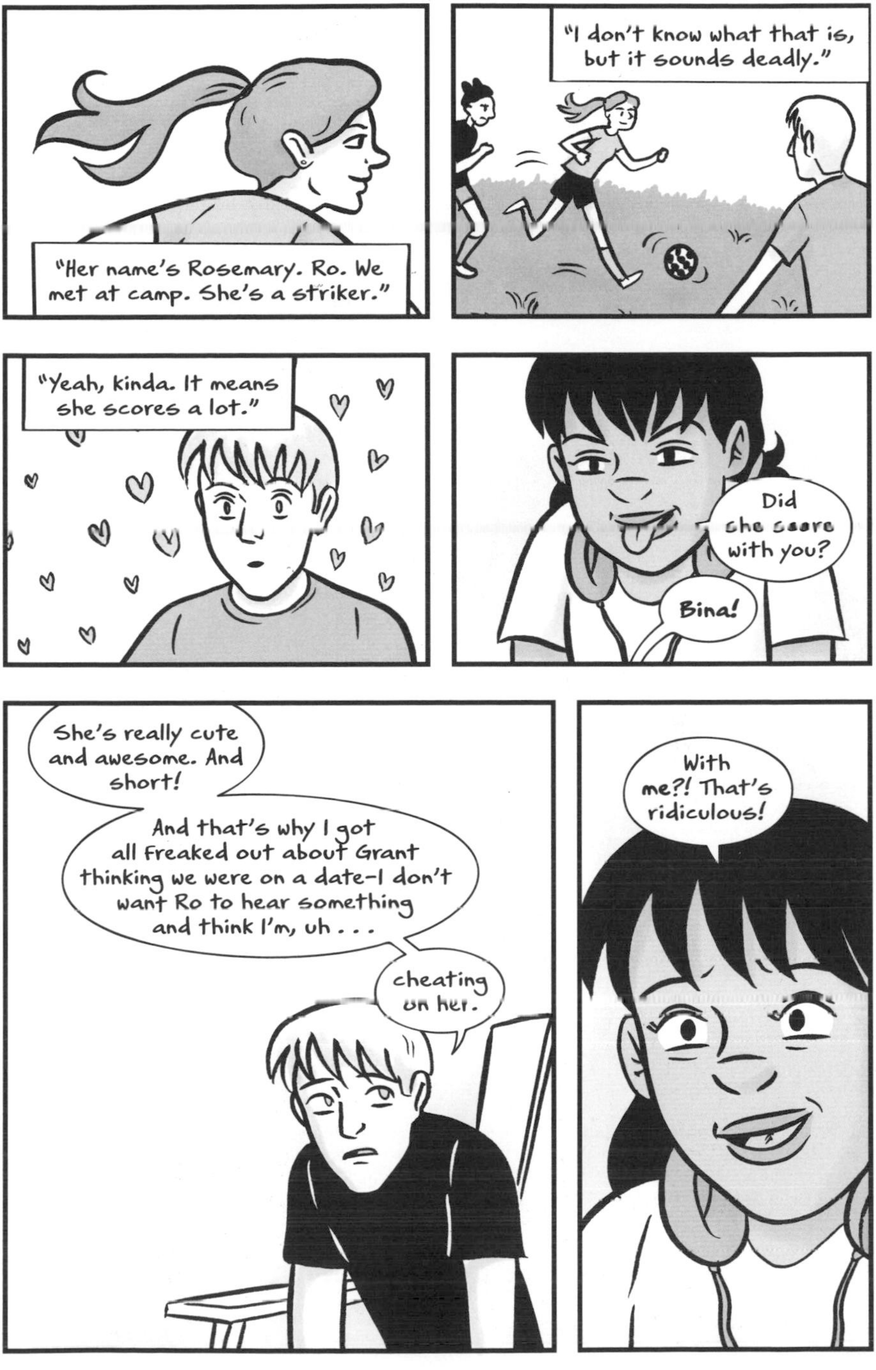
"Her name's Rosemary. Ro. We met at camp. She's a striker."
"I don't know what that is, but it sounds deadly."
"Yeah, kinda. It means she scores a lot."
Did she score with you?
Bina!
She's really cute and awesome. And short!
And that's why I got all freaked out about Grant thinking we were on a date-I don't want Ro to hear something and think I'm, uh . . .
cheating on her.
With me?! That's ridiculous!

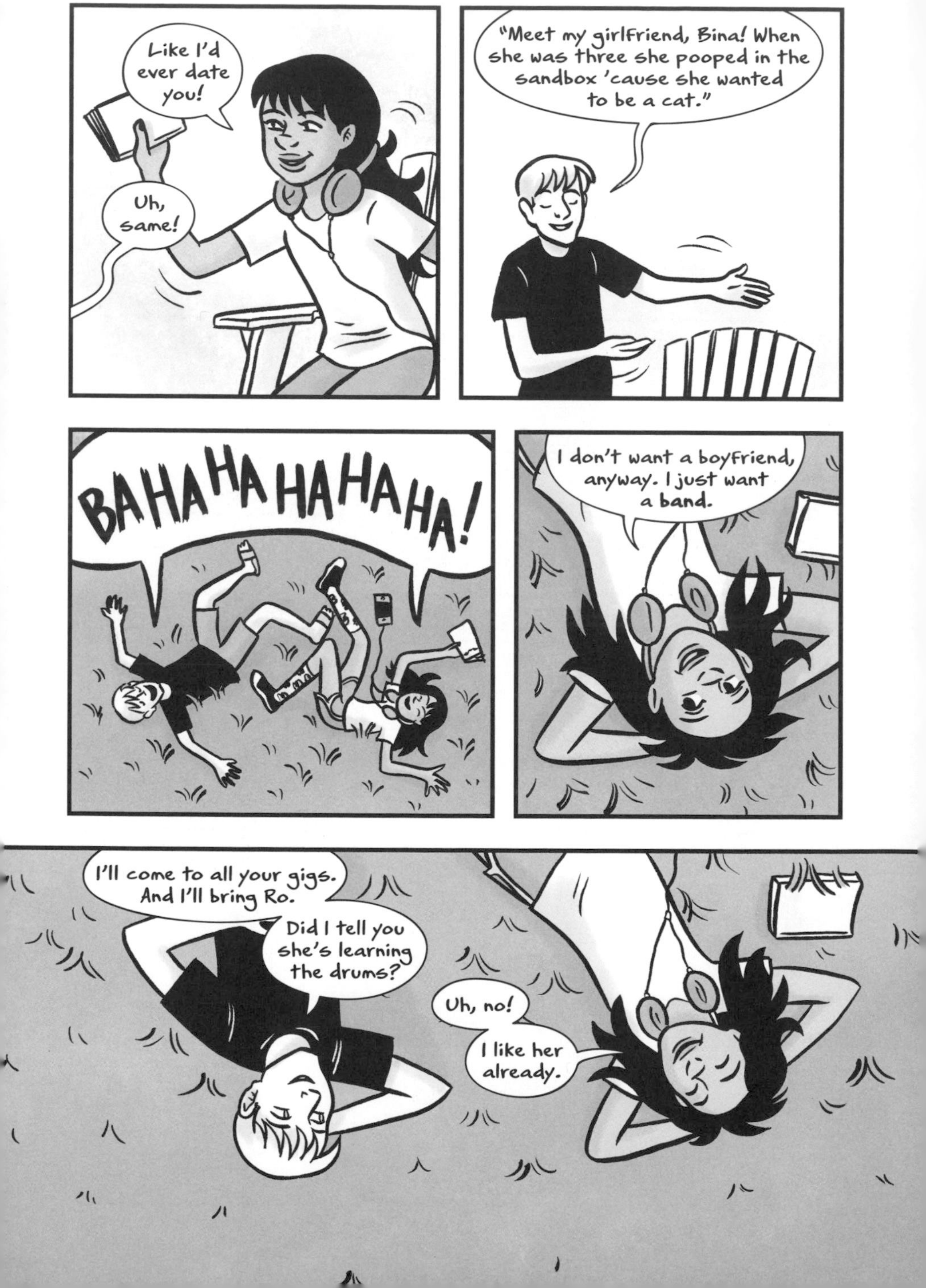
Like I'd ever date you!
Uh, same!
"Meet my girlfriend, Bina! When she was three she pooped in the sandbox 'cause she wanted to be a cat."
BAHAHAHAHAHAHA!
I don't want a boyfriend, anyway. I just want a band.
I'll come to all your gigs. And I'll bring Ro.
Did I tell you she's learning the drums?
Uh, no!
I like her already.

Week Eight

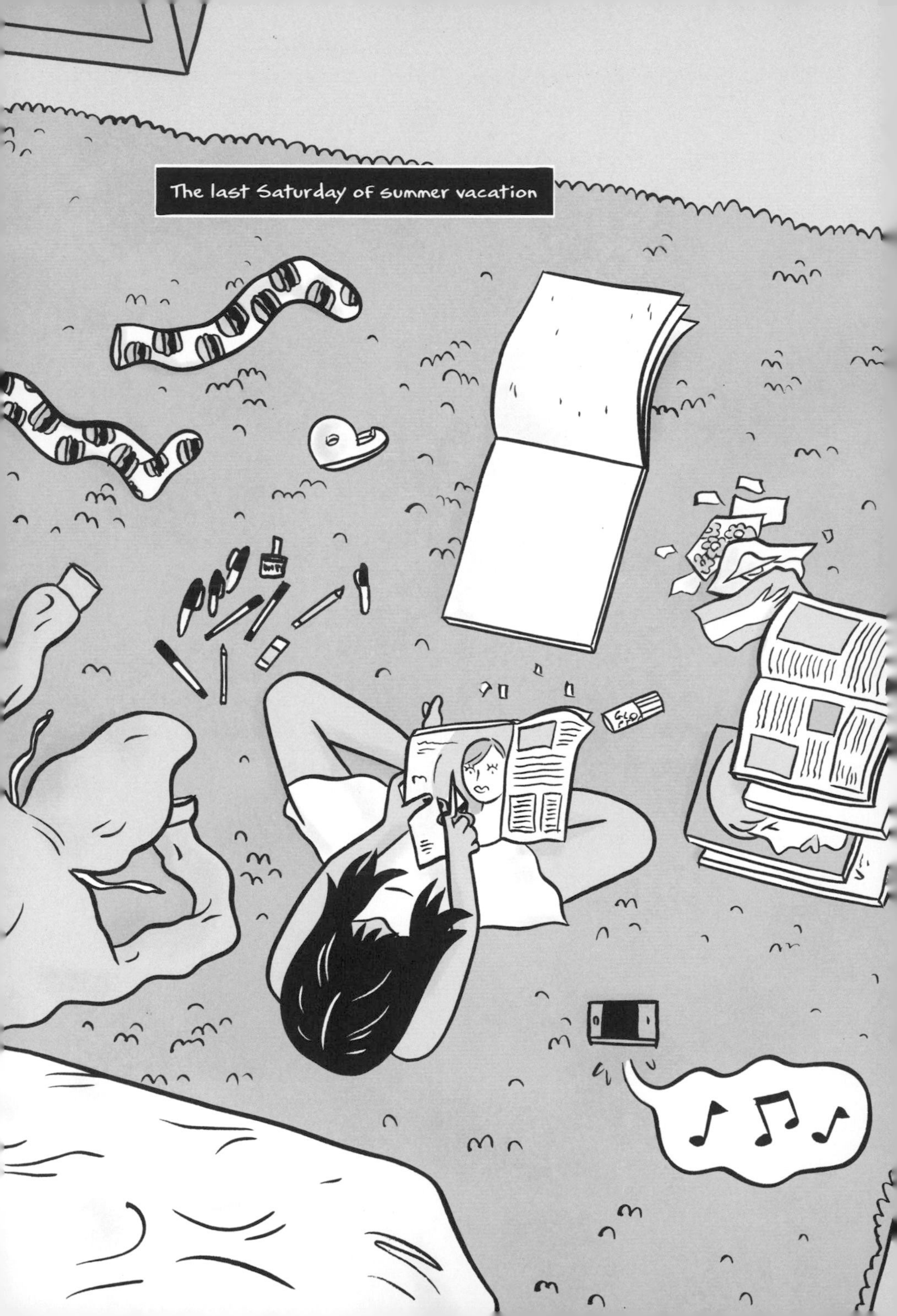
The last Saturday of summer vacation

HeY! YOU!
oin m
y

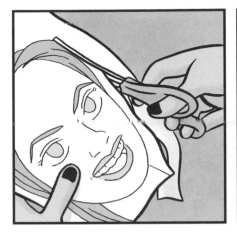

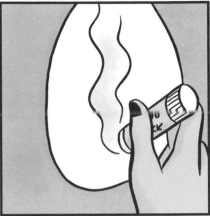

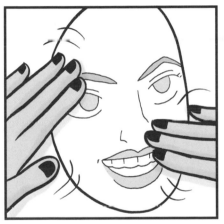

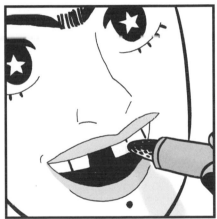

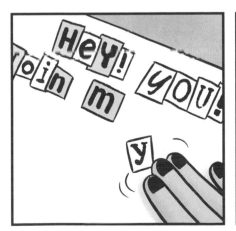

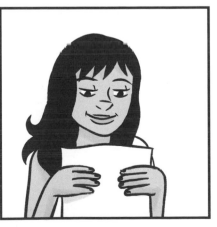

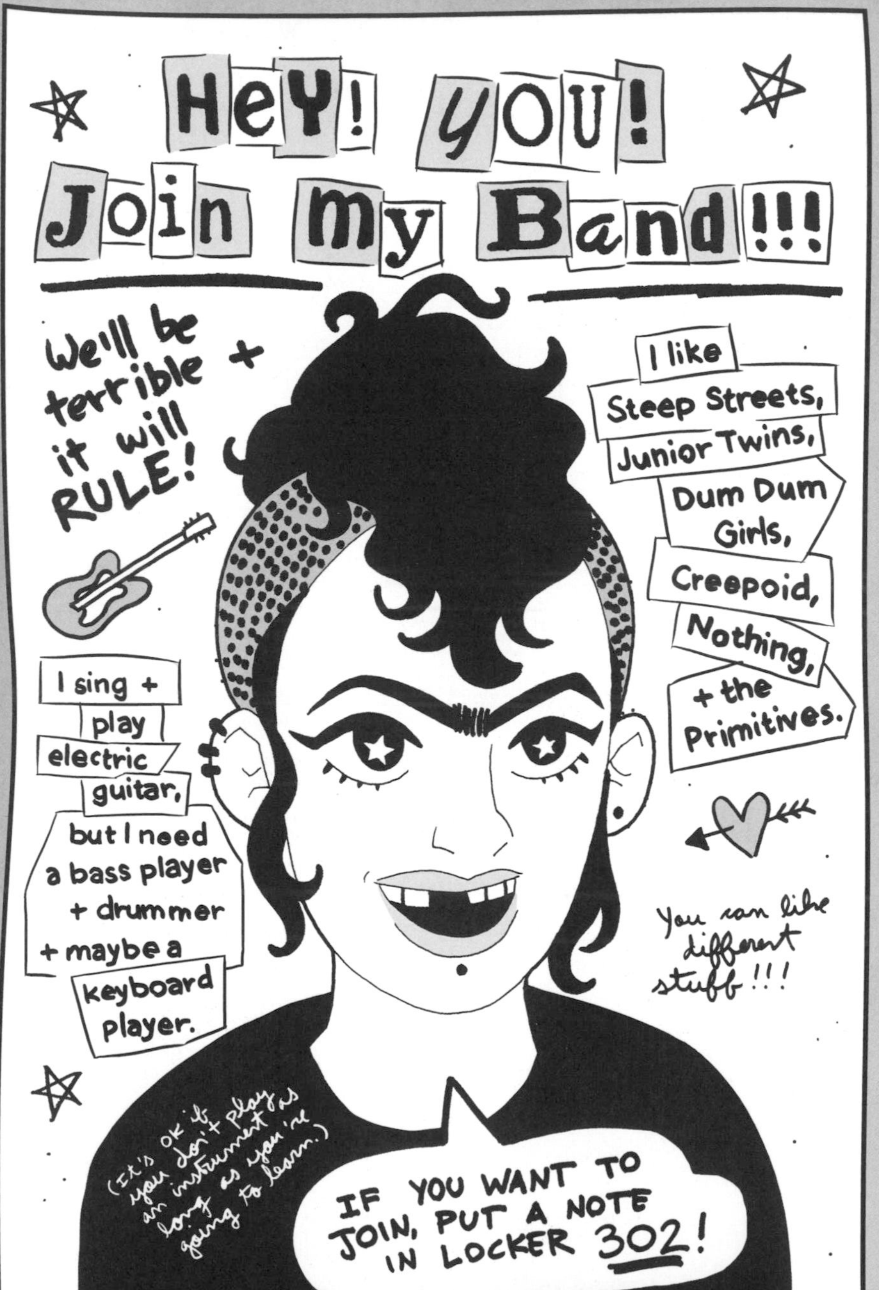
HEY! YOU! Join My Band!!!
We'll be terrible + it will RULE!
I like Steep Streets, Junior Twins, Dum Dum Girls, Creepoid, Nothing, + the Primitives.
I sing + play electric guitar, but I need a bass player + drummer + maybe a keyboard player.
You can like different stuff!!!
(It's OK if you don't play an instrument as long as you're going to learn.)
IF YOU WANT TO JOIN, PUT A NOTE IN LOCKER 302!

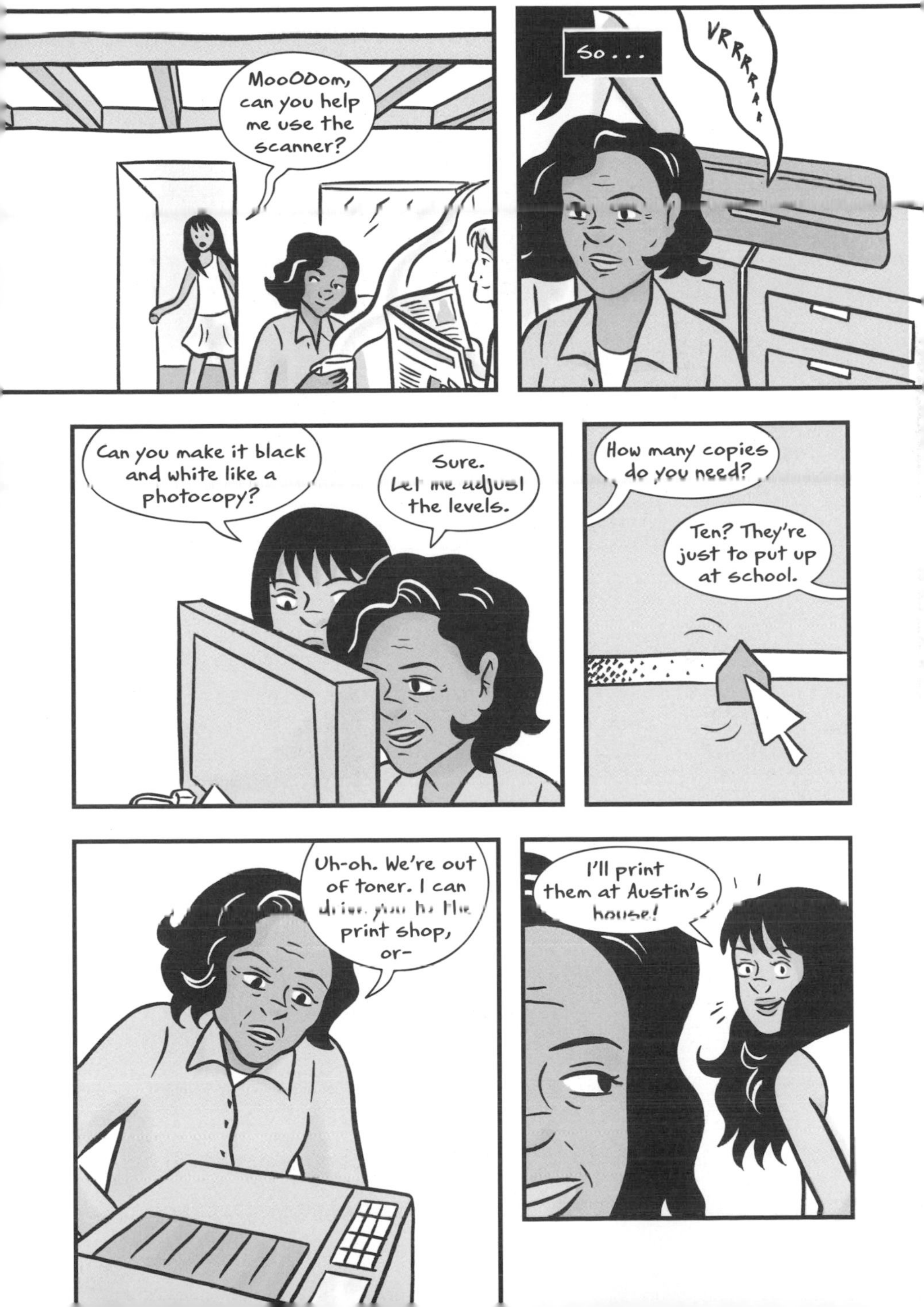
MooOOom, can you help me use the scanner?
So . . .
VRRRRRRR
Can you make it black and white like a photocopy?
Sure. Let me adjust the levels.
How many copies do you need?
Ten? They're just to put up at school.
Uh-oh. We're out of toner. I can
print shop, or–
I'll print them at Austin's house!

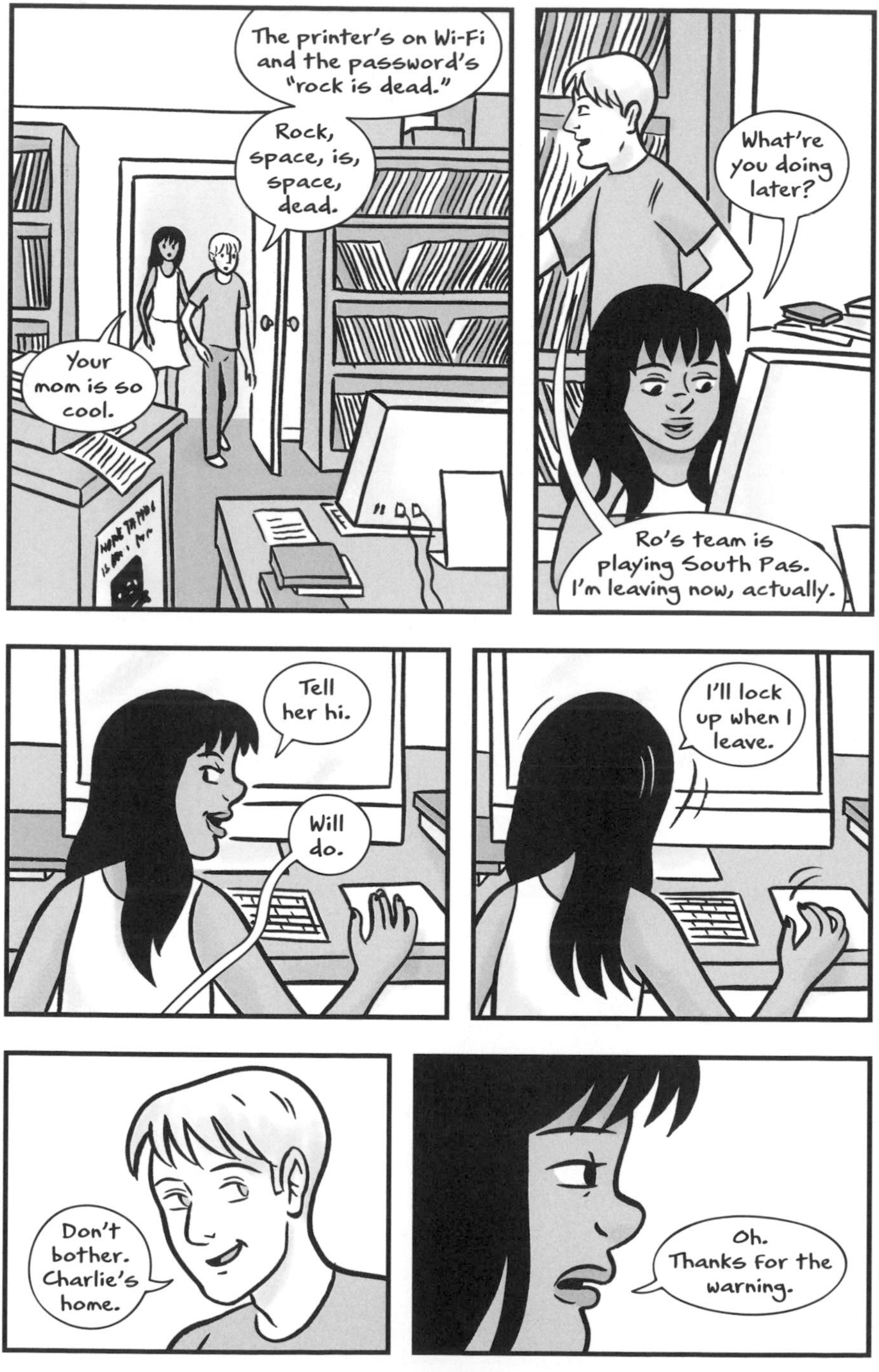
The printer's on Wi-Fi and the password's "rock is dead."
Rock, space, is, space, dead.
Your mom is so cool.
What're you doing later?
Ro's team is playing South Pas. I'm leaving now, actually.
Tell her hi.
Will do.
I'll lock up when I leave.
Don't bother. Charlie's home.
Oh. Thanks for the warning.

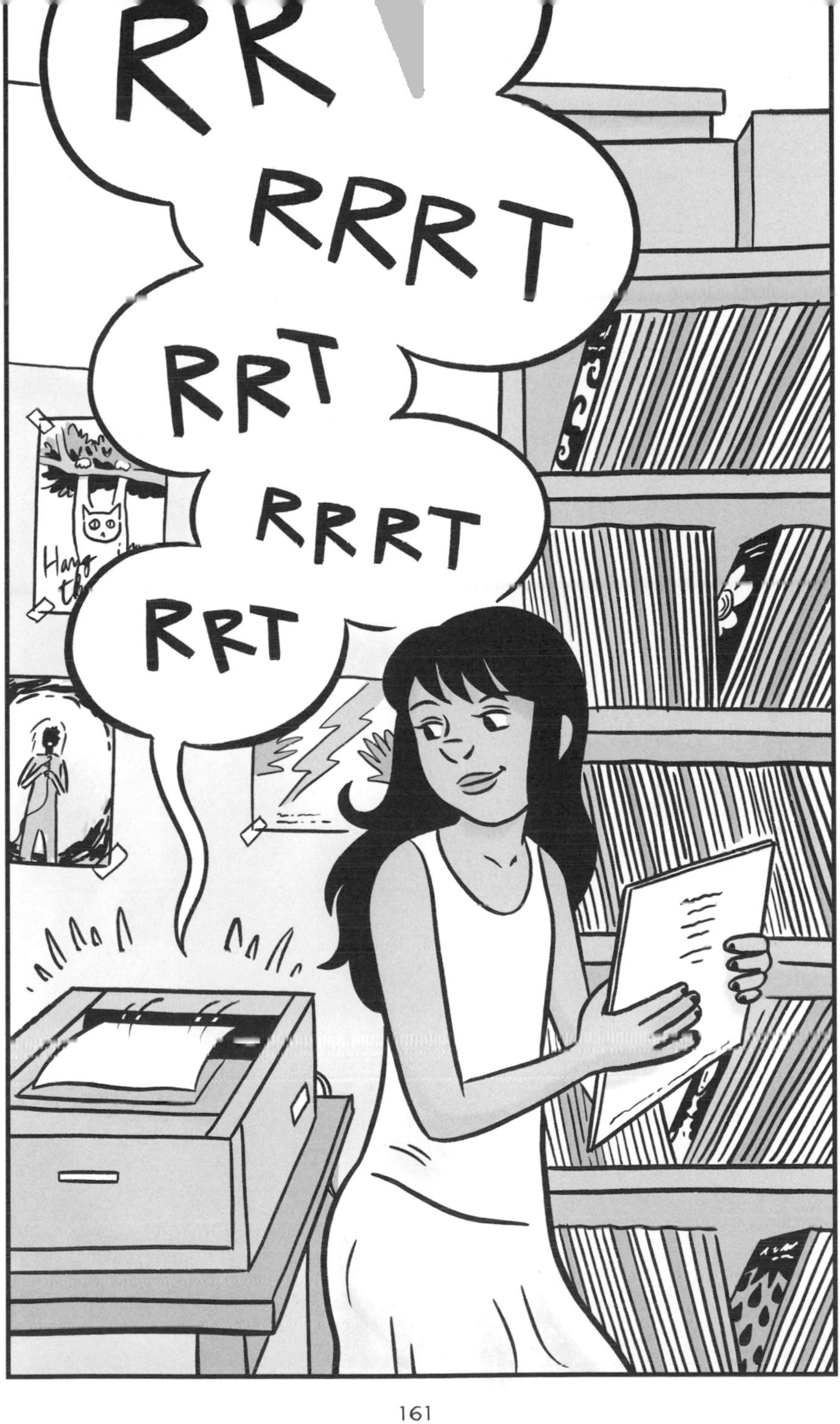
RK
RRRT
RRT
RRRT
RRT

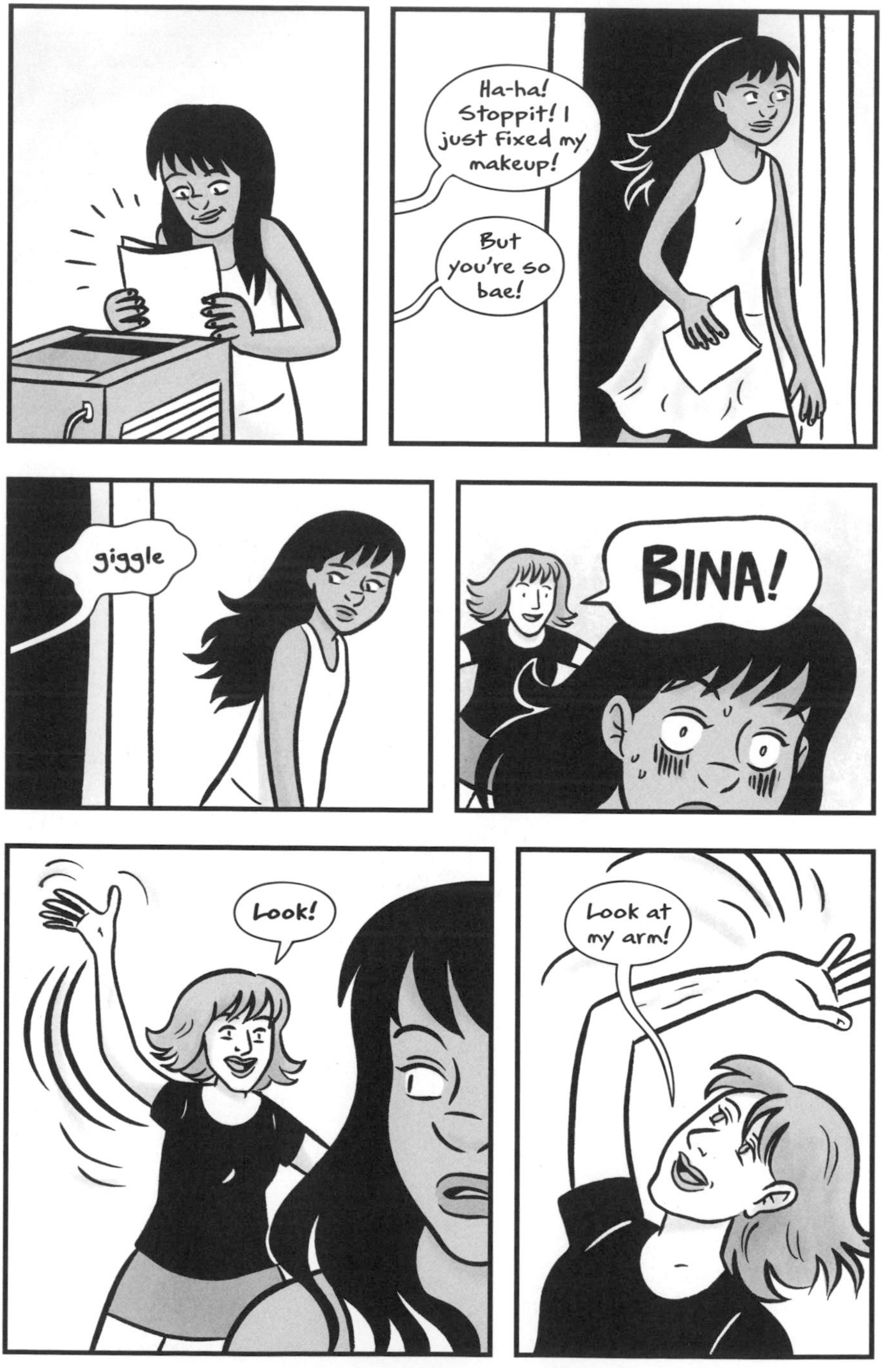
Ha-ha! Stoppit! I just fixed my makeup!
But you're so bae!
giggle
BINA!
Look!
Look at my arm!

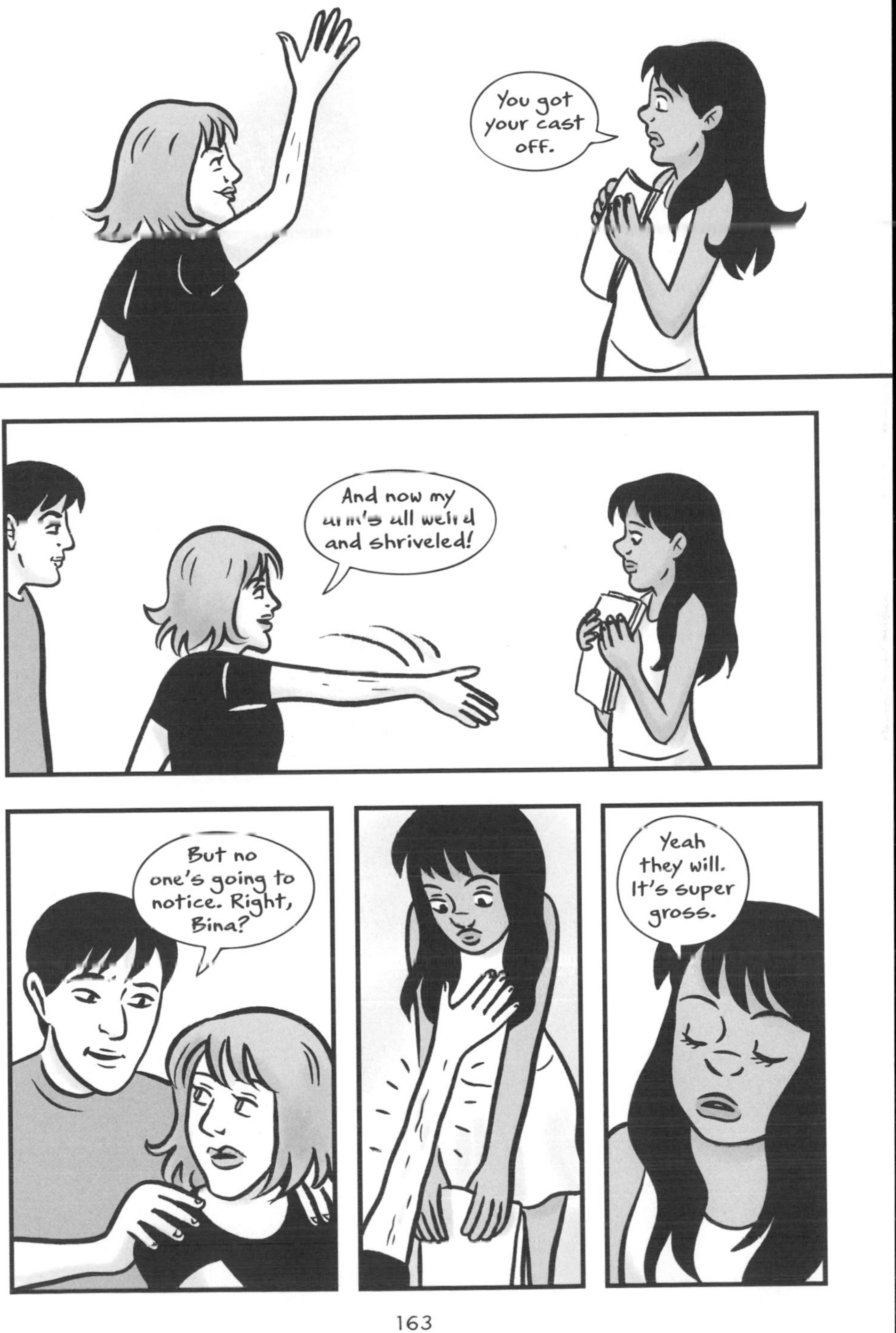
You got your cast off.
And now my arm's all weird and shriveled!
But no one's going to notice. Right, Bina?
Yeah they will. It's super gross.

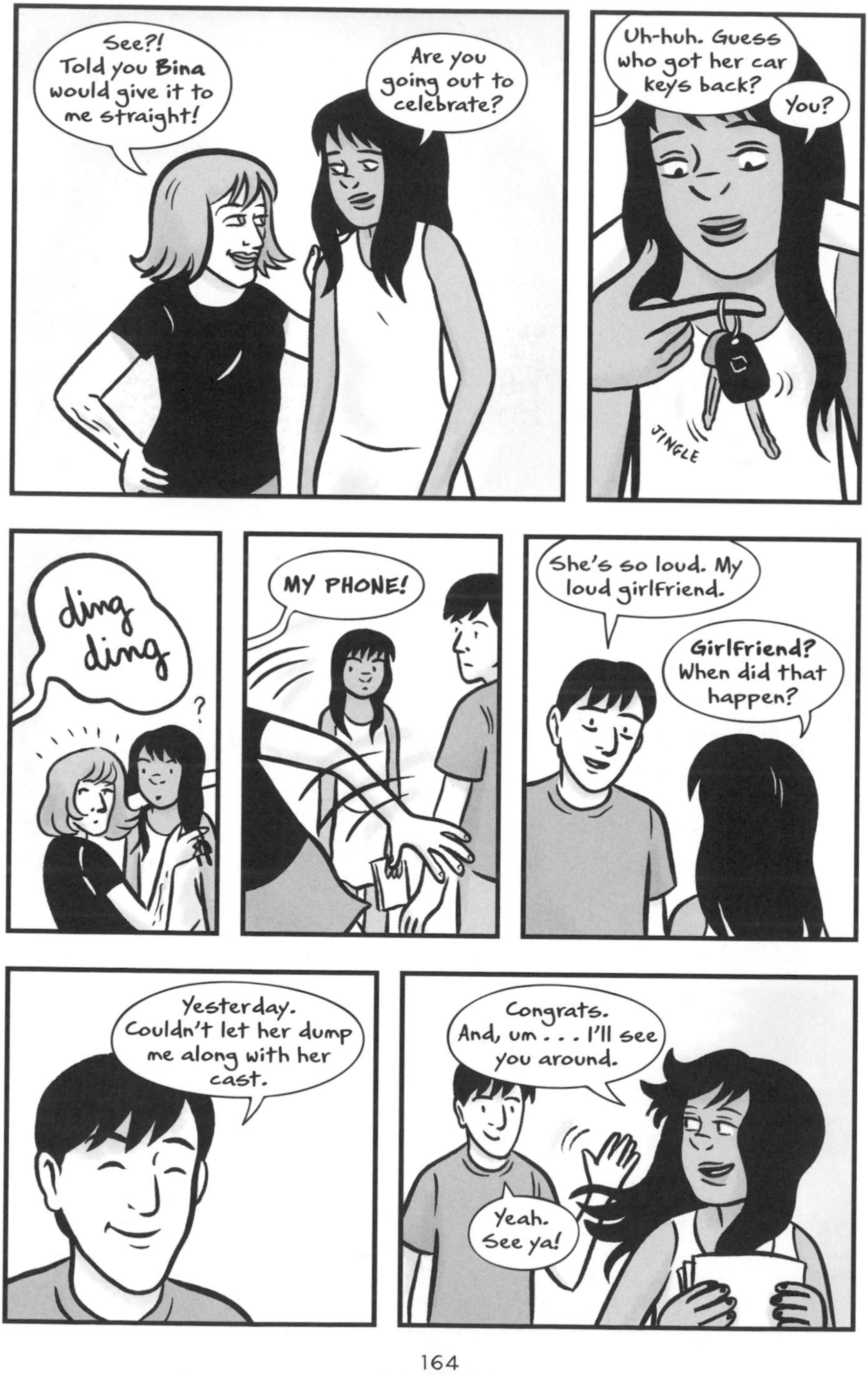
See?! Told you Bina would give it to me straight!
Are you going out to celebrate?
Uh-huh. Guess who got her car keys back?
You?
JINGLE
ding ding
?
MY PHONE!
She's so loud. My loud girlfriend.
Girlfriend? When did that happen?
Yesterday. Couldn't let her dump me along with her cast.
Congrats. And, um . . . I'll see you around.
Yeah. See ya!

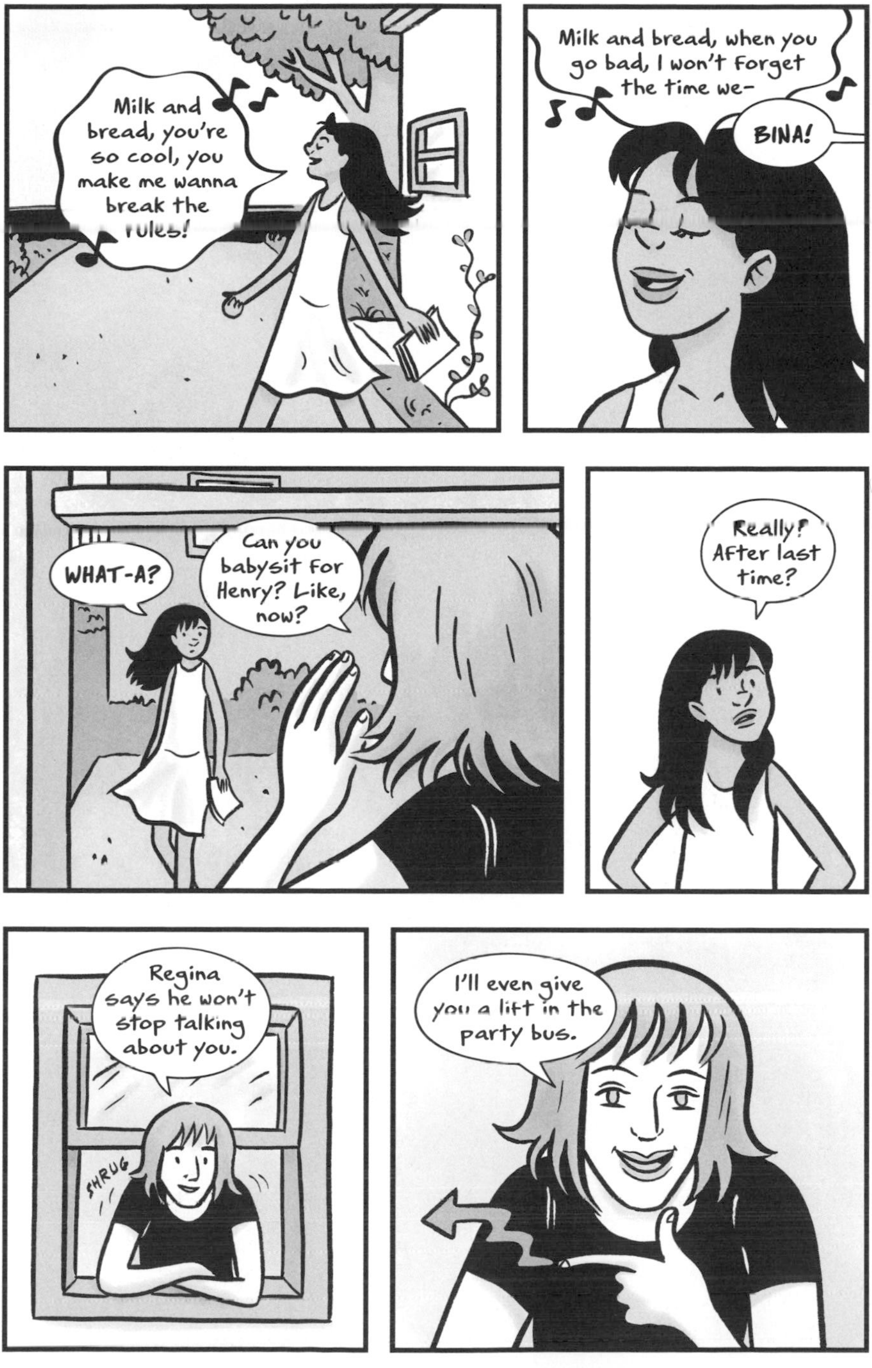
Milk and bread, you're so cool, you make me wanna break the rules!
Milk and bread, when you go bad, I won't forget the time we-
BINA!
WHAT-A?
Can you babysit for Henry? Like, now?
Really? After last time?
Regina says he won't stop talking about you.
SHRUG
I'll even give you a lift in the party bus.

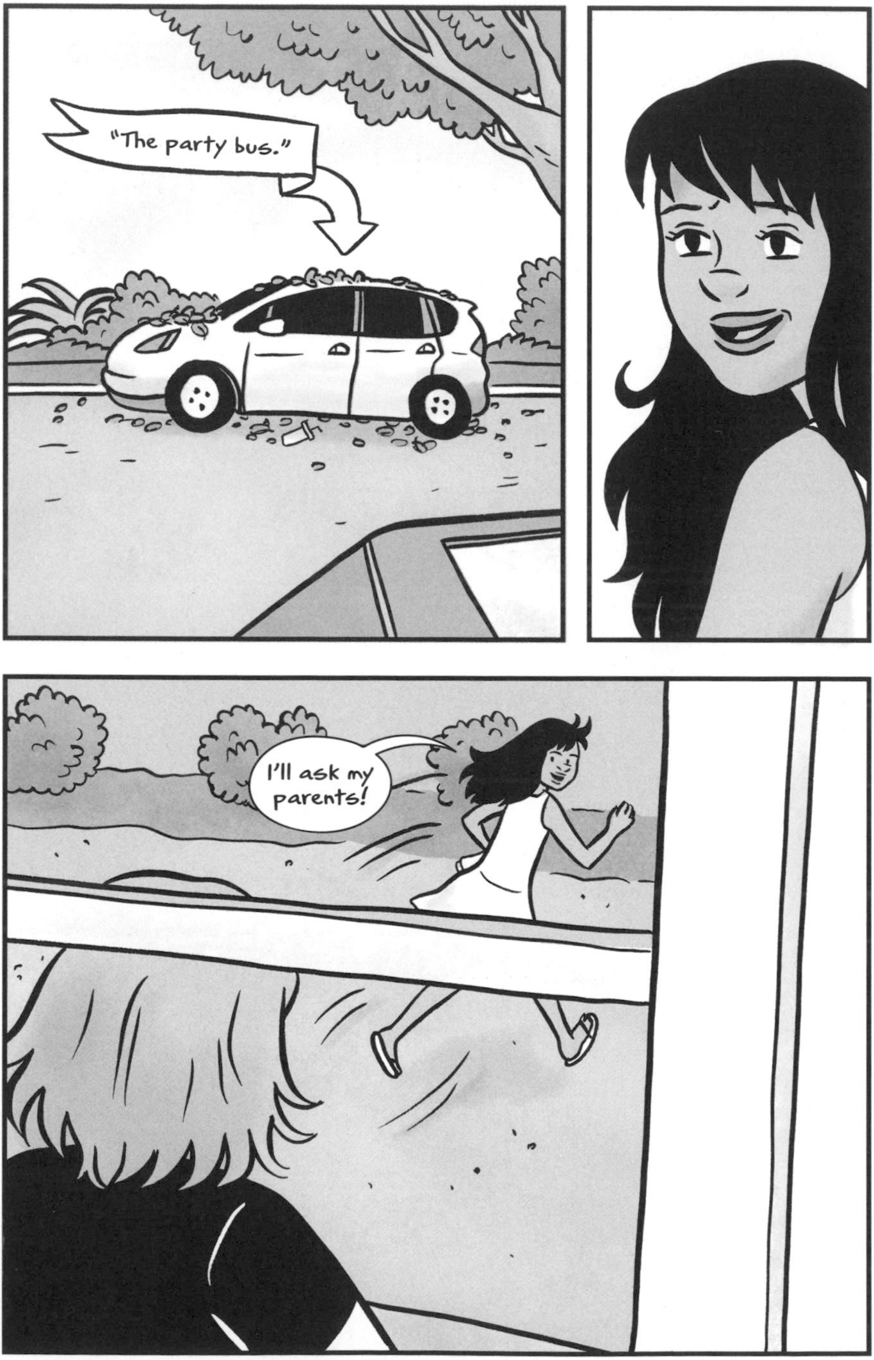
"The party bus."
I'll ask my parents!

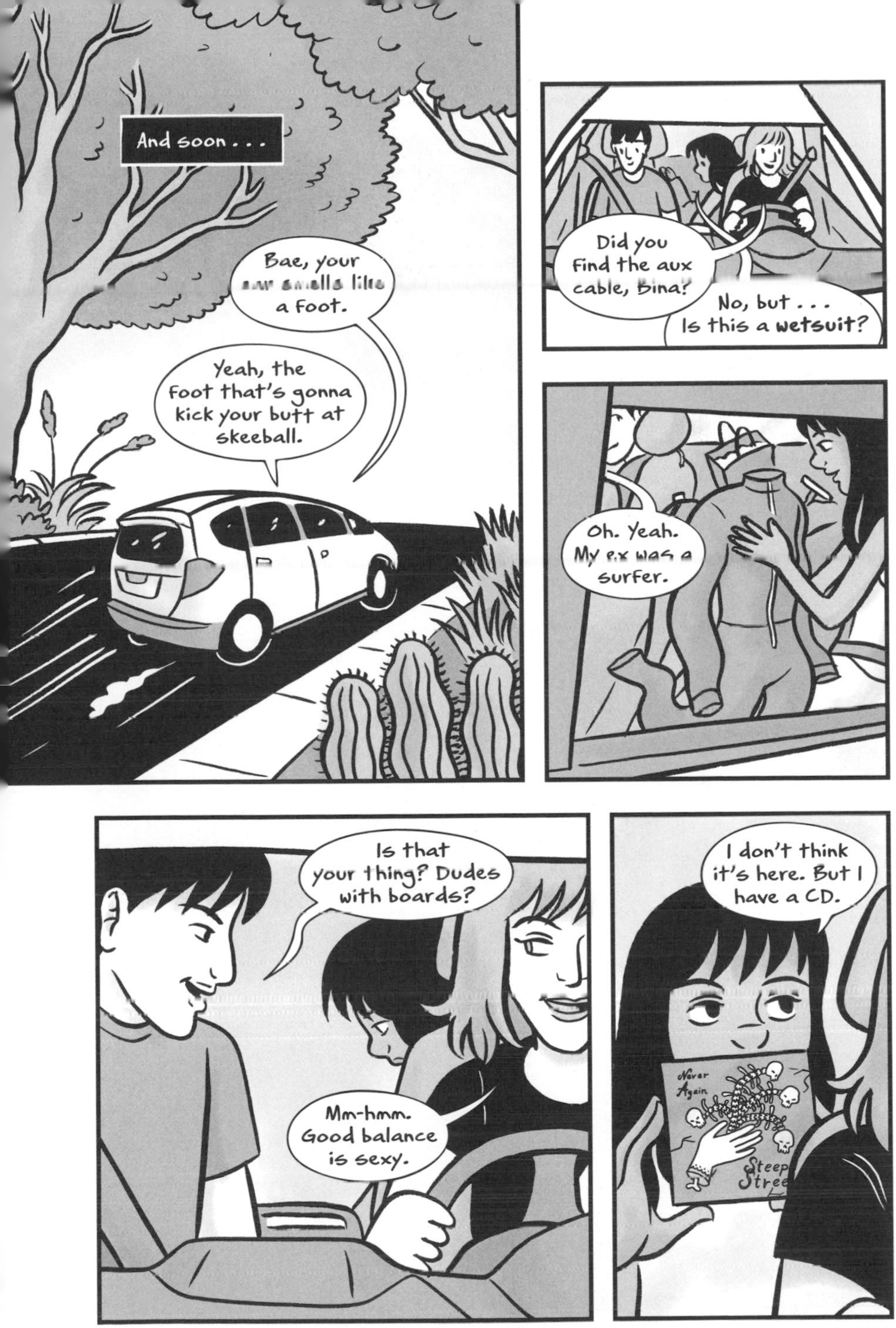
And soon . . .
Bae, your smells like a foot.
Yeah, the foot that's gonna kick your butt at skeeball.
Did you find the aux cable, Bina?
No, but . . . Is this a wetsuit?
Oh. Yeah. My ex was a surfer.
Is that your thing? Dudes with boards?
Mm-hmm. Good balance is sexy.
I don't think it's here. But I have a CD.
Never Again
Steep

A CD?! Is this the '90s?
It's Austin's. From your mom. I keep forgetting to give it back.
Who is it?
Steep Streets. I know they're a baby band, but you're gonna love them.
A one-way track, a bad-
You grab my hand, pull
And fly me where she'd never go
You're through with her
If you say so
If you say so
An empty flask, a Virgo moon
Her ghost is lighting up your
Unfinished busine
You're
Wow.
If yo
Right?
I wish I'd gone to that show.
So do I.
Next time.
Yeah. Next time.

Week One

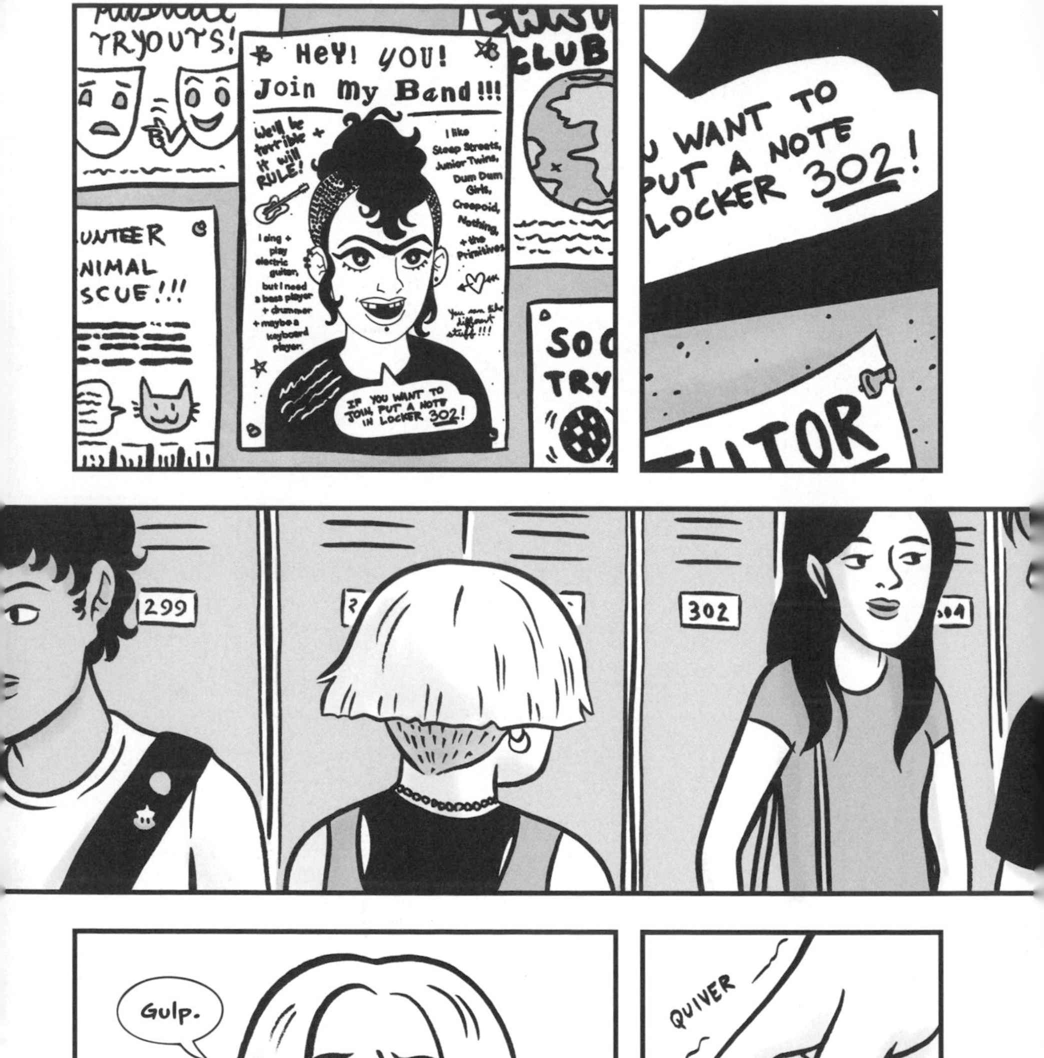
TRYOUTS!
HEY! YOU! Join My Band!!!
We'll be terrible + it will RULE!
I like Steep Streets, Junior Twins, Dum Dum Girls, Creepoid, Nothing, + the Primitives
I sing + play electric guitar, but I need a bass player + drummer + maybe a keyboard player.
You can like different stuff!!!
IF YOU WANT TO JOIN, PUT A NOTE IN LOCKER 302!
CLUB
UNTEER
NIMAL
SCUE!!!
SO
TRY
U WANT TO
PUT A NOTE
LOCKER 302!
TUTOR
299
302
Gulp.
QUIVER

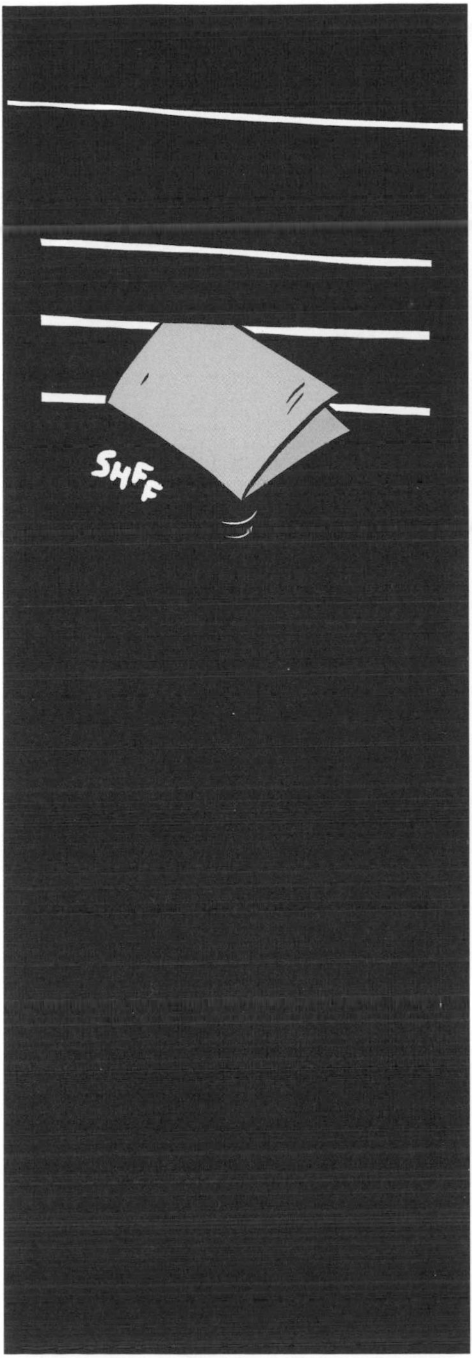
SHFF
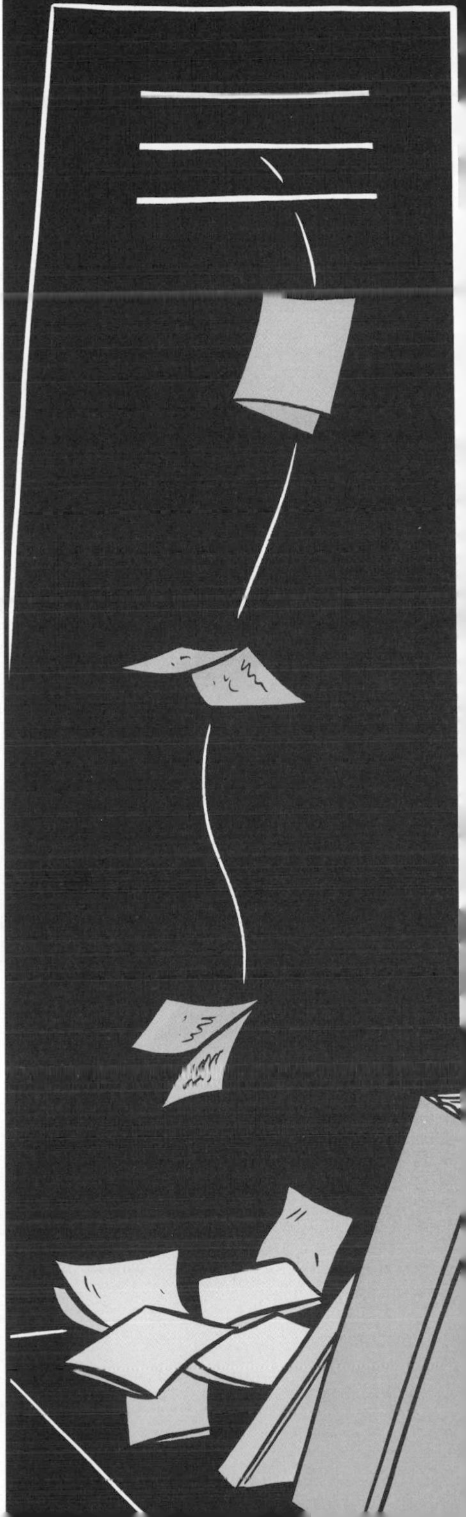

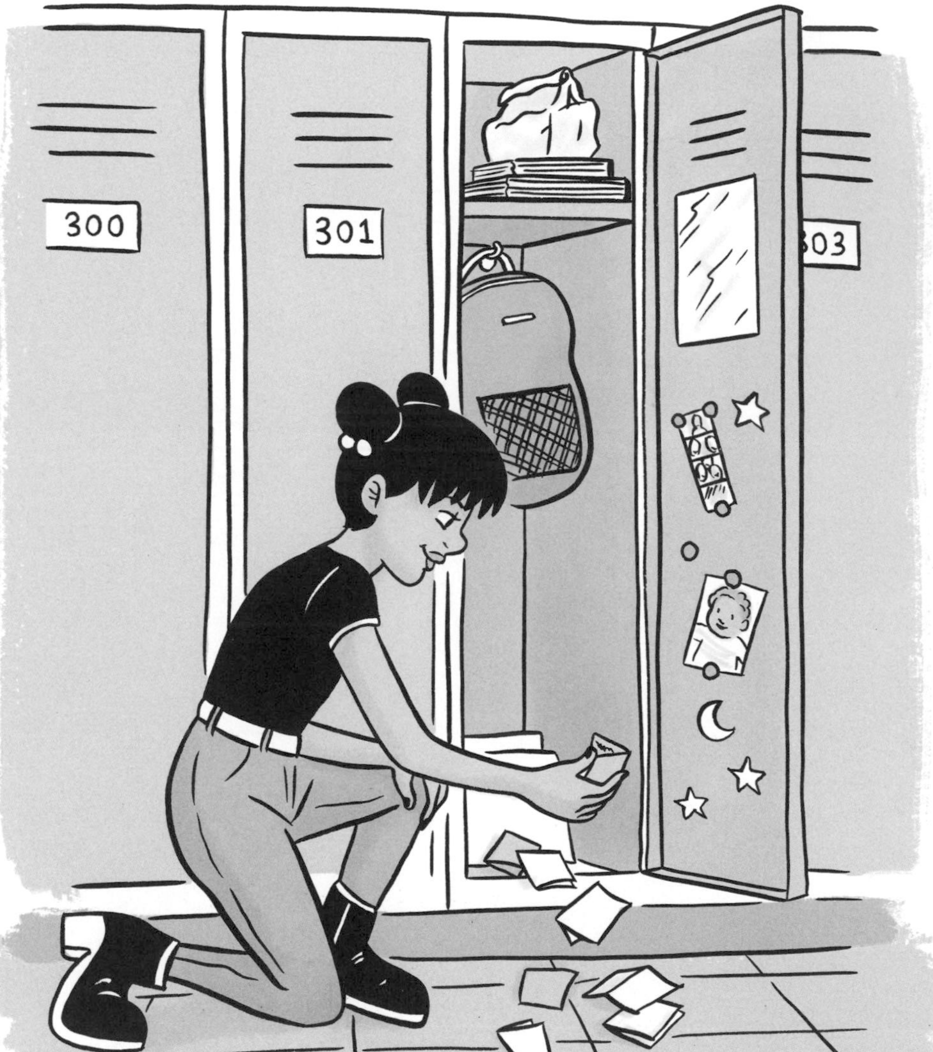
300
301
303